SOME OF TH[
PRAISING THIS N[

"OLIVIA'S

***

"This book is described as a roller-coaster-ride, and it is. It reads like a life history, and wh[...] redemption in it, there is also an underlying darkness, pe[...] [indi]cative of the Author successfully parlaying the sadness that li[...] bring. This is not a light-hearted book… I found it to be a com[...] story, with an obviously interested and engaged writer. It is a w[...] addition to the newest genre of late, chick-lit."

Angela Hailey….Black-Butte[...] 'ook-Review-Grou[p...] Maryland-United-States-of-Am[...]

******

"Dear Judi Emm,…I cannot thank you enough for a[llowi]ng me the privilege to read your wonderful novel. I have rea[d h]undreds of novels and I must admit, that "Olivia's Full Circle" was a complete page-turner for me. And I was compelled to read it at every oppo[rtun]ity I had. I was captivated within the first few pages and became co[mp]letely enthralled in Olivia's story. I couldn't wait to read what was going to happen next!! This is a novel that I will recommend to my friends and family. There is no doubt in my mind that this could definitely be the next 'BEST SELLER'!! I simply cannot wait until you publish the sequel!!"

Tracy Jodoi[n] Canada.

"Dear Divine Ms. Emm,…I've j[ust c]ompleted reading your engrossing, captivating novel. We need more women like Olivia, headstrong, confident and independent. She certainly went the distance to exercise her demons and achieve "A FULL Circle".

Judi, never stop putting pen to paper, thoughts into ides, churning out novel after novel. You're an inspiration to all womankind."

Ennia Mulfati….Montreal Canada

"Judi Emm is everything I am looking for in an Author. She's daring and has a take control attitude. I thoroughly enjoyed her novel from beginning to end. It certainly was a "Roller Coaster Ride" that even her readers got to go on. It is a book to enjoy. I Can't wait for Olivia's next book "Another Full Circle" to arrive on the Shelves."

Claudette Owen….Ontario-Canada.

******

"Dear Ms. Judi Emm,…Congratulations on your book! I couldn't put it down, a real page turner. Read it in two days flat and thoroughly enjoyed it. I loved the twist at the end. Hurry up with your next book, there had better be one!!"….

Linda Bell….Shelly-Beach, South-Africa.

******

"The cover of the book is candy to my eyes! The story is such a reality Olivia stole my heart, I could feel all her pains and joy. Kudos to you Judi Emm what a wonderful page turner!"

Connie Leroux….Ontario-Canada.

******

"Hi Judi Emm,…..It was lovely to read your book and to see what Olivia's life was like, and how she got treated! The book was very well put together, and was a very good read all the way through. It was one of those books you didn't want to put down, as you wanted to know what was going to happen next!! Yes, I would highly recommend this book."

Angela Wilson….Hope-Valley-England.

******

OLIVIA'S FULL CIRCLE

BY
JUDI EMM

Bloomington, IN   Milton Keynes, UK
authorHOUSE®

AuthorHouse™
1663 Liberty Drive, Suite 200
Bloomington, IN 47403
www.authorhouse.com
Phone: 1-800-839-8640

AuthorHouse™ UK Ltd.
500 Avebury Boulevard
Central Milton Keynes, MK9 2BE
www.authorhouse.co.uk
Phone: 08001974150

© 2006 JUDI EMM. All rights reserved.

No part of this book may be reproduced, stored in a retrieval system, or transmitted by any means without the written permission of the author.

First published by AuthorHouse 11/27/2006

ISBN: 978-1-4259-7919-5 (sc)

Printed in the United States of America
Bloomington, Indiana

This book is printed on acid-free paper.

This book is a fiction novel. All names, characters, places and incidents are the product of the writer's imagination or are used fictitiously. Any resemblance to actual events, or locales, or persons living or dead, is entirely coincidental.

Exception.
The Inclusion in this Novel of the Character, Places and Incidents, regarding the 'Yorkshire Ripper' are factually correct.

This Novel Is Dedicated To My Wonderful Relatives & Family Members,

To My Caring And Loving Dad Keith, And Uncle John.

Grandparents Gwendolyn And Arthur, Claire And Samuel & Great Grandparents Ernest & Elisa-Jane.

My Very Emotionally-Strong, Caring, Example-Setting And Loving Liggins Aunties,
Aunty Mabel, Aunty Hetty, Aunty Annie, Aunty Gladys and Aunty Jane /Jinney.

My Wonderful, Darling & Loving Cousins,
Dee, Tony & Mike And Very Good Author, Linda Liggins.

And My Wonderful, Loving, Always There For Me No Matter What, Cousins,
Michael & Diane, Bob & Carol And Ken & Linda.

Whom I know Would All Have Been And Will Be Proud Of Me, In My Accomplishment In The Writing Of This Book. Thank You All Very Much For Being There For Me & Giving Me Your Support & Strength.

This Page Is For My Darling-Wonderful-Loving Husband And Manager Pierre.

Who's Spent Many-Many Months And Years Of His Time Helping Me With The Story-Line-Places-Proof-Reading-Editing-Layout And Format of This Book.

Thank-You So Much For All-Of-Your Time, Patience And Belief In My Work Pierre,

Because-Without Your Help I Could Never Have Done This!!

With Special, Loving Memories This Page Is For Angela,

My Very Own Angel.

Thank-You Angela For Always Being By My Side Guiding Me,

And I Will Always Love You.

This Page Is For My Wonderful, Loving, Caring Friend Claudette, Who Took The Time Out Of Her Very-Busy-Non-Stop-Working-Life, To Do The Editing Of My Book For Me. Making A Point Of Arranging And Moving Most Of Those,,,,,,,,, In The Way!!!

OLIVIA'S FULL CIRCLE.
PART ONE.
1967 - 1968.

Chapter 1

APRIL 1967. MANCHESTER, ENGLAND.

She was rolling around on the stretcher in intense pain, holding her stomach with both of her hands, while the ambulance men were carrying her into the Emergency Room of the hospital. They carefully laid her on the examining table, and could see by the hurt look in her eyes, how much pain she was feeling. One of the men put his hand on her shoulder to comfort her, saying, "Don't worry kid, it will be over soon."

The ambulance men were leaving the room when a nurse arrived. She looked at the teenage girl laying there, rolling around in pain on the examining table, and said, "Hello, what's your name?"

"Olivia, and can you give me something for this pain please? It's so bad, it's nearly killing me."

"No, I'm afraid not just yet Olivia, not until the doctor has seen you, then you can have something. And I'm sure the doctor will be here soon. How old are you Olivia?"

"Sixteen," she replied, still holding her stomach with her hands, and rolling around in intense pain.

While the nurse was busying herself getting medical instruments and sterile gloves ready for the doctor's examination, Olivia began to cry with the pain. There was no break in it, not even for a few minutes like there had been with her first baby.

Doctor Jones, the admitting doctor, a tall dark haired young man, came into the room. He walked over to Olivia, and pulled back the sheet that was covering her, while asking, "What's wrong? Why are you crying?"

"I'm having a miscarriage," she moaned through gritted teeth. "And I'm in such pain, I can't stand it."

"Well, you will have to keep still, and stop moving around so I can examine you," the doctor said, feeling Olivia's stomach with his hands. "Gloves please nurse."

The nurse passed the doctor the sterile gloves that he pulled on over his hands. He then spread Olivia's legs apart, before putting one of his hands inside her vagina, to examine her internally.

She let out a loud, piercing scream before shouting, "Bloody hell! Get your damn hand out of me. You're killing me!"

"Don't you scream and swear at me young lady. I didn't get you pregnant; I'm just trying to help you. From what I can feel this baby is dead, and coming away from you, but this is no two or three month old fetus, this feels about five months. How come you are miscarrying at five months?"

Olivia was crying and didn't answer him.

The doctor asked again, "How come you're miscarrying at five months? And where is the Father of this baby?"

Through her tears she cried out, "Gone! He's bloody left me. Gone to live in bloody Australia."

"Oh I get it, your boyfriend got you pregnant, and when you told him about it he didn't want to know, so he packed his bags, and took off to Australia. And then you aborted the baby."

"No! No! No! It wasn't like that," Olivia cried. "He didn't know I was pregnant with this one, and I didn't abort it. Please Doctor I beg you, please give me something for the pain, it's just killing me and I just can't take anymore."

"What do you mean, 'this one'? Have you had another baby?"

"Yes," Olivia replied, between sobs that were now beginning to wrack her body. "Yes I have another baby."

"Yes, and I feel sure that you aborted this baby," the doctor said, shaking his head in disgust at her and the situation that he felt he was dealing with. "Do you know that it's still illegal to have an abortion girl? And I want some questions answered about this very soon. But for now nurse, put her into bed, and give her something for the pain. This baby is coming away from her, but I'm not going to help her as much as I could. Let her feel some pain and suffer, because I am sure she killed this baby. How old is she? And where are her parents? I want to see them, I wonder what they know about this."

"She's sixteen years old Doctor. I'll put her in a bed on the ward, and keep an eye on her," the nurse told the doctor, before he left the examination room. She then went to Olivia, saying sympathetically, "My name is Nurse Wendy. It will be over soon Olivia, and the pain will be gone. I'll get another nurse, and we will get you into a bed where you can sleep for a while."

Olivia was given a couple of injections in the thigh; the nurse told her one was for pain, and the other was to help her sleep.

Nurse Wendy and Nurse Susan then wheeled her out of the examination room onto the ward, and lifted her into a bed.

The ward was full of women who were all talking, and looking at her. She fell asleep hearing the strange voices, and wishing the pain would go away.

***

It was dark outside, and the rain was beating against the window above Olivia's, bed, when she began to stir after hours of dreamless sleep, due to the injections she had been given. She opened her eyes and found the lights in the ward very bright, and could hear lots of people talking. She sat up in bed looking around her, and seeing people sitting on hard, straight-backed chairs around the beds of the other patients, she realised it was visiting time at the hospital.

Her head felt groggy from the drugs she had been given, but she knew she must get to a bathroom, because her bladder felt very full. Olivia didn't know where the bathroom was, and not seeing any nurses on the ward, she began to panic and look around her, but no one seemed to notice her.

No one cares, she thought, *they're all so bloody busy talking to their families, and I need to get to a toilet.* She shouted to a lady sat on a chair, at the bed next to her. "Excuse me!" She shouted again, louder this time, "Excuse me!"

"Yes dear," the lady said, turning to face Olivia.

"Could you please get me a nurse, and tell her I need to get to the toilet right now."

"All right dear, I'll get the Nurse for you. But just lie down luvie, you look really ill, your face is so white."

The lady in her high-heeled shoes disappeared into another room off from the ward, to find a nurse.

A few minutes' later three nurses came out of the room, with one of them carrying a bedpan. They went to Olivia's bed, where one of them drew the curtains around her, for some privacy from the rest of the ward.

"Did you have a good sleep?" Nurse Wendy asked.

"Yes thanks, but I need to go to the toilet," Olivia replied.

"Okay, we are going to sit you on this bedpan now," Nurse Susan said.

Susan and Wendy helped Olivia lift herself up, while Nurse Janet put the bedpan underneath her.

It was a great relief for Olivia to pass water, until she suddenly began to have a strange, horrid feeling between her legs, and grabbed hold of Wendy's hand tightly saying, "Oh God! It feels like something is coming out of me Nurse."

"It's okay, just relax, let it come, don't try and stop it, it's the baby," Wendy replied, patting her hand.

Olivia then felt herself give birth to a small baby. "It's out of me, it's gone," she said, as it dropped into the bedpan.

Wendy and Susan helped lift Olivia off the bedpan, as Janet took it out from underneath her, saying, "Don't look down into the bedpan Olivia."

But as the bedpan was taken from underneath her, Olivia felt she must look, and glancing down, she saw a perfectly, formed, tiny, pink baby, the size of her hand, laying very silent and still, as though it was just sleeping, in the bottom of the bedpan. It was another boy!

Wendy and Janet left Olivia's bedside, and Susan stayed with her saying, "We'll get you cleaned up, and make you comfortable in a minute, then you can get a good nights' sleep."

Olivia was silent, as many different thoughts began to whirl around inside her head.

Wendy arrived back with warm water, towels, and a pad for the blood Olivia was losing, whilst Susan went and made her a strong cup of tea.

"Here drink this, it will help you feel better," Susan said, passing Olivia the hot cup of tea. "And is there anything else I can get for you? Are you hungry?"

"No thanks, I'm just tired."

When Olivia had drunk her tea, Wendy gave her an injection in the thigh.

"What was that for?"

"To help you sleep,"

"Where is the Father of the baby you just lost? And are you married?" Susan asked.

"No, I'm not married."

"Do you already have a baby?" Wendy asked with compassion in her voice.

"Yes, I have a beautiful nine-month-old baby boy, called Antony."

"Where is the Father of your babies?" Susan asked again.

"Gone! Gone far away down under."

"Can't you contact him at all? Did he know about this baby you've just lost?"

"No, and he will never know, never. All I know is we had a big fight, and he left me and our son to go and live in Australia, and anyway, I don't know where in Australia he is living, and Australia is a big place. I don't want to talk about him now, I just want to sleep, I'm so tired. Maybe I can go home tomorrow," Olivia replied, in a sleepy voice, with the injection beginning to take effect on her. "Yes, tomorrow I will go home."

******

Chapter 2

THE NEXT DAY

She was awoken from her drug induced sleep, by a lady in a light brown, wrap around apron, who was shaking her and saying, "Wake up luv, it's morning. How do you like your tea?"

"Tea! What do you mean, tea?" Olivia replied, in a sleepy voice. "I just want to sleep."

"My name's Gladys, and I bring you patients your meals and tea. It's six-thirty in the morning and time to give you all your cup of wake up tea. So come on luv, wake up and have your tea. Then you can get washed, and I'll bring you your breakfast at seven. How many sugars do you take luv?"

"Bugger off! And take your sodding tea with you, I just want to sleep," Olivia muttered angrily.

"Now, now dear, there's no need to be like that. I'll leave a cup of tea on the top of your locker for you; I've put two sugars in it. Now you wake up luv and drink it."

She closed her eyes and went back to sleep. During the talking and moving about of the other patients she slept on, undisturbed by all the activity.

At six forty-five Nurse Wendy came to her bed. "Olivia please try and wake up, I want to take your temperature, and breakfast will be here soon."

Olivia slowly opened her eyes and looked into Wendy's kind face.

"Open your mouth please, I'm going to put this thermometer under your tongue."

"Ugh! My mouth feels stuck together."

"Didn't you drink your tea?" Wendy asked, while placing the thermometer under Olivia's tongue.

"No, I just wanted to sleep," Olivia mumbled.

"How are you feeling today?" Wendy continued, taking Olivia's pulse.

"Okay," she replied, when the thermometer was taken out of her mouth. "The pains gone, so do you think I can go home today?"

"Oh, you'll have to see what the doctor says," Wendy said, shaking down the thermometer. "Your temperature is okay. Do you want to go to the bathroom and get washed before breakfast?"

"Yes please, where is it? And when will I see the doctor?"

"It's down there at the end of the ward," Wendy replied, pointing her finger towards the end of the room. "And the doctor will be here at eight-thirty."

Olivia carefully eased herself out of bed, putting her feet onto the tiled floor, and stood up holding onto the side of the bed with one hand, thinking, *My legs feel a bit shaky, but after what I've been through I'm not surprised. And my parents thought they were doing the best thing for me. I wonder if they've phoned the hospital to see how I'm doing. I hope I'll see them later today at visiting time, and they bring Antony with them, I do miss my baby.*

"Bloody hell, what a mess," she said to herself, when she reached the bathroom. "I'm bleeding a lot, and I do hope that I'm not starting to hemorrhage."

After washing herself, she came out of the bathroom and walked down the ward passed the other beds, towards her own. Gladys was putting the breakfast trays out for all the patients, and pouring them more cups of tea.

"Hello, What's your name? I'm Veronica. You came in yesterday and slept all the time, didn't you?" A lady with blonde hair and a pretty face, said to Olivia, as she was slowly walking past her bed.

"What are you in for?"

"Hello Veronica, I'm Olivia, and I've had a miscarriage. I'm okay now though, and I hope I can go home today."

"Oh, there's no chance of that, you'll have to have a D and C first. I've had a miscarriage and I had my D and C yesterday," Veronica replied. "Isn't that right Pam?" She shouted to a lady across the ward.

"What's that?" Pam asked, coming across to Veronica's bed, and introducing herself to Olivia.

"I was just telling Olivia, she won't be going home today after having a miscarriage yesterday, she'll have to have a D and C first."

"Oh yes," agreed Pam. "They will give you a D and C if you've had a miscarriage. I had to have one after my miscarriage, and Veronica's just had one, everybody has a D and C after a miscarriage."

"Well, they do here, that's for sure!" Added Veronica, laughing.

"What's a D and C?" Olivia asked, feeling a little scared now.

"It's a scrape," replied Pam.

"Well, what the hell's a scrape?" Olivia asked.

"Olivia," Nurse Susan shouted. "Olivia, come and get your breakfast before it goes cold."

"Okay," Olivia shouted back. "And I'll talk to you ladies again after breakfast."

"Yes, we'll see you after breakfast," Veronica replied.

"Or after the doctors," added Pam. "Let's hope that they come to see us on time. I get sick of waiting for them, when they're late."

Her breakfast looked good but she didn't have much of an appetite, after being on her feet and walking about she was starting to have bad cramp pains in her stomach. She drank her tea and ate a piece of toast; but the tea was too sweet and the toast tasted soggy and bland.

Gladys came up to her bed carrying a large teapot. "More tea luv?" She asked.

Olivia just nodded her head.

"Two sugars is it dear?"

"No, not two bloody sugars, two makes it taste like syrup, one and a half please."

"All right," Gladys sighed. "But I wish you wouldn't swear at me luv."

Olivia just gave Gladys a blank stare with her big, bright emerald green eyes.

***

After the breakfast trays were cleared away, the nurses were busy getting the ladies into their beds because it was time for the doctors to make the morning rounds of their patients.

Olivia was lying down because the cramp pains in her stomach were now very bad. She did not take any notice of the doctors going to the other patients, and after a while they were at the side of her bed.

"Olivia can you sit up please, we would like to talk to you."

She opened her eyes, to the sound of an Indian woman's voice.

"Hello, how are you feeling today?" Continued the doctor, when Olivia began to sit up. "I am Doctor Mehta and this is Doctor Stevens. One of the doctors told me you came in yesterday after a five month fetal abortion."

"I did not have an abortion," Olivia replied, glaring at Doctor Mehta and her long, bright red-painted fingernails.

"Well, your fetus was sent to the lab, and the report came back that there was no reason why it would have died spontaneously, there was nothing wrong with it, it was perfectly normal. So are you going to tell us how the baby died Olivia? What did you do to kill it?"

"Nothing! I did not kill him" Olivia replied, beginning to cry. "Nothing! And stop accusing me of killing my baby, I didn't kill him."

She remembered the echoing words of her concerned parents, as she was laying in her bed at home, crying and rolling around in such pain, whilst she waited for the ambulance to bring her to the hospital. *Don't tell anyone Olivia or we'll all be in trouble, promise us you won't say a word to a living soul!*

"Why are you crying Olivia, have you something to tell us?" Doctor Mehta asked.

"No I don't, the baby just died, and I don't know why he died," she replied defiantly. "But I'm in a lot of pain now, and I just want to go home."

"Well lie down and let me feel your tummy," said Doctor Mehta, who then pushed her hand hard into Olivia's pelvic area.

"Owe! That bloody hurts," she screamed. "And why don't you cut those bloody long finger nails of yours?"

Doctor Mehta ignored Olivia's remark, turning to speak to Doctor Stevens. "Her womb is very swollen Doctor Stevens, don't you agree?"

Doctor Stevens put his hand on Olivia's pelvic area probing gently. "Yes," he agreed, "it is very swollen. I think we will leave it another day or two before she is given a D and C."

"What's a D and C?" Olivia asked in a frightened voice, sitting up in bed, and opening her large, green eyes very wide, looking from one doctor to the other. "I've been told it's a scrape, what's a scrape? What will you be scraping?"

"You will be having a small operation, a D and C, that is a Dilation and Curettage. It will be done under an anaesthetic," Doctor Stevens replied. "We will clean the inside of your womb, using a medical instrument, and get rid of all the clots of blood that are still in there, after the fetus came away."

"Is that necessary? Really necessary, won't my womb clean itself? I am bleeding a lot."

"Yes it has to be done," Doctor Stevens replied. "But don't worry, you won't feel anything, it won't be painful and the operation only takes about twenty to twenty-five minutes."

"All right then," Olivia said sighing. "If it won't hurt you can do it, but God I've felt enough pain. Can I go home then?"

"As soon as you are strong enough," Doctor Stevens replied.

"Your chart says you are only sixteen Olivia. What is your date of birth?" Doctor Mehta asked.

"The twenty-fifth of October nineteen-fifty."

"Doctor Jones, the Doctor who saw you yesterday, told us you already have a baby. Is this so?"

"Yes, I've got a nine month-old boy, called Antony."

"So you were only fifteen when you had him?" Doctor Mehta asked with a raised eyebrow.

Olivia just nodded her head in reply.

"Was Antony's Father also the Father of the baby you've just lost?" Asked Doctor Stevens.

"Yes and he's left me. We were going to get married, I thought he loved me, but he left me and our baby."

"Oh why do these stupid young girls keep getting themselves pregnant. When will they ever learn?" Doctor Mehta commented to Doctor Stevens, with a disgusted 'tut' added at the end of her sentence, as she closed Olivia's medical record notes that she was holding.

"Just sod-off you," Olivia shouted, feeling that she had to defend herself against doctor Mehta's opinion of her. "And don't you call me stupid."

Olivia and Doctor Mehta glared at each other as their eyes met. Doctor Mehta had an evil smirk forming around her mouth, with evil thoughts beginning to go through her mind.

***

"Hello Olivia. I am Sister Cole, the ward Sister. How are you feeling?"

"I haven't seen you before," Olivia said, to the lady in the dark blue dress, white apron and hat.

"No, I have just come on duty. Are your parents coming to see you this afternoon?"

"I think so, why?"

"Well, when they arrive would you tell them that Doctor Jones would like to see them?"

"Okay. But I've got awful cramp pains in my stomach, could you give me something for the pain please?"

"Yes, your womb is very swollen, I'll get you a couple of tablets that will help to ease the pain. Are you bleeding heavily?"

"Yes I am."

"Well I want you to stay in bed, and keep off your feet as much as you can. That will help to stop the bleeding. You will be having a small operation in a couple of days, so get plenty of rest."

Olivia took the pain killing tablets and started to drift off to sleep thinking, *Oh God, when will this all end? And what's going to happen in my future? Is it true no one will ever want or love me?*

My Father says I am just a bloody whore. Why did you leave me Stan? I loved you so much; you were my life; will I ever be able to love again? Come back to me Stan, save me, I love you so much.

******

Chapter 3

Olivia awoke at lunchtime, and tried to eat a little of her lunch, to keep up her strength. She was missing her baby Antony so much; she hoped her parents would bring him to see her when they came to visit in the afternoon.

After the lunch dishes were cleared away by Gladys, the women were getting themselves washed and tidied up for their afternoon visitors.

At two thirty a nurse opened the big doors to the ward, to let the visitors in. A crowd of them marched in going to different beds, and she saw her Mother and Father dressed in their expensive, smart clothes, walking into the ward with the other people.

Eric, her Father, was a tall, broad shouldered, handsome man, with neatly trimmed, short, black hair and green eyes, dressed in his very smart, expensive, blue suit. He was a hard working, outspoken, quick-tempered, tough, headstrong, but very honest, kind-hearted man. With a good sense of humour, who could not tolerate idiots or fools, and demanded respect, and obedience from his family.

Olivia had always loved and admired her Father as a child, and always saw him as her hero. She thought he was so strong and that nothing in life could or would ever beat him down. But now as she was growing older, she began to feel that her Father was far to old fashioned, to protective of her, and to cynical about life and changes in society, and should try to understand things and get with it a bit more.

Her Mother Margaret, a small, good looking, blue eyed lady, was heavily made-up with lots of powder, and bright, pink lipstick, with not a hair out of place in her lovely, brunette, hair style. She was wearing her well-tailored cream suit, with a pink blouse that matched her pink, high-heeled shoes, handbag, and nail polish. She was a person who felt that smart appearances, and the way people spoke really mattered in her life. She was also a very calm, quietly spoken, hard working, self-centred, procrastinating lady; who enjoyed, and expected, the finer things in life to make her happy.

She hated the problems or things that she felt life had dished out to her, without her asking for any of them, when all she wished for was a quiet, peaceful, happy life. She also cared very much, what other people thought and said about her, especially her neighbours and the rest of the people in the village.

Olivia loved both of her parents dearly, but always saw her mother as being too weak a person at the side of her Father, as she always seemed to be there at his beck and call for everything, instead of standing up to him. But she did want to always think of her mother as being a kind lady, who would never dream of hurting anyone intentionally, even though Olivia would never be able to understand why her mother never seemed to have the time for anyone else, but only herself in her life, with this making her mother seemingly to be just like she was a snob, especially to other people whom she could and would easily snub. And now as Olivia was getting older and began to analyse her mother, she felt that she had sometime, somewhere, put a wall up between herself and her daughter, and had pushed Olivia, as far away from her as she could, especially when she felt she really needed her mother the most in her life. But Margaret always seemed to be afraid of her daughter's problems, and getting too close to them, and afraid of loving her daughter too much. Yes Olivia felt that her mother could and would only love her, as one of her daughters, from a distance.

"Hello luv, how are you?" They asked, when they reached Olivia's bed and kissed her on the cheek.

"Oh I suppose I'm okay."

"I've brought you some grapes," her mother said.

"Thanks, and where's Antony?" Olivia replied, putting the bag of grapes on her bedside locker thinking, *I'm sure a bunch of bloody grapes will help me to get better.*

"He's staying with Mrs. Mason," her mother replied.

"Why didn't you bring him to see me? I'm missing him and I want to see him."

"Don't be bloody stupid," her father said. "We can't bring him here."

"Why not? Why can't you bring him here to see me?"

"Don't tell me, that you've told the people here, that you have got a baby," her mother said, in a disgusted tone of voice.

"Why not? Why shouldn't they know I have a baby?"

"Have you no shame?" Her mother asked, glaring at her.

"No, I am not ashamed of Antony, I love my baby, he's my love child."

"Shut up," her father snarled. "Shut up, don't start."

"I'm not starting anything, it's a fact," Olivia replied, looking at her dad defiantly. "And by the way, Doctor Jones wants to see you two before you leave."

"Why? What have you told him?" Her mother asked in a panicky tone of voice.

"Nothing, I'm leaving that up to you two. But I hope you both have a good story made up between you, because abortions are still illegal. And the doctors are convinced the baby didn't die by itself, they said there was nothing wrong with it."

"Are you sure you didn't say anything Olivia?" Her father asked.

"No, I told you I didn't, your secret is safe with me for now. And you can tell Aunty Mary, not to worry about it either."

Eric turned to his wife saying, "I could bloody slap her, Margaret, the ungrateful little bitch, after all we've tried to do for her, to save her reputation."

"Shush don't start Eric," Margaret replied in a loud whispered voice.

"Oh look! There's Doctor Jones, he's just going into his office right now. And I think he's come especially to see you both, because he's a very busy man you know," Olivia said, with a smile, feeling that her parents would have a lot of explaining to do, to the doctor.

"All right, we'd better go and get this over with Margaret. Are you sure you didn't say anything to anyone Olivia?" Her father asked once again.

Olivia just stared at him with her big green eyes.

Her parents left her bedside and went to the Doctor's office, while Olivia rested her head back against the pillows, as tears began to roll down her cheeks, while she was thinking, *I wish you'd stop fighting me Mum and Dad, and let's try and be friends. Oh, how I wish I could tell them how much I love them and how sorry I am for hurting them so much. But are they hurt? I just feel they care more about themselves and what other people would think and say if they knew I'd gotten pregnant again. Yes, that would really hurt them more than I ever could. Oh, why do they have to put such a nice face on for the rest of the world, and appear to be so hard, cold and uncaring to me? I wonder if they know what I went through having that abortion and losing my baby. My poor little baby boy, who I would have called Oliver, after my Granddad. My poor little Oliver, who I never said goodbye to. You never got to know me Oliver, my poor little baby, but I will never forget you, and will always love you forever.*

***

After about twenty minutes in the Doctor's office, she saw her parents coming back towards her bed with stern looks on their faces.

"What's happened? What did he say to you?" She asked, wiping the tears quickly, away from her cheeks, so her parents wouldn't notice that she had been crying as Margaret and Eric sat down on chairs that they pulled up very close to the bed, so no one would hear them talking.

"He asked us if we knew that you were pregnant, and we said no," Margaret said, in a whispered voice. "He also asked us if we knew where you would be able to get a back-street abortion, because he feels that's what you've had, but we told him we didn't know."

"Don't worry Mum and Dad, I promised you I wouldn't tell anyone," Olivia said, giving a deep sigh, feeling sorry for her parents and what the Doctor must have said to them.

"That's a good lass," her Father replied, putting a comforting hand on her arm and giving it a squeeze. "We do love you, you know Olivia and everything will be okay now and you'll be coming home soon."

"The Doctor told us you are going to have a D and C on Tuesday, the day after tomorrow, so we will come and see you on Tuesday night," her Mother said.

"Why can't you come and see me tomorrow?" Olivia asked. "And bring Antony with you, 'cause I want to see him. I'm missing him so much."

"Tomorrow we are going to see your Aunty Mary, and tell her that everything went okay, and she's no need to worry, no one knows anything," her Father replied.

"Oh yes, Aunty Mary, the great abortionist. Do give her my love," Olivia said sarcastically.

"Shut up and keep your bloody voice down, will you? Just be thankful it's gone," her Mother hissed through her teeth. "You already have one baby, and there's not much chance of anyone wanting you with that one, never mind two. And we only did what we thought was the best thing for you, with the mess you went and got yourself into again."

Olivia just stared at her parents and bit into the corner of her bottom lip, as her eyes began to fill up with tears again as she remembered, how her Aunty Mary had demanded that she go upstairs to the bathroom with her, and then forcefully inserted an enema tube, filled with a soapy liquid, deep into her womb, to abort her baby. Her parents had arranged for this abortion after they told her about the family's great secret. The now old, but very strict, Aunty Mary, who used to be a midwife, had always been there for the women of the family, whenever any of them needed help in getting rid of their unplanned pregnancies. But when Olivia had told them very positively, that she did not want to have this abortion, that she did not want to get rid of her baby, no one would listen to her cries of protest.

When visiting time was over, her parents gave her a kiss on the side of her cheek, before they said good-bye. They both walked away thinking that they were leaving their daughter, in the safe hands of the Doctors and Nurses who worked in the hospital, and she would soon be coming home, and that life would start to go forward for them all again. Just carrying on as if none of this had ever happened to any of them, because now it had all been so carefully swept away underneath someone else's carpet, so that it could never come back to haunt any of them.

******

Chapter 4

The next morning Olivia was feeling stronger, she'd had a good restful nights sleep, due to the sleeping tablet she had been given. The pain in her stomach had finally gone, and she felt well enough to take a bath. She had stayed in bed all day and kept off her feet, like the Sister had asked her to. During the day the other women in the ward were friendly to her, and came over to her bed to talk to her, bringing her magazines to look at, making sure she wasn't lonely when she wasn't sleeping, this helped her to pass the time of day while she was resting up.

***

Before going off duty for the evening, the ward Sister, told her that she would be having her small operation the next morning. So not to eat or drink anything after eleven o'clock that night, and to abstain from having any tea or breakfast the next morning, because she would be going down to the Operating Theatre at about nine o'clock.

Olivia was feeling good at nine-thirty that night. She'd had her drink of hot, milky Ovaltine, and had taken the sleeping tablet that Nurse Sally had given to her, so she would have another good night's sleep. The other patients were saying good-night to each other, and when Veronica came back from her visit to the bathroom, she got into her bed and shouted, "Good-night," across to Olivia, adding how much better she thought, she had looked today, that her face wasn't as pale looking.

"Yes," replied Olivia, shaking her pillows before lying down and getting comfortable in her bed. "I've felt much better today, I'll be glad when the operation is over tomorrow though and then I can go home."

Home to see her lovely baby son Antony, whom she so much wanted to hold in her arms, and tell him how much she loved him, and had missed him. She closed her eyes and soon began to drift off to sleep, as the sleeping tablet started to take effect.

***

An hour later at ten thirty that night Olivia was in a deep sleep, when Doctor Mehta came onto the ward, and went into the examination room off the ward, calling out, "Nurse, can I see you please?"

"Yes Doctor Mehta," Nurse Sally answered, entering the examination room, and seeing the Doctor getting sterile gloves from the shelf.

"Are the patients asleep?"

"Yes, most of them are."

"Good. Bring Olivia Howard here to see me, tell her I want to give her a little examination."

"Okay Doctor," an anxious, Nurse Sally replied.

The nurse left the examination room feeling confused and apprehensive, about the doctor's unusually late arrival in the ward for a patient exam, but her strict training denied her the right to question the doctor's motives, or even ask her why she wanted to see one of her patients at this late hour of the night. She had been taught and was led to believe that the Doctors were to be treated like Gods, and whatever their requests and orders were they had to be carried out, respected, and obeyed without question, especially by nurses who were felt to be very inferior to the knowledgeable Doctors.

"Olivia wake up, wake up," Sally said softly, gently shaking her by the shoulder.

"Mmm...." Olivia mumbled in her sleep.

"Olivia can you wake up please?"

"What? Nurse, what's wrong?" Olivia asked, trying to open her eyes and stir herself from her deep sleep. "What's wrong? What's happening Nurse? Why are you waking me up?" Olivia now asked feeling very confused.

"Nothing's wrong Olivia, and I'm sorry to have to wake you, but Doctor Mehta is here and she wants to examine you. So would you be good enough to come with me to the examining room?"

"What now! Jesus Christ! What a time to want to examine me. Is she bored with her life or something? Why can't she wait and do it in the morning?"

"I understand how you feel Olivia, but I'm sure this won't take very long. She probably just wants to feel your stomach to see if the swelling inside has gone down enough for them to operate on you in the morning."

"Okay I'll come with you then, but it better not take her all night to see if my tummy's still swollen, 'cause I'm tired and I want to get back to sleep."

Olivia went with the nurse to the examining room, and walking through the door Doctor Mehta turned around to face them both, with a big smile on her face.

"Oh come in Olivia my dear, don't be afraid now, come and lay on this examining table."

"I'm not afraid, but why the hell do you want to see me at this time of night? I was fast asleep."

"Oh, I just want to give you a little examination Olivia, to see if you are okay for your operation in the morning. Come on now get up onto this table, this isn't going to take me very long."

"Shit! I think all this could have waited until morning?" Olivia replied with a deep sigh, before reluctantly getting onto the examining table.

"That's it my dear just lay down and put one foot in there and the other foot in there," Doctor Mehta said, taking hold of Olivia's feet and placing them into the stirrup type foot holds, before pulling on a pair of sterile gloves over her hands. "That's it Olivia just rest your feet in the stirrups. And Nurse place your hands firmly on Olivia's shoulders and hold her down for me."

"What the hell are you going to do to me?" Olivia asked, now beginning to feel afraid.

But instead of answering her question, Doctor Mehta made a clenched fist with one hand, and pushed it into the top of Olivia's pelvis, pressing down hard to make her womb drop lower in her vagina. She inserted her other hand into Olivia's vagina searching to find her cervix, which she then forced open with her long, pointed finger nails, pushing her fingers deep into Olivia's womb, and began scraping the blood tissue from the walls of it.

Olivia let out a blood-curdling scream, when she felt the doctor's hand plunging deep into her womb. "Stop! Stop!" She screamed loudly. "Stop it, you fucking bitch, get your fucking hand out of me now."

She lifted her head up and tried to sit up and stop her, when Doctor Mehta's hand came out of Olivia's vagina, with large, blood clots hanging off her fingers. With a shake of her hand they dropped onto a large white paper tissue at the side of Olivia's leg.

"Hold her down nurse, hold her down firmly," insisted the doctor. "Just a few more times and I'll have all this out of her womb, and then she won't have to go to theatre tomorrow."

The nurse pushed Olivia's shoulders back down onto the bed, hating herself for doing this to her, but because she was afraid that if she didn't do what Doctor Mehta told her to, she would report her to the matron in the morning for disobeying Doctors orders.

"Just one more time Olivia," Nurse Sally said, in a very upset voice. "I'm sure the doctor will only do it once more, please try and be brave."

"Brave!" Olivia shouted, "I don't want to be fucking brave."

Doctor Mehta pushed her fingers deep into Olivia's womb again, continuing the scraping process with her long, red-painted fingernails.

"No!" Olivia screamed, feeling even more intense pain surging through her pelvis, and stomach. "No! No more, please I beg you," she yelled, beginning to cry.

Doctor Mehta pulled her hand out of Olivia's vagina, with more blood clots hanging from her fingers, which she shook and wiped onto the paper tissues. In went the doctor's hand again, filling Olivia's womb with her fingers, in and out went her hand, continuing the process of searching for more blood clots, while Olivia was rolling around on the bed screaming. She had never known, or felt, such pain before, she was sure the doctor was tearing her womb out.

"You fucking bitch. You fucking witch. You fucking monster, stop it," she screamed at the doctor.

Doctor Mehta had a big smile on her face as she looked at Olivia thrashing around on the bed in such pain. "You silly little girl, I will teach you. You will never want another man again, you will never let another man inside your body again, and you will never kill another baby. And you will never forget this night."

Nurse Sally was holding Olivia's shoulders down on the bed. Olivia's eyes looked into Nurse Sally's; they were pleading with Sally, begging her for help.

Sally had tears running down her cheeks, she was so sorry this was happening to Olivia, she wished she had the guts to stop Doctor Mehta, but she was so afraid of her.

Eventually Doctor Mehta stopped violating Olivia's body, stopped pushing her fingers deep into Olivia's womb, but the evil smile was still on her face.

"There now, that's over with," she said, in a very matter of fact tone of voice. "That's a good job done, and it will save Doctor Stevens from having to operate on her in the morning. Take her back to bed nurse, clean her up and give her an injection for the pain, and one to stop the bleeding."

Doctor Mehta pulled off her gloves, and threw them on top of the pile of blood clots, on the paper tissue.

"Good night nurse," she said leaving the room.

***

Olivia was lying on her side curled up in a ball, clenching her stomach. She felt as if her womb had been torn out. She was crying softly, with wracking sobs coming deep from her soul, she thought she was going to die and she just didn't care, she only hoped it would be soon, then the intense pain in her stomach, would end.

"Olivia, can you get into this wheel chair? And I'll take you back to bed. Olivia come on, let me help you, I'm so sorry this has happened to you, I had no idea the Doctor would do anything like this to you," Nurse Sally said, laying her hand gently on Olivia's shoulder.

"No! Go away you! You should have helped me, you could have stopped her, but you didn't! So don't bother helping me now! Anyway

I think I'm dying, so just leave me alone!" Olivia Shouted, between her gut wrenching deep sobs.

"Come on Olivia, let me help you to sit up and I'll get you back to bed."

"No! Just bugger off. Just fuck off will you, I feel too ill to sit up, I just want to die!"

"Come on Olivia, please let me help you, I can't leave you here. Come on I'm going to get you back to bed," Sally said, gently putting her arms around Olivia, and trying to pull her up.

Olivia very slowly, began to move her body, turning her head to one side before vomiting all over the floor. She vomited because of the torture her body had been put through, and wishing she had vomited all over Doctor Mehta, instead of the floor. She then began to shake uncontrollably, and started to shiver, she felt so cold, as her body went into convulsions. The nurse knew that Olivia was going into shock, and she had to get her into bed, and get her warm as quickly as possible, or she may die from the shock that her body had just endured. So she lifted her into the wheel chair, before wrapping a blanket tightly around her, to help to keep her warm.

When she pushed Olivia through the doors, back onto the ward, all the other patients were sitting up in their beds, wide awake, and looking very concerned.

"Nurse what happened?" Veronica shouted. "We heard Olivia screaming, what did that fucking doctor do to her?"

"God! She looks like death," Pam said, getting out of bed and going over to Olivia. "Here nurse, I'll help you get her into bed. How do you feel Olivia? Are you okay?"

Olivia didn't answer, she felt too ill, she just wished she could soon die, then this intense pain and evil nightmare, her quiet, secret grieving for the loss of her baby boy Oliver, whom she never got to say goodbye too, telling him that it was not the time for him to be born, would at last all soon be over, because mentally, physically and emotionally, her whole being, body, spirit and soul just could not take anymore.

Sally, put extra blankets on her bed to keep her warm, and then gave her a couple of strong injections.

"How are you feeling now?" Sally asked, gently stroking Olivia's forehead. "Can I get you anything?"

"Yes, I want a drink of water."

"Okay, here, just lift your head up," Sally said, putting her hand under Olivia's head and putting the glass of water to her lips.

"Thanks, I'm going to die now, but it's okay 'cause I have to be with my poor little baby Oliver, he's got no-one to look after him, " Olivia said, with a deep sigh, closing her eyes and laying her head back against the pillows to go into a deep sleep.

"Stop saying that, you're not going to die. You're going to get a good nights' sleep and you will feel a lot better in the morning," the nurse replied, feeling she had to say something positive to Olivia, to keep her going. "You have your other baby son to look after, he needs you. And I'm going to write a report about what Doctor Mehta did to you tonight, and Sister will read it in the morning. And I'm sure she will show it to the Matron. I really hope they can do something about that doctor, because she is evil doing what she did to you."

***

THE FOLLOWING DAY

The day-nurses came on duty the next morning, Nurse Sally rushed over to tell Nurse Wendy, and Nurse Susan what Doctor Mehta had done to Olivia last night, before placing her night report containing the written events on the ward Sister's desk for her to read.

"Oh my God!" Said Wendy. "How is Olivia? Come on Susan, we must go and see her. What kind of a night did she have?"

"Well, I looked at her half an hour ago and she was still asleep," Sally replied. "I put a tranquilliser in with the injection for her pain, because she went into a state of shock, and she kept saying that she wanted to die and be with that poor baby that she lost. She seems to have had a good night, she slept soundly. I think she will be okay now."

"Poor kid, I'm going to see her," Wendy said.

"She's still asleep," Susan said, when they reached Olivia's bedside. "I want to take her temperature, so I'm going to have to wake her up."

Putting a hand gently on Olivia's shoulder, Wendy said, "Olivia, Olivia, its Nurse Wendy, can you open your eyes Olivia?"

There was no response from Olivia; she continued to sleep deeply.

"Olivia," Wendy said again in her gentle voice. "Olivia it's morning, can you wake up."

Slowly Olivia began to stir and opened her eyes.

"Good morning Olivia, how are your feeling?"

"I'm thirsty, can I have a drink?"

"Yes you can," Susan replied. "I'll get you a nice hot cup of tea."

"Can you put this under your tongue Olivia?" Wendy asked, shaking the thermometer. "I want to take your temperature. How are you feeling?" She asked again, while checking Olivia's pulse. "Are you in much pain?"

"No," Olivia replied, when the thermometer was taken from her mouth. "No, the pain seems to have eased."

"Good. I heard what Doctor Mehta did to you last night, it must have been hell for you?"

"Yes it was. I can't believe how I let her do it. I had no idea she was going to do that to me and I couldn't stop her. It seemed to happen so fast, but go on forever. I thought she was tearing my womb out and the pain was so bad, it was worse than having a baby, I've never felt anything like it before."

"I should hope not, it was barbaric what was done to you," Susan said, passing Olivia her tea. "Here drink this while it's hot. Doctor Mehta is a bad doctor, none of the staff like her, not even Doctor Stevens. It will be a good thing when she's gone back to wherever it is she comes from. She's just a very sadistic and cruel woman. Now can I get you any breakfast?"

"No thanks, I just want to sleep, I'm still very tired" Olivia replied.

"Okay, you go back to sleep, you do have bit of a temperature, so we'll keep checking on you. We'll give you a bed bath later, before we change your bed," Wendy said.

"Could I have a bath in the bathroom, instead?" Olivia asked.

"Yes, I'm sure you can, if you feel up to it," agreed Susan.

***

Olivia went back to sleep for a few more hours, waking when she felt very wet and sticky between her thighs. *God! Why am I so bloody wet?* She thought, pulling the bed covers back and seeing blood, lots of it, between her legs and on the bottom sheet of the bed. "Nurse," she shouted anxiously, "nurse, can I see you please?"

"Yes, what's wrong?" Nurse Susan asked, running over to Olivia's bed.

"Blood, lots of it look, it's all over my legs, why the hell am I bleeding so much? I hope I'm not starting to haemorrhage. I need to have a bath, I've got to get myself cleaned up."

"Yes okay. No I don't think that you're haemorrhaging, but yes come on, I'll run you a warm bath. Can you manage to walk, or shall I get you a wheel chair?"

"I think I can manage, though I do feel a bit weak."

Olivia was glad to climb into the warm bath and stretch out and relax. "This feels so good, can I put some more hot water in?"

"No," Susan replied, handing Olivia a bar of soap and a washcloth. "Don't have the water any hotter, because it will make you bleed heavily, and we want to stop the bleeding. I'll leave this bath towel on the chair here for you, with a clean nightdress and a pad. Press that button on the wall there, if you feel faint, or need any help when you are ready to go back to your bed. I'm going to change your bed now. Don't stay in the bath too long Olivia, lunch will be served soon."

"Okay then," Olivia answered, beginning to soap her body vigorously, rubbing more and more soap onto herself, her legs and the inside of her thighs, as though she was trying to wash, and cleanse Doctor Mehta, from her body.

After her lunch she felt very weak and tired, and just wanted to sleep. She had been given another injection to stop the bleeding and her temperature was still a little high at ninety-nine degrees Fahrenheit.

***

The dishes from the evening meal had been cleared away, and Olivia was sitting up in her bed eagerly waiting for her parents to arrive at visiting time, as she had so much to tell them. Especially her Father, as she thought, *I'm going to tell my Dad, about that bloody doctor, and what she did to me last night. I know that he'll sort her out, just like he used to sort my teachers out at school, when I was younger, if they picked on me, hit me, or bullied me, just because I couldn't get my sums right. He'll pin that horrid Doctor Mehta, up against the wall, with his large hand around her throat, and shout in her face, frightening her to death, telling her that he'll break her bloody neck, if she comes near me or touches me again. Just like he did to that miss Parker, who shouted at me and slapped my hand, in Junior-school, just because I got a few of my sums wrong. My Dad never lets anyone hurt me and get away with it. Yes I can't wait to see my Dad, he'll sort that evil bitch out, and everyone in this ward will see my Dad taking care of her, 'cause he doesn't care who's around; no one would dare stop him. I wish that he'd been here last night, and I wish that he'd hurry up and get here now.*

The nurse opened the big doors to the ward, at seven o'clock and Olivia's parents were some of the first visitors to enter the ward.

"Hello love, how are you feeling?" Her Mother asked, giving her a kiss on the cheek, when they walked up to her bed. "Your looking a bit flushed. Isn't she Eric?"

Eric just nodded in agreement, after he also kissed her on the cheek.

"Hello Mum, Dad. When I tell you what happened to me last night, you'll know why I am looking so bloody flushed."

"Why, what happened to you love?" Her Mother asked.

Olivia began to tell her parents of the nightmare ordeal, she had been through the night before, and how she felt that Doctor Mehta, was trying to tear her womb out, with her long, bright red finger nails, just to punish her, for losing her baby. And how she had wished that her Dad had been there to protect her. But by the time she got to the end of her story, she felt that her parents were not interested in the pain and the violation that her body had been put through. That they just didn't seem to care, or even wanted to know about it, all the pain she'd had to endure.

"Well what do you expect us to do about it?" Her Mother asked, in a haughty tone of voice, feeling rather helpless.

"I want my Dad to see that bloody Doctor Mehta and do something to hurt her, and make her suffer, like she did me, she just can't get away with what she did, can she Dad? You've got no idea how much she hurt me."

"Well I can't do anything about it now," her Father replied, making his hands, which were at the side of him, into clenched fists. "Anyway when you go messing around with boys and getting yourself pregnant, what do you expect? People won't put up with this kind of behaviour from young girls like you, who keep getting yourselves pregnant," her Father replied, trying to justify his means for not seeing the Doctor, who had hurt his daughter. "She probably thought that you, deserve all you've been through, and hope it's taught you a good lesson."

"Mess around with boys," shouted an upset Olivia, dismayed at their response as she looked from one to the other. "But I haven't been messing around with boys. Stan was my boyfriend and I love him, and we were going to get married in a few months time."

"Yes, and you were having another baby," her Mother replied in a loud whisper, with a disgusted 'tut', added to the end of her words. "Anyway, it's over with now, and Stan took off to Australia the other month, so it's no good crying over spilt milk anymore. You're just going to have to pull yourself together and forget about all this now, just try to put it out of your mind, as if none of it has ever happened."

"We've told the customers who come in the pub, and we've also heard that it's around the village, that you were rushed into hospital to have your appendix out," her Father said, with a slight laugh in his voice, trying to change the subject.

"Have my appendix out! But I've still got my bloody appendix," Olivia shouted in disbelief.

"Just listen to her Margaret, I could bloody slap her one, the ungrateful little bugger."

"Don't you realise that the people in the village didn't know, that you were having another baby, so they won't be talking about you, thank God," her Mother said

"I don't bloody care what people know or say about me. And at least while their talking about me, they're leaving someone else's life alone," Olivia shouted. "And if it keeps them all bloody happy talking about me, then let them get on with it. But it certainly seems to worry you two very much, what people say, doesn't it? But then again it always has, hasn't it? Now will you please go?"

"We've just driven about twenty bloody miles from the village to see her, and she wants us to go now," her Father said, with a shake of his head.

"We've only just got here we're not leaving yet," added her Mother, trying to take control of the situation.

"Please go," Olivia told them again. "Go home, I don't want to argue with you two anymore and that's all we seem to be doing. Anyway I don't feel too well, I feel so hot and tired."

"Well then, if your feeling poorly, we'd better go and let you get some rest," her Father replied.

"Oh all right, and I suppose after what you've been through, we should let you get some sleep. You'll be coming home soon, and you'll be all right then," her Mother said, giving her a good night kiss on her cheek.

As Olivia watched her parents walking out of the ward, she was feeling very hurt and painfully thinking. *I thought that they cared about me and loved me, but my Dad wouldn't even see that Doctor Mehta, when I told him what she had done to me. They just want me to forget the whole thing, the illegal abortion, and my baby boy, Oliver, who I've just lost. They've never even asked me what sex the baby was; I suppose it was just a thing to them. And after all this pain that I've been through just for them, and I should now act as if none of it has ever happened to me. Well fine, if that's what they want, I will never mention this, or think of it, ever again, for as long as I live.* So it was that for the next twenty years, these memories were to remain buried very deeply in Olivia's subconscious mind.

******

Chapter 5

LATER THAT EVENING

Sally, the night nurse came on duty, pushing the drink trolley, and going to each bed asking the patients what they wanted for their night-time milky drinks, before she made them. She finally came to Olivia's bed, bringing Olivia, the hot, milky Ovaltine drink, that she usually asked for. "Hello Olivia, here's your Ovaltine. And how are you feeling tonight?"

"Hot, very hot. And I don't want a hot drink tonight, only cold water please."

"Let me take your temperature, you do look flushed."

After looking at the thermometer when it was taken from Olivia's mouth, Sally continued, "Yes I'm not surprised, 101 degrees. Do you have any pain? And are you bleeding much?"

"Yes, I've got a bit of pain but the bleeding isn't heavy. I'm going to drink a couple of glasses of cold water, and go to sleep now, 'cause I'm feeling very tired."

"Okay but I'll keep checking on you during the night. Do you want something for the pain?"

"No thanks, I'll be okay."

***

Olivia fell into a very restless sleep, and began to develop a fever during the night. She was starting to moan loudly in her sleep, when Nurse Sally came to take her temperature again at 2:00 a.m. On finding that it had risen to 103.5 degrees, Sally decided to call in the Emergency Doctor on night duty.

"My God!" Said Doctor Allan, a small, young man, with bright blue eyes, and blonde hair, when he read Olivia's file and charts. "This Doctor Mehta did this to her?"

"Yes, and it was horrid," Sally replied.

"Well, I'm not surprised she has a fever after all that she's been through. She's more than likely got a bad internal infection raging inside of her. Here get me these medications from the narcotic medicine cabinet, nurse," Doctor Allan said, in an angry voice, giving Nurse Sally the piece of paper he had written them on. "And double check that you bring the right ones, because these are very strong drugs. I'll also need three large syringes."

"Yes Doctor," Sally replied, hurrying away to get the medications.

"You will be okay soon kid, I hope," Doctor Allan said, pushing Olivia's damp, dark hair gently off her face. "I wish I'd have been called to this ward last night, I would have put a stop to that doctor's evil antics."

Olivia did not hear Doctor Allan's words as she rolled about in the bed delirious, with her temperature continuing to rise.

"Here you are Doctor," Sally said, handing Doctor Allan the medications and syringes.

"Thank God!" Doctor Allan replied, checking the labels on the vials. "I have to get this into her fast, to try and stabilize her. She's delirious now, check her temperature again nurse."

"104.8 degrees," Sally said, reading the thermometer.

"God! I hope it doesn't go any higher," the doctor said, in a concerned tone of voice. "Get some tepid water and sponge her all over, lets try and get her temperature down."

"MY BABY!!! I WANT MY BABY OLIVER!!!!! I HAVE TO FIND HIM!!!!! NO STOP DOING THIS!!!!!! LISTEN.... HE'S CRYING FOR ME!!!!!! NO, DON'T TAKE MY BABY... GIVE OLIVER BACK TO ME!!!!! DON'T.... NO.... DON'T TAKE MY BABY... MY BABY.... HE'S SO LONELY WITHOUT ME!!!!!!!!" Olivia began shouting and screaming incoherently, while she was burning up with a fever.

"It's okay, your going to be just fine," said Sally, while wiping Olivia's face, and neck with a cool damp cloth.

"HELP ME!!!!! STOP HER!!!!! DAD HELP ME.... HELP ME PLEASE DAD!!!!!! HELP ME FIND MY BABY!!!!! DAD WHERE ARE YOU?????" Olivia continued to shout.

"Those injections should start to work soon," Doctor Allan said. "Check her temperature in another hour, I'll stay here until she stabilises. I also want to see this Doctor Mehta, do you know when she comes on duty, nurse?"

"Not really, maybe it's around 8 a.m. I think you'll catch her then."

Olivia's fever and delirium continued well into the next day, with her temperature fluctuating between 103.5 and 104.8 degrees Fahrenheit. Every three hours she was given three large injections for her infected pelvis, and the nurses were giving her tepid bed baths every hour along with sips of cold water, when they could get her to drink. Everyone was very concerned about her and hoped she would pull through.

***

At ten-thirty the next evening her fever began to break, her temperature dropped to 101, then later to 98.4 degrees Fahrenheit.

"Hello there!" Said a smiling Doctor Allan, when Olivia at last opened her eyes, "Welcome back to the land of the living. How do you feel?"

"Strange, what happened to me?"

"You have been very, very ill, but you are going to be okay now."

"I'm thirsty, can I have a drink please?"

"Yes, would you like a nice cup of tea?"

"Yes please and who are you?"

"Nurse, get Olivia a cup of tea will you please?"

"Yes Doctor I will," Nurse Sally replied, holding Olivia's hand and smiling at her.

"I am Doctor Allan, and I was called from Emergency last night to help you when your temperature rose very high, and you became delirious. I came to see how you were doing tonight, because you have been very ill."

"Thank you for helping me Doctor."

"That's our job, to help people and make them well again."
Olivia drank her cup of tea and had a restful nights' sleep.

***

The next morning when she awoke, she asked Gladys to bring her a big breakfast because she was now feeling very hungry.

"I will luv," Gladys said, smiling at Olivia. "And its only one and a half sugars in your tea isn't it dear? It's good to see you are feeling better this morning; we were all very worried about you. It's because of what that awful Doctor Mehta did to you the other night, that you've been so ill."

"How do you know what Doctor Mehta did to me? I didn't tell you."

"Oh, everybody's still talking about it luv, and some are saying that Doctor Allan, has reported her to the Medical Superintendent Administrator, so she'll soon be gone from this hospital."

"Good. That's what my Dad should have done."

***

Olivia was sitting up in bed and feeling much better. She had taken a bath, washed her hair and was wearing a clean, fresh nightdress. She had no more pain now and the bleeding had stopped. She was eagerly waiting to see the doctor, so she could ask him if she could go home today?

When Doctor Stevens, a medium built, young man, with red hair, came onto the ward to do his morning rounds; there was no Doctor Mehta with him today.

Good she's gone, she thought, with a happy smile on her face, when she saw Doctor Stevens by himself.

"Hello," Doctor Stevens said, when he approached Olivia's bed smiling. "My, my, I'm pleased to see you look much better today. How do you feel after being so ill? You certainly gave us all a fright."

"I feel much better today Doctor, I think I have Doctor Allan to thank for saving my life."

"I suppose you could say that, our Doctor Allan is a very good doctor."

"Can I go home today please? I'm really missing my baby, I can't wait to see him."

"Nurse, has Olivia been complaining of any pain this morning, and has the bleeding stopped?" The doctor asked, gently feeling around Olivia's pelvic and stomach area.

"No Doctor," Nurse Wendy replied, smiling at Olivia. "She says the pain has gone, and the bleeding has stopped."

"Good, I'll tell you what Olivia, you can go home tomorrow, but today I want you to stay in bed and get plenty of rest, because I'm sure you are still feeling a little weak. I'll get Sister to phone your parents, and ask them to come and pick you up in the morning, is that okay?" Doctor Stevens said, feeling a surge of compassion for Olivia after what she had been through.

"Great," Olivia replied, with a big smile on her face. "And thank you doctor."

"Just you take it easy and look after yourself. I don't want to see you in here again."

***

Olivia walked through the large doors of the Manchester Royal Hospital with her head held high, when she went with her parents to their car. She had to hold her head up very high, she was a sixteen-year-old unmarried Mother, in the year of 1967, who would now still have to find her own identity, because other people would be so eager to stick their own labels on her, for her to live with.

******

Chapter 6

Olivia did not talk very much, during the journey in the car, on the drive back from the General Hospital, in Manchester, about twenty to twenty-five miles from the Hope-Valley-District of Derbyshire, to her home in Bradwell. A small country village, nestled amongst a group of other small villages and hamlets named, Bamford, Calver, Eyam, Grindleford, Padley-Mill, Hope, Edale, Brough, Great-Hucklow, Little-Hucklow, Ashton, Thornhill, Abney, Grindlow, Dove-Dale, Stony-Middleton, Froggatt, Millers-Dale and Tideswell.

Also included amongst this group of villages, are two of the more interesting, popular and much better known to most of the people in the North of England, the villages of Castleton and Hathersage. Where in the village church graveyard in Hathersage, was buried and laid to rest, the body of 'Little-John' who used to be a member of 'Robin Hood's-Band-Of-Merry-Men', whom all lived happily together in Sherwood-Forest, Nottinghamshire, and who always took from the rich and gave to the poor.

Castleton village has its 'Blue-John-Caverns', high up in it's hilly mountain sides, making it a very popular tourist attraction, and tourist village area. With people coming from all around England in the summer time, to visit and look around these 'Blue-John-Caverns.' Seeing the lovely, 'Blue-John-Crystalline-Rock' with it's beautiful shades of different colours of blue and bluish-purple-crystal. Which the Romans discovered, about 2,000 years ago, found in veins of some 3-inches thick, in nodular-forms, lining the inner walls of these cavities here in the hillside caverns. It is only here in these country hillside caverns, in the village of Castleton in Derbyshire, where the only known and very extremely rare deposits of beautiful crystalline 'Blue-John-Stone' can be found in the world. The mining and work done with this crystal rock, began on a grand scale about 250 years ago, done by existing, Marble-workers, consisting then mainly of the making of solid, 'Blue-John-Urns'. 'Blue-John' was then later popularised in the latter part of the 18th century, with large vases, chalices and clocks then being made from it. The mining techniques of the 'Blue-John-Crystal' have changed very little at all, since the times of the Roman-Empire. It is still essentially all done by hand and in its natural state when mined, but it is an extremely difficult material to work with, because of the brittleness of its crystalline nature. It is now still made by very artistic marble craftsmen, into beautiful pieces of jewellery, with the stone set into real silver, or gold mounts, including rings, necklaces, bracelets, watches, broaches or lighters, vases and sculptured figurines. Which the tourist can then buy in the lovely sparkling-gift shops, which are placed at the exits of each 'Blue-John-Cavern', where they are all so eager to go into and purchase as many pieces of the beautiful expensive, crystal jewellery, along with pictures and post-cards of the 'Blue-John-Caverns', that they can afford to buy. Usually promising each other, that they will definitely, come back soon, in the not to distant future, to buy a lot more of this wonderful, very rare, hardly ever seen anywhere else in the world, 'Blue-John-Crystal-Jewellery'.

The tourists can go into and visit these fascinating, 'Blue-John-Caverns', by going into the 'Speedwell-Cavern', high up on the hill called 'Winnats-Pass'. They go around this cavern on board a boat tour, but the boat does not speed around the cavern as the title of the cavern suggests. Every one, of about 20-people at a time, get into a long, rowing-boat. And the tour-guide of the rowing-boat, instead of using oars to row it, lays down flat upon his back, on the bottom of the boat, placing his feet upon the ceiling, of the low, roofed cave, slowly guiding and pushing the boat along and around the cave with his feet. And while laid on his back, talking and pointing out with his hands the things of interest to the people, especially the 'Blue-John-Crystal-Rock' that can be seen twinkling and sparkling, in the walls of the cavern, for the tourist in the boat with him, to look at.

There are also two other 'Blue-John-Caverns' to visit, the one on the hill of 'Mam-Tor', and the 'Treak-Cliff-Cavern' at the bottom of 'Mam-Tor'. The tourists can take a leisurely walk around these caves, going through narrow-tunnels and up and down a lot of very, steep steps, on these tours they are able to feel and touch with their hands, the 'Blue-John-Crystal-Rock-Veins', that have formed and are sparkling in the cavern walls. They also see the funny, unusual looking, beigey/brown coloured, Stalagmites and Stalactites that grow inside of these caves. Which of course are always pointed out to them, by the tour-guide for everyone to notice, telling his tourists, that they have been growing inside the damp, wetness of these caves, for hundreds of years now. And also to try and remember the fact, that the Stalagmites grow up, and the Stalactites grow down, taking many-many years, before the tips of them, ever get to touch with each other and then joining together as one.

The 'Blue-John-Caverns' are always closed to the public during the wintertime, so that the 'Blue-John-crystal-rock' can be mined, dug out from the walls. To make more beautiful jewellery to sell to the public, in the pretty, sparkling, glittering, glassed-shelves of the 'Blue-John-Shops'. For the next summers' tourists, who will all arrive again, to come to visit the caverns and purchase more of this very rare, pretty jewellery, from these gift shops.

***

Olivia lived in the rarely visited by tourists, boring village of Bradwell, which only had a very large, high hill called Bradwell-Edge, at the start of the village, running along one side of it. She lived with her parents, who owned a public house called the 'White Hart', and her Sister Suzanne, a pretty blue-eyed girl, with blonde hair, who was twelve months younger.

She was excited about seeing her baby son Antony again, and was thinking about him while looking at the countryside through the car window. Knowing that any grieving she may have done, for the loss of her dead-baby-boy-Oliver, must now be over and done with. She knew that she must not take any of the pain, or the sadness of his loss home with her, or she would be in trouble with her parents if they saw her, shedding one single little tear for him. Yes Olivia knew what was expected of her from now on, about any grieving problems she may have, that they must all be swept under the carpet!!!

"How's Antony? I can't wait to see him," she asked.

"Oh he's fine, he's at the pub with Mrs. Mason," her Father replied. "And I suppose he's missed his Mummy, but you know he's okay with us."

"I'm sure he was. But I'm glad I will be back home with him soon," Olivia replied.

"Mandy came to see you at the pub last night. And I told her you were in hospital, and you'd had your appendix out, and would be home sometime today," her Mother said.

"Yes," added Olivia's Father, "don't forget to tell your friends, that you've had your appendix out, okay!"

Oh yes, my bloody appendix! I mustn't forget them, must I. That's what I left at the hospital, instead of a dead baby! Olivia thought with a sad smile, as she stared out of the car window. *Here's hoping I never get appendicitis, or what would the story around the village be about me then? That they must have grown back one day, so I had to have them taken out again!*

***

She was asleep in the back seat of the car when they pulled into the 'White Hart' car park.

"We're home," her Mother said. "Wake up Olivia, we're home."

When opening her eyes and realising where she was, she pushed the car door open and jumped out. Running into the pub and through into the living room, looking for Antony.

Antony was sitting in his high chair, and threw his little arms into the air, squealing with glee and laughter when he saw his Mummy.

"Antony, my wonderful, adorable baby Antony," Olivia said, lifting her green-eyed baby, out of his chair, and kissing his little chubby cheeks. "Oh! I have missed you my baby. I'll take you out for a walk soon, I'm sure you'd like that wouldn't you?"

"Goo-goo," Antony replied, laughing and blowing bubbles. He was so pleased to see his Mummy again.

"Hello Olivia, how are you?" Mrs. Mason asked, coming into the living room from the bar.

"Hello Mrs. Mason, I'm fine, but I'm sure Antony has missed me."

"Oh I'm sure he has, haven't you Antony?" She said, while squeezing his little hand.

"Ga-ga," Antony replied, laughing and blowing raspberries.

"Have there been many customers in yet?" Eric asked Mrs. Mason, when he came into the living room with Margaret his wife.

"No, only a couple, and Mrs. Wright returned some beer bottles," replied Mrs. Mason. "Would you like me to make you a coffee now Margaret?"

"Yes please, I think we'll all have one, and a ham sandwich for lunch. Then I'll have a sleep because I'm feeling quite tired after that long journey."

Mrs. Mason took her coffee and sandwich with her back into the bar, because the lunchtime customers were beginning to arrive.

"I couldn't stop thinking about you Olivia, a couple of days ago," her Mother said. "And I was dreaming about you in the night, I woke up in a cold sweat and came downstairs and made myself a cup of tea."

"That's when I had the bad fever. Didn't you think of phoning the hospital to ask how I was?"

"No, because what could I have done for you?"

"Didn't you think I may have been reaching out with my mind and asking for you?"

"No! Anyway you were in the best place. Now then I must call Ellen my hairdresser, I think I'll have some silver streaks put in my hair tomorrow," continued her Mother, looking at her nails to see if they needed another manicure, as she got up out of her chair, walking over to the telephone.

Olivia's large green eyes, just stared at her Mother, wondering what she could ever do to get her Mother to care about her, just a little more.

"Do you want any groceries from the Co-Op this afternoon Mum? Because I am going to give Antony his lunch now, and then I'll take him for a walk in the village, to see the ducks and give them some bread."

"Yes, I'll write you a small list of things to get for me, and it will certainly save me a journey."

After giving Antony his lunch she changed his nappy, washed his hands and face and combed his hair, telling him he was a pretty little boy, before taking him out for his walk.

***

LATER THAT AFTERNOON

Antony was sat up in his big, blue pram smiling, and feeling a happy boy as his mummy wheeled him through the village. It was a bright sunny afternoon, and she was pleased to at last be back home with her baby son, and to start to get on with her life once again.

"Hello Olivia, where have you been this last week?"

She turned around on hearing her friend, David's voice behind her. David was nineteen years old and good looking, in a rugged sort of way, with brown hair and dark blue eyes. He was a very definite but caring and honest, fun-to-be-with type of person. He had only lived in the village of Bradwell for about a year now, and was finding life very different and strange, to adjust to here in this small village, compared to the big city of Manchester, where he'd grown up and originally came from, with his parents and two Sisters. He was very popular with all of the teenagers in the village, and they just loved the way he talked, with his Manchester accent, most of them never hearing an accent like that before.

"Hello David, I've been in hospital."

"Yeah, so I heard. Some people are saying you had a miscarriage, and others are saying you had your appendix out, well which ever it was, are you feeling okay now?" David asked with a kind smile.

"Yes thanks I'm fine now, I just got back this morning. I'm taking Antony for a walk, and to get my mum some things from the Co-Op."

"Anyway it's good to see you girl. And are you going to come out, down the village tonight with Suzanne, Brenda, Sandra, Jane, Jill, Cheryl and Angela?"

"I suppose so, what else is there to do around here?"

"I know, I wished I'd never left Manchester, and it's great night life there. This village life does take some bloody getting used too, for a city bloke like me."

"Yeah, I suppose it will. Anyway okay Dave, I'll see you later, on the bridge tonight. Bye for now," Olivia replied, putting the brake on Antony's pram, outside the very big window of the village Co-Op shop.

***

While inside the shop, as she was walking around it, filling one of the metal shopping baskets with groceries from the shelves, a voice at the side of her said, "Hello Olivia, How are you? Are you all right? We heard about you, didn't we Jean?"

"Yes, and we're ever so sorry for you," added Jean, in a sad tone of voice.

Olivia just nodded at Mary and Jean, saying, "Yes thank you, I'm all right. But what are you sorry about?"

"Well," continued Mary, "We heard that you'd been-int hospital, and had a miscarriage or your appendix out."

"Which was it?" Asked Jean, eagerly.

"What?" Olivia replied.

"Well was it a miscarriage, or was it your appendix?" Mary asked, hoping to be one of the first people, to get the story of the village gossip about Olivia right, so that she would be able to inform everyone else of the facts.

"That's for me to know, and for you to think about," Olivia replied, turning away from Mary and Jean, and walking across to another shelf of groceries, to get some of the other things on her shopping list.

While paying for her groceries at the check out counter, she looked across at the big window of the shop, noticing Mary and Jean standing outside at the other side of the window talking together, with their babies in their pushchairs, knowing they were waiting to talk to her, to ask her more questions.

Olivia did not, and never had liked, these very nosey girls, who were four years older than her, she usually never had anything to do with them. She pitied them really because she felt they were so dumb, stupid and very dirty looking, and both always smelt as though they had not had a wash, or taken a bath in weeks. Jean had short brassy-bleached-blonde hair that was black at the roots. Mary had mousy coloured hair that hung in greasy strands on her shoulders. Both girls had thick foundation make-up on their faces, that looked as if it could be scraped off with a knife, and eye shadow that lay in crease lines on their eyelids, instead of being smoothed and blended evenly. Their mascara stuck all their eyelashes together in thick blobs.

Seeing Olivia walk towards Antony's pram with her groceries, Mary and Jean pushed their babies' pushchairs towards her, with Mary saying, "Hey-Olivia did you hear about Doctor Oswald, our local Doctor? Well his son Mike got his girlfriend Sylvia pregnant, and she's only 14-years old yu know, isn't she Jean?"

"Yeah I know that she's only-14. And our Doctor's-son-Mike, well I heard that he's 15-years old himself, or he might have just turned-16 by now!" Jean replied.

"Anyway Olivia, Sylvia gave birth to this baby at home on the bathroom floor, all by herself! Yes her mother heard her screaming in the bathroom, so she went in there to see what she was screaming about, and saw Sylvia laid on the floor giving birth to this baby, it was coming out of her!" Mary eagerly went on to say. "Anyway we don't know if that baby is still alive or not, 'cause her mother could have drowned it in the toilet yu know! Or I suppose she could have given it away to somebody else to bring up. And I still don't know if that baby was a boy or a girl, or if Doctor Oswald knows that he's a grandfather yet. I've still got to find that out, haven't we Jean?"

"Oh yes we have to and if it's still alive, poor little bugger. And have you heard about your friend Mandy?" Jean asked.

"What about Mandy?" Olivia replied.

"Well we think she's also had a baby," Jean continued excitedly. "'Cause she went away pregnant the other month, and came back last week without the baby."

"So we think, that she must have had it adopted," added Mary.

"Why are you telling me this?" Olivia asked.

"Because we know she's your friend, and we thought she would have told you," Jean replied.

"Oh did you?" Olivia asked, in an angry tone of voice. "And if I did know anything, do you honestly believe I would tell you two? Or anyone else? If I did know that she's had a baby and told you all about it, would that make your boring little life's any happier? Would it make you better and greater people to have your stupid heads, full of more useless village gossip information?"

"No! But we were just wondering that's all," Jean replied.

"Yes just wondering and talking about things that are of no concern of yours. You girls' just love to bloody gossip about everyone, don't you? And what you don't know you very quickly make up, or add to a story to make it sound a lot more interesting, don't you? And the bloody awful things that you say about other people can hurt them," Olivia stated. "But that doesn't bother you two does it?"

"Oh no you've got it wrong there luv. We wouldn't want to hurt Mandy," Mary replied quickly, "Would we Jean?"

"No! No! Not us luv," Jean added.

"Well I know all about you two and have done for years," Olivia replied very positively, looking at each of them in turn. "And for the last three years, before you both got yourselves pregnant, you were in every bloody barn and hay stack in this village and the other villages, screwing anyone who was desperate, or pissed up enough to want either of you two. Then you started going in the cars with the men, who came over from Manchester and Sheffield, and the big rumour has it in all of the villages, that you both got VD. Then you found out you were pregnant and the boys in the village, who you said were the Fathers of your babies married you. So you are not unmarried Mothers like some of us are you? Now girls, if you don't stop all of this nasty gossip of yours about Mandy and I, I might just have to have a word with those poor husbands of yours. And when I tell them that, they are not the real Fathers of your babies, what do you think will happen to you both then?"

"Oh God! Mary, no! She wouldn't do that, would she?" Jean asked, in a fearful tone of voice.

"Oh yes I would, and I promise you I will," Olivia stated. "And remember this you two, Olivia doesn't get mad, she gets even."

She then screwed her face up in disgust, when Jean's 12 month-old-baby boy, picked his dirty bottle up off the rusty foot rest of his push chair, and put the dirty teat into his mouth. "Poor kid. Why don't you girls take your babies home, bath them and put some clean clothes on them, then give them a clean, sterile bottle to drink their milk from? Then clean yourselves up, take a bath and wash your hair."

"Okay Olivia, I think we will," Jean said nervously, now knowing that she had meet more than her match, with Olivia, and wanting to eagerly get away from her.

"Yes come on Jean, let's go. We'd better go and get our babies bathed right now, I hope we've got some hot water. But please don't go saying anything to our husbands about us, please Olivia," agreed a very nervous Mary.

Mary and Jean both began to hurriedly push their babies' pushchairs home, both chatting in a high pitched tone of voice, nervously to each other at the same time. Hoping that Olivia never sees their husbands soon in the village.

***

Baby Antony had fallen asleep, so she covered him with his warm blankets, and walked back through the village towards the bridge. A trout filled shallow brook ran underneath the small, quaint looking, natural-stone built bridge, with the water coming out on the other side of the very narrow, busy major village road, continuing it's journey passed the back of some houses and fields, flowing out of the village and into streams which continued onto the other villages. The bridge was a very focal point, the place where the teenagers of the village of Bradwell, gathered to meet each other during the evenings and afternoons at weekends. The bridge had a brightly painted fire-engine-red telephone box, stood on a corner of it right next to the brook, overlooking the football and playing field. She hoped Antony would soon be awake, to help her throw some bread into the water for the ducks to eat. The ducks lived and nested in the green plants, which grew on and around the brook.

***

The green and white Hope-Valley-College school bus came to a stop on the small road, outside Mr. Howard's plumbing and storage-garage across from the brook.. Suzanne, Cheryl, Brenda, Jill, Sandra, and Angela, got off the school bus and came running over to them. They all put their arms around Olivia, giving her kisses and hugs, saying how much they had missed her, asking her if she was better now, and how good it was to see her again.

Olivia had grown up with these school friends of hers, and they were all very close, doing everything and going everywhere together. Angela had always been Olivia's best friend, their close friendship began when they started school together at the age of four, and she always called Angela, 'Angel', because she said, she could always see a halo around her head.

Antony woke up with all the talking and laughing noise that the girls were making. He was so excited to see everyone and especially the ducks, who were quacking. He was laughing, and squealing and trying to make the same quacking sounds that they made. Suzanne showed him how to throw the bread onto the water for them to eat, and he clapped his little hands in glee when the ducks ate the bread. Angela then lifted him out of his pram, and was dancing around with him in her arms; he loved this, and was laughing and began blowing raspberries at everyone.

"Are you coming out tonight?" Jill asked.

"I think so," Olivia replied.

"Good, I'll bring my radio so we can listen to radio Luxembourg, and we'll party in the playing field," Sandra said.

Suzanne linked arms with Olivia, to walk back up the hill to the pub, saying, "Okay, we'll see you all on the bridge later."

"Call for me about six-thirty," Jill shouted to Sandra and Angela. "And don't be late."

"Yeah I'll see you all on the bridge around seven," Cheryl shouted to everyone.

"Right see you all later," Angela replied. "And let's get some cigarettes, so all bring some money out with you, okay."

***

Their mother Margaret, was cooking the evening dinner when the girls arrived home. "Dinner smells good," Olivia said, passing the groceries to her Mother. "Is there anything I can do to help you?"

"No love, Suzanne can set the table for me. You can put some of the cabbage, mashed potatoes and skinned sausage, in Antony's baby dish, with some gravy over it."

"Oh yes Antony, will love that, I'll mash it up with a fork so there are no lumps in it. I'll just change his nappy first though, so he'll feel fresher."

Antony had climbed up onto his Grandfathers knee, when Olivia lifted him off saying, "Dad, is it okay if I go down to the bridge tonight, with Suzanne, to see my friends?"

"Who! Who're these friends that your in such a hurry to see?"

"Jill, Cheryl, Brenda, Sandra, Angel and the other girls. Please Dad? 'Cause I want to see them all?"

"I suppose so, but I want you back home at nine o'clock."

"Okay, I will be."

***

LATER THAT EVENING

After they had eaten their evening meal, Olivia helped her Mother to wash and dry the dishes. She then gave Antony his night-time bath, and he soon went to sleep when she put him in his cot with his teddy bears.

"Are you ready?" Suzanne asked, when Olivia went back downstairs.

"Yes, I'll just get my coat."

As they walked passed the bar to go out of the pub, their Father shouted, "Don't forget girls, be home for nine o'clock."

"Okay Dad," answered Suzanne.

***

A group of village-men were sitting in one of the rooms, down the hallway away from the bar. They ranged in age from twenty to thirty-six, and were all drinking beer from pint-pot glasses. A few of them were married but the rest were either engaged to be, or preferred to stay still single.

When Suzanne and Olivia passed the door of the room that the men were in, one of them called out, "Hey Olivia, come here a minute."

"Yes," Olivia said, entering the room. She had known these men for many years in her life now, and they had always been very kind and polite to her in the past.

"Hey Olivia," one of the young men said, putting his pint-pot on the table after taking a drink of his beer. "We were just talking about you. Some of us heard you'd been in hospital and had your appendix out, and some of us have heard you'd had a miscarriage."

"Which was it Olivia?" One of the other men asked.

She looked around the table, at the faces of all the men sat there, with her green eyes, wide in disbelief at them, she really did not want to think that they could be laughing, and talking about her, but they all had smiles on their faces.

"Well Olivia?" She was asked again. "Aren't you going to tell us which it was?"

"Huh, you can all sod off, 'cause that's for me to know and for you to find out," she replied.

"But how can we find out Olivia?" One of the older men asked. "Your boyfriend Stan took off to Australia, and left you and Antony, didn't he?"

"Why did he leave you Olivia?" Another man inquired laughingly. "We heard he beat you up and tried to strangle you. Was it because you said no to him one night?"

"Don't worry Olivia, I'm free, you can go with me, if you like. And I'll give you another baby anytime," another man volunteered.

"Me too," added another man laughing.

"Sod you, sod you all, you fucking animals," Olivia shouted at the men in a hurt voice, walking out of the room.

"What was that all about?" Asked Suzanne, who was waiting for Olivia by the outside door of the pub.

"Nothing, just the local farm boys enjoying their sick, little jokes. Let's go."

Olivia now felt like an avenging phoenix, trying to rise from the ashes of the pain, of the loss of her dead baby Oliver, after all the hurt and emotional upset, that she felt Stan had caused and put her through. She was filled with such a deep emptiness, knowing that she would never rest, or feel complete again, until she had found Stan. She needed to ask him why he had made her pregnant again, and then left her to face the consequences alone, knowing himself how hard life could be for someone, whom the village people thought had done wrong. She didn't know when, where, or how long, it would take her to find him again, but one day she knew, deep down inside of herself, that she would eventually find him, and he would have a lot of questions to answer for her.

***

They walked down the hill from the pub to the bridge, seeing that they were late and all of their friends were now gathered as a large group in the playing field. "Hello," Jill shouted. "Come on over, we're trying to get a small fire started with these branches. Sandra's brought some crisps, and Angela's asking for money off us all to get some cigarettes. David, Ian, Graham and Les have gone over to the Shoulder pub, to get some cider for us all to drink."

"Here Angel," Olivia said, putting her hand into her pocket. "I've got some money, how much more do you need?"

"About two shillings," Angela replied, holding her hand out to Olivia, waiting for her to put some money into it. "Thanks, I think I'll have enough now."

"Oh, and get some more matches please," Cheryl shouted. "'Cause we're running out of them trying to get this bloody fire started."

David, Ian, Graham and Les arrived back onto the playing field carrying some bottles. Suzanne's boyfriend Ian, passed her a bottle of cider, saying, "Here Suzanne have a drink of this. But don't get pissed, 'cause your Father will fucking kill us."

"No I won't," Suzanne answered laughing, taking the bottle.

"Olivia, can I talk to you?" David asked.

"Sure, what about?"

"Come and sit on the swings away from the others, because it's kind of private what I want to ask you."

They both went to sit on the swings and drink cider from the bottle. David lit two cigarettes and passed one to her saying, "Well Olivia, you are my friend and I care for you a lot, but I'm fucking sick of hearing the people in this village talking about you, and putting you down. They're saying you are nothing but a little whore, a tramp, and a slag. I want to marry you Olivia, and be a Father to Antony, and then all this talk about you will stop."

Olivia looked into his eyes, saying, "Thanks David, that's very good of you, but I can't marry you because I don't love you, I still love Stan."

"Yes, and where the fuck is he?" David replied nastily. "The bastard fucked off and left you when you needed him. He never loved you Olivia, he just fucking used you, and he should have known better because he was four years older than you."

"Don't you think he loved me?" Olivia asked, with tears welling up in her eyes.

"No I don't, and I'm glad he's gone. I hope you will soon get over him and start a new life for yourself."

Olivia started to cry really hard, while saying, "In time, I hope I can forget him."

David put his arms around her, and began to kiss her on the cheek and around the lips, while tenderly saying, "Don't cry Olivia, please don't cry, I didn't mean to upset you, I feel that you've been through enough. Let's be close friends and remember I'll always be here for you, and tell me if and when, you would like us to be married okay. The offer is always open."

Olivia responded to David's kisses eagerly and wrapped her arms around him. She felt so alone in the world and hoped that feeling would go away soon.

"Hey David, Olivia," Ian shouted. "We're all thinking on Friday of going down to that discotheque that's opened near Bamford at the 'Marquis of Granby', it's about four miles away from here, are you two coming also?"

"That's a good idea," agreed David. "Do you want to go Olivia? It will be fun."

"No thanks I've never been to a discotheque before," Olivia replied, wiping her tears away with the back of her hand. "And I can't go 'cause I've got nothing to wear."

"Well we're not going without you, and don't worry, I'll lend you some of my clothes if you like," Angela said.

"Okay then I'll go," Olivia said with a smile.

"Right, Friday night it is then. We'll get the seven-thirty bus to Bamford, and a taxi back to Bradwell at twelve o'clock," Ian said.

"Great," everyone shouted.

They were all looking forward to this new adventurous night life scene, because it would be so different to what any of them had ever experienced in their young life's before.

******

Chapter 7

Olivia was giving Antony his lunch at twelve o'clock the next day, when she heard someone knocking gently, on the living room door.

"I'll get it," her Mother said, putting her green coloured, coffee cup and saucer down on the table, before opening the door.

"Oh hello Mandy, I told Olivia that you came round the other day. She's just giving Antony his lunch right now."

"Hello Mrs. Howard," Mandy replied. "I hope I haven't called at an inconvenient time."

"Mandy come on in," Olivia shouted happily, when hearing Mandy's voice. "It's so good to see you, how are you?"

"I'm fine Olivia, how are you?"

"Oh, I'm okay thank-you," she replied, with a shrug of her shoulders.

Mandy was twelve months older than Olivia, but looked about twenty-two instead of seventeen. She was five-foot-eight tall with copper coloured hair and blue eyes, a very attractive girl who had a lovely shaped figure.

She walked over to Antony and held his little hand saying, "Hello Antony, you are a big boy now, you were just a tiny baby the last time I saw you, you are a lovely boy."

Antony replied with his usual 'ga-gas' and laughter.

"Olivia, could we go over to my house when Antony's finished his lunch? I have something that I want to show you," Mandy asked, in a pleading tone of voice.

"Yes, he's nearly finished, I'll just wipe his hands and face and change his nappy. You don't need me for anything this afternoon, do you Mum?" Olivia shouted to her Mother, who was in the kitchen.

"No love, why?"

"Because I'm going over to Mandy's for the afternoon."

"Yes that's okay then."

The two girls were walking by the side of the brook, and Mandy was very quiet, while pushing Antony in his pram.

"Are you okay?" Olivia asked, in a concerned voice, "Because you're not very talkative. Is something wrong?"

"Yes, I'll be okay. We'll be home soon and then I want to talk to you. I don't want to talk about anything yet, because you know what these bloody village people are like. They snoop around and hide everywhere, just to hear what other people are saying, so they have something to gossip about, to keep their bloody boring, little, life's happy."

***

When they arrived at Mandy's house, Antony had fallen asleep in his pram, so Mandy gently lifted him into her arms, took him inside, and laid him on the living room carpet, covering him with a blanket so he would stay warm.

"Will he be all right there, Olivia?"

"Oh yeah, he'll be fine."

"Good, come into my bedroom will you. I want to show you something."

Olivia followed Mandy into her bedroom, and saw her go over to a set of white-topped drawers. She pulled open the bottom drawer putting her hand underneath a pile of thick sweaters, searching for something. Then pulling out a white medium sized envelope, taking six large photographs out of it, and passed them to Olivia saying, "Here I want you to look at these."

Olivia took the photos from her and her eyes grew larger, when she saw pictures of a beautiful, new born baby dressed in pink, with lots of dark brown curly hair. "Wow, this baby is adorable, just look at that little dimple in her chin, she's just gorgeous, who is she?"

"She's my baby, my sweet little Susie, and she weighed seven pounds three ounces, she was a breach baby she came out of me bum first. And I love her so much my heart is just breaking, and my arms just long to hold her again."

"But where is she now?" Olivia asked, feeling tears starting in her eyes.

"Gone! I had to put her up for adoption! I had to give my baby a last sweet kiss goodbye from me, and then walk away from her! Leaving her! All completely all alone in that hospital! And after I left her there, later-on someone came and took my baby, and have given her to some strange people, whom I will never know. And my little Susie will call some other lady Mummy! And I will never be allowed to see her or hold her again! And it's just bloody killing me!" Mandy replied, laying down on her bed and crying.

After looking at the beautiful baby photo's once again, Olivia put the photos of baby Susie, back into the envelope before placing it on top of the set of drawers. She then put her arms around Mandy to comfort her, crying along with her as they both knew what each other was feeling, as they tried to cry away their pain. Yes Olivia was now feeling a lot of Mandy's pain, along with her own about losing a baby that she shouldn't care anything about.

They laid with their arms wrapped around each other, holding on so tightly together, both crying so very hard. They both had so much hurt and pain that for a long time now had been bottled up, concealed very deep inside of them, painful secrets that they were both hanging on to, too scared to ever let go of. Secrets that their Mothers, had told them that they must never feel, talk about or show to anyone.

'No! Shush! Don't say a word to anyone in the world! And it will very soon get better and all go away!'

They were expected to push all of their pain to one side, to ignore it to walk away from it, to sweep it away underneath the carpet, so they would feel absolutely nothing at all, as if nothing had ever happened in their life's, to live their life's in a deep denial of it. So that their life's could and would, hopefully continue to go forward again one day, on a very different road. Yes go forward with a new clean slate, just wiping all of this out, as if nothing different or unusual had ever happened or taken place in their life's. Acting as though they had never been pregnant or conceived a child, never carried a growing embryo, a fetus, a baby inside of them. Feeling it start to kick them one day and punch the insides of them with it's little fists, as their babies grew and stretched and moved around inside of their wombs, telling them… *'Hey feel me! I'm alive! And you made me! I belong to you! You are my mummy!'*

No they must never ever think again of the unbearable pains they felt, when they went into the long, slow hours of labour pain, pains that were so strong with the feeling that it was just wracking and tearing apart their naive young bodies, at times making them really think that their punishment was going to be death, yes a very painful death for having these out of wedlock babies. This was their justice these pains that no one had ever told them or warned them about, violent breath-taking-gagging-pains, that made some of them scream out for forgiveness. Pain that they had to endure all alone, with no husband or relative to encourage them, telling them that they were doing fine and everything would soon be okay, to help them get through it by holding onto their hands or wiping their brows. And finally when at last they did give birth, to their must hide away get rid of and always deny ever happened, dark, dirty secret, little babies, which they had carried and felt grow as they developed inside of them for nine-months. When the umbilical-cord was cut by the doctor or midwife, and the healthy, kicking, crying babies were wiped clean, before being passed to these girls to hold, nurse and love, there was no other member of their family there with them in the delivery room, to rejoice or congratulate them on a job well done!!!!

Yes they must hide all of this, their hurtful, tearful, sorrowful, physical and mental pain, from the rest of the world forever and to forget all about it, as no one else must ever know!

So that when their mothers had been putting on their make up and dressing in their smart outfits, keeping up their very smart appearances for everyone else to see. As they so rightfully felt that they should, in their kind and caring so-self-serving ways, carrying themselves with their heads held high and shoulders pulled straight back, with so much pride and self-respect still oozing from them. When they would walk through the village streets of Bradwell, to do their shopping, go to the bank, the post-office, a visit to the hairdressers, or go out for a drink to one of the local pubs in the evenings with their husbands. If anyone should dare to enquire or ask them. 'How are Olivia or Mandy doing?' Their Mother's would be able to reply with a very comfortable smile, which would instantly form so falsely around their carefully, lipstick-painted-mouths,--- *'Oh, she's doing very well, thank you, she had to leave the village, to take a very good job that was offered to her!!!!'*

***

Later that afternoon when Mandy and Olivia felt that most of their gut-wrenching, deeply hidden, secretive pain, was all cried and sobbed out of them, they reached for a box of tissues at the side of the bed; to wipe their tears and blow their noses on. They eagerly lit cigarettes inhaling the smoke from them deeply, as if it were a tranquillizer they were trying to inhale.

"Let's have a coffee?" Mandy suggested. "And my parents have got a bottle of brandy. I'll pour us both a large drop into our coffee, it will help to make us feel better."

"Great! Right on, just what the doctor ordered," Olivia replied, smiling through her tears.

While Antony continued to sleep on the floor, Mandy and Olivia sat on the couch in the living room with their brandy-coffee and cigarettes, and began talking about the experiences of their pregnancies.

"What happened when your parents found out you were pregnant, Mandy?" Olivia asked.

"Well my mother guessed that I was pregnant when I was about three months, but I lied and kept telling her I wasn't, and that I'd been having my periods. So she kept asking my boyfriend John, if he'd got me pregnant, and he would just grin and say no way. Anyway when I hadn't had a period for five months, my mother took me to the doctor one Friday night and he confirmed it."

"What happened then?"

"Well my mum told John that I was definitely pregnant, and asked him if he was going to marry me. He said he couldn't yet because he hadn't got a job, but not to worry about it because he would marry me sooner if not later. My mother then asked him when he thought he would be getting a job, and could he marry me before the baby was born. But John said that he really didn't know."

"God! What did your parents say to that?"

"Well as you know it's always been my mother's rules here, she rules the roost, and my dad doesn't have much to say about anything, more's the pity. When she started to pack my bags, I asked my dad why I had to be sent away, and told him that I wasn't going anywhere, that my home was here with them. But my dad told me that it was up to my mother, and if John wasn't going to marry me, I had to do what my mother thought was for the best. Yeah probably what was the best for her, so no one in this bloody village knew that I was having a baby. Anyway she packed my bags, 'cause I wouldn't pack them, and drove me over to my Aunty and Uncles in Blackpool. She'd phoned them the week before, and told them that I was going to have a baby, but it was going to be put up for adoption as soon as it was born, so could I stay with them until it was all over with. My Aunty and Uncle said yes, so there I stayed until a few weeks ago. Tell me what happened to you Olivia, when your parents found out about your pregnancy. Where did they send you to?"

"Well I went to the doctors, and he told my mum that I was five months pregnant. My dad gave me a few hard slaps across the face, asking me who the father was. I did eventually tell them that it was Stan, and my dad said he was going to bloody kill him. Anyway about a week later I was taken to my Grandparents in Cleethorpes. They were very kind good and loving towards me, and my wonderful grandad always brought me home from work with him, a box of chocolates every Thursday night when he got paid. It was his way of telling me that he luved me, and that he wasn't angry with me for being pregnant. And I will always be forever thankful to them for being there for me, they were so good to me. Also my wonderful cousin Anton who was there for me, he was just like the big-brother that I never had, and he never sat judgment on me, never looked down on me shamefully, never told me how stupid I was for getting pregnant, he seemed to take me under his wing, and he was very loving caring and kind towards me. When I was just a scared, frightened little girl, and he became my very very good friend, the only friend that I felt I'd got at the time. And it was because of Anton, and his kind caring friendship that I didn't go and drown myself in the Cleethorpes-North-Sea. Because before I went over to stay at my gran and grandads, I had seriously thought about doing that, a few days after I arrived there. You know? Just going out for a walk one afternoon, along the promenade the sea front, waiting until the high tide came in over the sandy-beach up to the sea wall, and then just walking into it. Oh yes I'd got it all planned out, feeling that it would be so easy to do."

"Do you think you could have really done it? Drowned yourself I mean?"

"Oh yes I'm sure that I could have, 'cause then I felt that I'd got nothing more to live for. I was having a baby that no one wanted; I wasn't even allowed to feel anything for it at that time. And it was going to be taken off me as soon as it was born, and put up for adoption. And the thought of going through all of that was so hard, as I think you now know yourself? And also being so far away from home, and all my friends over here whom I'd grown up with. I was just living in shame and was so very lonely. Anyway I will always luv my cousin, my now adopted brother Anton, so very dearly forever, for being there for me for saving me 'cause he always had lots of time for me. And he had his own life to live and get on with you know? Anyway that's why I named my baby after him, calling him Antony. He even gave me a job in his lovely top high-class expensive hairdressing-salon. So that I'd got something to do to occupy my time, instead of having just many upsetting boring days to deal with. Yes my Cousin Anton is also a top of the line hairdresser, he's even better than that famous hairdresser Vidal Sassoon, and if he could get the same publicity as him, he would so easily take over from him. You should have seen some of the wonderful hairstyles that he does, and the ladies just purr like pussy-cats while he's doing their hair, and of course flirting with him, as he's doing his best to make even the ugly women look attractive. I learnt a lot of and about hairdressing from him; he was a very good teacher. Also at the beginning of the week, Mondays and Tuesdays when we weren't to busy. Anton used to use me and my hair to practice his new hairstyles on, adding and putting false hairpieces into my hair, and cutting and styling it with great new hairstyles. So my hair always looked lovely. "

"Yeah I bet it did."

"I've never really known or met before, an adult person as kind and caring, as our Anton is and was towards everyone. And he's so full of confidence, it just oozes out of him. I really wished that he wasn't my Cousin, then maybe I could have married him. But you can't marry your Cousins can you?"

"No I don't think you can."

"More's the pity, 'cause yeah I think it's now safe for me to admit, I did really fall in luv with my Cousin Anton."

"How old is he?"

"Oh about 30."

"Do you think he knew that you were in luv with him?"

"No, and anyway he also has lots of girlfriends, all of his own age of course."

"Yeah what a pity you can't marry someone whom you luved so much, for being there for you, who was so good and kind towards you. And did you stay there with your granparents until your baby was born?"

"No, my stupid parents decided to move me from my loving granparents. When and where I did get myself very comfortable and settled, with all the rest of my family around me there, and they were all so good to me. Anyway my mom and dad decided to put me into this unmarried-mother's-home, somewhere off Ecclesall Road in Sheffield, after they had spoken with Stan, and he told them that he loved me, and wanted to marry me. So they decided that I could keep my baby, but I had to go into this unmarried- mother's home until it was born. It just broke my granparent's hearts, when I had to leave them and go to live there. And also mine to, I cried all the way in the car, on the journey to that home. I so much wanted to stay with my gran and grandad. And my cousin Anton wasn't very pleased about any of their plans for me at all either. So he made it very clear to them when he told my parents, in a confident contempt tone of voice. That they were making a very big mistake, it was all a very stupid idea of theirs, and that I was far too young to be forced into a marriage. He had no problem with me keeping my baby, and not putting it up for adoption, but being forced into getting married was another thing. But my mother told him, that she thought it was for the best. Yeah the best for her! I also think there's a big part of my parents story missing somewhere, because this all came about after my gran had talked with me, and told me that I wouldn't have to give my baby up for adoption when it was born. And I could carry on staying there living with her and my grandad. And that you don't go giving babies away when they are born, just because it doesn't suit you at the time of their birth. So I think that my gran phoned my mom and dad and told them that. She also told me not to go blaming my dad, because I was thrown out of my home and had to be there at my Granparents house. She said my dad was sat in the chair with tears in his eyes in their house, the day he went over to tell them about me, and ask them if I could go and stay with them. And he told them *'that he didn't want me to leave his home at all. That I was his daughter and he wanted me at home with him, where he could look after me and see that I was doing okay'.* He told my gran and grandad, *'that he couldn't understand Margaret, why she wants to throw our daughter out of the house when she really needs us now, her parents.'* So it was my sodding mother who insisted that my dad find somewhere else for me to go and live, until the baby was born and then adopted. And I will never forgive her for doing that to me. My gran told me that my mother said to my dad, *"she can't stay here in that condition, I just don't want her here."* My gran told me that because of something that I'd said to her about my dad. And she thought that I hated my dad, for throwing me out of my home. So she thought that she should tell me, so that I'd got the story right. Oh yes she told me over and over, *"don't you go blaming your dad 'cause you have to be here, this isn't his doing it's your mother who doesn't want you around her."* And I'm glad that she told me 'cause I was thinking that it was my dad, who decided to throw me out, 'cause you know my dad and his temper don't you? And he was so angry with me and kept shouting at me. But my mother the old cow, led me to believe that it was my dad's decision to throw me out of the house."

"Yeah I know your dad can frighten us all to death when he starts shouting, he's just like Marion's Dad."

"Yeah he is. Anyway my mom kept saying to me in a very sad tone of voice, *"how can you do this to me?"*

"But why did she keep saying that to you? You did this to yourself not to your mom. It was you who got pregnant not her."

"Yeah I know, I just couldn't understand why she kept on saying that to me. Anyway when my parents told me that I could keep my baby, I asked them if I could please now come back home to live. But my mom not my dad was very quick to reply, *"no of course you can't and don't start causing us any more trouble now, when we're doing the best that we can for you."* The sodding bitch."

"Yeah I would have thought it was your dad, who decided that you had to get out of the house, 'cause you were having a baby, 'cause your dad can be so bloody strict with you like my mom is with me. And after what us two have been made to go through, we both know now who is in control of us and our life's, our Mothers."

"Yes if we didn't know it before we certainly do know now, our Mother's are in great control of us, their Daughters life's."

"But thank-God that your gran and grandad were there for you. Is this your Dad's parents that your talking about?"

"Yeah my gran and grandad Howard."

"God I wish that I had some granparents like them. But mine do what my mom tells them to, more's the pity. How do you feel about your mom now?"

"Distant! She always keeps me at a distance from her, she thinks that I'm to much trouble. And of course I've always known from being a young child, that our Suzanne was always her favourite, being her blue-eyed-daughter. I always felt that my mom never really wanted me from when I was born. I don't know why she didn't let my gran and grandad Howard adopt me, 'cause I spent most of my baby-time and childhood years before I went to school, growing up with them. And they are the ones who always loved me and were always there for me, no matter what. Not my bloody mother, with what she did to me or thought of me as a child. I could tell you some real horror stories about what my mom used to do to me as a kid. And I know deep down that I suppose I should prepare myself really, 'cause I do think that one day my mother will disown me completely, for whatever reason. But I can't think of anything worse than her daughter being an unmarried mother can you? But she'll think of something one day, she'll invent a good reason. She does that to most people you know? Drops them when she's had enough of them. If any of her friends do something or say anything to her that she doesn't like, she ignores them forever, as though they never existed. And she makes my Dad's life hell, and you should see how her bottom lip drops down at the corner of her mouth, while she's sulking, if he doesn't buy her, the fur coats that she tells him she likes, or the jewellery especially the gold that she sees and wants him to get for her. And now people have started going abroad to Majorca for their holidays, my Dad better soon get down to the travel-agents and start getting the holiday brochure's, so my Mom can start bragging to everyone in the pub, where my Dad's taking her to in Majorca."

"So even though you've always thought, and I've always thought, and everyone in this bloody village thinks that your dad's in charge of everything, it's really your mom? Yeah well I've always thought your mother was a bloody snob the way she talks to people, in her posh-voice and like looks down her nose at them. She always thinks that she's better than everyone else. Don't you think so?"

"Oh yes definitely that's always been my mother. But I hoped she'd never do it to me her daughter, but it's done now so there's not much that I can do about it is there?"

Anyway tell me what's happened between you and Stan, Olivia? I haven't seen him for months around the village. And I heard that you two were going to get married soon. But have you now split up with him?"

"Yes, we finished just after last Christmas, so my parents' great plans of me getting married didn't come to be" Olivia replied, with a deep sigh. "But Stan was always drinking and getting drunk, he only went to work if he felt like it, and he was very jealous if any other boy looked at or spoke to me. I couldn't take it anymore the way he started to treat me, we were always arguing and fighting, and even though I think that I loved him I didn't like to be with him. I didn't really understand him anymore, so I was getting afraid for me and my baby. And I couldn't see what, if there was any future for us together. So one night when we were taking my dog for it's walk, I told Stan that we were finished, if he didn't start to change himself. Get a job and go to work and start giving me some money, to help me buy things for our baby. Stop all of the drinking that he was doing, and always getting drunk every night. And start to treat me better than he has been doing. Well when I'd said all of that to him, we started to have a big argument which turned into a fight, and I mean a real fist fight, and I was so bloody angry with him that I smacked him across the face with the chain-linked dog leash. So he decided to put his hands around my throat and began to strangle me, and I lost consciousness when everything went black and I passed out. When I came to, my friends Jane, Angela, Brenda, Jill, Cheryl and Sandra were there with my dad the police and an ambulance. Now I've heard Stan's living somewhere in Australia."

"Christ! What a bloody ordeal you went through Olivia, but why did Stan try to strangle you?"

"Because he was losing the fight, and he said, "That *if he couldn't have me, he'd make fucking sure no one else could*." And they are the last words I heard or remember of him."

Olivia and Mandy were both sat silent for a while, deep in their own thoughts and painful memories, drinking their second cup of brandy-laced coffee, as they smoked more cigarettes.

"Well," Olivia said after awhile, "surely you've heard what the villagers are saying about me now Mandy. Some say I was in hospital last week because I had my appendix out, and some are saying I had a miscarriage."

Mandy turned her head, and looked deep into Olivia's green eyes, saying in a vicious nasty tone of voice, which Olivia had never heard Mandy use before. "It's none of their fucking business what you had out."

"What about you Mandy, aren't you curious to know which it was?"

"No I'm not, it's none of my fucking business either," Mandy replied, taking hold of Olivia's hand, and holding it in a close bonded friendship.

"Did your mom go over to the hospital to see her Granddaughter, baby Susie when she was born?" Olivia asked, while lighting another cigarette.

"No she didn't want to see her at all, she wanted nothing to do with her. I still don't know how anybody can be like that, about a wonderful new born baby, especially my mother towards her own granddaughter. I so much wanted her to see my baby, hoping that if she saw and held our Susie, she would change her mind and let me keep her, 'cause you couldn't help but love her. But no my mom didn't want to come and see her, she didn't even want to know what name I'd chosen for her, what I'd called her."

"Well don't be so surprised about that. Because I saw a very strange thing happen in the hospital when I had Antony. There was a young blonde haired girl about nineteen years old, she was also an unmarried mother who had given birth to adorable twin babies, a boy and a girl, they looked so alike just like identical twins, oh they were just perfect wonderful precious new born babies, just like little angels. Anyway the mother, I forget her name now, she didn't want anything to do with them at all, she told me that she just didn't want them, that she was putting them up for adoption, and the sooner she got rid of them the better her life would be. And that she'd just passed her driving test and she couldn't wait to get out of the bloody hospital, 'cause her mom was buying her a new car. And that's all she could talk about the car that her mother was buying for her, and what colour it would be. She would only do the routine things for those poor baby twins that she had to do, she fed them changed them bathed them, and then put them back into their cribs. She never held them in her arms or smiled at them, nursed them rock them kissed them, or even picked them up when they cried, or said one kind loving word to them. She never bonded with them, had no feelings what-so-ever for them, never even gave them a name, she couldn't have cared less if those precious baby angel twins, had died in their sleep. And when the doctor discharged her from the hospital, she got out of bed got herself dressed and then said goodbye to us other mothers on her way out. But not a word a glance or a tear for her baby twins that she was leaving, she never even said goodbye to them or looked to see if they were awake, she just left them there and walked away from them, leaving them all alone in their hospital cribs behind her. As she happily linked arms with her mother chatting with her so excitedly about seeing her new car, all that mattered or was important to that girl in her life, was getting back home to see her new car. So how's that for being so bloody cold uncaring and callous for you?"

"Oh my God! How could she do that to them?" Mandy replied, in total shock.

"I just don't know she must have had a bloody screw loose in her head somewhere. So after she'd gone some of the other mothers and I, went and picked the twins up and held them close to us, telling them what beautiful precious babies they were. God it was just heartbreaking to see them left there, by a mother who couldn't care less about what would happened to them!!"

"Well she's nothing more than a fucking cold-hearted fucking bitch. And I hope she got her lovely new shiny car, and I hope she has a very bad accident in it and she's paralysed for life, and can never have anymore babies to give away."

"Mandy are you still going out with John?" Olivia asked, while rushing to change the subject when feeling tears beginning to start in her eyes again, over the memory of the twins that were left behind in the hospital. "And when are you two going to get married, and get your little precious baby Susie back?"

"Oh God I don't know, I don't bloody know anything anymore. I don't think it bothers John about losing our baby Susie, he didn't give birth to her he never held her feed her or saw her, only on the photographs and he never bonded with her like me. And he just keeps saying over and over, don't worry about her or fret over her, she'll be okay. And that we can have another baby anytime that we want one. But it's okay for him to say that, he didn't give birth to her and then have to leave her at the hospital.

The night before I knew that I would be leaving my baby Susie the next day, I held her so tightly in my arms rocking her, telling her how much I luved her and would never ever stop luving her, while I cried my eyes out. I felt that I just couldn't bear to lose her, and if I did let her be adopted I would just die. I was thinking of sneaking out of the hospital and running away with her and hiding somewhere, where no one could ever find us and take her off me. But after it was nearly daylight and I'd got no more tears left inside of me to cry, because I'd cried more than a river. I began to think where could I run to with her, where could I take us to. I'd got no money no job no food or clothes for her nothing, and with just no place to go to. There was nothing I could give my little Susie but luv, and my luv wouldn't have done much for her in the long run. So in the end I had no choice, it wasn't and never would have been my decision to let her go, but I just had no choice in the fate of my own babies life. I had to be cruel to be kind to her and me. To let her go hopefully, to some other very loving parents and a very happy home. I will never know if she is still called Susie, her new Mummy and Daddy have probably given her another name. But I do know this Olivia, I will never ever forget this year of 1967 when I gave birth to my darling precious baby Susie, and I will never ever stop loving her!!!

But as for John, huh well I feel and know he didn't go through any of this, nothing that ever really touched him, except losing me for a while. And I feel that he let me down when he didn't want us to get married, so that we could keep our precious baby Susie. I don't know if we'll be together for much longer though, or if he's worth all the sad sick pain that I've been through alone.

My mom wouldn't care if I finished with him, in fact she keeps telling me, that after all the pain that he's put me through I should finish with him. And she also keeps telling me, *"that there's always plenty more fish in the sea."*

"Hey!" Olivia said in a brighter tone of voice, thinking that Mandy was now going to quite rightly so sob her heart out once again. "There's a crowd of us going to Bamford on Friday, there's a discotheque that's opened up at the 'Marquis of Granby.' Why don't you come with us? You might find someone else that you like there, and remember it's true what your Mother says?"

"That there's always plenty more fish in the sea." **They both said together laughing.**

"That's a good idea, who's going?"

"People you like, that you went to school with not so long ago, Suzanne, Cheryl, Jane, Sandra, Jill, Angel, Brenda, David, Ian, Graham and Les."

"Yes I think that I will go with you all, it should be fun. And it will do me good to get out for a while, instead of waiting for John to turn up when he feels like it, after he's had a few drinks of course. I've just bought myself six lovely mini dresses, and I haven't worn them yet. Would you like to borrow a few Olivia?"

"Yes please I'm short of clothes. I've got to get myself a job somewhere and buy some."

"Here do you like any of these?" Mandy asked, while taking some lovely bright coloured dresses out of her white wardrobe, as Olivia followed her into her bedroom.

"Wow yes I really do like these," Olivia replied, choosing three of the lovely mini dresses, with Mandy insisting that she should now keep them, while also giving her a couple of pairs of dark-tan-coloured tights to wear with them.

***

Baby Antony woke up and began started crawling around on the carpet floor, pulling himself up on the furniture while laughing and squealing.

Mandy quickly rushed over to picked him up, giving him big kisses on his little fat cheeks, "Oh Antony you are a lovely baby and such a happy little boy, I do wish you were mine. And you know what Olivia? The next baby I have I will kill anyone who tries to take it away from me."

"Yeah I know how you feel Mandy, but one day soon I feel sure you will have a baby of your own to always keep."

"Yes you're right, I know I will," Mandy replied with a deep sigh, as she held Antony close to her. "One day I will have another baby to love and always keep close to me."

"I must be going home now, as Antony will be getting hungry soon. But don't forget we're going out on Friday, so you come up to the pub about seven o'clock, okay Mandy."

"Okay I'll see you at seven o'clock on Friday," Mandy replied, waving good-bye to them at her front door.

******

Chapter 8

Antony was having his nightly bath earlier tonight, and when he was laid down in his cot to go to sleep earlier than usual, he didn't seem to mind and after playing with his teddy bears for a while he soon fell asleep. Olivia was going out to the discotheque with her friends for the evening. It was the first time she had been to a discotheque, and she was starting to feel excited about it.

She took a lovely hot bubble bath, soaping her body vigorously; she did this religiously every day now since leaving the hospital, still always trying to wash and remove the horrid deeds, of that evil Doctor- Mehta, from her body. After a nice long soak, she got out of the bath, drying herself with a large bath towel, using deodorant under her arms and lavishly coated her body in body lotion and talcum powder.

She went into her bedroom and sat at her dressing table, and began to apply liquid-foundation-cream to her olive-skinned face, dark green eye shadow and black eyeliner to her eyelids, and black mascara to her long black eyelashes. This made her large emerald green eyes, look even bigger and very cat-like.

She pulled on her dark-tan coloured tights before putting on a bright red mini dress, and pulling the zipper's large metal-ring up the front of the dress to fasten it. The dress had a short collar around the neck, which she adjusted to make it lay flat at the back of her neck. She then stepped into a pair of black patent high-heeled shoes, and picking up her hairbrush she began to brush her long, dark-copper-highlighted hair, making it very shiny and healthy looking.

"Yes!" She said to herself looking into her full-length bedroom mirror. "Not bad in fact very good. This is the new look for me, I'll just have to work on myself a bit more and I think I could become perfect in time."

She then kissed her sleeping baby, picked up her coat and handbag before walking out of her bedroom, with a newfound confidence in herself.

***

Mandy was sat waiting in the living room when Olivia came downstairs and walked into the room "Wow!" She said when she saw Olivia, "You look great in that dress, I've never seen you look as good as this before."

"Thanks, and I do feel good tonight this is the new me. And I love the length of this mini dress, it's the first time I've ever worn a mini. Are the other two dresses you gave me the same length, or are they shorter?"

"They're about the same. I have no idea yet how short mini dresses and skirts will get. They are very big in the fashion world, but I think they have only just taken off up north. They came out here in England in sixty-six, a girl called Mary Quant, down in London designed them. I don't know about America, or if the girls are wearing them over there yet."

Suzanne then came into the living room, and Mandy and Olivia told her how pretty she looked in her new lemon mini dress.

"Thanks, you two look good yourselves," Suzanne replied. "And I do like the colour of your dress Mandy, it is a pretty pink."

The three girls were picking up their coats to put on as Eric came into the room. "Where are you two going?" He asked.

"To the new discotheque at the 'Marquis of Granby' in Bamford," Suzanne replied. "You did say it was all right for us to go when I asked you."

"I said you could go Suzanne, but I didn't know our Olivia was going," Eric said.

"Well if Olivia can't go Dad, I'm not going then," Suzanne replied.

Margaret walked into the room and smiled at everyone.

"Mum, Dad says I can't go to the discotheque tonight with my friends," Olivia told her.

"I didn't say that," Eric replied. "I've just not decided yet whether I should let you go or not."

"Oh, let her go Eric, it'll do her good. And she needs to get out," Margaret said, winking at the girls.

"But have you seen what she's wearing Margaret?" Continued Eric. "Have you seen the length of that bloody dress, she's showing all her legs and backside, she looks like a bloody whore."

"Dad, really! That's not very fair," Suzanne said in a protesting voice. "Mandy's and my dress are the same length as Olivia's, it's the new mini look. Everyone's wearing dresses this length now, and have been since last year. We're late starters with this fashion."

"Christ I don't know, what are things bloody coming to?" Eric replied, with a 'tut' at the end of his words. "Go on then, get off all of you, and Olivia no boyfriends, stay away from boys. What time are you coming home?"

"We've ordered a taxi for twelve o'clock when the discotheque closes," Suzanne replied.

"Twelve o'clock," Eric said in a shocked voice. "I never thought I'd allow my daughters to stay out until twelve o'clock at night. Just make sure you both come straight home then."

"Okay Dad, we promise we will," Suzanne replied, hurrying through the door with Olivia and Mandy following.

"Let's get out of here, before your Dad changes his mind about you two going out," Mandy said, when they were walking through the pub hallway, to the outside door.

Waiting outside the front door of the pub were Sandra, Jane, Jill, Brenda, Cheryl and Angela. David, Ian, Graham and Les were just walking up to join them. When they had all exchanged greetings, David looking at the time on his watch said, "Come on let's go for the bus, it will be here in five minutes, and we don't want to miss it, 'cause the next one doesn't come for another two hours."

***

Bamford was about four miles away from the village of Bradwell, and the bus stopped just across the road from the 'Marquis of Granby'. They all got off the bus, and stood staring at the flashing, red-neon lights that spelt out Discotheque.

"Come on, let's go," Olivia said to everyone. "I can't wait to see the inside of this place. Have any of you been to a discotheque before?"

"Yeah I have," David replied. "I went to one in Manchester last year, and it was fab. Discotheques have been opening up all over England for over twelve months now."

Walking through the large glass-panelled doors of the discotheque's entrance, they were greeted by the sound of loud music coming from another room. They each paid a five-shillings' entrance fee, and had a blue rubber stamp pressed onto the back of one of their hands. So if they left during the night they could show the stamp on their hand on the way back in, and not have to pay again.

The two doormen Jim and Cheyenne were also the bouncers there, just in case any of the lads started any trouble. Jim was a tall man, with dark wavy hair, and Cheyenne was a very large built, muscular looking guy, with blonde hair, they greeted everyone with a welcoming hello and a cheery, happy smile, before showing them where the cloakroom was. The girl's coats were taken from them by a lady who gave them a numbered ticket.

After telling David, Ian, Les, and Graham that they would meet up with them inside the discotheque, Suzanne, Sandra, Jane, Jill, Mandy, Cheryl, Brenda, Angela, and Olivia went into the ladies' room to re-do their hair, and check their make-up.

***

Inside the ladies' room there was a crowd of other young teenage girls, whom they knew from school and the other villages. They all exchanged warm, happy smiling greetings to each other, admiring each other's dresses and asking where they bought their clothes. They were all stood in front of a very large mirror, that took up the length and width of one wall, where they were doing their hair, spraying it with hair-spray, applying fresh lipstick to their lips and more mascara to their eyelashes, before spraying themselves with more lovely smelling perfumes and admiring themselves in the mirror.

"God! Just look at Angela and Olivia," said Delia, a tall, very good looking girl, with long dark hair and hazel coloured eyes, who used to be a long time friend of, and went to school with Olivia. "They look like twin Sisters, and they seem to look more alike every time I see them. I don't understand it, it's weird. They're both about the same height, have the same slim figures, the same coloured hair, and hairstyles, and they both have large, emerald, green eyes. Are you sure you two aren't related in some way?"

"No they're not, I'm sure of that, they just look alike," Suzanne replied laughing. "And don't forget Delia, I'm Olivia's Sister, but I know I look nothing like her, and my hair is blonde, not dark like hers."

"When Olivia went to school with me, the teachers used to get us two mixed up, didn't they Olivia?" Added Angela laughing.

"Yes they did Angel, and wasn't it fun?" Olivia replied happily. "They used to call me Angela and her Olivia."

"Are you girls ready?" Jill asked. "'Cause I am, and I think we all look lovely, well at least we tried to. Now let's go and have a look at this discotheque, I can hear some good music coming from it."

***

Olivia, Suzanne, Mandy, Jane, Sandra, Jill, Brenda, Cheryl and Angela all came out of the ladies, and walked over to the room where the loud music was coming from.

They stopped at the doorway and looked into the discotheque in fascination, but at the same time trying to look very composed and cool, as if they had been there before.

They saw a large, long room with a dance floor that went the whole length of it and almost to the sides. There was lovely red carpeting all around the outside of the dance floor, and on it were square tables, covered in red and white chequered tablecloths, with four to six chairs around them.

The lights above the dance floor were long ultraviolet fluorescent tubes, which made anything that was white have a bluish white, glowing effect, and people who were wearing anything white looked as though they had a lovely golden suntan. Above the dance floor, at each end of the room, were two glass-mirrored globes, slowly turning with different coloured spotlights shining on them.

There were people sitting at the tables with drinks and smoking cigarettes, and others dancing on the dance floor. The loud, music was coming from a jukebox at the far end of the room, with people continually putting money into it and selecting records, so the music was non-stop.

David came through a doorway from another room with a large bar in it. He was holding two drinks, and passed one to Olivia saying, "Here, I got this for you."

"What is it?" She asked, taking the drink from his hand.

"Try it, see if you like it."

"It's good," she replied, after taking a sip. "What is it?"

"It's Bacardi and Coke, I thought you'd like it."

"I'd like to get a drink," Mandy said.

"Yes me too. Is the bar through there?" Angela asked, pointing to the doorway David had come through.

"Yes, it's a big bar," David replied. "And a lovely large carpeted room through there, with low tables and chairs in it. Then there's another doorway that goes through to a smaller room, which has another bar with a carpeted floor, low lights, and seating, it's very plush. I think Ian and the other lads are getting drinks for you girls."

"Come on," Suzanne said, to the other girls. "Let's go and have a look."

"Let's dance girl," David said to Olivia, taking hold of her hand, and putting their drinks and her handbag on a table close by.

"I love this record," Olivia said to David, dancing close to him. "Is it the Four Tops?"

"Yes, it's one of those American, Tamla Motown records, that are doing so well in the charts over here. They've got some fantastic groups and a good new sound."

"Oh yes, the Tamla Motown sound is just great, and I love this one," Olivia said, as they danced to 'You Keep Me Hanging On'.

Olivia and David were dancing to 'Jimmy Mack', when she noticed four men in their early twenties, drinking pints of beer and stood watching her.

They moved closer to Olivia and David, and while they continued to watch her, she began to hear what they were saying.

"Not bad at all," one of the men said laughingly, to the other three. "I wouldn't mind having her for the night."

"Get em off Olivia," another man shouted.

"She never has them on," added someone else, who was laughing, and talking loud enough for Olivia and David to hear him.

Olivia, while still dancing, looked at the four men, and then at David, when she heard these remarks.

David, now looking very angry, stopped dancing and said to Olivia, "Do you know these fucking blokes?"

"No," she replied. "I've never seen them before in my life."

"Well I want to know what the fuck they're talking about, especially if you don't know them."

David turned to one of the men saying, "'Scuse me pal, but I don't like what I fucking heard you say about my girl Olivia, and how do you know her? 'Cause she tells me she has never bloody seen you before."

"My name's Paul not pal," the man, with blonde hair and blue eyes, replied. "And no I haven't met Olivia yet. But I've heard so much about her, same as everyone else, and I would very much like to meet her."

"Oh yes, and why is that then?"

"Because I hear she's easy," Paul replied laughing.

His laughter was joined by the other three men when he turned and looked at them.

"Well pal, Paul or whatever your fucking name is, you've got the wrong idea about Olivia. And you shouldn't listen to bloody rumours."

"Oh yeah," Paul replied. "Well I bet I could get her off you tonight, if I wanted to."

"That's it. Come on prick, let's sort this out outside," David said to Paul. "You can put your bloody fists where your mouth is."

"Okay then if you fancy your chances," Paul replied, with a cocky grin on his face. "I'll see you outside."

"Oh No! No!" Olivia shouted, grabbing hold of David's arm. "No David, don't go fighting because of me, I don't want you to. You might get hurt."

David put his arms around Olivia, holding her close to him saying, "Olivia, no one will say things like that about you, and get away with it, while I'm around. No one ever."

"But Dave it doesn't matter, it really doesn't matter what people say about me. I've got to the point where I don't care anymore, it doesn't bother me now what anyone says. Come on Dave, calm down, let's have a drink, or dance, please."

Olivia was pleading with David with her big green eyes, and he kissed her tenderly before saying, "Olivia, you can come outside and watch me punch the shit out of that prick, or you can stay here and finish your drink. It's up to you, but you can't stop me."

"I'll come outside with you Dave. But I'm scared you'll get hurt."

David laughed saying, "I won't get hurt but I'll show you someone who will, and that's a promise."

He then took Olivia by the hand and they made their way out of the discotheque.

Ian, Les and Graham, Suzanne, Mandy, Jane, Sandra, Brenda, Jill, Cheryl and Angela, came up to them. "Hey Dave, what's happening?" Ian asked. "And I hear there's going to be a fight outside."

"That's right, definitely. Do you want to come and watch?" David replied.

"Oh yes," said Ian. "I'll watch, I love to see a bloody good fight, who is it?"

"Me," David replied, laughing.

"You! Fucking hell, why?" Ian asked, in a shocked tone of voice.

David told Ian and the others what had happened, and how he thought Olivia had been insulted, whilst they were all walking towards the entrance door of the discotheque.

***

When they got outside there was a crowd of other people, stood in the car park with Paul, all waiting for David to arrive.

"We thought you might have chickened out," Paul shouted to David.

"Thought or hoped?" David shouted back. "Here luv hold this please," he said to Olivia, passing her his jacket.

"Oh David please be careful," Olivia pleaded. "I don't want you to get hurt."

"Don't worry, I won't get hurt luv. Just stand out of the way Olivia, I don't want him to fall on you when I smack him."

"Oh God, please don't do this Dave," Olivia pleaded with him again.

Paul took his jacket off, and passed it to his friends who had started to cheer for him.

"Go on Paul," someone shouted. "Fucking hit him good."

Paul came towards David with his right hand made into a fist, and took a swing aiming at David's face. David moved fast, putting his left arm up to block Paul's punch, as he hit him in the face with his right fist. It was such a powerful blow that it knocked Paul flying over a beautiful, brand new, white MG sports car, and he landed on the ground on the other side of it.

Everyone was stunned and silent for a few seconds, because the fight seemed to be over very fast. The shiny white, sports car, had blood splattered on the front and side windows, and along the roof. Paul's friends started cursing and swearing about David, as they made their way over to Paul to pick him up off the ground where he was lying.

David walked across to them all saying, "anyone else while we're out here? Come on, any one else want to take me on?"

No one answered David. They all just walked away from him.

Olivia ran up to David, wrapping her arms around him tightly, hugging and kissing him, asking, "Dave, are you okay?"

"Of course I am luv, and I told you not to worry about me."

He took his jacket from her, and handed her a pound note saying, "Here girl, get us both a drink, I'll have a pint and I'll meet you in the bar. I'm just going to the gents to wash this blood off my hand."

***

Olivia went back inside with her friends, and at the bar got a pint of beer and a Bacardi and Coke. She felt a little uneasy, and Angela asked her if she was all right.

"My first hour in a discotheque and all this happens," she said, to Angela and the others. "I think I should go away for awhile, 'cause I don't want Dave to have to keep fighting for me. It's just not fair to him."

"Oh, Dave will be okay, and he doesn't mind fighting, he's good at it he always wins," Les replied.

"That's not the point," Olivia said, picking up the drinks, and going to sit at a table by the dance floor.

The record that began to play was Jimmy Ruffin's soulful voiced, *'What Becomes of the Broken Hearted.'* She had never heard this song before and began listening to the words, *'As I walk this land of broken dreams, I have visions of many things, but happiness is just an illusion, filled with sadness and confusion. What becomes of the broken hearted, who had love that's now departed, I know I've got to find, some kind of peace of mind, maybe! ......'*

David came over to the table where Olivia was sitting, and he noticed tears on her cheeks. *Oh God,* he thought, *I hope I haven't upset her.* He then realised what record was playing.

"Hey Olivia," he said to her cheerily. "Don't sit and cry to this song, come on girl, let's dance to it."

He pulled her by the hand on to the dance floor, and put his arms around her when they started to dance together. He began to kiss her tears away, saying, "Don't cry Olivia, these words aren't for you. There is someone out there for you, and if it isn't going to be me, there's someone else who will care for you and luv you."

She put her arms around David and her head on his shoulder, and continued to cry, feeling the words of the song said just how she was feeling, and could have been written for her.

***

They danced to *'Happy Together'* and returned to sit at the table where they had left their drinks. They were in deep conversation, when Ian came rushing up to them in a panic. "Dave, Dave," he shouted, in a frightened voice. "You'll never ger-out-a-ear-alive, they're all after you."

"Who's after me?"

"All his fucking mates are. And I've just been told by one of em, that some of his other mates have taken that Paul to hospital. He's got a broken nose, a split eyebrow, and a bad cut below his eye."

"Good," David said laughing. "He'll be fucking careful who he talks about next time, won't he?"

"It's not bloody funny. They're all after you, and look they've circled the room, they're all watching you. I've heard they're going to kick your fucking head in Dave. What the fuck are you gun-a do?"

"Well," David replied calmly, as he got up from his chair. "If they're all watching me, I'll put on a bloody good show for them. Come on Olivia let's dance, she's a good dancer is Olivia, did you know that Ian?"

"Shit! Can't you try and keep a low profile?" Ian asked, in a panicky voice. "I'll try and find a way for you to ger-out-a-ear, wi-out them seeing yu, then you'll be safe. Hold on to him Olivia, will you? And don't let him start anything. He's fucking crazy, and they'll kill him if they get the chance."

Olivia and David went onto the crowded dance floor, and began dancing.

Olivia began to look around the discotheque, and saw male faces everywhere watching them. "Shit! Ian's right," she said to David. "Look, they're all bloody watching us. Look Dave, Paul's friends are everywhere we've gor-a-get-out-a-ear."

"No! We're going nowhere," David replied, smiling at Olivia. "I like dancing with you, and I love the way you move your hips. Come on girl, enjoy dancing with me."

"Sod it, Dave, have you seen how many of them there are?" Olivia said angrily.

"Stop worrying Olivia, I don't care how many there are. We are not leaving until the disco closes, so just enjoy yourself girl."

Suzanne, and the other girls, came to join Olivia and David on the dance floor. Angela, Jane, Sandra, Brenda, Cheryl and Mandy had got some good looking guys with them, who had their arms around their waists, these guys had bought them drinks, while chatting them up, Jill was still looking around for someone that she fancied, and Suzanne asked where Ian, Les and Graham were.

"Looking for a way out for me," David replied, with a laugh.

"Oh are they. I was wondering where Ian was, I thought he was ignoring me. I've hardly seen him all night," Suzanne said angrily.

"Don't worry, he'll be back soon. He'll be scared that one of these spare blokes, will try to get off with you Suzanne," Mandy replied with a laugh, before snuggling up to and kissing her guy on his neck.

"Oh that's good Mandy, and you smell beautiful, where did you say you lived?"

"I see that you've caught yourself another fish," Olivia shouted over to Mandy, above the noise of the music.

Mandy just replied to Olivia, with a big, very pleased, looking smile on her face.

While they were all having fun, dancing with each other on the dance floor, and getting more drinks from the bar. Paul's friends were spread out around the room, and seemed to be continually watching David and Olivia for the rest of the evening, but it had no effect on David whatsoever. He just acted as though they weren't there and continued to enjoy himself dancing with her.

At eleven thirty, Ian, Les, and Graham came back, and joined the rest of the crowd. "Where the bloody hell have you been?" Suzanne asked Ian nastily. "I've been waiting hours for you to dance with me."

"We've been in the other bar talking and planning things out for most of the night," Ian replied, kissing Suzanne on the cheek. "I'm sorry luv, but we're scared what's going to happen to Dave. Anyway Dave, don't worry I've found a way you can-ger-out, and Les and Graham will help me bar the door until you've managed tu-ger-outside."

"What the hell are yu going on about?" David asked.

"Listen to me will you?" Ian said in a worried voice, grabbing hold of David's arm. "There's a small window in the gents toilet, and Les, Graham and me will hold the door closed, while you ease yourself through the window. Then wait about a mile down the road, and we'll pick you up later in one of the taxis, when all the other cars have gone, then no one will see-yu. If you go now Dave, my plan should work."

"Sod off," was David's reply to Ian's plan. "You must think I'm as fucking scared and crazy as you are. Pass me my drink please Cheryl, it's on that table to the right of you. And Ian," David continued, in a very controlled voice, whilst looking at his watch. "This disco closes in about fifteen minutes, then Olivia's going to get her coat from the cloakroom, and I'm going to leave this place with her, at the same time as everyone else, not before. Understand?"

"But David, they're all still watching you," protested Ian. "And I've heard their all guna bloody get-yu outside. They're just fucking waiting now."

"Ian, why don't you go and crawl through the bloody window? And we'll pick you up later in the taxi, about a mile down the road, okay? 'Cause you're the one who's bloody scared of them all, not me."

"Shit! I don't fucking believe him," Ian said, turning to the others, hoping for some support from them all. "You've got some fucking guts Dave."

"Oh for Gods sake, will you cool it please Ian, you're spoiling a good night for us all," Angela said to him. "Why don't you go and dance with Suzanne? Look she's stood there glaring at you."

"Yeah I'll have a dance with her before we go, but I'm worried about Dave, right now."

"Well I'll tell you what Ian, if they're all going to get me outside," David said to him, after knocking back the rest of his beer in his pint glass. "It should be a bloody good fight this time. Better than the last one eh, and you said you liked to see a good fight, didn't you Ian?"

The music playing on the jukebox finally stopped, the big lights came on overhead, and everyone finished off the last of their drinks. David looked at his watch saying, "Well it's twelve o'clock. Are you ready girl, let's go and get your coat.

Olivia, David, and the rest of their crowd started moving slowly out of the discotheque with everyone else, while they were all laughing and talking.

Olivia got her coat from the cloakroom, and joined David by the outside door, where two taxis were waiting for them all.

***

A gang of about twenty of Paul's friends were stood outside, near the wall of the car park. David made sure everyone else was in the taxis before he went to join Olivia in theirs. When he was about to open the door to get in, he stopped, and turned to the gang, who wanted to kick his head in, and shouted across to them all. "Well you tuff looking bunch of pricks, this is your last chance 'cause I'm going now. Don't any of you feel brave enough to carry out what you said you were all going to do to me? 'Cause I know you've been watching me all night, so come on then. I'll wait two minutes for you all to decide which one of you is brave enough to take me on."

David looked at the minute finger on his watch as it moved around before shouting to the gang again. "Well your time is up now, and I haven't got all night to wait around for you blokes to get brave. Pity, we could have had a good fight, fuck there's enough of you." Before getting into the taxi, he shouted across to the gang, one last time, "And don't let me see any of you trying to pick-up Olivia, okay. Just stay away from her understand? Or you will be very sorry."

******

Chapter 9

That weekend Olivia told her parents, that she wanted to go away and spend some time with her Grandparents, uncle Brian and cousin Anton. She was sure they would like to see her baby, Antony. Eric's parents, and his Brother Brian lived in Cleethorpes, a seaside town on the east coast.

"Yes, I'm sure they'd love to see our Antony," her father said. "But what about us? We'll miss him being away from us, won't we little boy?" Antony just giggled, when his grandfather squeezed his little foot. "Our Brian's got a good job as chef in a top night-club over in Cleethorpes, and he says he's making good money there."

"Yes, I heard you and mum talking about uncle Brian's new job, so I'm going to ask him if there's any chance of him getting me a job there," Olivia replied.

"You're not old enough to go working in a night club, you're only sixteen," her mother said, in a scolding voice. "So if that's what your thinking of going over there for, I should think again."

Olivia ignored her mother's remarks, and asked her dad if he would be good enough, to drive her over to her grandparents in Cleethorpes, the next weekend.

"I don't see why not," Eric replied. "We'll go next Saturday, that will give you a week to pack. How long were you thinking of staying for?"

"I don't know, about a month, maybe longer, I really don't know yet."

"What about asking your cousin Anton, if you could go back and work for him? So you can get back into hairdressing again?" Her mother asked.

"I'll see, I don't really know what I want to do. Right now I just feel that I want to spend some time with my uncle Brian, I haven't seen him for ages."

***

Olivia went down to the bridge to meet with her friends, from the village that Monday night, to tell them she was going away to stay with her Grandparents.

"How long are you going for?" Angela asked.

"About a month I think," Olivia replied.

"We'll all miss you," said Sandra.

"Thanks, but I won't be away for too long. And I'm not going to stay at my gran's forever," Olivia replied.

"Olivia, can I talk to you?" David asked her.

"Yes, come on, let's go for a walk down to the shop, I need to get some cigs."

"I've got the chance of getting a good job in London," David continued, when they were walking through the village, to the shop. "And I would like you and Antony to come with me. I would like to marry you, and be a father to Antony."

Olivia stopped walking and took hold of David's hand, as she turned to look him in the eyes, while saying, "Thank you for asking me Dave, thanks for everything, and for being so kind and caring towards me. But no thanks, I don't want to get married yet, I want to do some living and have some fun first."

"Don't you love me Olivia?"

"Yes, I do love you, but not enough to marry you. Oh please don't go getting upset about me Dave, and refusing your kind offer of marriage. I'm very fond of you, and always will be. But I'm only just sixteen, and how old are you? Nineteen? Well can't you understand, at the moment I feel to young to get married? And I don't know anything about life yet, or what goes on in the big wide world, and when I feel I do, I maybe will want to get married, one day."

"Yeah I suppose I understand yu. But don't forget, I've told you before, if you ever do feel you want to marry me, just let me know, okay?"

"I will, but please don't go through your life waiting for me, promise?"

"I promise. Hey, I can borrow my dad's car on Wednesday night. Would you come out for a drive with me?"

"Yes, I'd love to. What time?"

"Oh about seven-thirty. There's a small country pub called the Crows Nest on the Derbyshire Moors, on the way to Sheffield, I think we'll go there."

"Do you think I look old enough to get served in a pub? 'Cause I don't usually go in pubs. My mom really doesn't like me to?"

"Oh yes you do look old enough to go into a pub, and Christ you live in one. And when you have your make-up on, you look about eighteen or nineteen."

"Is that how you see me Dave? When you look at me? About eighteen or nineteen? Instead of a sixteen year old girl, who's got her life in a mess?"

"Yeah, when I first met you, I thought you were at least eighteen or nineteen. And you seem to act a lot older than your friends do, especially the sixteen year-olds, they just seem to act like babies who just want to play, at the side of you Olivia."

"Well that's okay. Anyway I just luv my friends for being like that and enjoying themselves, I wish I could have the same innocent fun as them all, with no worries or serious responsibilities to think about. But I had to grow up very fast, when I had my baby, didn't I? He's a big responsibility for me, you know?"

"Yeah, I suppose you did have to start thinking like someone older very fast, after you'd had your baby. And I feel that you went through a lot, when I found out that you were kicked out of your home, when I think that you must have needed your parents so much, especially your Mum at that time."

"Oh don't worry about it, I'm getting over that now. And I'll always have my mother to thank for that anyway, kicking me out. But she doesn't care about what she did to me, so why should anybody else care? She only thought that she was doing the right thing, like most of our mothers do, in that situation. They have to do something like that to save themselves, and in today's polite, correct society, when mothers feel it's best for everyone included, to kick their too young to be, unmarried pregnant daughters out, it's secretly known as doing the best thing, for keeping up appearances."

***

"Where have you two been?" Suzanne asked, when Olivia and David went back to join their friends on the bridge.

"We just went up the village to get some cigarettes, do you want one?"

"Yes please, I'll have one," Angela replied.

"Here, all have one," Olivia said, passing them the pack.

After about an hour of socialising, with laughter over funny jokes and exchanging local gossip about the other village people. Especially Stella, Cheryl's mother, who became a very liberated, outspoken person while she was still a teenager, long before the 'Women's-Liberation-Movement' had even been thought of. Everyone else in the village always knew where they stood with Stella, when she felt that they should know, exactly what she thought about them, due to their doings and actions. Stella was also a very, sexy looking lady, with her blonde hair and short skirts, which she always wore short, above her knees, long before the design of the 'Mini-Skirt' had even been thought of in the 60's. Always showing off her lovely pair of long, shapely legs, in her black stockings, and 3-inch high-heeled shoes, to her husband Tom, whom she admired and was very much in love with. Or for any other man in the village who cared, or dared, to look at her lovely long legs. But these men would soon get a quick, sharp, slap across their face from Stella, if they admired or stared at her legs for too long. Or just happened to put one of their hands on her knees, while talking with them, when she was sat down in one of the pubs in the evenings, having a drink with Tom. These girls all very much liked, admired and respected Cheryl's mother, Stella, for being such a gutsy, liberated, lady, who could and would always never think twice about standing up for herself, especially if she thought that anyone had been talking about or badmouthing her. So they were always interestingly asking Cheryl, who was the latest male victim in the village, that had recently had his face slapped, by her mother Stella? For looking at and admiring her legs for to long, and which pub the incident had taken place in?

Later with a yawn, Olivia told her friends that she was going home, to have a nice long soak in a hot bath.

"But you've already had a bath today," Suzanne stated.

"Yes well I feel like taking another one, I love having baths," Olivia replied with a silent shudder, at the thought of who and what, she was still trying so hard to scrub and cleanse from her body.

"What are you trying to do? Turn your skin rusty?" Jill asked laughingly.

"Maybe! Bye all see you tomorrow," Olivia said, with a forced laugh instead of trying to give any explanation to her friends, of why she felt she had to always be bathing and cleansing her body. "And Dave, I'll see you down here, on the bridge Wednesday night at seven-thirty."

"Okay, see you then," David replied.

***

The next day Olivia told her Parents, that David had the chance of a good job in London, and he'd asked her to marry him, but she had turned him down.

"Why? You might never get another offer of marriage. And don't forget, you've got a baby to think of now," her Father said, pleased at the thought of someone responsible wanting to marry his daughter, and give her and her son a good home.

"Is it because you would be going down London to live, and you feel that it's too far away from us?" Her mother asked.

"I suppose it's a bit too far away to take our Antony, 'cause we wouldn't see him very often," her father added. "You couldn't take him as far away from us as that, Olivia. But why don't you marry this David, and leave our Antony here with your mother and me, and let us adopt him. 'Cause you know he'll be okay with us and wouldn't want for anything."

"No! I will never let you adopt my baby, so don't even think about it," Olivia shouted in a protesting voice. Trying to make what little independence that she felt, that she had, clear to her Parents. "And no, it's not because David, may be going down London to live, I just don't want to get married to anyone yet. And one day, you never know, I may go a lot further than London to live. And you both know you could never stop me, wherever it is I decide to go, and I'll always take my baby Antony with me."

***

David picked Olivia up in his father's car on Wednesday evening, and they drove out to the Crows Nest pub. They talked a lot and had about four drinks each.

On the way home David drove the car off the road, pulling into an entrance of a field, before switching off the engine. "I've got a bottle of beer, do you want to share it with me?"

"Okay, I'll take a couple of swigs, but you know that I don't really like beer."

"Come on let's get over into the back-seat of the car, there's more room there."

They had both kicked their shoes off and were lying across from each other, in the back-seat of the car, with their heads resting on the arm of each door, passing the bottle of beer across to each other. When David decided that he felt, that there was something that he now should tell Olivia.

"Tell me what?" She asked.

"Well, it was back sometime in January, and Ian and I were in the Bowling Green pub, that very old pub in the village that's had the inside of it altered recently."

"Yes, I know which one you mean, my dad is friends with the Land-Lord and Land-Lady there."

"Well, Stan was in there one night having a drink by himself, so when Ian and I went in, we went over to join him."

"Yes so well, why are you telling me this?"

"Because I think you ought to know what was said. Ian asked Stan what his plans were now for the future, now that you'd finished with him? And if he was still working at Earls cement works? Anyway Stan said no, he'd packed his job in there, and at the moment he'd got no plans for the future and had no idea what he was going to do. And was hoping that you'd change your mind and get back with him again. He then asked Ian if he'd seen you? And if he had got a message from you, for him? Ian said no, why? So Stan said that he wanted very much, to see you and his son Antony again. To ask you, if you two could get back together and get married sometime?" At this point after taking a drink from the beer bottle, before passing it across to Olivia, David began to laugh before he went on to say, "So I told Stan that I didn't think he'd be hearing from you anymore now, or in the near future, because I was now going out with you, and that you had got over him already."

"You bloody said what?" Olivia shouted, throwing the beer bottle at David. "How could you Dave? Why did you tell him that bloody shit? You knew we weren't going out together. Christ, I didn't even really bloody know you then, you hadn't lived here that long, and I just saw you around the village sometimes. You bastard! It's because of you he took off to Aussieland, isn't it?"

"I think so. In fact yes, I suppose it is," David replied nonchalantly. "'Cause it's after I talked with him that night, and I told him that I was now seeing you, that the next month I heard, that he was going to live in Australia."

"Well thanks very much, friend!" Olivia said, beginning to cry. "Thanks a fucking bucketful. What kind of a friend are you anyway?"

David moved across the seat to her, putting his arms around her saying, "I'm sorry don't cry Olivia, Stan's not worth your tears. Have you forgotten what he did to you? Have you forgotten how he tried to strangle you? And if your friends hadn't of been there to save you, you would be dead now."

"But I loved him," Olivia said, between sobs. "And I still love him, and he was the first and only man I've ever had. He was my first love, and I miss him and still love him so much it hurts. We had a baby together and I thought that he cared about our baby. It doesn't matter about me, but how can he turn his back on Antony, our baby?"

"Because Stan's no good Olivia. He's no fucking good for you, or your baby, all he cares about is himself. You can do better for yourself, and Antony. You're a good-looking girl with a brain, and I think you're right, you have to start living and looking out for yourself now. But please Olivia, don't do this to yourself, Please try and stop crying, he's not worth it, all these tears of yours, come on Olivia," David said, gently kissing her tears away from her cheeks.

"Oh! I'm so hurt David, and I don't know what to do!"

"I know, I know you are, but this hurt will eventually go. Please believe me Olivia, it will soon go forever," David replied, while continuing to kiss Olivia's tears away.

Her crying slowly beginning to cease, as he began to gently kiss her on the lips, with her lips now responding to his as she put her arms around his shoulders. Their kissing became deeper as he began to explore her mouth with his tongue, and to caress her breasts through her sweater before going underneath it to explore them further. He undid her bra and felt her breasts swell and her nipples begin to harden. As he stroked her thighs with his other hand, moving his hand down the top of her tights and panties, beginning to explore between her legs, she began to moan with such warm pleasure, feeling his hardness now against her leg.

"No I can't do this! Stop it Dave! No more!" She moaned almost breathlessly, pushing his hands away from her body.

"But why not? What's wrong? You seemed to be relaxing and enjoying yourself. What's just happened to suddenly change you?"

"'Cause I'm scared! I'm afraid of making love with anyone else! And I sure don't want to get bloody pregnant again!"

"It's okay Olivia, you don't have to be afraid, and I promise you that I won't get you pregnant. I just want to show you how good it will be making luv with me. And there's always got to be a first time with someone else, so come on just relax yourself now," David replied, lovingly kissing her.

As she surrendered to his passionate embrace, he began to slowly remove her tights and panties, stroking her gently between her legs, before tenderly caressing her love button. Oh how she moaned with such now found pleasure, clinging fiercely with her fingers onto to his arm as her climax was beginning to slowly build up, when she let out a deep-throated squeal of pleasure, and sigh of delight when she finally reached a climax, that she felt go through the whole of her body. A feeling that she had never experienced or thought was possible to have before now. David also felt these wonderful, strong vibrations now surging through her body, knowing that this was the right time to enter her gently, as she began to feel his hardness penetrating the now wet and very open entrance to the inside of her womanhood. She began to have another strong climax and arched her body up to meet his, while he put his hands underneath her small but strong hips, coaxing her gently to move with him, her body slowly but eagerly began to move with his, thrusting her pelvis up and down in rhythm with his movements. They were so now together and moving as one, with them both moaning in ecstasy with these wonderful, beautiful, feelings that their bodies were experiencing and giving to each other, before they finally climaxed together, clinging onto each other breathlessly not wanting any of it to go away, stop or end!!! As they kissed each other so passionately with David promising her, his love forever!!!!

******

Chapter 10

The following Saturday Olivia rang the loud doorbell as she opened the front door, of her Grandparent's Howard's house. Shouting happily to them as she walked down their long, hallway to the living-room, carrying Antony in her arms. "Hello Gran, Grandad, we've arrived."

Her Grandmother Marjorie, was a tall, good looking, brown eyed, dark red headed, hard working, positive no nonsense lady, came out of the living-room to meet her and their Great-Grandson in the hallway, giving them a big, hug and a kiss on the cheek. "Hello Olivia, it is lovely to see you again. Let me take Antony, your grandad's been waiting eagerly to see him." She carried Antony into the living-room to her husband saying, "He's here grandad, our precious baby's here."

"Well you are a lovely big boy aren't you Antony?" Olivia's grandfather Oliver, a brown haired, green eyed, dapper, very, gentle, quietly spoken gentleman, said happily with a warm smile on his face, to his great-grandson. "I said, only a few minutes ago they'll be here soon. That little lad will be with us soon."

Antony was clapping his hands and laughing, when his great-grandmother sat him on her husband's knee.

Olivia gave her grandfather a hug and kiss, before sitting down on the arm of his chair, putting her arm around his shoulder. She could see how very pleased they were to see her and Antony again. "How is my favourite Grandad feeling? I have missed you and I do love you."

"I know you do luv, and I'm feeling okay in myself. I've got a job working at the zoo and the fresh air is good for me."

"Oh I didn't know that, what do you do there?"

"I take the entrance money to the zoo, I started working there a couple of weeks ago. I work five days a week depending on how busy they are. You must bring Antony to the zoo to see the animals one day."

"Oh yes I will he'll love that, and you know how much I love animals to."

"Hello mum, dad," Eric said, entering the room.

"Hello Eric how are you?" His father asked.

"Oh, I'm doing okay thanks dad. I've just put Olivia's cases in the hallway for now, I'll take them upstairs when I know which bedroom she's having. Where's our Brian?"

"He's taking a bath but he'll be down soon," Eric's mother replied. "I'll put the kettle on and make some tea, do you want anything to eat? Did you have any breakfast before you left?"

"I didn't have any breakfast this morning, I'd like some bacon and eggs please gran," Olivia replied.

"Okay, I'll cook you some bacon and eggs. And what about our Antony? Do you think he would like a fried egg with some fried bread?"

"Oh yes please gran, he'd love that. But he'll make a lovely mess dipping his bread into the egg yolk, he loves to do that."

"That doesn't matter, so long as he enjoys eating it," her grandmother replied. "We'll put a big bib around him, so he doesn't get egg all over his clothes. We can clean his hands and face up afterwards."

"Uncle Brian," Olivia said, jumping and smiling, when Brian a small, good, looking, dark haired, green eyed, plumpish, young man, came into the room.

"Hello luv," Brian answered, giving Olivia a hug and a kiss. "It is good to see you again. And our Antony is a lovely baby isn't he? He's certainly grown since the last time I saw him, he is a big boy. Hello Eric, how are you?" He said shaking hands with his brother. "Didn't our Margaret come with you?"

"No, she's looking after the pub for me this weekend," Eric replied.

"Well I was hoping that she'd have been with you. I would have liked her to come to the club with you, and my dad tonight. It's a lovely club I'm working at," Brian said.

"Yes so I've heard, tell me about it, I'm very interested. What's it called? The Flamingo?" Eric replied.

"Yes it's across from the Beach-Comber holiday camp. It's been open for about fifteen months now. It's a private club, members only, and has a very select clientele of a few hundred people. It's not a big club and it's quite cosy really, but it's very plush and expensive. And it attracts the wealthy people who like to get together for a good evening out, with first class service. We even have people making sure the ashtrays are always emptied and clean. Anyway you and my dad come down tonight about eleven o'clock, and I'll reserve you a table for the cabaret."

"You even have a cabaret there?" Eric asked.

"Oh yes and dancing girls. I think it's a magician and comedian from London that starts tonight, he'll be there for a week. After the cabaret dad likes to go into the casino room and play American Roulette, and then he has a game of blackjack at the card table. Don't you dad?"

"Oh yes when I've watched the show, and seen those lovely dancing girls, I like to do a bit of gambling in the casino."

"Yes I'd like to have a look at the place tonight," Eric replied. "I'd love to go to the Flamingo-Club. Are you going to come with us mother?"

"No oh no," Eric's mother answered firmly. "I'll stay here with our Olivia and Antony. Actually I'm knitting our Antony a red-jumper, that I want to finish for him tonight."

After Olivia had eaten her bacon and eggs, she washed Antony's hands and face and changed his nappy, when he had finished eating his fried egg. She put him into his pram to go and see her cousin Anton, whose hairdressing salon was only at the bottom of the street and across the road, a short distance away from her grandmother's house.

"Our Anton will be pleased to see you," her grandmother told her before she left the house. "I told him you were coming over today to stay for awhile. I think he's bought a teddy-bear for our Antony, and he asked me if you would go and see him, before he closes the salon today."

"Yes his last customers should be leaving very soon," Olivia replied looking at her watch. "Does he still close at one-o'clock on Saturdays?"

"Yes he does."

"Well I'll just catch him before he goes out for the afternoon."

"Yes, and ask him if he's going to that Flamenco-Club tonight? Tell him that your dad and grandad are going about eleven o'clock, and our Brian's reserving them a table."

"Yes I will," Olivia replied, laughing at the way her gran pronounced the Flamingo-Club as Flamenco.

***

Olivia saw, a very large, blue teddy-bear, sat in a pink, Queen-Anne-arm-chair, in the pink and gold, ambience painted, reception area of Anton's hairdressing salon. Antony spotted the teddy-bear immediately and pointed to it as he began squealing with delight.

"Hello Anton," she shouted, from the reception through to the salon. "Guess what? Antony's seen this teddy-bear, and he wants to play with it."

"Hello there," Anton shouted, from inside his salon, which was separated by two medium sized, white painted, swing salon doors. "Bring the teddy-bear through with you, it is for our Antony. I hoped he'd like it."

Olivia picked up the teddy-bear, pushing the two swing salon doors open with her elbow, carrying it under her free arm into the salon saying, "It's bigger than our Antony is, this teddy-bear, it will be years before he can pick it up."

She sat Antony down on the floor with the teddy bear next to him. He was laughing and poking at the teddy's eyes and trying to pull its pink tongue off. "He loves it Anton, thanks for getting it for him."

"Yes I thought he'd like it. And it's lovely to see you both again, Olivia," Anton replied, leaving his client for a moment who's hair he was combing out, to greet his cousin, going over to her to give her hugs and kisses. He then picked Antony up giving him a kiss on the cheek, but he screamed and began to cry, because he just wanted to be next to the teddy bear. "Oh! It's like that then is it?" Anton said, sitting Antony back down on the floor. "I'll be finished soon Olivia then we'll have a drink and talk. And you can tell me about yourself, and what you've been doing lately with your life."

Anton's last client of the day walked out of his hairdressing salon, with her hair done in a beautiful, coiffure of a Birds-Nest-style, with a touch of gold coloured spray on the top of her own dark-brunette colour. After she had paid him and said thank-you before her goodbye, he locked up the main, small-paned glass-panelled, Georgian-style front-door, to the salon.

He then went and picked Antony up, along with the teddy-bear, saying, "Come on we'll go upstairs to the lounge. I've done enough hairdressing for this week, and I'm ready for a break."

She followed her cousin through the salon into the colouring and tinting room, through a sliding doorway into a hallway, walking up the deep, cerise-pink carpeted stairs, and through a glass-panelled door off the landing, into a big lounge.

Anton sat Antony down on a thick-piled, turquoise-coloured carpet, with the teddy-bear next to him.

"Would you like a drink of sherry? It's a lovely sherry that I've brought back from Spain."

"Yes please. This room is still beautiful Anton, I love these new antiques you've got in here."

"Yes I like antiques to, and I pick them up whenever I see them, at very good prices."

"You're right Anton, this is a lovely tasting sherry, and I don't usually like Sherry. You say you got it from Spain, when did you go there? And who with?"

"Well it was Majorca I went to actually, that's an island just off Spain. And do you remember the very pretty blonde lady called Allison, who comes here to have her hair done twice a week? Well that's who I went to Majorca with this time."

"But I thought she was married, if it's the Allison that I'm thinking of. I remember her telling me, her husband had bought her a lovely red sports car, for her twenty-fifth birthday last year."

"Yes that's her. But she's not with her husband anymore, she left him about four months ago, and she's filing for a divorce."

"So she's going to marry you next, is she?"

"No way," Anton replied laughing. "She might think she is, but I know different."

"So why does she think she is? My wonderful, good looking cousin Anton, I bet she thinks you're the perfect catch for husband number two. Just look at yourself, age thirty, six-foot-tall-blonde-hair, blue-eyes, sun-tanned-skin, a very good looking bachelor, no make that playboy, with a beautiful big car, and a very successful hairdressing salon, and plenty of money in the bank. You're also much better looking, and a far better hairdresser, than that Vidal Sassoon you know? Anyway what have you been telling Allison, for her to think you could be husband number two?"

"Nothing, it's just what she thinks, I should be. Anyway I've told her I've no intentions of getting married, and I also told her, not to get too deeply involved with me, on the rebound from her failed marriage. She also knows she's not the only lady in my life, that I just have a few others."

"Oh really, well how come she went to Majorca with you?"

"Well I wanted to go, and she was free, so we thought it was a good idea for us to go together, and share a room. And I'm glad we went, we both had lots of fun. But enough about me." Anton replied, taking another sip of his sherry, before pointing his hand towards Olivia. "Tell me about yourself my darling Cousin? What's been happening to you? And what do you plan on doing with your life, now that Stan's out of it? And I can't say I'm sorry he's gone. I always thought you could do better for yourself than him, a good looking girl like you."

"Well thanks, that's good of you to say so," Olivia answered, with a deep sigh.

"Well I've always told you, that you look like a Howard, with your dark, hair and green eyes. And when you were just a little girl, I always told everyone, that when our Olivia grows up, she'll be very good-looking and sophisticated. And our Suzanne will be all plump, and chocolate-box looking"

"Thanks again our Anton, that's a very nice complement. But as a Howard, I've no plans made for my future yet, I'm just taking it day by day, not really knowing where I'm going to, or what I want to do. I just want to do a bit of living and see life, I feel I'm very naive about everything, and it's time I opened my eyes and saw what's out there. I certainly don't want any more babies, so I've just started taking this birth-control-pill that's come out. My doctor has given me six-months supply of them, just in case he said, and to go back to see him when I need some more."

"Yes, most of the ladies I know are taking the birth pill, and us men love it. As long as you ladies remember to take it, no more unwanted pregnancies. Let me get you another drink Olivia." Anton said, walking across the room to take her glass. "I'm thinking of opening another hairdressing salon a few miles away from here, in Louth. So would you like to work for me as an apprentice hairdresser? You would go to college, and in five years be a qualified hairdresser. Then I'd open another salon for you to run, and we could go into partnership together."

"Wow!" Olivia gasped, coughing while drinking her sherry. "That's some terrific offer you've just made me. Do you want an answer now? Or can I have some time to think about it?"

"No, you don't have to give me an answer right now. I'm not going to open another salon until next year, so you have plenty of time to think about it. But do think about it seriously, 'cause I don't want to start making plans for you, if you say yes, and then you go and change your mind about it all later on."

"No Anton, I won't mess you around, and thank you very much for making me the offer, which does seem too good to be refused. It does seem like the chance of a lifetime, to do something good and very interesting with my life, yeah I promise you I'll think about it seriously. And thanks for everything else that you've already done for me, I will never forget how good you've always been to me Anton, you're a one-in-a-million cousin to have you know?" Olivia said, standing up, and giving Anton a kiss on the side of his cheek, before going to pour herself another small glass of sherry. "Oh! By the way before I forget to tell you, my dad and grandad are going to the Flamingo-Club tonight, and uncle Brian is reserving them a table for eleven o'clock. Gran asked if you will also be going to join them there tonight?"

"Yes, tell them I'll be there just before the cabaret starts," Anton replied, offering Olivia a king sized cigarette before lighting one for himself. "And will you ask our Brian if he'll make that table reservation for four."

"Why four?"

"Because I have a date," Anton replied smiling, blowing the smoke from his cigarette into the air. "Her name is Grace, and she owns a fur, shop down-town. And yes Olivia, you have met her, she's the lovely slim lady, who has blue eyes and dark hair. And she still comes to the Salon at 2 o'clock every Friday afternoon, to have her hair done."

"Oh yes! I remember her," Olivia said laughing. "She isn't married yet is she? Don't tell me, she's waiting for you? My good looking Cousin."

***

The next morning they were all sitting at the breakfast table, and Eric said, "Yes, it's certainly a beautiful club Brian. I really enjoyed the cabaret, and they do have some lovely dancing girls. Our Anton had a lovely bit of stuff, with him last night, didn't he?"

"Yes he did," Brian replied. "I think her name is Grace, and she owns a fur, shop down-town. But our Anton always has some lovely looking, wealthy young lady, with him."

"Did you have a good time last night Grandad?" Olivia asked, squeezing her Grandfathers arm.

"Yes thanks luv. And I certainly did okay at the blackjack table, I had a good time there," her Grandfather replied, pushing a ten-pound-note into Olivia's hand. "Yes a very good time indeed."

"Thank-you Grandad," Olivia replied, while giving him a hug. "What a pity I'm not old enough to play blackjack, if this is the sort of money you can win."

"No, I'm afraid you're not. You have to be twenty-one before you can go into a casino, or any betting shop for that matter luv," uncle Brian stated. "Last night I asked Peter the manager of the club, if you could have a job at the club for a few weeks. I told him you were eighteen years old of course. Anyway he said yes, he could find you a job."

"The manager said I could work there?" Olivia asked, in a very happy surprised voice.

"Yes, he says that you can start tomorrow night."

"Oh great! What will I do?" Answered an excited Olivia.

"The manager will tell you tomorrow night, and I'm sure you'll enjoy working there, it's a lovely atmosphere. The staff are a great bunch of people, and I've told everyone my niece will be coming to work on Monday night. And they are all looking forward to meeting you."

"Yes it's certainly a beautiful club. And I must bring Margaret over to see it, the next time I come for the weekend," Eric said, not minding at all that his brother Brian, had got his daughter Olivia, a job working there. "I think I'll set off home tonight, about six o'clock, I want to get back before the pub closes tonight. Mrs. Mason is helping Margaret behind the bar this weekend, but I do want to get back to make sure everything's been okay."

******

Chapter 11

"I'm feeling a little nervous," Olivia said to her uncle Brian, when he was driving them to the Flamingo-Night-Club, the next evening.

"There's nothing to be nervous about luv, I'm sure you'll be okay," Brian replied. "And don't forget I've told them your eighteen not sixteen, and don't worry, 'cause you certainly do look that age, now you've got all your make-up on. And if you have any problems with anything, or anyone, just come and see me. As I've told you, you'll enjoy working at the Flamingo Club, and I'm sure you'll get on with the staff okay, they're a very friendly and easy going crowd."

"I've never even asked you where this club is?"

"Well, do you remember the big holiday camp on Sea View Road?"

"Yeah the Beach-Comber, that's the one very similar to a Butlins holiday camp."

"Well it's across the road from that. It's owned by the same people, a big company of solicitors called Chetmen and Sons."

"Do the people from the holiday-camp go to the Flamingo Club at night?"

"Oh God no, they wouldn't allow that lot of white-trash into the Flamingo, to do their bloody-hoki-kokie-dancing. Anyway they have their own club across on the campsite. It's members only at the Flamingo, and everything would be far too expensive for the holiday campers, even the cloak-room tickets."

"Oh well who are the sort of people, who go to the Flamingo Club then?"

"Doctors, Dentists, Solicitors, Company-owners, all very wealthy people."

"God! I feel even more nervous about working at the club now."

"Well I've told you don't be luv, anyway we're here," Brian said, driving his car into a white-gravelled-car-park. As Olivia saw a white-pebble-fronted building with a flat roof. On top of the flat roof stood a figure of a large, pink-Flamingo-bird, with flashing coloured-lights outlining it, and over a large, solid looking white- wooden door, in pink lights, was the name 'FLAMINGO'.

Brian drove his car around the gravel-car-park to the back of the club, and parked it outside in front of the large, white painted kitchen door.

***

They both got out of the car and went through the door into a very large, clean kitchen, that had a big wooden table in the middle of the floor. All around the kitchen next to the walls were fridges, grills, cookers, deep fat fryers, stainless steel sinks, and worktops.

"This is the staff entrance and my kitchen where I work," Brian said, hanging his car keys on a hook at the side of the door.

"Good evening Chef," said a slim, young, teenage boy, with dark hair and blue eyes, who followed them in through the kitchen door.

"Good evening Stewart," Brian replied. "This is my niece Olivia. This is my commis-chef, Stewart."

"Good evening Olivia, I'm pleased to meet you. Chef tells me you will be working here with us, for a while," said Stewart.

"Hello Stewart," Olivia replied. "And yes I hope to be working here for a few weeks. I can't wait to start."

"Come on Olivia," Brian said.. "I'll show you around and introduce you to the staff, then we'll find Peter the manager, and see where he wants you to work. The club will be opening soon, it opens at nine thirty. Stewart, light the grills please and get the steaks, scampi, caviar, truffles, pate' and trifles out of the 'fridges, the salads made and the eggs boiled. And. I'll be back soon."

"Okay Chef, I'll start getting things under way," Stewart replied.

"First of all this is my kitchen, the kitchen belongs to the Chef no one else, so they're my rules in here," Brian stated to Olivia, waving his arm around the room. "And no one is allowed to smoke in here, or sit around the big table, drinking coffee and talking. The meals for the restaurant are taken from this kitchen, by the waiters through the swing doors over there, and the meals for the people sat at the bar, go through that door there to the bar. And that long corridor past these doors, is the way to get backstage, to the manager's office, the staff toilets, and staff cloak-rooms are also down there. This other kitchen is where the coffee is made, the pots are washed, and the staff take their breaks and meals in here," Brian continued, walking through into another smaller room. "This is my niece Olivia," he said to two ladies, whom both looked to be in their fifties.

"Hello Olivia, I'm Hilda," said the lady, with her silver hair fastened up in a bun.

"And I'm Joyce," said the other lady with curly blonde hair. "Chef told us you'd be working with us, and I hope you'll enjoy it. I make coffee and wash the pots in here, and help Chef and Stewart out in the big kitchen, if they get very busy."

"I work behind the food-bar, that's over at one side of the long bar. And hopefully keeping Chef and Stewart continually busy, don't I?" Hilda said, giving a wink to the Chef, with her right eye.

"So the Flamingo has a food-bar as well as a restaurant?" Olivia inquired.

"Yes," Hilda replied. "The customers can also order sandwiches at the food-bar, but not in the restaurant. Most meals at the food-bar are scampi and French fries. It's also cheaper to eat at the food-bar than in the restaurant."

"This door goes into the bars," Brian said, pushing open a swing door at the side of the kitchen. "Come on through and I'll show you the club."

Olivia followed Brian through the door into a very long curved bar, that also continued around a corner. "Good evening Pat," Brian said, to a tall man with sandy coloured hair and blue eyes, who was fixing a bottle of Scotch on to an optic, on the wall behind a well stocked bar. "This is Pat the bar manager. This is Olivia my niece."

"Good evening Olivia, I'm very pleased to meet you," Pat said, offering his hand for her to shake. "Chef tells me your going to be working with us for awhile, and I can always use some extra help behind the bar. We're always very busy with serving customers, and there's always plenty of glasses to be washed. By the way Chef, did you know we've got a stripper performing at the club tonight?"

"Yes," Brian replied. "The manager was telling me last night. And it's the first time we've had a stripper at the Flamingo."

"Yes," agreed Pat. "And did you know? That only in a private members club, is a stripper allowed to remove her G-string?"

"A female stripper?" Olivia asked, in a surprised, hopefully not to shocked tone of voice.

"Yeah," Pat replied, with a big grin on his face. "Have you ever seen a stripper before Olivia?"

"Come on our Olivia," Brian said, walking to a small lift-up hatch in the bar, "Pat's only trying to shock you, so just ignore him. Come and have a look at the club."

"I wonder how many waitresses will give their notice in tonight?" Pat said laughing. "I bet not many of them have seen a stripper before either. What do you think Brian?"

Brian just ignored Pat's jovial remark, that he knew was just to get him going about what his thoughts were, of a stripper appearing at the club. When Brain didn't really care one way or another.

Olivia silently continued to follow Brian through the bar hatch into the bright, yellow, pink and blue, very, thick carpeted floor of the club. There was a small stage at the front, with a small square dance floor in front of it. Low tables with pretty, pink-candle-lamps stood in the centre of them, and comfortable armed chairs around them, surrounded the dance floor, and filled the rest of the room. The restaurant with four wide, carpeted steps up to it, ran the length of one side of the club. The overhead lighting was dimmed very low, making the club look cosy and warm, against the lighted candle-lamps glowing on the tables.

"Wow! This is all very plush and expensive looking," Olivia said. "This place is great, it certainly puts the working-men's-clubs to shame."

"Oh God yes, the people who go to the working-men's-clubs never come in here, they'd be way out of their depth, they all go across the road to the holiday-camp. Come on let me show you the Casino, it's around here," Brian said, walking around the long bar, and through a pair of small-paned-glass-windowed-doors. "Good evening Peter," he said to a tall, broad shouldered, good-looking man, with blue eyes and blonde hair. "This is my niece, Olivia."

"Good evening Chef. And Olivia I'm very pleased to meet you, I'm Peter, the manager of the Flamingo," he replied, shaking Olivia's hand warmly. "What do you think of our club?"

"I think it's a terrific place. It looks very plush and expensive, and this casino is something else. It's the first time I've ever seen a casino, what's played in here?" Olivia asked.

"American Roulette, Blackjack and Craps," Peter replied, putting his arm around Olivia's shoulder and walking out of the casino with her. "Chef tells me you would like to work here with us for awhile?"

"Yes please, if you can find a job for me?"

"Oh yes I'm sure I can. How old are you Olivia, eighteen?"

"Yes," Olivia replied, thinking, *'God! I hope I do look eighteen? And everyone in this place sounds so grown up, polite and sophisticated around here. I've never experienced or seen anything like this before, it all seems so different and wonderful. I hope I don't let anybody down, especially my uncle Brian!'*

"Let's go into to my office then and we'll discuss this, because the club is open now and customers will be coming in soon."

***

A very pretty, blue-eyed, short-blonde-haired-lady was in the office, taking a large, blue canvas bag of money out of a safe.

"This is my wife Naomi," Peter said. "I'd like to introduce you to Olivia, Naomi, the Chef's niece."

"Hello Olivia," Naomi said, greeting Olivia with a very warm, welcoming smile while shaking her hand. "I heard from Chef, that you are going to be working with us."

"Yes," Olivia replied nervously. "And it seems that my uncle Brian has told everyone about me, coming to work here with you."

"Oh yes he has," agreed Naomi. "We all know about Chef's niece Olivia, and we've all been looking forward to meeting you. Chef told us you have a baby son. What is his name?"

"Antony," Olivia replied quietly, in a very surprised kind of, how did they know my disgusting hidden secret? "Has my uncle Brian also told everyone else who works here about my baby son?"

"Oh yes of course he has," replied Naomi, instantly picking up on Olivia's nervousness. "And don't you go worrying about it, you should be proud of your baby son Antony. You must come over to our house with him one afternoon,. I'd love to see him, I just love babies. I'm having one myself in about six months time. I found out last week, that I'm three months pregnant."

"Oh you are? Well I'm very pleased for you," replied Olivia smiling, feeling that she had bonded with Naomi immediately, someone who didn't feel that she should hide her shame away.

"Yes," Peter said. " And you will have to stop working in a couple of months time Naomi. I don't want you standing as much as you are doing now, and working until nearly daylight. I want you to start getting plenty of rest."

"Oh soon Peter, soon," Naomi replied laughing, "I'm okay at the moment. I'll probably finish working when I'm seven months."

"What do you do here Naomi?" Olivia asked.

"I'm a croupier, and I deal American Roulette, Blackjack and Craps. And yes I suppose it sometimes can get to be a tiring job," Naomi continued with a deep sigh. "Especially when the punters are continually winning, and don't want to go home until they have tried continually to break the bank. What job would you like to do here, Olivia?"

"That is what we are going to discuss now," Peter said. "Do you like working behind a bar Olivia? I hear your father has a pub, so I suppose you are used to serving customers."

"I'll let you two get on with this interview," Naomi said. "I must go and open up the casino. See you later Olivia."

"Bye Naomi," Olivia said, before turning to Peter and asking him what other jobs he had that she could do.

"Well," Peter replied, offering Olivia a cigarette and motioning to her to sit down. "You can be a cocktail waitress, and we'll find you an outfit to wear for that job. Or you can serve behind the bar and help keep the glasses washed and dried, or you can work in the kitchen with Joyce. It's really up to you Olivia, which job you'd like to do? Chef tells me you will be here for about a month. So I'll pay you cash under the table instead of through the books, so you won't be paying any tax. I'll pay you two pounds a night for every night you come into work. Is that okay by you?"

"Yes thanks that sounds great. I'd like to work behind the bar washing some glasses, but not serving customers just yet, I don't feel I have enough confidence for that job. I don't want to be a cocktail waitress, because I haven't enough confidence for that yet either. I would like to get used to the club first, before I deal with the customers. So could I help Joyce in the kitchen, and wash glasses in the bar for now, please Peter?"

"Yes of course you can, if that's what you'd feel happy doing. Let's go and see Joyce and Pat, and tell them they've got some extra help."

***

Four very tall, good-looking girls, were in the smaller, kitchen when they entered, they were all stood together, talking, smoking cigarettes and drinking coffee. "These are our dancers, 'The-Foxy-Ladies'." Peter said to Olivia. "The two blondes are Bridgette and Fiona, and the brunettes are Jill and Tiffany. This is Chef's niece, Olivia, and she is going to be working with us from tonight."

"Hello Olivia, pleased to meet you, I'm Bridgette. Would you like a coffee?"

"Hello Bridgette, and I'm very pleased to meet you," Olivia replied, shaking hands with her. "Yes please, I would like a coffee."

"Hello Olivia, I'm Jill, and I'm also pleased to meet you, Jill said offering her hand for Olivia to shake. "How would you like to get together with us girls after work, and come over to the flat for a drink with us, Olivia?"

"Yes, we'll have a party so you can meet everyone Olivia," a smiling Tiffany said, as she shook Olivia's hand when introducing herself. "And I'll ask Chef, Stewart, Pat, and a few other people to join us."

"That sounds fab and I'd love to come, if it's okay with my uncle," Olivia replied, feeling very happy and relaxed in the company of the dancing girls, with the warm, friendly welcome they were all extending to her.

"Oh I'm sure it will be," Jill replied. "Your uncle Brian loves to party."

"What about you Joyce, would you like to join us later for a drink?" Fiona asked.

"I'll see how I feel after work, I'm not as young as you girls you know," Joyce replied.

"Come on girls," Tiffany said. "I can hear 'Angelo's' band starting to play. We must go and put our costumes and make-up on, it will soon be cabaret-time."

"Bye Olivia," Fiona said. "We'll see you after the show."

"They seem to be such nice fab-girls and so friendly," Olivia commented, feeling once again total acceptance, with no judgement passed on her, from these people in this adult world.

"They are lovely girls," Joyce agreed with Olivia. "And I'm sure you'll get on great with them. They're all single girls in their early twenties, and they just love to party."

"Yeah! And they all seem as though they want to be friends with me," Olivia replied, with a happy smile, and a good feeling about working with these very different, enjoyable people.

***

After a couple of hours the nightclub began to get very busy, and started to swing, as it filled up with customers. Pat put his head around the door of the small, coffee kitchen, asking Olivia, if she would mind coming behind the bar, to help wash some glasses for him. She began to help a lady called Julie, wash and dry the glasses, as the club's compere, Jeff, came onto the stage to began the cabaret show with a song, followed by a few jokes, before he then introduced the dancing girls, 'The-Foxy-Ladies' who all did a dance together, to the music from the Flamingo's, resident Italian band, called 'Angelo's'. After the dancers had finished doing their wonderful, choreographed dance and left the stage, Jeff came back out to introduce to the audience, for the very first time ever, at the Flamingo-night-Club. *'The very sensual, female stripper, 'Sexy Sonia'.'*

"If you think this might embarrasses you too much Olivia, you can go back to help Joyce in the kitchen while the stripper's show is over," Pat said, feeling some concern for this young girl, who had come to work along with the staff behind the bar.

"No I'll be okay, I don't think for one minute she'll have anything I haven't got, or seen before," Olivia replied, with a nervous giggle, as she began to watch the stripper do her show.

'Sexy Sonia' looked to be about in her middle thirties, with short blonde hair and blue eyes. She danced and moved her body very seductively, to the sound of strip music, that was playing on an LP record for her performance, as she slowly began to remove her clothes. Beginning with the shiny-very- silky-looking, long-sleeved-black-gloves, that covered her arms just passed her elbows. After removing her bra, she began to swing her breasts around and around to the beat of the slow sexy music, and the long-gold-coloured-tassels that were attached to the end of her nipples, also swung around and from side to side.

The people in the audience seemed to be mesmerised, by Sonia's sexy show, until she was at last finally stripped down to her matching-gold-coloured-G-String, dancing around in it for a while especially in front of the tables that only had the men seated around them, as she kept everyone in suspense before finally deciding to remove her G-String. Revealing to everyone in the club her pubic area, that had been carefully and artfully shaved and trimmed, leaving a small-heart-shaped-patch of black-pubic-hair. The spotlight on her was then quickly dimmed, as her manager stepped forward from the wing-area of the stage, to wrap a golden-coloured-cloak around her completely naked body, to cover her as she left the stage. To a gentle, very polite applause, from a mostly embarrassed, coughing audience, from some of the gentlemen and certainly most of the ladies, who had never in their life's been entertained by a stripper before, seeing a total stranger in their presence eagerly removing all of her clothes in Britain's early 1960's. No only the very lucky adventures men, who would go over to some countries in Europe on business, before then going out of their way to find the 'Striptease-Bars' over there, had ever experienced seeing a stripper so sexually removing her clothes before. So these were the gentlemen who did tend to clap their hands a little louder than the other guests in the club!!

"Yes I guess all the blokes enjoyed that, but I wonder what their wives thought of it? They were probably all very shocked, and hoped to God that their husbands don't expect them to perform for them, like 'Sexy Sonia', in their bedroom tonight," Pat announced, with a hearty laugh to his bar staff. "It was all very nice to see, but Sonia certainly isn't a natural blonde."

"What would you know about natural blondes?" Julie asked him, in a surprised voice.

"Well my latest girlfriend Fiona is a blonde, that's how I know," Pat replied, with a wicked grin on his face.. "You two can take a break now," he said, to Julie and Olivia.

***

The two girls were leaving from behind the bar as the next act, by 'Michael Bentein' began his show on the stage, introducing himself to the audience by saying, *"Ladies and Gentlemen, it gives me great pleasure, and has done since the age of thirteen."* The audience in the club all roared with laughter.

"I'll ask Chef if he'll cook us some scampi and chips," Julie said, when they went back into the small kitchen for their break.

"Hey Joyce, did you know that Pat's going out with Fiona?" Julie inquired, as she began to pour a cup of coffee for Olivia and herself.

"Yes I do," Joyce replied. "They've been going together for about three weeks now."

"I didn't know that, I thought he was after Tiffany."

"Yes he was, but he's got no chance with Tiffany. She's got a steady boyfriend down in London, who owns a large, 'Chinese restaurant'."

"Anyway Pat's been telling us that Fiona's, a natural blonde."

"Oh, he's just bloody sex mad is Pat," Joyce said laughing. "I'm very glad my daughter's married, and out of his reach."

"Scampi and chips for two are ready," Chef shouted from the big, kitchen.

"I'll get them for us," Olivia said to Julie.

Olivia walked into the large kitchen saying to her Uncle Brian, "We've been invited to a party after work. Is it okay if we go?"

"Hello luv, are you having a good time?" Brian asked. "And yes if you like, we can go the party. I've already told Jill we would be able to go, if you aren't to tired after your first night working here. And how do you like it? Working here Olivia?"

"Oh it's just fab, I've never had so much fun before. And it's a lovely atmosphere here, everyone seems to be so happy and friendly, as they get on with doing their jobs."

"Yes I thought you'd like it here. I finish cooking meals about one-thirty A.M. And then we clean the kitchen up. And we can go over to the party about two, to two-thirty, if you're sure you won't be to tired."

"Oh no I'm sure I won't be to tired. And I'm looking forward to going to this party and meeting more of these wonderful people."

***

The remainder of Olivia's first night's work at the Flamingo Club passed very quickly. She was kept so busy helping to wash and dry the glasses behind the bar, and wash and dry the dishes in the smaller, kitchen. Socialising with all the waitresses, the 'Foxy-Ladies-dancing girls and other staff members, who came into the smaller kitchen, to take their breaks for a coffee and to eat their meals.

This was her first real, big step into another adult world, especially one like this that her uncle Brian had introduced her to. It was so different to the one that she had been allowed to step into before, when she was living in shame, due to her pregnancy. Into her Cousin Anton's world of hair and nails, with beautifully styled coiffure-Bouffants, perms, colours, tints, hair-dryers, manicures, nail-polish and the lovely smell of all the different hair-sprays. Yes she had enjoyed very much her wonderful, experience with the please make me look beautiful people world, of hair and nails. But this so new, working in a night-club-world, in an exclusive, private members only club, was another wonderful surprise for her. Which she found to be very exciting, happy and full of wonder, especially mixing with the people who ran the show, in and behind the night-club scene, who seemed to be all so eagerly willing to accept her into their crowd, as one of them!!!

***

She was feeling so good and happy as her uncle Brian drove them across the road to the holiday-camp at about 2:15 A.M. the next morning. And still so very wide awake at this unearthly hour, without even a trace of tiredness in her body from all of the work she had been doing that night. As they went to this party that she had been anxiously looking forward to, where she would be meeting more different people and hopefully making more new friends, with other guys who also worked at the Flamingo-Club.

They went up some stairs to a large, flat which was over an amusement arcade, and could hear the record 'You Can't Hurry Love', playing loudly on a record player. Brian opened the door and they walked into a big room, which was full of people all stood around drinking, smoking and talking very, loudly above the music.

"Hello there you two, come on in and have a drink," a smiling Tiffany shouted, coming over to greet them, and taking Olivia by the arm leading her over to a wicker-bar, in a corner of the room, saying, "What would you like to drink Olivia? Do you like anything in particular?"

"Yes could I have a Bacardi and Coke please?"

"Oh you aren't a Scotch on the rocks drinker, like your uncle Brian then?"

"Oh no! I've not started drinking Scotch yet, I don't really like the taste of it," Olivia replied, as Tiffany handed her a drink.

Jeff the club's compere, a good-looking, brown eyed, dark haired man in his late twenties, came over to the bar to introduce himself to Olivia, and asked where her uncle Brian was.

"I think he's talking to some people at the other side of the room."

"Oh yes I can see him now," replied Jeff, looking across the room. "He's with Roberto he's the headwaiter in the restaurant, and that's his wife Tara. Come on Olivia let me introduce you to them, you must meet these terrific people. Roberto is from Italy and God knows where Tara is from, she's just very beautiful oriental and exotic looking. Hey Brian, Roberto, I've got something bloody awful to tell you blokes about what happened to me the other night!" Jeff shouted, as he walked over towards them.

"Yeah-a tell-a-us-a-thee-a-latest, a-that-a summa-tina-craz-ia-appen, in-a your-a life-a every fuckin-a week-a," replied Roberto, an olive colour skinned, small, fat Italian, with receding black hair and dark brown eyes, in his middle thirties. Who talked in an Italian, very broken English accent.

"You blokes remember Janet eh? The blonde that I was living with, and going to marry at the end of this month?" Jeff asked, beginning his story.

"Yes I do," Brian replied. "And I don't think she came into the club tonight."

"No she didn't," Jeff continued. "And I don't think you'll see her with me, ever again. She caught me in bed with another girl, a couple of nights ago. And when I got home a few days later, that fucking cow Janet, had cut up six of my suits. One hundred fucking pounds each, those suits cost me, from 'Savile-Row' in London. That was six hundred pounds down the fucking, drain or cut up."

Everyone burst out into fits of laughter over this news, before Jeff went on to say, how he had slashed the tires on Janet's new car, in retaliation.

"Yeah that'll get you all your suits replaced," Brain stated with a laugh.

"Why do you always live life so dangerously?" Tiffany asked.

"Oh I can't help it, and I do find it so bloody exciting," Jeff replied.

"Your-a just-a fuckin craz-ia," Roberto added, once again in his broken English accent, with a tut added at the end of his statement, followed by his loud laughter.

"You must come over to see us tomorrow Olivia," said Tara, the tall, slim, beautiful, oriental looking lady, with shoulder length, black hair and dark brown eyes, who looked to be in her early twenties.

"Yes-a and bring--a your-a bambino," Roberto insisted.

"Yes I would luv to, but where do you live?" Olivia asked.

"Oh don't worry about that, your Uncle knows, and he'll bring you over to our flat. Won't you Brian?" Tiffany replied.

"What's that?" Brian asked, breaking off from talking and laughing with Jeff..

"You'll bring Olivia over to our place, to have a glass of wine with us sometime tomorrow afternoon, okay," Tara said.

"Yes fine I'd love to," Brian agreed.

"Come on let's dance Olivia? I just love this record by "The Four Tops," Jeff suggested.

"No! No! You-a just-a leav-a her-a alone-a, you-ar-a to-a fuckin craz-ia for-a, get-a sum-a-one-a else-a-to-a-dance," Roberto said, protectively taking hold of young Olivia's arm. "Olivia, she will-a be-a safe-a-stayin a-her-a wiv-a me-a."

"Oh yeah but she's only safe with you Roberto, because Tara is here," Tiffany said with a laugh, taking Olivia's glass from her hand to go and refill it.

"This is a very big flat," Olivia said to Tiffany, walking over to the bar with her.

"Yes it really is a good size," Tiffany replied. "There is a big kitchen through here look, and we all have our own bedrooms, with bathrooms down the hallway there."

Olivia looked down the hallway seeing eight closed doors to the rooms. "How much does it cost to stay here?"

"Nothing. Anyone who works for the Flamingo or the Holiday-Camp, is allowed a flat, a chalet, or a room in here, and it's free any time of the year."

"Wow! That's good, and are all these places furnished?"

"Oh yes and we just provide our own bath-towels, they even supply the bedding for us. We have got a really good management team who look after us all here. We can also eat free across at the club, and at the holiday camp during the summer, when it's open. And the wages are good. And the staff all get on like one big happy family, that's why I wanted you to come over here tonight, to meet everyone and party with us."

"Thanks so much Tiffany, and it was so good of you girls to ask me over here tonight, to be with you all."

"Well while you work with us, consider yourself one of us!!! How long do you think you'll be staying for?"

"Oh about a month, I think. And when I've made some money, I want to go and buy a load of new clothes, to take back home with me."

"That sounds great and I'll come along with you, to help you choose some. We've got some lovely new boutiques that have just opened around town, that I must show you, so just let me know when your ready to do your shopping."

"Yeah thanks I will."

***

The next afternoon at three o'clock, Brian and Olivia arrived at Roberto and Tara's flat. "Cum-a in-a, cum-a-in-a," Roberto said, greeting them at his door. "Ah! You ava brought-a the bambino, let-a-mea-old-a-im-a. What a lovely bambino, what's is-a name?"

"Antony," Olivia replied.

"Come-on-a-sita-down-a, and-a I'll get-a some-a-vino," Roberto said, walking into the kitchen carrying Antony.

Brian and Olivia moved some clothes and newspapers over to one side of the couch, so they could sit down on it.

A few minuets later the bathroom door opened and Tara walked out, stark naked and dripping wet. "Hello," she said, walking over to the couch, and picking up the clothes and newspapers. "I'm sorry, I have not had time to clean all this mess up, I slept in very late today."

"Tara leave those things alone will you, Olivia and I have moved them so we've got room to sit down," replied Brian. "And why don't you go and dry yourself off? And put some clothes on?"

"Yes I will soon," Tara answered. "I've just had a bath, and I like my body to dry by itself. My skin feels better that way."

"Well why don't you wrap a towel around yourself until you dry off," Brian suggested. "I should have told you about Tara, most of the time she walks around the flat naked. She says her body feels better that way, and Roberto likes to see her like that. I don't think I've been here once yet, and found her dressed. I really should have warned you Olivia."

Olivia was sitting on the edge of the couch looking bemused, at Tara's very shapely body, but swollen stomach.

"Yes-a," Roberto said, coming out of the kitchen, holding Antony in one arm, a bottle of wine under his other, and carrying glasses in his free hand. "I luv-a to see-a my-a Tara's body, Olivia. It-a really turns-a me on-a, and I don't-a mind-a other men lookin, as long-a they don't-a fuckin touch-a. But now Tara, go-ana put-a some fuckin-a clothes on-a, weev-a got-a bambino here-a, he-a can-a see-a you."

"Are you pregnant Tara?" Olivia asked.

"No, no I'm not, but I think I'm due for a period though, and I'm a bit late," Tara replied, trying to push her swollen stomach in further with her hands.

"Well your stomach looks very swollen to me, and you look about three months pregnant, are you sure your not carrying a baby in there?" Olivia continued.

"No! No! I don't want to have a baby yet! I will be okay very soon. My stomach will go down next week, when I have my period," Tara replied, in a dismissive tone of voice, still holding her stomach in with her hands.

***

"Didy-a hear-a who came-a in-a club last-a nigh-ta, looking for-a Petea?" Roberto asked Brian, while they were drinking their wine.

"Well I heard something about some heavies, asking where the manager was," Brian replied. "They told Peter that they were the 'Kray-twins', and that they wanted so much of the club, and casino's profits each month, or bad things will happen to him. Anyway Peter told them that he doesn't own the club, he is only the manager there, and they should get in touch with Chetmen and Sons, they are the owners."

"We'll-a we-a just-a ave-a to-a see-a wha-ta-appens," Roberto added. "I was-a talkin to-a Mist-a Gillroy, the jewella, last-a night-a. He-a told-a-me-a, that-a the 'Kray-twins', have-a taken-a over-a most-a the-a big-a clubs, in-a London, an-a they-a known-a as-a thee-a Mafia down-a there-a, and-a people av-a been-a hurt-a and-a killed by-a them."

"Yeah I hope Peter's phoned the police today, and they know that they've been around to our club. 'Cause they should know all about these 'Kray-twins' by now. And they hopefully are gathering enough evidence to stop them very soon, before they take over our club," Brian said. "'Cause I'm not staying around here if the "Kray-Twins' move in on us and take things over, it will be to fucking dangerous for us all to even breath, let alone work at the club. "Because I've been hearing about some of the violent things that the 'Kray-twins' have been doing to people around the London area, like having peoples legs chopped off."

Olivia had been listening to all of this and didn't want to believe what she had just heard, as she remembered her dad Eric talking about these violent gangster 'Kray-twins' with the customers in his pub the other month. Looking at Brian first and then Roberto, with her green, eyes wide open in disbelief, she asked them,. "Is what you have just said for real, about these 'Kray-twins' were they in the 'Flamingo-Club last night?"

"Don't-a worry bout-a it-a Olivia," answered Roberto, squeezing her hand reassuringly. "No-a one-a is-a gonn-a hurt-a you-a, just-a forget what-a you-ave-a-eard-a-ere-a. I will-a phone-a my-a Father, in-a Italy, ana tell-a- im-a, 'cause he-a works in-a the Government-a-ova-der."

"Yeah that's a good idea Roberto, 'cause the people in your Government talk with the people in our Government, and they might be able to get someone to put a stop to what these blokes are doing to other people. And don't you go say anything to your Gran and Grandad about these 'Kray-Twins' coming to the club our Olivia luv, Will you?. Or what you've just heard Roberto and I talking about," Brian warned her. "Because it will frighten them to death, and they won't let you work at the Flamingo anymore."

"It just all sounds like something out of a bloody American film, that you're talking about," Olivia stated. "But could it really happen over here? Could the 'Kray-Twins' take over the 'Flamingo-club'?"

"Oh yes quiet easily, if the police aren't ready to put a stop to them on the east coast. I've already heard that the 'Kray-twins', are making a move up the north of England on the Casinos there," Brian replied. "And remember not a word to your Granparents about any of this okay!!"

"I'm dressed now," Tara announced, coming out of the bedroom. "Come on let's all go out and get something to eat, I'm starving. Then we'll go and visit Peter and Naomi."

***

Olivia stayed with her Grandparents and Uncle Brian until June. She continued to work full time at the Flamingo Club, always until it's closing time at 2 o'clock in the morning, then socialising and partying with her co-worker-friends, until the daylight used to break. When most of them would all pile into each others cars, driving around to find somewhere to eat breakfast. On the days that the Grimsby outdoor market would be open, they would all go over to the market-place there, saying their good-mornings to the market people, and the barrow-boys, who were there setting up their market-stalls, to sell their goods for the day. They would all go into a small, cafe' very close to the market, ordering the delicious smelling, bacon, sausages, mushrooms, fried tomatoes, eggs and fried bread. All freshly cooked, along with endless made pots, of freshly brewed tea, by the people who ran the cafe there, to cook the early morning breakfasts for the people who opened their market stalls.

When they had all been refreshed and woken up by their breakfast's and cups of tea, sometimes they would get themselves a second wind, and instead of going straight home to their beds for a much needed long, sleep. They would instead for the next couple of hours, go for a walk along the Grimsby-docks.

To breathe into their lungs some of that wonderful fresh sea-air, and the smell of the freshly caught fish, that was being unloaded from the fishing trawlers, that had just recently sailed into the docks. They would sometimes asking a Captain, of one of the Grimsby fishing, trawlers, if they could have his permission to have a look around his ship, that was now being prepared to go back out to sea, for a few more months, for another fishing trip. Because no stranger was ever allowed onto these fishing trawlers, without the Captains permission.

***

On her last night at working in the Flamingo-Club, Olivia said her tearful, sad, goodbyes to all these wonderful people, who had become such dear, special, caring friends to her. Hoping that they would now stay and remain in her life, as a part of her life for many years to come.

These people whose life's Olivia had been allowed to enter into, in her young teenage years, had opened her eyes to a very, new way of life, ideas and thinking. Not one of these friends in any way, sat in judgement of her, questioned her, or put her down for being an unmarried mother. They had been willing to accept her just as she was, without any airs and graces of how she should be, or what she should do with her life.

It seemed to her, as if she, had been guided towards these people in her life, by her wonderful, caring, uncle Brain, who knew how she had been talked about and put down, and he felt that she had been living her life in sadness, shame and disgrace, for far to long now, because of the baby son, she had given birth to out of wedlock.

Brian knew and felt that these people whom he worked with, would be kind and caring towards Olivia, and never sit in judgement of her. Like the mistake that the people, in today's society thought that she had made. No these were the people whom he knew, would be so good for his Niece to mix with now, to help her to recover, boost her ego, show compassion and give her, all the morale support, that he felt she needed.

And these were the people whom Olivia felt, were good enough to give her another chance in life, without any questions of why did you do this? Or you shouldn't have done that, no matter what she had done or been through. They had also made her now feel, that her life was important and that it must now go forward, filled with happiness and fun.

It was with all of these thoughts and feelings, that she thanked them all very much, for all the good times that they'd shown her. That she'd had with them all, and how each of them had helped her to see another kinder, way of life, that was very unprejudiced.

She also told her Uncle Brian, that she would never be able to thank him enough, and that she would never forget his kindness and what he had done for her. It was with all of these good, happy thoughts, and memories, that Olivia left her Grandparents home in Cleethorpes. To return to her parents' home again, with her baby son Antony, to the small, isolated, village of Bradwell. In another frame of mind, to get on with her life in, now what was becoming, the swinging sixties.

******

Chapter 12

The ideas, the fashion styles, the morals, thoughts and attitude towards life, of the young people went through a very radical, rebellious change during the mid, sixties, and England was leading the way for the rest of the Western World, full of creativity and excitement. The revolution began in London with people who came from working class backgrounds. It was far better to have a Father, a Dad, who was just a plumber, a bus driver, a train driver, an electrician, a dustbin-man, a coal man, a window cleaner, or one who worked in a factory, than to have one who was a Duke or a Lord. People born with titles, began to shed them so that they would be accepted. No one wanted to have anything to do with anything that appeared to be conventional, as it was considered to be so boring and just not fab, at all.

A young fashion designer named Mary Quant, changed the look in the women's fashion world, with the 'Mini Skirt' and 'Mini-Dresses', which became shorter and shorter over the years, as the girls began to feel very comfortable about showing off their legs. They would often wear mid-drift shirts and tops with their short skirts, or hipster bell-bottom jeans and trousers, showing of their shapely figures and belly-buttons. A narrow side street in London, called Carnaby Street, was full of shops, now called boutiques. It was the place to shop for the new fashions and cosmetics, with that idea soon spreading and growing all around England.

Long hair for men, a fashion started in the early sixties by the Beatles, called the Beatle-cut, became the 'In' look for men, and the top women's hairdresser was Vidal Sassoon. Instead of the backcombed, beehive, Haut-coiffure, bouffant, and lavishly hair-sprayed, crowning glories for the hair, which their Mothers had always favoured. The young-teenage, fashion-following girls, grew their hair long and straight, parting it down the middle to let it hang, all shiny and loose around their shoulders.

To look- 'in fashion'-'with it'-'sophisticated' and 'trendy', people had to be thin figured, pale faced and look very bored. The eye-shadow colours at this time were either a soft pale blue, pale green, pale lilac or white. The girls were now using a very black, Kola eye pencil or liquid eye-liner, to paint the thick- black-lines on their eyelids, with a triangle towards the outer corner of the eye, and a crease line painted just above the crease in their top eyelids. With a line painted underneath the bottom eyelashes, extended to the outer corner of the eye, and artistically painted eyelashes, applied underneath the bottom of their real lashes. After this artistic work was applied to the eyelids, lots of black mascara was then applied to the eyelashes, making them look thicker. With some of the girls preferring to wear false eyelashes over the top of their own lashes, to make them look thicker, curlier and longer. The girls also plucked their eyebrows with tweezers, to shape them into a lovely-high-arch, starting past their noses, above where the inner part of the eye began, with a thin line tapering off past the arch, towards the end of the shape of the eye. With some girls also just shaping their eyebrows into an arch and shortening them, and then drawing the rest of the brow on, in a very thin line, upwards and towards the end of the eye, with a black or brown, eye-brow-pencil. Doing this plucking and shaping of the eyebrow, gave them more space to work on their eyelids, with the eye-shadow and black eye-liner, making their eyes look wider and much bigger. The colour of the lipsticks that they wore, were usually a pretty-soft-pale pink.

The top fashion models were Jean Shrimpton, Pattie Boyd and Twiggy. Pattie Boyd became George Harrison's wife, one of the Beatles. Twiggy's manager was a hairdresser named Justin, and most teenage girls dreamed of finding themselves, someone just like Justin, who could turn them into top models, as he had done with Twiggy.

The top actors were Michael Caine and Terence Stamp, who both spoke with very-working class, 'Cockney' accents. One of the popular female actresses with beautiful, very-long-red hair, was the lovely

Jane Asher, whose lifestyle was always closely watched, especially when she became engaged to one of the Beatles, Paul McCartney, before staring in the very popular, much talked about movie with Michael Cain, called 'Alfie'.

The hottest and biggest actors, soon to hit all of the news media, were Richard Burton and Elizabeth Taylor, who both played staring roles in the very, successful, popular, movie 'Cleopatra'. With their passionate affair together, on and off the film set, seeming to spin out of control.

The new Pop-music sound had taken off first from Liverpool in England, with the 'Beatles', followed by 'Gerry and the Pace Makers', 'Cilla Black', 'Herman's Hermits', 'Billy J. Kramer', 'The Tremeloes', 'Lu-Lu', 'The Dave Clark Five', 'Procol Harum', 'The Kinks', 'Sandy Shaw', 'Dusty Springfield', 'The Rolling Stones', 'The Hollies', 'The Bee Gees', 'Donovan', 'Cat Stevens', 'Manfred Mann', 'The Who' and 'Pink Floyd'. With 'Joe Cocker' and 'Dave Berry and the Cruisers', coming from Sheffield in England. 'Dave Berry' having a smash hit with his song, 'The Crying Game'.

The British teenagers loved the new sound that was coming from America, of 'The Beach Boys', 'The Byrds', 'Dylan', 'The Mamas and the Papas', 'Sonny and Cher', 'Grace Slick' with 'Jefferson Starship', 'Janis Joplin', 'Joni Mitchell' and 'Jimmy Hendrix'. And the new soul-sounding music that was coming from the black singers, 'Stevie Wonder', 'The Four Tops', 'Jimmy Ruffin', 'Mary Wells', 'Edwin Star', 'The Supremes', 'Martha Reeves and the Vandelles', 'Marvin Gaye and Tammi Terrell', 'The Temptations', 'Smokey Robinson and the Miracles', just to name a few of them who came from Detroit, in the state of Michigan. They recorded on Berry Gordy's, 'Motown' record label, better known as the 'Tamla Motown' record label in England.

The favourite TV programs that this younger generation stayed in their homes and chose to watch, were- 'Top Of The Pops' and 'Ready Steady Go'. All of the top groups and solo artists, who had a record climbing up the pop charts towards number-1, would appear on these pop shows, for all of the young people to see and hear them, and to hopefully go out the next day to buy more of their records.

Artists were starting to paint what was called 'Pop-Art', and it was beginning to appear in the art galleries. The very famous artist, who always seemed to be under discussion in the artistic world, as to what he was now painting, and who had made his fame with his paintings of the 'Campbell's Soup Cans', was Andy Warhol, who always said *'Everyone wants and deserves their fifteen minutes of fame.'*

The affordable in-car to drive and to own was the 'Mini', which many people painted in bright colours, following the 'Pop-Art' trend.

Jobs and money were plentiful, and the only adults out of work were those who chose to be.

Morals and sex, which was practised and talked about without shame, became very free. Girls discovered that they could have orgasms, which they enjoyed frequently without feeling ashamed about, as their mothers and grandmothers would have been so ashamed to admit to it, if they had ever been lucky enough to experience the powerful feeling of one. And the now preferred sanitary protection, which the girls chose to use, was the Tampax-tampon.

Everyone seemed to now be smoking cigarettes, even during their own weddings that would be taking place at the registry offices in different cities around England. And Marijuana joints slowly crept in everywhere, soon followed by LSD, which was made popular by the university students.

Comedy became satirical, and everyone was looking for the next-new-radical- 'happening', because things were changing very fast all the time.

During the sixties' revolution of the 'British-teenagers,' which all began in early 1963/64, with the 'Mods' and the 'Rockers' eventually evolving into the 'Hippy-Movement,' with all of the 'Mods' becoming 'Hippies.' This was a movement which soon began to grow around the world, with most of the teenagers, becoming 'gentle-loving-Hippies'--'Flower-Power-Children,' who began to hand out flowers to people, always carrying the same message for everyone, as they passed around the flowers saying, *'Peace- man,-make-love-not-war.'* They were part of a great, worldwide movement where radical ideas and happenings went to extremes, never to be forgotten by those who took part in them.

******

Chapter 13

Olivia's parents Eric and Margaret and her sister Suzanne, were all very happy when Olivia arrived back home with her son Antony, to be with them again. She was showing them her new clothes that her friend Tiffany, had helped her to choose when she took her on a shopping spree, around the new Boutiques. She was telling them all about the 'Flamingo Night Club', where she had been working, when her uncle Brian had got her a job there. And about all the great-people that worked there, and the wonderful-fab, new friends that she had made. This made her mother Margaret, a little envious of her, and she made some remark about, *'some people have all the luck, and maybe Brian could get her a job there?'* But Olivia quickly told her mother, *'to forget it, that it just wouldn't be her scene, working there and socialising with her new friends.'* There was a lot she felt she could not tell her parents, about her new friend's world, and their way of life, because she knew they would not understand them. And she could just imagine the look on their faces, if they went to Roberto's and Tara's for a glass of wine, and Tara greeting them with no clothes on, how that would shock and horrify, them both so much!

***

Suzanne was very eager to go upstairs with her sister, and talk to her while she unpacked her clothes, because she had a lot to tell her, about the big change in her social life, that had happened while Olivia had been away from home.

"While you were staying in Cleethorpes, David went to live down London. He said to tell you, he'll always be there for you, if you want him. And I've finished with Ian," said Suzanne.

"Yes, I knew David was going to live in London soon, but why have you finished with Ian? I thought you two were in love, or something?" Olivia asked in a surprised voice, while hanging her dresses on the coat hangers and putting them into her wardrobe.

Suzanne sat down on Olivia's bed, and continued in an excited voice, "Because some lads from a place called Dronfield, turned up in the village a few weeks ago, and they're Hippies. They're just fab and so much fun, and they're all very different from our local village lads, they make our village lads seem very boring. And I've started seeing someone called Kenny Dee, so I had to finish with Ian, didn't I? Kenny's got long black hair and blue eyes, he's six feet tall and just fab looking. He's nineteen years old, and drives a red Mini car, that most of them pile into. And he seems to be the leader of them all."

"Wow! You seem to be very impressed with this Kenny. But I bet poor Ian's hurt."

"Yeah I think Kenny's fab. And I'm really sorry about hurting Ian, but he was my first boyfriend and I wanted a change. And I didn't love Ian the way you think I did. Anyway Olivia, you've just got to meet them, I'm sure you'll like them all. They're coming over tonight to meet you, 'cause we've told them all about you, and that you'd be coming back home today. They used to go up to the 'Bowling Green pub' to drink, and I've got them to come to my Dad's pub, and they like his 'John Smiths' beer. They're called Dee, Snifter, Bucket, Lassie, Spud, Skippy, Egg, Bozo, Willie and K and K."

"Slow down Suzanne," Olivia said with a laugh. "And what do you mean? 'We've told them all about you'? Who's told them what about me?"

"Me and the other girls have. Sandra and Angela are going out with K and K, Jill's going with Lassie, I'm with Kenny, who they call Dee, Bucket's going with Pim, Spud's going with Sly, and Egg's going with Dill. They're girls from the next village in Eyam. They come over here with them most nights, and Fridays and Saturdays, we've all started to go down to the 'Marquis of Granby's disco. Anyway, now I've told you who's going out with who. That leaves Willie free, I don't think you'll fancy him though, he sulks and has a bad temper, but he's tall and not bad looking. There's Skippy he's fun, he's just got back from working in Australia for a couple of years. There's Bozo now he's very good looking, he's over six feet tall, has long blonde hair and lovely blue eyes, I think you'll like him Olivia. Then there's Snifter, he's free and a lot of fun, but I don't think you'll fancy him though, 'cause he's got a big nose, that's why the other lads call him Snifter."

"Well they've all got funny names, who the hell gave them strange names like that? And do they know about my baby, Antony?"

"Those are their nick-names, they've had them since they were all in school together, I don't know their real names, except Kenny's, no one ever uses them. And yes, we've told them about Antony, but that doesn't bother them. We've also told them what a great person you are, and they're just dying to meet you."

"I'm looking forward to meeting them, they all sound very interesting. But don't you and the other girls, go setting me up with anybody okay?" Olivia said, pushing her long, hair back off her shoulders with a flick of her hand. "Now let's go and help Mum with the Sunday dinner, I can even smell the roast beef cooking in the oven, up here."

***

Olivia, Suzanne, Sandra, Jane, Cheryl, Jill, Brenda and Angela, were walking through the village, early, that evening, after they had been to the shop to get a packet of cigarettes. When they heard a car behind them blowing its horn loudly, they all stopped, and turned around to look. Suzanne grabbed hold of Olivia's arm, squeezing it tightly in excitement. "It's them, it's Dee and the others."

"Where are you girls going?" Dee asked, after he stopped his red Mini car, at the side of them, opening his window.

A few seconds later a blue Mini car pulled up behind Dee's, and Angela said excitedly, "Look it's K and K."

"We're going up the Dale to the rocks," Jill shouted. "Wow! Where did you get the blue Mini from?"

"K and K picked it up this afternoon," Dee replied. "They each paid half for it. Do you like it?"

"It's fab!" Angela said. "Do you lads want to come up to the rocks with us? 'Cause if you do, carry on driving on this main, road, through to the end of the village, that brings you to the Dale where the rocks start. Then take the first sharp right bend, onto a dirt road, and that will bring you up to the rocks. You can't miss it really, and we're going to listen to Radio Luxembourg."

"We're just going up to Suzanne's dad's pub first, to have a drink, then we'll meet you up at these rocks. We'll bring some bottles of beer and cider, and some crisps, we'll have a party up there while we listen to Luxembourg," said Bozo, the Hippy with blue eyes, and long blonde hair, that touched his shoulders. Bozo was sitting in the passenger seat next to Dee, looking at Olivia very admiringly.

"I take it you're Olivia?" Dee asked her, with a friendly smile on his face. "We've all been looking forward to meeting you."

"Yes, I'm Olivia, and I'm pleased to meet you all," she replied, smiling and waving to everyone in the two 'Mini' cars.

"Hello Olivia," the Hippies all shouted, and waved back to her.

"Lets go, I'm dying for a pint," Bozo said. "And Bucket wants us to go and pick up Pim, Sly, and Dill, from Eyam. So we'll see you girls up by the rocks later. Bye for now Olivia."

"Yes, I'll see you later Bozo," Olivia replied with an interested smile.

When the cars drove away, the girls were very happy and excited that their new Hippie friends had come to the village to see them.

"What do you think of them Olivia?" Angela asked her eagerly, hoping Olivia did like them, as the other girls were all talking happily together, when they all started to walk through the village towards the Dale.

"Well, I'll tell you when I get to know them a bit better, but they seem to be okay, and very far out. And I do like the look of that Bozo," Olivia replied, with a smile.

***

'*Mellow Yellow*', was playing on Angela's radio, and Angela and Brenda had used twigs to make a small fire in a dirt hole, Jill, Cheryl, Sandra and Jane, were gathering more branches to burn.

"We don't really need a fire Angel, it's a warm night tonight," said Olivia, who was sitting on a large, rock near the bright, burning fire.

"I know," Angel replied, "but I thought it would be cosy."

"Don't forget Olivia, Angela always luves to feel so cosy, wherever she is," stated Cheryl.

"Yeah you're right about that, she always does, I suppose it's her way of feeling secure," Jane replied.

The two Mini cars drove up the dirt road towards them, and when they stopped a lot of Hippies, with long hair, wearing bell-bottom-jeans and T-shirts, all seemed to fall out of the cars.

"How do you get so many people in those cars? When they're so small," Olivia asked, her eyes wide in amazement.

"Oh there's plenty of room in the back of these Mini's," replied Skippy, who had long, brown-hair and soft, hazel-brown eyes. "We sit on each other's knees in the back, it's quite comfortable really."

"If you say so," laughed Olivia.

"Wow! It's great up here," Kenny Dee said, looking all around him. "Look at these walls of rock surrounding us, it's just like a big, 'Rock-Canyon'. That's what the Americans would call a place like this yu-know? 'A-Rock-Canyon'. And it's very, very private up here, you can't see any of this, from the Dale-road at all."

"Yeah it is very, private up here," Jill replied. "That's why we thought we'd come here, it's away from the stuffy old villagers and adults. Our parents never come here, they don't even know about this place or where it is."

"Well this can be where we all meet from now on. This will be our 'Rock-Canyon'," Dee announced happily to everyone.

"How was this 'Rock-Canyon' formed then?" Asked Willie, "How did it get here? It looks to me as if these rocks, were all blown apart at some time, 'cause look the face of these rocks are all jagged."

"Yeah they would be jagged," replied Dee, in his confident voice. "'Cause if my memory serves me well, on what I know about the history of these Derbyshire villages, Bradwell in particular. At around the sixteenth, seventeenth century, these rocks up here, were all blown apart by the people of the village, who were then still just living in straw-and-mud-huts. And they got all the large stones from here, to build themselves all those stone houses, that ye-see around the village. So that's how this 'Rock-Canyon' was formed many years ago. And that pub that yer Dad's got, Suzanne and Olivia, it was originally built as a farm house, and the stones used to build it, were probably taken from here."

"What the 'White Hart' used to be a farm?" Sandra asked in surprise.

"Yeah and if yu look on the wall, outside the front of the pub, it's got the date written on it 1676, the year the stone farm was built," replied Dee.

"Do you know I've seen that date 1676 on the front of the 'White Hart' wall, and I've always wondered what it was written there for," stated Angela. "I wonder when it used to be a farm, if it had some pigies, cows, sheep, hens and chickens kept in it?"

"Yeah I bet it did," Cheryl agreed eagerly.

"This is all very interesting to know Kenny, about our village, and that the pub that my Sister and I live in used to be a farm, I must tell my Mom and Dad. And none of us had any idea how or why this 'rock-canyon' was formed. You're quite the historian Kenny," said Suzanne, eagerly complimenting her boyfriend.

Kenny just smiled, feeling very pleased at the knowledge he remembered, about the Derbyshire villages, in the Peak District, from his school history books.

"Yes it's all very interesting," said Jill thoughtfully. "And I wonder how old my house is, 'cause that's built with natural stone, that probably came from these rocks also."

"Yeah well, I don't think that anyone will be blowing up any more of these rocks, to build more stone houses with. Because this 'Rock-Canyon' is now guarded by a nasty little goat, that you all should watch out for," added Sandra. "The old lady, who owns this place, has a black and white goat with big horns, that I call Patches, and he's left loose up here most of the time, and he bloody chases and butts us, he can be very nasty."

"Yeah, he's worse than a bloody guard dog," Angela said laughing. "So always be on the look out for Patches up here, for your own safety."

"Yeah well us girls from Bradwell, are all forgetting to tell Kenny Dee, this great Derbyshire historian among us, that he hasn't just found this wonderful, 'Rock-Canyon', today. That all of us girls, during our growing up period in this village, used to come up here often and climbed these rocks. And if we could get up them and then back down them, without falling or breaking an arm or a leg, we all used to feel very brave and pleased with ourselves," Olivia proudly announced.

"What you girls were all tom-boys? Who used to come up here to climb up the face of these rocks?" Snifter asked, in a surprised tone of voice.

"No not up the face of them, that would be far to dangerous, but if you look around them, you can see that there are small, ridges and ledges around the sides of them, over there," Sandra replied, pointing across to some other rocks. "And that's where we used to go climbing up them."

"What all the way to the top?" Lassie asked. "'Cause it's still quite a height to get up there."

"Yep, all the way up to the top," Cheryl replied proudly. "And I remember one year, when we were about thirteen or fourteen," she continued with a laugh. "When I was wearing my jeans and bumper-boots, and Olivia was wearing her tight-skirt, stockings and three-inch-high-heeled-shoes, and we came up here for a walk one afternoon. And I said to her, it's a pity your dressed like that, we could have climbed the rocks if you had your jeans on. But Olivia said, it's okay, I've climbed these rocks that many times over the years, being dressed like this won't stop me. So we climbed up them, and that was no problem, we got to the top easily, and after sitting there for a while sharing a cigarette and looking down, we then started to climb back down them. Well we got half way down them okay, until we got to that ridge over there, and that's where Olivia got stuck. Because of the way she was dressed in her tight-skirt and high-heels, she couldn't slide of the ridge and down the rock to the next ridge, so she thought she'd be up there forever, and it was starting to get dark. But luckily for her at that time 'Boss-Girl' came for a walk up here and climbed up to the ledge, and helped Olivia down. Do you remember that day Olivia?"

"Oh-God-yes I do, and if it hadn't of been for 'Boss' showing up and helping me down, I thought I'd be stuck up there forever, or until someone got my Dad to come and get me down, it was pretty scary. Yeah I think we were about thirteen or fourteen years old then Cheryl, and after that happening, that was the time that I stopped rock climbing forever. But no, none of us were ever brave enough to climb up the face of these rocks, there are no ridges or ledges on them, and they're to high up, they'd be nothing to break your fall if you fell down them, so you'd definitely be dead when you got to the bottom, eh girls."

"Yeah right," all of the other girls agreed with her.

Bucket who had dark, brown, hair, and brown eyes, had been stood around with the others, listening with interest, to hear of how Dee explained that this 'Rock-Canyon' was originally formed. And about Olivia's near death experience, getting stuck on a ridge, while trying to get back down them one-day, now began to get some bottles of beer and cider, and bags of crisps, out of one of the cars saying, "By the way Olivia, I'm so pleased you didn't fall down those bloody rocks that day, or we wouldn't have had the pleasure of meeting you tonight. And this is my girlfriend Pim, and these are her friends Sly and Dill, Spud and Egg's girlfriends."

"Pleased to meet you," Olivia said, taking a bag of crisps from Bucket. "How come I've not seen you girls before? Which school do you go to?"

"We're in our last year at Lady-Manor's High School," replied Pim, who had long brown hair and blue eyes. "I'm taking shorthand and typing so I can become a secretary. And Dill here wants to be a hairdresser. But Sly doesn't know what she wants to do yet, so she's just taking all the 'O'-level exams, that she can."

"Shur-up all of you," Dee shouted in a very bossy voice, when the song *'All You Need Is Love'*, started to play on the radio. "Snifter, switch the car radios on and tune them into Luxembourg, I just love this record by the Beatles."

Everyone was sitting around the fire, as it was going dark, and they all began to sing in full voice, *"All you need is love, love is all you need...."* The song seemed to go on forever, and they all liked the message they were hearing in the words.

"I've got an idea. Let's all go to that 'Ice-skating-rink', what's it called? 'Silver-Blades' in Sheffield, next Saturday night," Dee suggested to everyone, when they had finished singing.

"But I thought we were going to the disco in Bamford?" Suzanne replied.

"We'll go to Bamford on Friday night. And when we've done some ice-skating on Saturday, we can go to that disco, above the ice-rink later on at about eleven o'clock," Dee replied confidently.

"That sounds like a good idea," Angela agreed. "We'll get the bus from the village into Sheffield, and meet you blokes outside 'Silver-Blades', and catch the last bus home at twelve thirty. I've just bought a lovely maroon coloured trouser suit, I'll wear that."

"Yes," Jill added, "we'll all wear trouser suits, then if we fall down on the ice we won't get cold wet legs."

"I've just bought a lovely pale-blue trouser suit," Olivia replied. "And I was thinking of wearing it Friday night, but I can't wear it Friday and Saturday."

"Yes you can, you're going to two different places," Sly replied. "And I love the way you do your eye make up, Olivia, with white eye-shadow and black eye-liner. I like the crease line that you draw, I'm going to try and do my eyes like that."

"Yeah the beautiful dancing girls, called 'The-Foxy-Ladies' that I meet at the 'Flamingo Night Club' and became friends with, showed and gave me a few tips about eye-make-up, and how to apply it."

"I wish you girls would fucking shut-up, about your clothes and make-up," Kenny Dee shouted impatiently. "Listen what's playing, my favourite record, I just love this song 'A Whiter Shade Of Pale', so just all shut up, will you?"

"You just sod off Kenny," Olivia replied angrily. "I've been listening to you, and you're so bloody bossy, telling everyone when to shut-up, what to do, where we're going, what to talk about. Who the hell do you think you are? And you're just pissing me off."

"What star sign are you Olivia?" Kenny asked her, in a very calm curious tone of voice, with a smile on his face, looking at her.

"Scorpio, why?" She replied, staring back at him.

"Well so am I, so you'd better watch out," Kenny answered, in a threatening tone of voice.

"Oh no!" Olivia shouted back, now glaring at him with her large green eyes. "You'd better bloody watch it Kenny, because Scorpio's are also very similar to witches. You have good witches, and bad witches, and you have good Scorpio's and bad Scorpio's. So it's your choice Kenny, because I can be either."

"Yeah I think you could, and you can also look like a cat, with those green eyes of yours. I bet you can give a nasty big scratch, just like one as well eh?"

"Oh yes definitely, if I feel like I have to," Olivia replied, glaring at him intently.

***

The fire that the girls had made was now starting to burn low, when Lassie suggested that they all go up to the 'White Hart', because they had run out of beer.

"That's a good idea," Kenny replied. "Anyway, I want to talk to Suzanne's dad, about putting a juke-box and some disco lights, in that room in his pub that only we seem to use. 'Cause I think it'd be great, having our own little disco in the 'White Hart' pub."

"What do you think of that brainy idea of mine, Olivia?" Kenny asked her, thinking that it was now time, for the two of them to become friends, instead of becoming mortal enemies.

"Yeah, I suppose that's a good idea, but don't go asking my Dad, just yet, because I know he'll say no, right now. He doesn't know you all very well, you've not been drinking at his pub for very long yet, and my dad can be funny about things like that. Wait until he's got to know you better, or he'll be telling everyone, *that the bloody Hippies, have turned up here, and are now trying to take over my pub.*"

"Okay I'll wait a bit longer then before I ask him," Kenny agreed with a laugh, and hoping that he and Olivia, would now start to get on better after this their first meeting. "Just tell me when you think the time will be right, then I'll have a talk with the old bugger, and I'll expect some support from you lot also."

"Yeah Dee, you've got it," the others all agreed.

***

Eric and Margaret became very concerned about their daughter's future with her son Antony. As Olivia eagerly became one of these Hippies, very strongly believing in their ideas and philosophies on life, informing her parents, '*That it was now a more peaceful, kinder, gentler time for everyone to get into, and go along with.*' Her parents reluctantly came to accept that these kind, gentle, fun loving lads that called themselves Hippies, were now her new friends. But no matter how often it was explained to them, her parents could never really understand what it was that they were all trying to do or prove. That their intentions were to change everything, including morals and attitudes that the generations before them had respected and believed in, which had all seemed to go so wrong. So everything in the life's of the Hippies was definitely going to be so very different now!!!

Oh yes so very different to how Eric and Margaret had both grown up, in a fearful generation during the Second World War. Where everyone tried so hard to be orderly and obedient while following the strict, accepted rules of living, in the do-as-you-are-told time and way of life. Along with the rationing-cards for food, clothes, furniture, and other supplementary goods, that people were allowed or restricted from having. With most people always trying to keep up their appearances, by being as smartly dressed as they could, by keeping up the front no matter what, with everyone following someone-else's orders or rules, in their chaotic life's of who will win the 'Great Second-World-War,' that will end all wars!!!

As this generation would all be so anxiously listening to their, plugged into the socket on the wall- wirelesses, fading in and out of the station, to the fighting and winning war-talk messages, of their Prime Minister, Mr. Winston Churchill. Telling them how *"Everyone shall fight on the seas and oceans, shall fight in the air, shall fight on the landing grounds, shall fight on the beaches, shall fight in the fields, shall fight in the hills and on the streets, we shall never surrender or be defeated."* In this their great, country and Empire of England, in keeping Hitler and his German, soldiers out of and away from their country. And to the most, kind, gentle and thoughtful words of their King, George VI and his wife, Queen Elizabeth, who tried so hard to give everyone encouragement to keep going and to stay strong as families. During the bombs dropping from the German aeroplanes around them, and their houses and homes being destroyed. As the loved ones close to them, who didn't run for sanctuary to the bomb shelters, instead taking shelter underneath their stairs or a table, were killed or lost and buried in the rubble after the bombing raids, of the towns and city's where they lived. With the children of that generation, thinking that they now had new playgrounds, as they played on the rubble of the bombsites, always looking out for unexploded bombs.

Eric and Margaret knew that the Hippy called Bozo, was now her new boyfriend, and noticed how she seemed to keep him at a distance from her, with no intense passionate involvement shown on her part, towards the relationship with him. They had no problem at all with this Hippy being her new, boyfriend, because he seemed to be a very nice kind and gentle person, who had a job and went to work. And one day when they had been going out together for a longer period of time, they thought that in about twelve months time. Bozo the Hippy may come to ask them, if he could marry their daughter Olivia.

But they felt that she should have something more than that Hippy boyfriend, and her baby Antony, in her life right now. They wanted her, especially her Father did, to have a job and later preferably a career, for herself.

Olivia told them about the work, that she'd done at the Flamingo Club, and that she'd been told by the manager Peter, before she left, that she could always go back to work for them again. She also told them about the job, and the wonderful hairdressing offer, that her Cousin Anton had made to her. Informing her Parents that she knew, that she could also, always go back to live with her Grandparents, but her Dad told her that he did not want her to leave home again. Instead her Father told her, that he could get her a job, as a hairdresser, if that's what she wanted to be. Because he knew a lady in the village of Hope, who had given him the job to do the plumbing work for her, when she was going to open up her own hairdressing- salon next year, so she would need an apprentice hairdresser. He also told her, he thought it would be better if she took the hairdressing job in Hope, so her Mother and him would be able to look after Antony for her, and that she'd know, that her baby would be okay, while she was at work. It would also be the best thing for Antony, if in time, she let her parents adopt him.

Olivia had begun to have many arguments now with her father about this, because she did not think that it was right, or his right, for him to want to adopt her Son. The son that she knew, that her dad could never have of his own, because her mother did not want to have anymore children. Margaret wouldn't even entertain the fact, even when Olivia tried to talk her mum into it, by saying, *that you'll probably have a boy this time mom, so why don't you try for one?*

She also felt that although her parents probably did love her, and care very much about her, and especially her future, they were now beginning to try and be too controlling with, and of her. But her attitude to this was, *how dare they now begin to do this to me, after disowning me and throwing me out, when I was pregnant.* Because for her, it was far to late to start now, to forgive her and want her back into their family, just like everything used to be before she had her baby.

Not only had her sister Suzanne accepted her and her new predicament, but her new Hippie friends whom she would meet up with, in the 'Rock-Canyon', had accepted her and loved her baby Antony.

Bozo had even been hinting and making suggestions about them getting married very soon, and was treating Antony, like his own son, being so kind and caring towards him, concerned about his welfare and beginning to love him dearly.

But for now as long as Olivia felt that she was accepted and loved by her friends, without any imposing questions about her life and why she had a baby, that's all that really mattered to her right now. Yes all her new friends beginning with the ones that she had made while working at the 'Flamingo-Night-Club', who had all now led her to believe that she should be proud, of her baby Antony. Feeling no shame over being an unmarried Mother, like some members of the older generation, thought she still should be.

******

Chapter 14

One bright sunny Saturday Morning, Eric was stood at the front, doorway of his pub, enjoying the feeling of the sun shining on his face. While he was deep in conversation talking to Stella, who had just been up the road to the 'Top-Shop' the small grocery store at the top of Town-Gate, to get a loaf of bread. Stella the lady who wore her skirts short, above her knees, with black, stockings, to show off her shapely legs to her husband, lived next door to the pub, and had been in 'The White Hart' for a drink with her husband Tom, the night before. Always made a point in her wonderful, infectious, throaty, laugh, of telling Margaret, Olivia and Suzanne. *I always know when Eric wants to talk with me, 'cause he always sits down outside, on that wooden bench, underneath his pub window. I come out every morning to have a look to see if he's sat there. And I usually shout to him, I'll be with you in a minute Eric. And other times I think, oh-u-can bloody wait a few more minutes, 'cause I want another cup-a-tea first.*

As she was telling Eric, about where her husband Tom, and kids Cheryl and Russell, were thinking of going for their holidays that summer. A bright pillar-box red, 'Standard Ten' car, drove up the hill of 'Town-Gate' from the bridge, pulling up and parking, outside the 'White Hart Pub'.

"Olivia, Suzanne," their Dad turned around and shouted to them down the hallway, inside the pub towards the living room. "Come and see what your bloody Hippy friends, have just arrived in."

"Where the hell did you get that from?" Suzanne asked laughing, when she arrived at the front door, to see what her Dad was shouting about, for them to come and have a look at the bright red car.

"We all put together for it," Bucket replied. "It's our flower power car. We're taking it up to the 'Rock- Canyon', and we're going to paint big colourful flowers all over it. Are you coming to help us?"

"Yes I am definitely, this should be fun," Olivia replied, joining her Sister and the others.

"Bring Antony with you," Bozo said. "And we'll let him have a brush to paint something on the car."

"No I don't think so. We'll leave Antony, here with my Mom and Dad for now, 'cause I don't think that my Dad, will be very happy, if I bring his Grandson home all covered in paint. Would yu-Dad?" Replied Olivia.

"No I wouldn't be," added Eric. You leave our Antony here with me and your Mother. 'Cause you bloody crazy Hippies, might just decide that he'd look better painted a different colour."

"A few days after I'd given birth to him, a Nurse in the hospital asked me if his father was black?" Olivia said.

"So what was your answer to that?" Asked Bozo?"

"I said well it looks like he was, doesn't it? By the colour of his skin. But no, unless I've now been given the wrong baby, from the nursery? But after a few more days in the hospital, his skin went the colour it is now, I think that he just had a touch, of yellow-jaundice when he was born, and a lot of babies are born with that, which makes their skin look darker for a while," Olivia replied.

"Well how would they know if a black baby, had a touch of jaundice? When their skin is already dark, when they are born?" Bucket enquired laughingly. "That would be hard for them to tell, wouldn't it?"

"God knows, I never asked them, how they would work that one out," Olivia replied laughing.

"Come on, we don't want to be stood here all day, just gossiping with each other, let's go and get this car painted," Lassie suggested eagerly, to everyone.

**

When they reached the canyon, Kenny, Egg, Snifter, and Skippy had just arrived in their car, and were getting out of it, when Kenny asked, "Whose got all this paint? For this job then?"

"I've brought it, and some brushes. They're in the boot of our car, I'll get them," Egg replied.

"I hope someones brought some paint remover, like turps," Skippy said with a laugh. "Or we're going to look weird at the disco tonight, all covered in paint."

"Not if we painted white shirts on ourselves," Snifter laughed.

"And don't forget the white, trousers to match," Egg added.

"You'd all be matching up with me in my white-suit then," Kenny stated.

"I'll drive down, to the hardware shop in the village, and get us some turpentine, to clean the paint of us," Willie offered.

"Yeah okay you do that Willie. And for everyone else, here's all the paint cans, and the brushes, let's get started then," Egg announced, very enthusiastically.

"Someone turn the music up on the car radios, 'cause this is going to be a very big happening," Kenny announced, sitting down on a rock, and beginning to roll a joint. "I can't wait to see it finished, and if we do a good job, we can all paint some flowers on my Mini-car."

They were all working very hard, on the car that afternoon, with everyone using their artistic talents, painting pretty, coloured flowers all over it, with some of the flowers having green-stems and leaves painted around them, and the black wheels of the car, were made to look as if they had flowers, growing out of them. Suzanne put her hands and feet in white paint, and then pressed them onto the boot of the car, feeling very pleased with the results, of how her prints looked. Bucket wrote in the fancy writing, that he was an expert in doing, 'Flower Power' and 'Peace Man! Make Love Not War!' across the roof, and on both sides of the doors. Then suggesting to everyone, that they all take a drive in it, and go into Sheffield, some time the next week, and hand out flowers to all of the people, they see around the 'Peace-Gardens' there.

"Yeah." Everyone agreed with Bucket that it was a good idea, and they would all go along to the 'Peace-Gardens', to hand out flowers to people, to help to spread their message.

"Have any of you heard about that university, scientist in America, and what he's preaching to the Hippies over there?" Egg asked, whilst he was cleaning paint off his hands, with a rag covered in turpentine.

"Yeah I've heard about him, he's called Timothy Leary," Willie replied. "I was reading about him in a magazine, the other day. And I think he's just some, fucking nutter of a scientist, who's been experimenting on people with this LSD drug. He's now telling everyone to turn-on, tune in, and drop-out. Tune-in to the youth movement's music, with all its messages in its lyrics, turn-on with all the different drugs they can take, and drop-out of school and jobs, and then go where? Which commune should we all go to live on? To find his great happenings? He's not told us where to go yet, to find that."

"Well maybe this bloke might let us stay in his house, if we decide to go over there to visit him. He lives in America, doesn't he? We should all go and see him one day, to ask what he thinks, that we should all do with our life's? When we've all dropped out, huh?" Lassie suggested.

"Yeah, I think we can all agree about the music and the drugs, we just love all of that. But if we'd had no education, we wouldn't have jobs, and without jobs we wouldn't be able to buy clothes, or have cars, or go out anywhere and do anything, or be able to feed ourselves. So what's his point?" Snifter asked.

"I don't think that Hippies, are supposed to work or drive around in cars. We are supposed to walk everywhere," stated Sandra.

"Oh yeah, that would be just great for all of us, wouldn't it?" Snifter added. "So how long would our 'Jesus-Boots', last us before the soles of them are full of holes?"

"We could always put some cut-out cardboard in them for soles," Egg stated happily, after having a few tokes of a joint.

"We could always buy a fucking Donkey to ride on, to get us around. I think one of them would be cheap enough to buy," Lassie added, to this weird, funny conversation.

"Well I think there should be a good farmer around here somewhere, in one of these villages, who'd sell us his donkey cheap enough. We'll just have to make some inquiries," Willie stated, after having a few tokes of a passed around joint that Bozo had rolled.

"And how many of you, do you think, will be able to ride on this donkey together?" Cheryl asked them all.

"Well all of us of course, it will be a fucking, big Donkey," Skippy replied laughingly. "But Kenny may have to walk for a while, if the Donkey gets to tired, won't-yu Kenny?"

"No I fucking won't. And we're not getting any fucking donkey, so stop playing sweet, fucking, Mary, Joseph and Jesus games, 'cause they're the only ones that I know about, who rode around on stupid, fucking donkeys," Kenny replied, putting everyone whom he thought had smoked to many joints, in their places. "But if everyone starts to listen and take notice, to what this Leary bloke, is saying that we all should do. I suppose yu-could be right, we'd all be riding around on fucking Donkeys one-day or walking, but certainly not me."

"Yeah I suppose your right Dee, and who wants a fucking Donkey anyway? Not me," Egg agreed, finishing the last of the joint off.

"What would we feed the Donkey on, if we had one?" Asked Willie.

"Eggs I suppose," replied a laughing Snifter.

"Eggs? You'd feed a Donkey on bloody, stupid eggs? Well I'm sure glad that I'm not, your poor Donkey," stated Angela. "You'd feed a donkey on grass and hay."

"Yes your so right Angela. And fuck the idea of us getting a bloody stupid Donkey. But without any schooling I wouldn't have been able to become an electrician. Anyway, who does this fucking bloke think he is? Who's out there preaching to a bunch, of lost kids, in America, who don't seem to know what they're doing or where they're going to. 'Cause I'm not going anywhere with them, to their fucking never- never land. Let's just phone um-up and ask um to tell us where it is that they've got to. And if it's somewhere nice, well we could all go and visit them. Anyway I think that he's just some nutty, out of his head scientist, who likes preaching to everyone and us kids, 'cause he thinks that we'll all follow him. And he thinks he's a Hippy does he? Well he's too fucking old and a has-been, to be a Hippy," Dee said, in a very matter of fact tone of voice. "I still think that he's a nutty scientist, who's probably lost his job at some university over there."

"Yeah!" Everyone agreed laughing, while talking together. "He's just an old man, who thinks that he's one of us, a Hippy."

"*If you go to San Francisco be sure to wear some flowers in your hair...*" began to play on the car radio, someone turned the volume up, as they all started to sing together, the happy words to it in harmony.

"I'd love to go over to America, there's a big Hippy movement happening in California. And I'd like to be part of it, and join the thousands of kids who are flocking to Haight Ashbury in San Francisco. I think that even so far away in England, we can feel the paradise that those Hippies have found over there. Oh! I wish and wish that I could, just go over there and join them. And when I'd arrive in San Francisco, I'd be wearing some flowers in my hair. 'Cause that's what Scott McKenzie, says we should all do," Olivia stated dreamily.

"I'd love to go too, and live in a Hippy, commune in California, with the other Hippies over there for a while," Kenny said. "But I wouldn't want to get drafted, like a lot of the lads over there are doin, because then I'd be sent to fight in their Vietnam War."

"No neither would I," added Bozo. "That's not being peaceful and making luv, instead of war. What's this stupid, Vietnam war all about anyway? It just seems to go on forever, and when one-country thinks that it's starting to loose the war, they all pull out and go home. The French were in there for long enough, fighting the Vietcong, until they realized it was a no-win war, for any outside soldiers. Then another country America, had to go in, to show everyone how they can win this war."

"Christ that's a fucking big statement, coming from you Bozo. What books have you been reading lately?" Kenny said sarcastically.

"Probably the ones that you lent me the other week Kenny, so now I know as much as you do," Bozo answered smugly. "And in case you didn't know, I can read, really."

"Well good for you Bozo, and don't forget who those books belong to, when and if you ever do, finish reading them," Kenny said, to remind him.

"Well the car looks good, don't you all think so?" Suzanne said happily, hoping she could stop any argument developing between

Bozo and Kenny. "Let's polish it up now, and take it over to the pub, to show my Dad, and see what he thinks about it."

"First I'm going to paint a big flower high up on those rocks," Bucket said, trying to find some ledges on the rock face, to put his feet on, holding different coloured cans of paint and a brush in one hand. "Shit, how the hell do you get up these rocks?"

"With great, difficulty," Kenny replied laughing. "Remember the girls told us? That you can't climb up the face of these rocks, 'cause there are no ledges or ridges to put your feet. But I'll tell you what, let's find that small road that runs along the top up there, and I think that we've got a bit of spare rope, in the boot of the car. So when we've driven up there, Willie and me will tie that rope around your waist, and then, with Bozo, who's as strong as an ox, and all the rest of us, who can help him, by holding on to you, and lowering you slowly, down the face of the rock, so that you can paint the flower. Then in many years to come, when all of us Hippies, have long, been forgotten about, and no-one even remembers us anymore. That flower that you paint will always be there forever, in memory of us all."

"Yeah that's why I'm going to paint a flower up there," Bucket stated. "So that us Hippies are never forgotten about, and this 'Rock Canyon' was our luving meeting place."

"As if anyone could ever forget us lot in a hurry," Cheryl added, with a laugh.

"As if anyone would ever want to forget, the beautiful people that we all are," Sandra replied.

***

"Christ," said Eric laughing, when he came outside his pub to see the painted 'Flower Power' car. "I can see that you've all worked very hard on it, but what a bloody eyesore. I've never seen anything like it before in my life. And I do hope that you all know, that you'll get pulled over by the police, if you drive around in that, you'll all get yourselves arrested and locked up. And don't park the bloody thing right outside my pub, it'll frighten away my customers, park it around the back somewhere out of the way."

***

The Hippies went in their newly painted 'Flower Power' car, to the city, of Sheffield the next week. They slowly, drove by the 'Peace-Flower-Gardens' in the city centre, and saw that it was full of other Hippies, who were all gathered there, holding arms full of beautiful, coloured flowers.

When they had parked their car and were all getting out of it, these other Hippies, in the garden came over to greet them, admiring their car very much, asking them where they had got such a beautiful car from? These garden, Hippies, were so welcoming, friendly, kind and chatty towards these new Hippies, who had just arrived amongst them, handing a flower to each of them, asking them where they had all driven from, in their lovely 'Flower-Power-Car?'

'We're from the country villages in the 'Hope Valley' of Derbyshire. And we all meet up in our 'Rock-Canyon' in Bradwell, and you should all come over to see us, in our Canyon sometime,' they were told. These Hippies who had come to greet them, in the 'Peace-Gardens', loved to meet up with each other, here, and around other parks and gardens in the city. They were always carrying beautiful, coloured flowers, laid in their arms, which they would hand out to people, with the message saying, *'Peace man! - Make love not war - Love is beautiful.'* So with their arms full of lovely, flowers, they asked Kenny and all the other Hippies, with him, if they had flowers that grew in their Canyon?

"Yes weeds, we've got lots of lovely flowering weeds," Willie answered, in a fun making voice, with all of the rest of his Hippie crowd, now glaring at him.

They were then asked by the flower holding Hippies, if they would like to help them, pass out their flowers, and spread the word to everyone who passed by.

"Yes, that's what we've come over here for, to pass out flowers to people and spread our message of peace," Bucket genuinely replied.

So they all eagerly began taking some flowers, from the arms of the other Hippies, and walking away with them, handing them out to people, as they spread their words of peace.

Bozo was carrying Olivia's baby, Antony, while they were all having fun, passing out the flowers to people who would stop to take one. He had bought an ice cream cornet for Antony, who now had a cornet in one hand, with a flower in the other, which the baby also thought was to eat. Bozo was trying to get him to give the flower, to a little old lady, who had stopped to look at them.

Antony finally did let the lady take the flower, from his hand, and this brought tears to her eyes, when she took it from him, giving him a kiss on the cheek. Asking Bozo, if Antony was a little flower power baby.

"Yes he is and I'm his Dad," Bozo replied proudly, with a smile while looking at Olivia.

***

The city streets of Sheffield were now beginning to fill up with boutiques, that were opening everywhere. The Hippies would meet up in them, buying cheesecloth, skirts, shirts and brightly, coloured patterned, tops and dresses, long wrap-around skirts, and leather opened toed sandals called 'Jesus-Boots'. They also liked to meet together, in the psychedelic 'head-shops', where they would buy trinkets, bracelets and rings made out of inexpensive silver, and lovely assorted coloured, and different lengths, of love-beads, posters, pipes to smoke, cigarette papers for rolling their marijuana joints in, and incense sticks that, when burnt, had a very mystical smell. The boutiques and 'head-shops' were continually playing the Beatles 'Sergeant Peppers Lonely Hearts Club Band' album, which was the album of the psychedelic sixties, the album everyone wanted to hear and listen to everywhere they went.

******

Chapter 15

"I'll put Antony to bed for you if you like?" Margaret said, going into the bathroom, and seeing that Olivia had just given Antony, his night-time bath, and was putting his blue fluffy pyjamas on him.

"Thanks Mum," Olivia replied, brushing Antony's damp hair with a soft hairbrush. "I'm just going to take a quick, bath myself, then I'll come and give him a goodnight kiss."

"Is it okay if I take him downstairs first though, to give your Father a kiss goodnight?" Margaret asked, walking out of the bathroom, carrying a happy, laughing Antony.

"Yes Mum, of course it is," Olivia replied, closing the bathroom door after her Mother, before undressing to take her bath.

***

After taking her bath and drying herself off, Olivia went into her bedroom and began to dress. She heard the sound of a car, with a noisy engine, pulling up across the road from the pub.

She looked out through her bedroom window and saw a lovely white, open-top, Triumph-Spitfire sports-car. Two men got out of the car and went into the pub.

While sitting at her dressing table, putting make-up on her face and brushing her shiny long hair. She began to wonder, *who these men were, because she had never seen them come to her Dads, pub before.*

***

She went downstairs and, on opening the door at the bottom of the stairs. She saw the two men who had arrived in the sports car.

They were sitting at the bar having drinks, and talking to her Father, who was stood behind the bar holding Antony.

One of the men had blonde hair, and blue eyes, and the other man had light brown hair and blue eyes, and wore glasses. They both looked to be in their late twenties and about six feet tall. They were wearing casual clothes, and had gold watches on their wrists, with the blonde haired one, wearing a wedding ring, on his third finger, of his left hand.

"This is my daughter Olivia, Antony's Mum," Eric said, introducing her to the men, when she came into the bar.

"Hello," said the man with brown hair and glasses, looking very interestingly at Olivia. "I'm very pleased to meet you. I'm Clive, and this is my friend Jack. You've got a lovely baby son."

"Thank you, I think so too. I'm going out now Dad, and Mum said she'll put Antony to bed for me. So I'll just give him a goodnight kiss before I go. Goodnight my darling baby, I'll see you later," Olivia said, kissing her son goodnight.

"Are you going somewhere nice this evening?" Clive inquired.

"Why? And I've not seen you two around the village before, where are you from?" Olivia asked.

"We're from Sheffield, and we're looking for a country pub with a tap room. Where we can come and play dominoes on a Friday night," Jack replied.

"We've just been telling your Dad," Clive continued. "That there's three more of us, and we all have a 'lad's- night' out together, on Friday's. We've been going to another pub in Bradwell, for a few months, but we fell out with the landlord there last week. So we've got to find somewhere else to have our 'lad's-night' out, and we heard about the 'White Hart', your Dad's pub. So we've come to check it out."

"Oh, how sweet. I do hope you find what you're looking for, in my Dads pub," Olivia said, in a sarcastic tone of voice.

"Do you have after-time drinking here at all? On Friday nights?" Jack, asked Eric, hopefully.

"Yes we do. And I'll reserve that big, table in front of the window over there, for you all, for your dominoes night. We can also do sandwiches for you blokes, if you get hungry."

"Well that sounds great. It looks as if we came and found the right pub, eh Jack?" Clive said looking over his shoulder into the 'Tap-Room', at the large, firm, very old table, underneath the window. Now feeling very pleased with himself, at this new pub his friend and him have found, for their 'lads-night' out.

"We've got our dominoes night all settled for here then Eric, and I'm looking forward to coming myself. We'll all be here about eight o'clock then, every Friday evening."

"Good, and I'm sure you'll all enjoy, your Friday evenings at my pub," replied Eric, feeling very pleased with himself, about getting some new customers.

"Well I'm so pleased, you've got that all sorted out. You must be feeling so happy, with your little-self's now," Olivia said to Jack and Clive, with a bored sigh. "But I must go and meet my friends now."

"You didn't say where you were going Olivia, when I asked you?" Clive said, looking at her intently.

"That's because I didn't tell you," Olivia replied, staring back at him.

"To meet all her bloody, Hippy friends, up the Dale somewhere, in what they call their 'Rock Canyon'," her Father replied, with a laugh.

"Where's that then?" Clive asked.

"Oh, up the Dale somewhere, where all those rocks start, just going out of the village, towards Tidesell," replied Eric.

"Don't worry about it, you'd never find our Canyon, bye now," Olivia said smiling, before she walked away from them.

"Bye Olivia," Clive and Jack shouted after her.

"Hope to see you again sometime Olivia!" Clive went on to say.

"I doubt it," was her reply.

**

Suzanne and Olivia arrived home at the 'White Hart' pub, just after midnight one Friday evening, after they had been at the 'Marquis' discotheque. They could hear the record 'Silence is Golden', playing on the juke-box, that Kenny Dee, had finally, talked and persuaded, their Father, Eric, into installing, along with the Black, fluorescent disco lights.

The girls went into the room where the jukebox was playing, and saw a lot of people in there. Their Mother, Margaret, was sat on a stool at a small table, with some of her and Eric's friends, having a drink and smoking a cigarette while singing along with them to her favourite record.

"Hello we're home," Olivia said, with a smile to everyone sat around the table.

"Hello girls," Everyone said, greeting them. "Did you both have a good time tonight at the Disco?"

"Yes thanks it was fab," Suzanne replied to her Mother and everyone else, while observing some strangers stood around their jukebox.

"Did you give your boyfriends a lovely kiss goodnight?" Asked Dave, who had a very sexual, intimidating sense of humour, especially when he'd been drinking.

"Yes of course we did, if your interested in knowing," Olivia replied haughtily, ready to give anything back verbally to him, that Dave could put up.

Clive, the man Olivia had met the other week, was putting money into the juke-box and selecting records, with Jack who was stood next to him, reading out the titles of the records on the juke-box. Olivia went over to them, to see what they were selecting.

"What are these songs like? *'I Was Made to Love Her'*, *'Bernadette'*, *'White Rabbit'*, *'Up, Up and Away'* and *'On a Carousel'*. Are they any good?" Jack asked her, with a smile on his face.

"Yes they're good, put them on and listen," Olivia replied. "Will you also put on *'San Francisco, Be Sure To Wear Some Flowers In Your Hair'*, that ones just great?"

"Here, put on *'A Whiter Shade of Pale'*, as many times as you can. I love to hear that record, I just wish I knew what it was they were singing about," said a tall, well-built man, with black hair and blue eyes, putting a pile of silver coins, into Olivia's hand.

"God this older generation. And who are you?" Olivia said, laughing at the man.

"This is Steve," Clive said. "And let me introduce you to the rest of the lad's. You've already met Jack, haven't you? Well, this is Allan and Gerry. Lad's this is Olivia."

"Hello, pleased to meet you Olivia," Allan, Steve and Gerry said, shaking her hand.

"And this is my Sister Suzanne," Olivia said, pulling her Sister by the arm, towards the crowd around the jukebox.

"Are you both Hippies?" Steve asked, smiling at the two girls.

"Yes, why?" Suzanne asked.

"I thought you were," continued Steve. "Because you look like Hippies."

"And what do Hippies look like?" Olivia asked defensively.

"Like you two," Clive replied.

"You mean we don't look bloody, old fashioned, and boring like you, thank God!" Olivia said, looking at them all, intensely, with her large, green eyes.

"Well, I think the Hippies all look great," Jack said, putting his arms around Olivia and Suzanne's shoulders. "And if there had been Hippies when I was a teenager, I'd have definitely been one myself."

"Me too," agreed Clive. "You must let us come and have a look, at this 'Rock Canyon', that your Dads told us about. Is this the place where you all have your happenings?"

"What would you know about happenings?" Suzanne asked, challenging them all.

"No! No never!" Olivia said defiantly, feeling the need to protect their Hippy world in the Canyon, from this outside intrusion. "It's ours, it's our world up there, and it's private. Anyway as our Suzanne has asked you, what the hell would you know about happenings? You look as though you've never had one in your life's before."

"What is a happening?" Clive asked her, in a very interested, serious tone of voice. "Tell us about them?"

"No I'm not," Olivia replied, "that's for us to know, and for you to find out, but not from me. And Kenny Dee, wouldn't be very pleased if you blokes, showed up one day, to just gork at us, he'd be really pissed off, and blame me. Anyway, I thought you came here to play dominoes tonight? Not to find out about Hippies and happenings, and to play our juke-box."

"We are, well we have been," Gerry said, putting more money into the jukebox. "We're just having a break, and some sandwiches for now. Here Olivia, come and choose some more records for us, will you please?"

"Can I get you girls a drink?" Clive asked.

"If you want to," Olivia replied. "We'll have Bacardi and Coke. And I'll have a cigarette, 'cause I've run out."

She took a cigarette, when Clive opened his cigarette packet and offered her one. He lit it for her, with his expensive, gold cigarette lighter.

"Fab lighter."

"Would you like to keep it?" Clive asked, passing it to her to have a closer look.

"No thanks," Olivia replied, passing the lighter back to him.

"Where do you go at weekends?"

"To the discotheque at the 'Marquis of Granby' in Bamford."

"Have you got a boyfriend?"

"Yes thanks."

"You have got lovely, green eyes Olivia."

"Yes I know, I get them from my Grandfather," she answered, looking at him. "Well, are you going to get us those drinks or not?"

"Yes I'm sorry, I'll get them for you right now."

***

"Whose is that silver-grey, Mark Ten, Jaguar? Parked outside the pub?" Olivia asked Clive, after he'd come back from the bar, and gave her and Suzanne their drinks.

"It's mine."

"Very nice car, we'll have to park our 'Flower Power' car next to it, I bet that would piss you off, wouldn't it?"

"No, I'd love to see your 'Flower Power' car. Your Dad's been telling us all, how hard you all, worked on it, painting the flowers all over it, and I bet it looks lovely."

"Well we think we all did a good job on it, and Bucket was very artistic with some good ideas for it. So tell us Clive where do you work?"

"I've got my own company."

"Oh! So that's why you can afford to drive a car, like a Mark Ten Jaguar, is it?"

Clive ignored her cutting remark, instead asking her, "Would you like to go for a drive with me? In my lovely car one day, Olivia?"

"Maybe," she replied, "maybe."

***

A few weeks later, Olivia and her Hippy friends were at the 'Marquis of Granby' discotheque, they had just come off the dance floor and gone into the bar, when Olivia saw Clive stood at the bar alone, having a drink. On seeing them all, he walked over to them saying, "Hello Olivia, I've been looking for you."

"Why? And I've never seen you here before," Olivia replied.

"Would you like a drink?" Clive asked her.

"What all of us? Yes please," Egg replied with a laugh, putting his arm around Olivia's shoulder, and asking her. "Who is this bloke?"

"Oh, let me introduce you to the crowd, this is Clive everyone, "Olivia said. "But there's a lot of us to buy drinks for Clive."

"Oh that's okay, I don't mind," Clive replied, hoping that he would be accepted, by trying to buy their friendship with his drinks, thinking this might impress Olivia, being kind to her Hippy friends.

"I'll have a Bacardi and Coke, just leave it on the bar for me and talk to my friends, I'm just going to the ladies," Olivia said before walking away.

***

While checking her hair and make-up in the mirror in the ladies' washroom, after washing her hands, she wondered to herself, *why Clive had come to the disco tonight, and what did he want with them all, because they were all so much younger than him.*

She went back into the bar to get her drink and to see how Clive, was getting along with her friends, she saw them all talking, joking and laughing together, and it looked as if they were getting on okay with Clive, and making friends with him. But Clive did seem to stand out like a sore thumb, in their Hippie crowd though, because of what he was wearing and his age. He looked a lot older than Olivia and her friends, but while he was buying them all drinks, most of them seemed to be accepting him.

Olivia took her drink off the bar and went to join Angela, Sandra, Brenda, Cheryl and Jill, who were sitting at a small table.

"Can I sit with you girls please?"

"Yes of course you can," Angela replied. "And we've all been wanting to ask you Olivia. Who's that old man, that's stood at the bar with Kenny and the others?"

"He's someone called Clive, and he goes to my Parents pub, with his friends on a Friday night, to play dominoes there," Olivia told the girls, with a shrug of dismissal of him, with her shoulders.

"Well what's he doing here tonight?" Sandra asked.

"I don't know, I've never seen him here before," Olivia replied.

"How old is he? 'Cause he looks a lot older than us," asked Jill.

"I don't know his age, so why don't you ask him? But ye, he is older than us, and doesn't he just look it?" Olivia replied, looking across the room at him.

***

Clive left the group of Hippies at the bar, with their drinks, and walked over to Olivia, and the other girls, sitting down at the table with them.

"Clive, how old are you?" Jill asked him.

"Twenty-eight, Why?" Replied Clive.

"We don't usually see you in here, and don't you feel a bit old for our scene? Why did you come down here tonight?" Angela asked.

"Well this isn't the first time I've been here, to this Disco, and no I don't feel to old for this scene, as you call it. 'Cause I've just told you I'm only twenty-eight, I'm not that old you know? My Niece wanted me to bring her here with me tonight, but I said no way, when you go there you can go by yourself. I'm not having my sixteen year-old Niece, hanging around with me, when she's only a kid," Clive said.

"Well I think you must be in the wrong company here tonight then. 'Cause most of us are only sixteen or seventeen, sat around this table, and we don't like to be put down for it," Olivia replied, as she stood up to leave them all.

"What, you're only sixteen Olivia?" Clive asked her, in a surprised voice.

"Yes, I've just told you that. Anyway how old did you think I was?"

"I thought you were about twenty, I really did think you were twenty, because you seem a lot older than sixteen."

"Yes well, I think I was just born old."

"How old is your baby?"

"One year old, why?"

"Well where's his Father?"

"What's that got to do with you?"

"Well I'm just interested that's all, I don't mean to be prying into your life."

"Well if you aren't prying, why are you asking me this stuff? Anyway just for your nosy information, Antony's Father got the chance of a good job in Australia, and I didn't want to go and live there, so I told him to go without us."

"Oh I see, so that's why you didn't marry him then?"

"Who said that I didn't marry him? Before he left? That's one for you to try and work out eh?"

"Well do you like my shirt?" Clive said, eager not to offend Olivia, and to try and get her attention back on to him.

"No not really, what's so special about it?"

"My Uncle sent it to me from America, and I thought it looked good."

"Well why ask me then?" Olivia replied, walking away from him to find her other friends, who were dancing in the discotheque.

***

"Have you managed to lose him, yet then?" Kenny asked her, as she began to dance with them to 'I was made to love her'.

"I've left him sat in the bar talking to the other girls, who are all giving him the third degree. I still don't know yet, what he's doing down here."

"Olivia luv, come and dance with me, it's *A Whiter Shade of Pale*." Bozo said, wrapping his arms around her.

"I wonder what that Clive wants with us then?" Skippy asked.

"Or who he wants?" Snifter replied, looking directly at Olivia.

"Hey, leave me out of this, I never bloody asked him down here tonight," Olivia shouted at everyone.

"Well I think he fancies you Olivia. But don't forget, you're Bozo's girl," Willie said.

"Yes she's mine, all mine, and I luv her so," Bozo said, wrapping his arms tighter around Olivia.

"No I'm not yours, I'm nobody's," Olivia said angrily, trying to push Bozo away from her.

"But I thought we were going to get married soon luv?" Bozo said, in a hurt voice.

"Well, I never said we were, you just thought that," Olivia shouted to him, above the music. "I'm not going to bloody, marry anyone, and I don't belong to anyone either."

"Yes I thought you two would be getting married soon," Kenny said. "That's what Bozo told us any way."

***

At the end of the evening, when the discotheque was closing, the Hippies saw their 'Flower Power' car, parked in front of the entrance doorways to the discotheque.

"What the hell is that doing parked here?" Kenny asked.

All the Hippies circled the car looking in through the windows, seeing Lassie and Pim, both naked and in the throws of passion, making love on the back-seat of the car. Everyone began to bang on the windows and the top of the car, laughing and shouting at them, to let them in, but nothing as loud as it was, could interrupt them in their lovemaking; they just didn't seem to care.

"When you two have finished," Kenny shouted with a laugh, through the partially, open window to them, banging on the roof of the car. "Would you be good enough to unlock the car doors, so we can get in, 'cause it's time to go."

"Fucking hell, I know it's the summer of love," Bucket said, looking in through the car window. "But I thought Pim was my girl?"

"Well, she doesn't seem to be anymore, does she Bucket?" Olivia said laughing, as she put her arms around him.

"So, this is what you Hippies get up to is it? Is this what you call a happening?" Clive said, in a patronising tone of voice, looking very amused, with a big grin on his face.

"Just fuck off you," Willie replied, in an angry tone of voice.

Lassie and Pim, in their own time, did eventually finish their lovemaking, slowly putting their clothes back on, while still kissing each other, before unlocking the car doors.

"Did you two enjoy each other? 'Cause it looked as if you did. Poor Bucket, he'll have to find himself another girl now, won't he? Well, who's going where, then?" Egg said, getting behind the wheel of the car.

"I can give Olivia, her Sister and friends, a lift back to Bradwell if you like," Clive offered.

"Thanks that's a help, and we'll take the other girls back to Eyam," Kenny replied, before he gave Suzanne a goodnight kiss, telling her that he'd see her the following evening.

***

"Wow! Look at this car, what sort of car is it?" Angela asked, sitting in the front seat, next to Olivia.

"It's a Mark Ten Jaguar," Clive replied proudly.

"But how can you afford a car like this? How can anyone?" Jill asked him.

"Because I own my own company," Clive replied.

"Oh really," Cheryl said.

Pulling up outside of the 'White Hart' pub, the girls started to get out of the car, shouting, "Thanks for the lift home, and goodnight Clive."

Clive got hold of Olivia's hand, before she could get out of the car, asking her, if he could see her the next evening.

"No," Olivia replied, pulling her hand away from him. "I'm meeting my friends at the 'Rock Canyon' tomorrow night."

"Well, can I see you sometime next week then?" Clive asked eagerly.

"No you can't, and goodnight," Olivia replied, slamming the car door shut behind her.

******

Chapter 16

A week later some of the Hippies were lying on the ground, or sat with their backs and heads, resting against the rocks, in the 'Rock Canyon'. There was a bright fire burning in the middle of a circle, that they had made around it. They were passing a marijuana joint to each other, and listening to the songs, that were playing on the car radio. 'Lucy in the Sky with Diamonds', started to play, and they all began to sing along with it, when they saw car headlights coming up the dirt road, that led in to their 'Canyon', approaching them.

"Who the fuck's this?" Kenny asked. "I didn't think other people ever came up here?"

A big Mark 10 Jaguar pulled up next to their 'Flower Power' car and stopped.

"It's that old, bugger Clive, that's his bloody car," Willie said angrily. "How the fuck did he know about this place? And what the hell does he want with us?"

"Hello, what are you all doing?" Clive confidently asked, while walking over to them, dressed in an expensive, looking pair of blue, trousers and a red sweater.

"Looking for tangerine trees and marmalade skies. Here have a smoke of this Clive, and see if you can find them for us," Egg said laughing, holding out the joint and offering it to Clive.

"No thanks, I'll abstain if you don't mind," Clive replied, smiling smugly, while sitting down on a rock next to them.

"No he won't have a joint with us," Willie stated. "It'll spoil his fucking rich, mans image."

"What do you do Clive?" Egg asked. "Who do you work for? To be able to afford a bloody car, like that?"

"I have my own company, and we make twist tools and taps and dies for car companies."

"What's your company called?" Asked Lassie, who had his arm around Pim.

"Clive Lemons and Sons," Clive replied.

"I've never heard of them," Kenny said.

"Why do you want anything to do with us?" Snifter asked. "We're all much younger than you, and we don't have any companies, or money. We're just a group of poor Hippies."

"He's after Olivia," Willie said. "And he knows she's always with us."

"Well Olivia's going with Bozo, and she's one of us, so he's shit out of luck there," a fact Kenny stated. "Anyway how did you find us up here?"

"Oh Olivia's Father, Eric, mentioned that you all hang out in a 'Rock Canyon', and that it was up the Dale, going out of the village, somewhere on the way to Tideswell. I saw this dirt road and looked up, and saw all these rocks and a bright fire burning, so I thought I'd take a drive up and see if you were here."

Bozo and Olivia were kissing deeply, especially when the Beatles record 'All You Need is Love' began to play on the radio. She could feel Clive's eyes watching her, and deep down she knew he fancied her, and that he had purposely, found the 'Rock Canyon', knowing that she would be there.

Bozo also knew Clive was after Olivia, and he didn't want to lose her. Not after he had fallen in love with her, and now wanted to be a Father, to her lovely, baby son Antony.

"Well we won't be coming up here at night for much longer," Kenny said. "Once the summer is over it'll get too bloody cold and wet, so we're making the most of it while we can. But we've certainly had lots of fun and happy times together, in our Canyon this summer, times most of us will never forget."

"Well, Bucket painted a flower on the rocks, in memory of us all. Did we tell you about that Clive?" Suzanne asked.

"Look, there's our flower up there," Kenny said, picking up a torch that he had at the side of him, and shining the bright light of it high up onto the rocks, across from where they were all laid.

"Hey, that's good," Clive said. "Who climbed up there to paint that?"

"Bucket did it," Kenny replied. "But he couldn't climb up the rocks, so we tied a rope around his waist, and dangled him down, as far as the rope would go, from that road up there, that runs along the top of the rocks."

"Yeah and if that rope had-a snapped, or if we had all dropped him, our poor Bucket, would have been splattered all over the rocks. Wouldn't yu-Bucket?" Lassie commented dryly. "Yu should have seen him dangling there, spinning around and around on that thin piece a rope. Holding about four cans of paint in one hand, and God knows how many, paint brushes in the other."

"Which would you have dropped first, to help save yourself? If weed-ave dropped yu, if yu were falling Bucket? The brushes or the cans of paint?" Skippy jokingly asked him. "Would it have been easy for you, to make that quick choice?"

"Probably everything at the same bloody time, 'cause if I'd of just let go of the brushes, I don't think that the cans of paint, would of been brave enough, to have done anything to help save me. And yeah if I had-a fallen down, from the top of those rocks, I would've expected you all, my wonderful Hippy pals, to bury me where I'd-of landed," Bucket replied.

"Yeah we would've done that for you all right. But it looked to us, who were down here watching you, that you were on a much, bigger, high, up there, spinning around on the end-a-that little bit-a-rope, than with any LSD that you could, ever have taken Bucket," said Cheryl laughingly.

"Yeah an he was even flying through the air as well," remarked Brenda, with a giggle.

"Well I hope you girls all got a fucking, good laugh at me, while you were watching me swinging around, and thinking that I was flying, through the fucking air, in memory of us all," Bucket replied, with a laugh, at the memory of it all, painting the flower.

"You must have been feeling very brave Bucket, because it's a long drop down, from the top of those rocks, it must be about a couple of hundred feet or more," Clive said, complementing him.

"I-an the rest, but somebody had to be fucking brave, didn't they? And I think it must have been me, on that day, the other week," Bucket replied.

"Well we couldn't have tied, that bit a-rope around Bozo, and asked him to do it for us, could we? Just look at the bloody size of him. That rope would have snapped straight away, and we'd have probably all been pulled, over the fucking top, of the rocks wi-him," Kenny said, with everyone laughing, loudly and agreeing with him.

"Yes your right," Clive agreed seriously. "But remember, that flower will still be there, for you all in a few years to come."

"I fucking hope so," Bucket said, with a laugh. "I could have fucking, killed myself, painting that, for us all."

"Shit, it's started bloody raining," Skippy shouted, getting up quickly of the ground, as large drops of rain began to fall on them all. "Come on before we all get soaked, let's get up to the 'White Hart'."

***

Kenny and his friends had a weeks' holiday from their work, later that summer, which they spent camping out in tents at the 'Rock Canyon'.

Clive also took a weeks' holiday from his company, and spent most of his time in the 'Rock Canyon' with his new, Hippie friends, who seemed to fascinate him, as he got to know them better. Most of the Hippies didn't mind him being there with them, especially when he provided food for the them to cook on their open, camp fire, and when he'd let them siphon, petrol out of the tank of his lovely, big Jaguar, when their 'Flower Power' and 'Mini' cars were getting very, low on petrol, and they told him that they couldn't afford to buy any more, for and during their trips to the other villages to see and pick their girlfriends up, to bring to the 'canyon'.

By the end of that week Clive, had managed to talk Olivia, into having a date with him, but the others were not too pleased about this, because they had all become very fond of her, and knew that Bozo's heart, would be broken if she finished with him. Because he had recently been telling them all, that he loved her so much, and wanted to marry her, and adopt her lovely baby son, next year. He had even been talking about taking her, to look at some big, old, houses, in

Dronfield, that were now going cheap. And if she liked one of them, he would buy them one, just before their wedding. So this break up with Bozo, to now go out with Clive, made some of the other Hippies very, unhappy.

***

About a month later the Hippies were all together in the Rock Canyon, and the atmosphere was unusually tense between them.

"What the fuck is going on between you two?" Willie angrily asked Olivia.

"I don't know what you mean," Olivia answered, walking away from him.

"Yes you do and come back here, I'm talking to you," Willie shouted. "We know you've started seeing this Clive bloke, and that you've been out on dates with him. And poor Bozo's really hurt 'cause you've finished with him. We never asked this old, Clive bloke, to join our Hippy group, he just wormed his fucking way in. And he's too bloody old, to be a Hippy anyway, so I want him out. So if you're encouraging him to stick around us, Olivia, you can get out of our Hippy group too."

"No, we don't want Clive to leave our group yet," Egg said laughing. "Bucket and I are trying to talk him into, letting us paint flowers, all over his lovely Jaguar, and then we hope we can get him to sell, his car to us cheap. 'Cause let's face it, he can't drive around in a 'Flower Power' car, not a man in his position, a company owner."

"I don't fucking care about his position, his car, his money, or how many bloody Lemon companies he owns, I just want him to keep away from us. So it's your choice Olivia, it's either him or us?" Willie finally told her.

Olivia looked around her, and from one Hippy to the other, as her green, eyes began to fill with tears, she answered Willie, slowly and angrily. "It's none of your sodding business, who I date or hang around with. And who the hell do you think you are Willie, talking to me like that? Your not my bloody Father. There's something I was going to tell you all, this weekend, but I suppose I had better tell you now. And if you don't want to be my friends anymore then that's your choice. But I want you to know, that I love you all, very much and always will do, and I will never forget the good times, and all the fun that us Hippies, have shared together."

Tears were now streaming down Olivia's cheeks, as she took a deep breath, to control her voice. When she told them that Clive, had asked her to marry him, and he had also told her, that he would be happy, to adopt her son, Antony, and become a Father to him.

Everyone was silent, this came as such a shock to them all. They could not believe Clive, had asked Olivia to marry him, after only knowing her for such a sort time, like a couple of months. Especially Willie, who now felt he had backed Olivia, into a tight corner, after telling her to make a choice between Clive Lemons and them. He was now very quiet.

She sat down on a rock, and began to cry harder, feeling she was now going to lose, her very, dear friends, who meant so much to her.

After a short time had passed, while Olivia was sat on the rock crying, Kenny walked over to her, putting his arms around her shoulders, and kissing her lovingly, on the side of her cheek, saying, "Olivia this news about you marrying Clive, has come as a shock to all of us. But you don't have to make any choice, you can marry Clive, and still have us as your friends. We don't want to lose you, you are special to us and we all luv you. And if Willie doesn't want anything to do with you, then that's his choice, but it's not ours, and you know I'm the leader, of our Hippy crowd, not him."

"Oh, thanks Kenny," Olivia said, wrapping her arms around him, and laying her head on his chest. "And I also luv you, I luv you all, so very much."

The other Hippies walked over to Olivia, each one of them giving her a flower, as they all said, "*'Peace', we love you Olivia, we won't leave you.*"

Willie, still feeling very angry, just stood by himself, staring at her and feeling very foolish. Knowing that he had, now been overruled by all the rest of the Hippies, who would always listen to Kenny Dee, and go along with his decision making for them all, before his.

******

Chapter 17

Eric and Margaret were more than overjoyed, when Clive Lemons, asked them one night, after closing time at their pub, if he could marry their Daughter Olivia, and adopt her Son, Antony. They were very pleased and enjoyed telling everyone, about their daughter's forthcoming marriage, to Clive Lemons.

Eric continually told Olivia, how lucky he thought she was, and how by a stroke of good luck, she had now landed on her feet. And did she realize how wealthy, Clive was, and that she'd never again find anyone, like him, or as wealthy as him, who would want to marry her, due to her circumstances of having a baby. He also thought it would be better for her now, to start wearing smarter, better, clothes. Especially since Clive, had told them, that he had told his Parents, he was going to get married, and he wanted to take Olivia, to meet them.

So instead of wearing her usual everyday Hippy gear, of jeans, or a cheesecloth skirt, love beads or her 'Jesus Boots', for the visit to meet Clive's, Parents. She decided to wear a pretty, yellow and white, chequered mini-dress, with puffed, out, short, sleeves and small, yellow bows, down the front of the dress, to the waist. On her wrist she wore a ladies, pretty, gold, dress watch, which her Grandfather Oliver, had bought her for her sixteenth birthday.

***

After Clive and her Parents gave their approval, of what she was wearing, she got into his car for the journey over to Sheffield, to meet his Parents.

Clive seemed to be very nervous during the drive, and he constantly talked about his Family. Informing her that his Mother, was almost blind, and that the old girl, had a few operations on her eyes, over the years. And please, not to stand, or sit, too close to his Mother, because if she got the slightest, nudge or knock, she would just lose her sight completely.

He also told her that he had a Sister, named Jane, who had married Howard Perkington, the owner of a big company called 'Perkington Gold and Silversmiths Company Limited'. They lived on the Derbyshire Moors, in a very big house, which used to be an old farmhouse, that they rebuilt themselves, and turned into a beautiful house, with horse stables next to it. They had a young, son named John, and two Daughters, named Janet and Jill, who were a similar age to Olivia.

"Where are we now?" Olivia asked, when Clive turned on to a quiet, tree-lined street, off Ecclesall Road South, a very wealthy area in Sheffield.

"We're nearly there," he replied, driving down a road that had big, Victorian-style, houses on each side of it.

***

He stopped the car outside one of the houses, and nervously took hold of Olivia's hand, and kissed it, saying, "I haven't told my Parents about Antony yet, I want them to get to know and approve of you first. My Parents are from the old school, they are very old people, like from the Victorian generation. They are not very modern thinking people, and I don't want to shock them too much just yet, so please Olivia, don't tell them about your baby, or that you're a Hippy. Now are you ready to go in and meet them dear?"

"What!! And no! I'm not ready to meet your sodding parents after what you've just told me! You bloody hypocrite," Olivia shouted, in an angry, surprised tone of voice. "And why didn't you tell me, all this about them, before you brought me here to meet them? You just kept on telling me, that your Parents were happy that you were finally getting married, and were really looking forward to meeting me. And you led me to believe, that you had told them about my Baby. And you know what Clive? I really don't need your sodding, judgmental, Parents in my life right now, and I certainly don't need their bloody approval. Christ! I've been through enough of that, with my own Parents, and other people."

"Now, now Olivia dear, please don't cause a scene, because I want them to like you. This meeting is very important for me, so do try and be a sweet girl, please dear," Clive replied, looking at her and hoping to calm her down.

"Don't you, bloody 'dear' me. I'm not, your fucking, 'old dear'. And have you got any more bloody stupid, surprises in store for me, that you'd like to now tell me about before we go into their house?" She asked angrily, taking a very deep breath, to try and calm herself, before opening the car door to get out.

Clive opened a big, heavy, dark-stained wooden door to enter the house, and she followed him into a big, hallway with a very, high, ceiling. A large Grandfather clock, stood against the wall, ticking away, slowly and loudly. To one side of the hallway was a large, wide, staircase, with a thick, shiny, banister rail, winding down from it. Clive opened a thickly-carved mahogany door, saying, "I think my Parents will be in the drawing room."

They went into a large, room, with a high, ceiling, and Olivia, saw a bright, coal, fire, burning in a big Victorian style, fireplace. The room was full of highly polished antique furniture, and had an expensive looking wooden clock ticking away on the wide mantelpiece, over the large fireplace.

An old man, with white, hair and blue, eyes, wearing glasses, and a pair of brown, slippers on his feet, was sitting in an armed, chair by the fireplace, smoking a pipe.

"Come in, come in," he said to them, getting up out of his chair. "I've been expecting you, for some time now."

"Father, I'd like you to meet Olivia," Clive said.

"I'm pleased to meet you Olivia," Clive's Father said, shaking her hand. "Come and sit by the fire, is it cold outside?"

"It's starting to get a little chilly Sir. Where's Mother?" Clive asked.

"She's just having a lie down, she's not feeling too well this afternoon," Clive's, Father replied. "She'll be down shortly, she knows your coming to see her."

Yeah not feeling well, because she doesn't want to really meet me. And God, he's bloody ancient, even my Grandparents aren't as old as him, Olivia thought, looking at the old man.

"What do you do Olivia? Where do you work?" Clive's, Father asked.

"I help my Parents in their pub."

"How old are you?"

"Seventeen."

"Yes you are so very young. What do your Parents think, about you getting married so young?"

Before Olivia could answer, the door opened slowly, and a white, haired old woman, with thick, tinted, glasses that had leather, blinkers, on the side of them, walked into the room.

"Hello Mother dear, how are you feeling?" Clive asked, going over to help his, Mother, across the room, and sitting her down in a comfortable, armed, chair. "I'd like you to meet Olivia, Mother dear, the girl I'm going to marry."

"Hello Olivia," the old woman said, turning to face her, as she began to pull her long, skirt, firmly, down well over her knees, to just above her ankles, while noticing the very, short dress, that Olivia was wearing.

God, another bloody antique, Olivia thought, smiling at the old woman, and saying, "Hello."

"I'm not feeling very well this afternoon Clive," his Mother said. "My eyes are hurting me, and I have got a touch of colic."

Horses get bloody colic, not people, Olivia thought, feeling that she would be out of place, in correcting Mrs. Lemons.

"Clive dear, will you and your Father go and see Mary, in the kitchen, and tell her we would like some tea and scones, now please."

The two men left the room, while Mrs. Lemons looked at Olivia, and began to ask her questions. "How old are you dear?"

"Seventeen."

"Don't you think, you're a little, too young, to be marrying my son?"

"No."

"Do you love him? Or are you marrying him for his money?"

"I've never even thought about his money," Olivia replied, in a very, honest, tone of voice.

"Clive once had a very, nice, girlfriend, you know? But that was many years ago, she was a school teacher, and I thought he would have married her. She would have been more suitable for my Son, I think."

"More suitable than me you mean? Well, what happened to her?"

But before Mrs. Lemons could answer, Olivia's question, Clive and his Father came back into the room, each carrying a silver, tray with a silver, teapot, cream jug, sugar basin on one tray and bone-china, cups, saucers and plates on the other. They were followed into the room by a middle aged looking lady, who was carrying a plate, filled with hot buttered scones.

"This is our maid, Mary," Clive's, Father, said to Olivia.

"Hello," said Olivia, smiling at the lady, who was taking the things off the trays, and putting them onto a small table, that was covered with a white, lace tablecloth.

I've got to get out of this place, before I bloody suffocate. I'll drink my tea nice and politely, then suggest we go, Olivia thought, remembering her manners.

"Where are you two going tonight?" Mrs. Lemons asked.

"To a Discotheque' to meet my friends," Olivia replied.

"Are you a Hippy?" Mrs. Lemons went on to ask, with a frown on her face.

"Mother dear, please," replied Clive. Quickly finishing off drinking his tea, and eating the last of his scone, because he could see that Olivia was now beginning to feel uncomfortable. "We must be going now, because Olivia's Parents will be expecting her home soon."

"Yes, and we'd like to meet Olivia's Parents, soon also," said Mrs. Lemons, when Olivia stood up, putting her cup and saucer down, on the laced, table clothed table, hoping Clive, realized that she was now wanting to leave.

"Oh I'm sure you will, meet them at our wedding. And thank you very much for the tea, it's been very nice meeting you both," Olivia replied, with a smile, before she said goodbye to them both.

***

"Don't you ever bring me here, to meet your bloody, Parents again," Olivia said angrily, when she left their house, and was getting back into Clive's car, for the return drive home. "It was so bloody, obvious to everyone, that your sweet, dear, darling, Mother doesn't like me, at all, and she certainly doesn't want you to marry me. God knows what she's going to say when she finds out I've got a baby. But with any luck she'll probably, drop dead before that."

"I'm sorry Olivia, I'll make it up to you tonight, I promise, and I want you to know, I love you very much. You didn't let me down at all, on your first meeting with my parents, and your manners were perfect. I think it went very well, don't you darling?" Clive replied smugly, ignoring Olivia's remark, about hoping his Mother would soon be dead.

"No I don't. And yes of course I will always have the most perfect manners, that was the way that I was brought up. But I think I was only brought here to meet them, for their disapproval. And I can't see how your dear Mother, will allow you to marry me, not if she has anything to do with it, especially when she finds out I've got a baby. So I'm warning you Clive, just be careful what you tell your Parents about me."

"Don't worry about anything Olivia, they don't know you, the way I do. And I could always tell them, that you are a poor, young girl, who got raped by one of the horny, village lads, one night, couldn't I?"

"Don't you bloody dare go telling them, or anyone else, bare faced lies like that, about me. 'Cause if I hear that you have, I just won't marry you," Olivia replied angrily. "And I'm now beginning to wonder, if this is all worth it? Maybe I should have married Bozo, 'cause I don't think that his Parents could be as snobby as yours."

***

The following week Clive drove Olivia and Antony, over to Cleethorpes, to be introduced and visit with her, Grandparents and Uncle Brian. They were all very happy, to meet Clive and hear about her forthcoming marriage, to him, as they felt that he would look after her and Antony.

"You must come to the Flamingo Club tonight," Brian said. "And I've told all your friends at the club about Clive, and they're all looking forward to meeting him, and seeing you again Olivia."

***

Later that evening Olivia, introduced Clive to her friends at the Flamingo Club, and Tiffany, one of the dancing 'Foxy Ladies' girls, suggested that they should have a party in their flat, after the club closed, to celebrate their forthcoming marriage.

Over at the party, Olivia told her friend's, that she planned on getting married at the beginning of the next year, and that after her marriage she would come over to see them all, at the club, that night, on the day of her wedding, bringing the rest of her wedding cake, for them all to have a piece of.

"Where's Tara?" Olivia asked. "And I didn't see Roberto, working in the restaurant at the club tonight."

"No Roberto's having some time off, 'cause Tara's just come out of the hospital," Brian replied. "She was pregnant, like you thought she was, and she had the baby at eight months, It was a boy, but the poor little thing died, at birth, he was born with the inside of his stomach hanging out."

"Oh my God! Poor Tara, what a dreadful tragedy for them to go through, I must go and see her and Roberto, and tell them how very sorry I am. They must be really upset."

"Yes they'll be pleased to see you Olivia, but leave things well alone for tonight, 'cause they'll be both sleeping. They are very upset and have both done a lot of crying with each other," Brian replied.

***

The next day, taking with her a lovely bunch of red Tulips for them, Olivia went to see Tara and Roberto, to offer them her condolences on the loss of their Baby Boy. But apart from giving them both, her comforting hugs and telling them over and over again, of how sorry that she was on the loss of their Baby. She found that there was not much more, that she was able to do, or could do, in staying much longer with them, to help them with their tragic loss. As she sadly left them both, heavily, burdened in their grief, trying to comfort each other, in the loss of their Baby Son.

Olivia took Clive, to meet her Cousin Anton, at his hairdressing Salon, later that afternoon and told him, while they were having a coffee break with him, in the kitchen. That she was sorry, but she wouldn't be able to take the wonderful, hairdressing job that he had offered her, now. But Anton told her, that it was okay, and not to worry about it, because all that mattered to him now, was her happiness, and he hoped that she'd be very happy, in her marriage to Clive.

***

"Now I think that it's time for you to meet all of my friends," Clive said, on their return journey home, from their very enjoyable visit to Cleethorpes. "I'll be playing dominoes with the lads on Friday night, and while you're at the Discotheque, I'll tell them that I've asked you to marry me."

***

Olivia had fun with her friends at the Discotheque the next Friday evening, and they drove her home in the 'Flower Power' car.

Jack, Steve, Allan and Gerry, were eagerly awaiting her arrival, when she arrived back home at the 'White Hart' pub.

"Olivia, congratulations," Jack shouted to her, from the large, table underneath the window, in the Tap-room, that the lad's, were all sitting at, with their dominoes, spread out all over the top, of the table.

"Come on over and sit with us. Clive tells us you two are to be married."

"Yes, that's right we are," Olivia replied, sitting down on a stool at their domino table.

"Well we hope you know, what you'll be letting yourself in for, with him? And we all wish you much happiness Olivia," Steve said.

"Clive's a bloody, dark horse isn't he?" Gerry stated. "We thought that he was seeing a girl, but we had no idea it was you Olivia, he kept it all very quiet."

"Well, I think this calls for a celebration, don't you lads agree?" Steve asked.

"Yes, definitely," the others all agreed.

"There will be a party at my house tomorrow night Olivia, and I want you to come with Clive, and meet our wives and a few others, who I'm sure would like to meet you, and congratulate you both. Is that all right with you Eric?" Steve shouted, across the room to Eric, who was serving behind his Bar. "I've invited your Daughter, to a party at my house tomorrow night, to meet our wives and celebrate her forthcoming marriage to Clive."

"Yes, that will be all right with me," Eric agreed.

"How does Clive get on with your Hippy friends Olivia?" Jack asked.

"Okay with most of them," Olivia replied. "But he can't really become one of us, because we think that twenty-eight, is a bit too old to become a Hippy."

"Yes I suppose it is. But who's twenty-eight? Clive?" Steve asked, in a surprised tone of voice.

"Yes," Olivia replied firmly.

"Twenty-eight eh?" Jack said.

"Well he's twenty-eight is he?" Gerry asked.

They all locked eyes with each other, in surprise and shock, before they began to grin, laugh and cough. While Jack scratched his head saying, "So that's how he managed to get you, is it Olivia? Well I do hope that he knows what he's doing, because marriage is a very serious business."

"What do you mean? What's wrong? What do you men know that I don't?" Olivia asked, in a concerned tone of voice.

"Nothing Olivia, absolutely nothing. And we all sincerely hope, that you will both be very happy. Now let's get some drinks, Lemon, where's Lemon?" Gerry shouted over to the Bar, after trying to make light of the situation.

Clive came walking over to the dominoes, table, putting down on it a tray that had pints of beer on it.

"Lemon, have you brought Olivia a drink?" Steve asked, looking intensely at Clive, as if expecting an explanation from him. "'Cause I feel that this girl, is going to need one, one day you bastard."

"Why do you all call him Lemon, when his name is Lemons?" Olivia asked, ignoring Steve's cutting remark to Clive.

"Well, sometimes he can be just like a bloody big lemon," Jack replied grinning.

***

Clive took Olivia into Sheffield the next afternoon, to buy her a new dress, for the party that they would be attending, at one of his friends' homes that night. She chose a very, pretty, bright pink, sleeveless felt mini-dress, which had gold, diamond-shaped pieces, stuck, across the front of it. He also bought her a pair of pink, open-backed, shoes, and a matching shoulder bag, to go with it.

***

They drove into Sheffield later that evening, to a very, large house on Manchester road, that had a long, wide, curving driveway, lined on both sides with fir trees. The house had lots of large, brightly, lit, windows, and a very big front door, with coach-lights, on the wall, at each side of it.

"Christ, this house looks like a bloody, mansion," Olivia said. "Who lives here?"

"Steve and his wife Caroline," Clive replied.

"But how can they afford to live in a house like this? How can anyone, ever afford to live in a house, this size?"

"Well, Steve's Family own the 'Shaws and Sons' butcher's shop's, all over the north of England. And they also supply fresh meat from their abattoir, to most of the restaurants in Sheffield. That's how they can afford to live in a house like this."

"And look at all these beautiful cars here," Olivia said, looking around at the cars parked outside the house, seeing an Alfa Romeo, two Mercedes, Rovers, E type Jaguars, and a Rolls-Royce.

"Yes these people are very wealthy, they either own or run their big, Family Companies," Clive replied, with a smug, easy smile around his mouth. Feeling very comfortable, in knowing that these wealthy, people, whom he was going to take Olivia to meet, were his friends, his class of people, whom he always felt very, comfortable with, being in their company. Now getting out of his own car, and going around to open Olivia's door for her.

"God, I don't know how I'm going to manage this scene, I wish Kenny and the others were here, I wish to God, that all my Hippy, friends were with me now, they'd just love this happening, in an 'Alice In Wonderland', time that I'm about to enter. "

"Don't worry about it, just watch and listen, you'll be okay, and they are a very, friendly crowd really."

"Oh really," Olivia said, now giving a big sigh, and holding on to Clive's hand, very tightly, as he rang the doorbell on the wall, at the side of the door, before they went into the house.

Steve greeted them both in the bright, massive, hallway, that had the walls covered in oil, paintings, and a tall, beautiful, slim lady, with short, dark hair and blue eyes, came out of a room to greet them.

"Hello Clive, Darling, we have all been waiting for you to arrive," she said, giving him a kiss on the side of his cheek.

"This is my wife Caroline," Steve said, introducing them to each other. "Caroline, this is Olivia."

"I'm very pleased to meet you Olivia," Caroline said, shaking Olivia's hand warmly. "Come on through, everyone is dying to meet you."

Olivia let Caroline, take her by the hand, as they walked into a very, large room, with the walls covered in more oil, paintings, that had about fifty, very well, dressed, people in it, stood around talking, drinking and smoking, or doing the same thing, sitting down in lovely, relaxing, looking, armed, easy chairs, with coffee, tables in front of them, which they could put their drinks onto, and use the ashtrays on the tables for their cigarettes, while a 'Beach Boys' record, was playing on a stereo system, somewhere else in the room.

"You all know Clive," Caroline said to everyone. "Well this is who you've all been waiting to meet, his fiancée Olivia, and isn't she just adorable?"

Steve went over to his beautiful, large, Wicker, Bar, in a corner of the room, to make Olivia, a Bacardi and Coke, then going back across the room, to pass her drink to her. With Olivia, almost falling down, rather than sitting down, in a chair that she was stood next to, in amazement at this whole new, never before seen world, that she felt she had just entered. Nervously she took a sip of her drink, as she slowly began to look around the room at all the beautiful, expensive furniture, priceless antiques, and the large framed oil paintings, that hung from the high walls. *Oh my God* Olivia was now thinking, *I've never seen anything like this before, and this is all really to much for me to deal with right now, I wonder how I can escape from all of this. I just wish that I'd brought a joint with me to smoke, then maybe I'd be able to handle this scene.*

A lady with long, shiny red hair, walked across the room towards Olivia, introducing herself, warmly and friendly, after noticing that she seemed to look lost, sat there in a chair by herself, "Hello Olivia, I'm Susie, Jack's wife. And please, don't go getting yourself intimidated by this lot will you? I don't know why Steve's invited so many people, here tonight, because they're not all personal friends of Clive's, or ours, there's only a few of us, about twenty that are. I don't really know some of these other people either, I think most of them just want to talk business, with our men, that's why they were invited."

"And I suppose that they also help to fill the room up," Olivia replied, with a smile, now thankful for Susie's company, after Clive had wandered off somewhere, to talk with different people that he knew around the room. "Because without all these people, in this large, room, it would look pretty empty, don't you think? 'Cause it certainly is a very big room," Olivia replied.

"This is only one of them, you should see the rest of the house," Susie said. "God knows why they bought a mansion, this size, you can so easily get lost in this place. And there's only Steve, Caroline and their son Andrew, that live here. I run a Dancing School, but my Parents own it, with me running it for them. We teach ballet, tap, ballroom and Latin-American dancing, and Jack and I live in a large, flat above the studios. And Clive and you really must come over, and have dinner one night, with Jack and I. Jack tells me you have a son, I'd love to meet him. I have two daughters myself, whom I'm trying to turn into ballerinas. You see those two people, sat across the room from you, over there both dressed in pink?"

"Yes, I see them," Olivia replied, looking at the dark-haired, good-looking couple who were talking to Clive.

"Well, they're the Taylor's, Jill and Peter, his Family owns a very, big, construction company, amongst many other things. Peter's okay, but beware of his wife Jill, she's just a bloody snob, who appeared in our crowed from nowhere. She came from a council, house, and never had a thing to call her own, until she became pregnant to Peter. Now that Madame thinks she owns the bloody world, and she will be ready to put you down Olivia, as soon as she can. Did you notice that Peter is wearing a pink, shirt, to match her pink dress? Jill always likes him to wear a shirt, the same colour as her dresses. You've met Caroline haven't you? She's great, a lovely personality, and quite a character, she's a model, you know. And I must introduce you to Sheila soon, Gerry's wife, when I can find her among all this crowd, she's a great person too, and I'm sure you'll like her and get on with her. And for the rest of them Olivia, just be very wary of them all."

Susie then excused herself, saying she needed to get another drink, and would talk with her later.

"Thanks for the warning Susie, and it was good meeting you, and yes I do hope to see you later," Olivia replied. Now somehow plucking up the courage, to get out of the chair, that she had wanted to feel glued into, for the rest of the evening, if only for her security.

She walked across the room to join Clive, who was still there, absorbed in some conversation with Jill and Peter. When he noticed that she was stood by his side, he took hold of her hand, as she heard Jill saying.

"Clive Darling, have you seen the lovely, blue, Mercedes, that Peter bought me last week, for my thirtieth birthday? Isn't it just a beautiful car, and so expensive looking?"

"Yes Jill, I think that I saw your, blue Mercedes, parked in the driveway. Now if you don't mind, I'd like to introduce you to my fiancée, Olivia," replied Clive.

"I'm pleased to meet you Olivia," Peter said, with a smile and a friendly wink, shaking her hand. "And I hope that you and Clive, will be very happy together."

"Thank you very much, and I'm sure we will be Peter," Olivia replied, smiling back at him.

"Oh hello Olivia Darling," Jill said. "Aren't you sweet looking? I think that you look a lot, like that 'Cher', that lovely girl singer, her that sings with that stupid looking man, what's he called, Sonny? Don't you think so Peter? Yes, we've heard a lot about you Olivia, and I hear that you're a Hippy, and haven't you got a love child? Or something like that? I've never met a Hippy before, well not one to talk with. Anyway I think that I'd like to become a Hippy, we are always hearing about you Hippies in the news, you people seem to have all the fun, you're all so free, and have no cares or problems, just lots of love-ins and happenings, it all sounds so exciting. Do you think I could become one of your Hippies Olivia? Could you introduce me to your Hippy friends? And do you think that I could 'hang out', as you people always seem to say 'hang out with you all', and enjoy some of your wonderful happenings, with you Hippies?"

"No, I don't think so," Olivia replied, staring hard at Jill, this drunken lady, who had so much to say for herself, and who seemed to be holding on to her husband Peter's arm, for support. "And I thought that you would have already known, you're far too old to become a Hippy."

"Oh Olivia Darling, you're so horrid, isn't she Peter? And I thought that maybe I was going to like you, but no, not now. I don't want to know you anymore, even if you do look like 'Cher'," Jill said, passing her glass to her husband, Peter saying, "Get me another strong, Gin and Tonic please, Darling."

Peter just shrugged his shoulders and smiled in an apologetic way at Olivia, in response to his wife's remarks to her, before taking her glass over to the Bar, to get it refilled with another strong, Gin and Tonic.

"Yes, you just keep on drinking your Mother's ruin, Jill Darling, and you won't be much of anything anymore, will you?" Olivia replied, before walking away from Jill, and going to find Steve and Caroline.

***

"Would you like something to eat Olivia?" Steve asked, putting a friendly arm around her shoulders. "Let me take you to the dining room, before all of the food has gone. Caroline and I have just had a small buffet, laid on and most people are eating now."

She went into the hallway with Steve, leading her to another very large room. Her eyes, opened wide, in amazement, when she saw a large, very, long, highly, polished, oak, dining table, that looked as if it could seat at least fifty people. The whole table was covered with food, there was Chicken, Beef, Pork, Lamb, Ham, Tongue, Coleslaw, different kinds of Salads, Sausages, Bread-Rolls, Potatoes, Sausage-Rolls, Pork-Pies and large bowls of Fresh, Cream Trifles, for dessert, with large, bright, shining, Silver, serving spoons and forks, laid at the side of them. Also more foods Olivia, didn't even know the name of. There were two, large, Silver, Candlesticks, with their candles-lit, stood in the middle of the table. And over at one end of the table, was a large, Silver, Coffee-Pot, with a matching Cream and Sugar Basin, Bone-China Coffee-Cups, Saucers and Plates, were next to them, along with beautiful, dark, blue, Cloth-Table-Napkins, with shining, Silver Rings, around them, and large, Silver knives and forks laid next to them. Hung above the table from the high, ceiling, was a very, large, beautiful, sparkling, Cut-Glass-Chandelier.

"Christ, Steve," Olivia said, still stood in the doorway with him, looking on into the room in absolute, complete, awe, of it all, with all of that food ladened on the table. "Steve I've never before seen so much food, and silver ware, and everything, all together before in my life, this just looks like a feast for a king. And if I did try to doubt it before, I certainly do now feel just like, 'Alice In Wonderland'."

******

Chapter 18

In the month of December, a few weeks before Christmas, Clive, Olivia, and Suzanne were driving around Sheffield, looking at houses that were for sale, when they saw a large, poster advertising,

'New Houses For Sale, With Show Houses To Visit'

Clive turned his car off the main-road in this area of Sheffield 8, onto a side road, at the corner of the street where the large, high, advertising poster was standing. He then drove down a recently, newly made road, with farm, fields, running along one side of it, and newly, built houses with long, driveways going up to them, all along the left hand side of the road.

He parked his car on this road, along with a line of other cars, at the bottom of one of these long driveways, outside a new house, before they all got out of the car and began to start walking around, looking at the various show houses.

"I like the look of that one," Olivia said, pointing to a detached, house, with a large, glass windowed porch on the front of it, surrounding the front, door.

"Well let's go and have a look at it then," Clive replied.

They walked up the long, cemented, driveway and stepped in through the opened, front door, into the square, entrance porch, with the 3 large, glass, windows. Opening a patterned, thick-glass door, and going into a lovely, bright, large, open-planned lounge. With two very, large, windows, on the wall next to the glass, door that they had just come through, they were in an orange, carpeted, furnished lounge, with a fireplace mounted on the chimney breast, that had a gas, fire burning on low, on the long, wall across from them. Straight in front, facing them, opposite the glass door they had just come through, was an orange-carpeted staircase, in this large open-planned lounge.

"Wow yes I do like this, and it's so very different, a staircase to the bedrooms going up from the lounge," Olivia said.

At the other end of the lounge, was a dining room, with large, windows, with a window sill, beneath them, on the back wall, next to a back-door, with glass in the top-part of the back-door, to go outside to the back of the house. Over to one side of the dining room, was a door to a separate, kitchen, with a large, glass window, through which the kitchen could be seen. The kitchen had the large, window above the sink, which had shiny, stainless, steel taps on it, and cupboards underneath it. Across from the sink, with the window above it, that looked into the dining room, the rest of the kitchen was fitted out with counter-tops, with cupboards above them, that had sliding, doors, with a tall, deep shelved, food pantry cupboard, at the end of one set of a counter-top, next to the window, that had a nicely, tiled window-sill on it, across from the window at the other side of the kitchen, behind the door, were more counter-tops. Yes the kitchen was very well planned and equipped in it's layout, using mostly and all of the kitchen space, with just leaving enough room for a cooker, fridge and washer and dryer.

At the top of the open staircase, going up from the lounge, was a landing, with three, nice size bedrooms, going off it, and a very, well, put together fitted bathroom, with a bath, underneath a window that had a tiled window-sill, the washbasin was on the other wall, standing next to the bath, and the toilet was fitted about two-feet away from the washbasin.

"I do like the big, picture window on this front wall, in the lounge here," Olivia said, pointing at the large window, with her finger, as she was walking back down the open-planned stairs, into the lounge.

"Yes, there are some lovely, big windows in all of the rooms. Plenty to keep you busy cleaning them all," Suzanne replied, with a giggle, following her Sister down the stairs.

"I just love this house, and its new open-plan layout," Olivia said smiling, after she had been all around the house, to have a good look at it all, and everything in its layout. "It's very different to anything else, that I've ever seen before."

"Well would you like to live, in one of these houses then Olivia?" Clive asked.

"Oh yes please, I'd just love to live in one very much," Olivia replied enthusiastically.

"Well, let's go and put a deposit down on one then," Clive said confidently, taking his chequebook, out of his inside, jacket pocket.

"What you mean just like that? Because I like it so much, you will go and buy us one to live in? I can't believe it can you Suzanne?" Olivia replied, grabbing hold of her Sisters arm, in her excitement.

"Well I wouldn't mind living in one of these beautiful houses myself, so would you like to buy me one also?" Suzanne replied, feeling now just as happy as Olivia. Knowing that her and baby, Antony, would both be so happy living here, and she would be able to come and stay with them, visiting her Sister often.

***

The salesman, whom Clive handed his down-payment cheque to for one of the houses, told them that the house that they had looked at, and Clive wanted to purchase, was already sold. But one, identical to it, which was not yet built, but with the building of it to begin very soon, now that Clive had put a down- payment on it. Would be built just around the corner, across from a wood there, in what was called Hunters Lane, and would be ready for them to move into, in the middle of January.

"Great, I just can't wait to move into my new home," Olivia said, now feeling very happy and exited at the thought of a house being built for her, her son, and her future husband to live in.

"If the house is going to be ready for us in January, don't you think we had better fix a wedding date?" Clive said, when they started to drive away.

"Why don't you get married on my birthday, January the eighteenth? And I'll be your bridesmaid," Suzanne suggested.

"Yes Suzanne, that's a good idea," Olivia agreed happily. "Now let's go and tell mum and Dad, about the house, and the wedding date, 'cause I'm sure they will be very pleased for me, don't you?"

"Yes I'm sure that they will," Clive agreed enthusiastically.

***

During the next few weeks, before the wedding, Clive and Olivia, shopped around Sheffield choosing, and buying carpets, curtains, furniture, beds, bedding, pots, pans, and anything else that Olivia, liked and wanted to fill her new house with.

And after a lot of debating between the two of them, over the last few weeks, Clive got his way in the end, by getting Olivia, to agree to a church wedding. After she had tried so very, hard to stand her ground, telling him, that she would much prefer, to get married in the Registry office in Sheffield. But Clive kept pointing out to her, that he very, much wanted his parents and his Sister Jane, along with her husband Howard, to attend their wedding, and that he knew that they certainly would not attend, a wedding in a Registry office. Telling her, *'That they had never attended a wedding there, in one of those places at all before, and they would certainly never expect, any son or Brother of theirs, to get married in one of those places, it was just not the done thing to do.'*

So in the end of all their debating, with the reasons of where and why they should, or why they shouldn't. The wedding date was booked and fixed, with the vicar at the small, stone built, village church, in Bradwell, and arrangements were made for their wedding, reception, to take place at the 'Rising Sun Hotel', just outside the village of Bamford.

Olivia did manage to stand her ground, on a couple of items in all of the arrangements and planning, of her wedding, making it very clear to everyone, whether they heard or listened to her at all, that she had no intentions of wearing a white wedding dress, or any other form, shape or colour of a wedding dress at all. And she did not want to have a big show of a wedding, with hundreds of people invited, she only wanted a very small quiet wedding, with the fewer the people attending the better.

On these things that they felt, were important to their daughter, her parents did agree with her. And they took her shopping around the Boutiques in Sheffield, where she chose for herself a lovely, red and black striped, double-breasted, short-skirted-suit, with a matching hat and shoes, to wear on her wedding day. They also helped to choose a matching green and black, striped outfit, for her only bridesmaid, Suzanne.

Clive bought her a beautifully patterned, wide, twenty-four-carat gold wedding ring, that she chose to wear on her wedding finger. With the ring then passed over to Jack to look after, when he was asked by Clive, to be his best man. With Jack's wife, Susie complaining, after she was shown the wedding ring, that Olivia, had chosen, 'S*he can't make pastry wearing that, she'll have to take it off first, or she'll get all the pastry stuck in the pattern off it.*'

Wedding invitations were sent out to about thirty, very close family and friends of Olivia, and Clive's, with arrangements then made, for them to spend their honeymoon at her Grandparents home, in Cleethorpes.

***

Exactly one week before their wedding day, Clive telephoned Olivia at the 'White Hart' pub, telling her that he was coming out to Bradwell, to see her in about an hours time. Asking her to go out for a short, drive with him, because he felt that he had something important to tell her, that he thought she should know about.

Clive picked her up at about 2 o'clock that afternoon, and drove up to the 'Rock Canyon', with her. Parking the car underneath, the large, flower, that her Hippy friend, Bucket, had painted on the face of the rock wall, in memory of them all. Clive turned off the engine of his car, leaving the radio on so that it was still playing their favourite records, on Radio 1.

He turned in his seat to face her, while he talked to her. "I'm afraid I have something horrid and not very nice to tell you Olivia. My Sister Jane, her husband Howard, and their two daughters Janet and Jill, came to see me this morning. My Sister, told me that she has no intention, of coming to watch her Brother, marry some young, pot-smoking, Hippy kid, who already has some other mans love child. It seems that the woman, who goes to clean Jane's house for her, has some relatives who live in Bradwell, and they told her, that earlier this year, you had an abortion at a hospital somewhere in Manchester. Jane also told me, to tell you Olivia, that she never wants to meet you, or have anything to do with you, because she doesn't think that you would be a very good influence to have around her daughters."

"Oh! So have you brought me out on this little drive! To this private, special, sacred place of ours! That belonging to my Hippy friends and I! Our 'Rock Canyon!' And you have the nerve to dare to park your car underneath our beautiful flower! Which my wonderful Hippy friend Bucket, painted up there in memory of us all! To tell me that our wedding is now off? Just because of what your sodding sister, and the sodding women, who cleans her sodding house, had to say about me? Because obviously you're all lacking, in some part of the brain department somewhere aren't you? As my Dad would say about you all! Because don't you all know? Abortions are still illegal! So if you don't want to marry me now Clive, if you've brought me here to my sacred place, to tell me that our wedding is off! Is this your choice Clive, or is it your sodding sister's choice? But before you answer me Clive, let me make my feelings about you all very clear to you first. Fuck your Sister and her fucking daughters, fuck her cleaning lady, and fuck you Clive also, for fucking listening to her, and everyone else's fucking shit!" Shouted a very, upset, angry and frightened Olivia.

With the thoughts spinning around in her head, of the secret that she had promised her parents, that she would always keep, and never to tell, to anyone at all. But now that it had been exposed and seemingly talked about, so openly, by it seemed to her, so many other people. How could she, still keep that secret? That now seemed to be coming back so fast to haunt her? But she had to and would always keep her promise, to her parents, knowing that she always would. And even now if because of it, that never must tell to anyone promised secret. She now felt and was prepared for the fact that she was now going to have to sacrifice her marriage to Clive, for it.

"Oh no no Olivia, don't go thinking that about me? Please? I just listened to them that's all," Clive replied, trying to put his arms around her, to comfort her, now realising that he had said something, that had really upset her.

He had never seen her so angry, upset and afraid before, saying and feeling such nasty, vicious things about other people, whom she had never met or seen before in her life. This was a side to Olivia, that Clive had never seen or could imagine, as he was now getting to know that she could be strong, if she was forced to be.

But he was beginning to be afraid that she would now open his car door, jump out and run away from him forever, and he knew that he must try and stop her somehow. "No that's not my choice at all, and I love you very much Olivia, please believe me, I will always love you forever. And I've told my Sister that she can think, and believe what she wants to, that's her choice. But I also told her that, I love you very much, and I am going to marry you next week, whether she attends our wedding, or not."

"You did? But why?" Asked Olivia, in a surprised tone of voice, wondering if it was now safe to let her guard down.

"Because, as I've told you Olivia, I love you very much."

"Well, thank you for standing by me, that was good of you, wasn't it?"

As she began to let Clive get close to her, and kiss her, the record *'Third Finger Left Hand, That's Where He Placed the Wedding Band',* began to play on the car radio. Olivia was listening to the words of this song, and wondering if anything else could now possibly go wrong , before her marriage.

"I've also got something else, that I feel I ought to tell you about Olivia, something that I think you should know before we get married," Clive said, now taking a deep breath. "I'm not really twenty-eight at all, my real age is thirty-eight."

"What!!! Oh God No!! No!!! I don't believe this, I don't want to believe this, I don't want to hear this!!!! That means your telling me, that you're twenty years older than me, right?" Olivia slowly moaned out loudly. Beginning to feel that her world of happiness and dreams, had only been just some sort of make-believe, that was now starting to all come crashing down around her. "Tell me? How could you do this to me Clive? What are you and your family trying to do to me? Destroy me? Chew me up then spit me out? As if I am nothing? I'm nobody? So you can all just walk all over me? And do your best to finish me off as a person? Why didn't you tell me your real age when you first went out with me? We could have still been friends. But get married to me? No way, I just can't do it!!!"

"Because I so much wanted to marry you Olivia, and I thought that if I told you my real age, you wouldn't even have gone out with me again, never mind thinking of marrying me. But I do hope you will still want to? Go ahead with our wedding and marry me? Olivia, please?"

"Oh God help me? I just don't know anymore, and my head is now spinning, with this tangled web of lies that you've spun, before carefully guiding me into your trap. Oh where's Kenny and my other Hippy friends? I've got to see Kenny, 'cause he'll know what I should do, he'll know what's right for me, and if I should still go ahead and marry you!"

"Why do you bloody Hippies always have to talk about everything together? Discuss everything that's going on, or about to happen in your life's? Is nothing secret or private? And no I don't want you running to Kenny, asking him about if you should marry me or not. I think that Kenny, has too much control over all of you Hippies anyway."

"No you don't want me to ask Kenny, what he thinks I should do, do you? 'Cause you know that he'd tell me not to marry you, 'cause you're far to old for me. And I think you've always known that Willie fucking hates you, don't you? Or did no one ever tell you that Willie and some of the other Hippies, don't really like you at all, and never trusted you?"

"Well I thought I got on with them all very well, during the summer time, and I thought that I'd got them to like me in the end."

"Well I suppose in that case, now that you feel that you've won everyone over in the end then, Clive. This little game that you've been playing with us all along, and you've caught your little Hippy girl in the end. So I suppose it was worth all your effort, in winning my Hippy friends over, so you could get to me. And how can I not marry you now? I really have no choice now do I? We have arranged everything for our wedding, someone is now busy, making our wedding cake, and my Mother has even arranged for all of the flowers, to be delivered. And we've even had a new, house, built for us, that we've filled with brand-new, carpets, curtains and furniture, all just waiting for us to move into it. And my parents would be so hurt and upset now, if I told them that the wedding was off, after all that money that it's costing them. I just couldn't do it to them, I don't want to hurt them or let them down anymore. So okay, yes, I suppose I will still marry you Clive," Olivia replied, with a deep, soul-searching sigh. "Just don't tell my parents, any of what you have told me today, 'cause it would just finish them. And my Dad would really sort you out, believe me, 'cause he can't stand liars or cheats in life. And don't go bragging to any of my Hippy friends either, 'cause you took me away from poor Bozo, remember? And I do now really know that Bozo, luved me, just for who I really am. And there are enough of them to sort you out Clive, and they will probably all beat you up okay. 'Cause I don't know if you know this, but as far as I'm concerned this summer of love is now over?"

"Yeah I suppose your right Olivia, in what you've just said. And no I won't mention the age difference, between us, to anyone. Especially your Father, because after getting to know him better, no, I don't think your Dad, would let you marry me, if I told him about our big age difference, just before our wedding. Would he? But do you still think you can love me Olivia, and we could make a go of it? Our marriage I mean? After I have just shocked and hurt you so much?" Clive begged her hopefully, with one very false crocodile tear, beginning to slowly run down his cheek from the corner of his right eye. But fully aware now that he had cleverly, managed to back Olivia, into a very, tight corner, with the knowledge that she was not old enough, or wise enough to have realized his game.

"I suppose I could, and yeah, I'll try to luv you. 'Cause after all, you have bought me a beautiful new house, for my son and I, to live in. But I so do wish this hadn't happened to me, I wish that you had done this to someone else, and not me, if it was just some very young girl, that you needed to get to marry you," she meekly replied, with a sad deep sigh.

Not really knowing what to say anymore, about the whole situation. Even though inside of herself she was full of very disillusive thoughts, and was starting to wonder what sort of new life, was in store for her, with Clive Lemons. Beginning with the feeling once again, that she had no choice, that her life had been decided for her, by other much older people. She felt trapped now, very trapped and very confused, but could see no way out of this nightmare, situation, that she had got herself into. Without hurting and disappointing, so many other people whom she cared about so much, people that were so close to her, and had high hopes for her. With better times to come her way, in a much brighter future, after her marriage to Clive. Especially her Father, and no she could never let her Dad, down again.

With her green, eyes looking very sad, she now began to stare very, intently at Clive, trying to work out in her mind, questioning things about him. *Why? Why? Why? Why did you lie to me when you say you love me? Why do you want me so much? How long have you been planning all of this? How many other lies have you told me, that I have without question, so stupidly believed? And what else have you got in store for me down the road? With all your wealth, and business and power Clive, you have subtly managed to buy me, and in the end how much would you be willing to also sell me for?*

It was with these thoughts now firmly installed into her mind, on the 18th of January 1968, with a sad, expression, instead of a happy, bride-to-be-smile, on her face. Holding very tightly onto Eric, her Father's arm, she walked down the aisle of the small, church in the village of Bradwell, in the 'Hope-Valley-District' of Derbyshire, and said, "I DO" to Clive Lemons.

******

OLIVIA'S FULL CIRCLE.
PART TWO.
1968 - 1975.

Chapter 19

As they pulled into the driveway of their new home, a tall, good-looking man, with dark hair and blue eyes, in his early thirties, jumped over the small wall that separated their driveways. He introduced himself to them, and offered his hand to each of them to shake, when they got out of their car. "Hello my name is James. Have you people just moved into this house next to ours? 'Cause if you have I'll be your new neighbour. "

"I'm very pleased to meet you James, I'm Clive, this is my wife Olivia, and our son, Antony. And yes we've just moved into the house. We've also just arrived back from a holiday in Cleethorpes with Olivia's Grandparents."

"Cleethorpes eh! That's on the East-Coast by the sea isn't it? Do you know that's a place I've never been to. Well I do hope you people had a good time there. Would you like to come inside and meet my wife and have a coffee with us?" James asked.

"Yes, please we will, that would be very nice. I'll just put our suitcases inside our house first," Clive replied, before they followed James into his house.

"Wow the inside of this house looks the same as ours, only it's the other way around. It seems like the only difference is, the carpets, curtains and furniture," Olivia stated, looking around the room.

"Hello," said a very tall, good-looking lady, with dark brown hair and blue eyes, who came out of the kitchen, carrying a baby and a feeding bottle.

"Darling," James said, to his wife, "this is Clive and Olivia, and their son Antony. They have moved into the house next door to us. This is my wife, Cassandra, and our three month old baby, Jema."

"Hello Cassandra, you've got a pretty baby there," Olivia said, walking over to have a look at the baby.

"It's her feeding time now," Cassandra replied, going to sit down on one of the chairs, at the dining-room-table, to give Jema her bottle.

"Coffee darling?" James asked Cassandra, after he had passed Olivia and Clive their cups of coffee.

"Please darling," Cassandra replied.

"Where are you people from?" Olivia asked. "You've both got very southern accents."

"We're from London originally, but we've just moved down here from a small village in Scotland, where I was working for a couple of years," James replied.

"What do you do?" Clive asked.

"I'm an estate agent and valuer, and I've just started working for 'Reeds Rains Estate Agents,' over here in Sheffield."

"Well, I own my own company, Clive Lemons and Sons, we make tap and die tooling for cars," Clive said, very proudly.

"Do you work, Olivia?" Cassandra asked, coming into the lounge, to sit with them, and drink her coffee.

"No, I spend my time looking after Clive and Antony. I get up at seven-thirty in the mornings to cook Clive his breakfast of bacon, sausage, mushrooms and eggs, followed by toast and marmalade. Oh! And orange juice for starters. Then I clean house, do the washing, and have dinner ready for Clive, when he arrives home from work," Olivia replied.

"God! You eat all that for breakfast in the morning, Clive?" James asked, in a surprised voice.

"Well, it's what I'm used to, mother always used to cook my father and I a big breakfast when I lived at home," Clive replied.

"How old are you Clive? If you don't mind me asking," Cassandra asked.

"I am twenty-eight," Clive replied.

James and Cassandra looked at each other; they both felt that Clive had deceivingly, lied to them.

"Oh are you are really?" James said, looking intently at Clive, and wondering what his game could be.

Olivia's green eyes glared at Clive, wondering why he had lied to these people. Because he was married to her now, so she felt his games were or should now be over. "Well, I'm only seventeen," she said, trying to make light of the matter. "And I've still got a lot of growing and learning to do."

Two young children, dressed in blue school uniforms, and carrying satchels, walked in through the door, and went to give their parents a kiss. "These are our other two children, Rachel and Andrew," Cassandra said proudly.

Rachel was a tall, very pretty girl, with long black hair in plaits, and big dark blue eyes, and Andrew was a smaller, good-looking boy, with black hair and dark blue eyes.

"This is Olivia, Clive, and their son Antony, they have moved into the house next door to us." James said.

"Yes I know," Rachel replied. "I've seen them before sometime the other week, I saw them through their window, when I was stood on our small, drive-way wall outside. And now that I've met you, please can I come around to visit, and play with Antony?"

"Yes you can." Olivia replied with a laugh, and thinking, *'This gorgeous Rachel is a very friendly, forward, kid, I do hope she's not too much of a precocious brat.'* She then asked, "How about you Andrew, would you like to come over and play with Antony sometime?"

"Yes, please," Andrew replied shyly.

"I must tell you Olivia, don't go thinking that Andrew is anything like Rachel at all, he's very different to his sister," Cassandra said. "He hasn't got half the confidence that Rachel's got. And she'd speak for them both if we let her."

"Oh, how old are the children?" Olivia asked.

"Rachel's seven and Andrew's five," James replied.

"Come on children, would you like a glass of milk before you take Shep for a walk?" Cassandra asked, going into the kitchen.

"Who's Shep?" Inquired Olivia.

"Shep is our lazy, bulldog, and I think she's asleep in the kitchen," James replied, with a laugh.

"Well, we must be going, it's nearly dinner time for us. And then Olivia has the cases to unpack, before she baths Antony and puts him to bed," Clive said, picking Antony up off the floor.

"You two must come over, and have dinner with us one evening this week," James suggested, before saying good-bye to them.

"Yes we'd love to. We'll leave it to Olivia and Cassandra to arrange shall we?" Clive replied.

***

One grey, very dull, and drab afternoon, Olivia saw at the end of her driveway, a tall, attractive lady with a small, blonde haired, boy, who was trying to pick up a black cat.

Antony also saw the cat, through the window and wanted to go outside. Olivia put Antony's coat on and went outside with him.

The two little boys became instant friends, when they began to talk and play with the cat, while Olivia introduced herself to the lady.

"Hello pleased to meet you, I'm Diana," replied the lady, who had curly, light brown hair and green eyes. "I live around the corner on Cedars Lane."

"Where the show houses were?" Olivia asked.

"Yes, but we don't live as far down as that, ours is the third house just around the corner."

Diana went into Olivia's house with her son Marcus, who played with Antony and his toys, while Diana and Olivia had a cup of tea and talked. Diana said she was twenty-seven years old, and her husband's name was David and he was an architect. She told Olivia, she had been quite lonely since moving into her new house, and she was glad that at last, she'd found Marcus a friend, his own age, to play with. Olivia and Diana became good friends, and Olivia said she must introduce Diana to Cassandra, because she was sure that they would also become friends.

Olivia became very happy with her life as Clive's wife, and she loved her new home, which every day she cleaned until it shone. She had fun with her new friends, Cassandra and Diana, whom were very good to her, even though she felt she was the baby among them, being something like about ten years younger. They met at each other's homes for tea and coffee each day, and talked about their husbands and children. They took their children for walks down Hunters Lane to a farm, where they could watch the cows being milked, and to the shops to do their grocery shopping.

Her Hippy friends came over to see her often, and the neighbours came outside to have a good look at their 'Flower Power' car, which they always proudly parked in her driveway. James, Cassandra, David, and Diana made friends with Olivia's Hippy friends, and they would go to her home, and party with them, listening to the Beatles 'Sergeant Peppers' LP, which they were always playing.

Olivia's parties went on until very late, and when her floor was full of sleeping Hippies, James and Cassandra would often allow one of them to sleep at their home, on the couch next to their bulldog Shep, who made a point of snoring all night. Which James told everyone jokingly, was in protest of sharing her bed with a Hippy.

***

Rachel came running into her home one Saturday afternoon in the summer, shouting excitedly, "Mummy, Daddy, do you like my hair? Don't you think it looks fab?"

James and Cassandra looked at their daughter in amazement.

"Rachel darling, what's happened to your plaits?" James asked, when he saw that her hair was parted down the middle and hanging lose around her shoulders. "And who's put that band around your head?"

"Olivia did," Rachel replied, spinning herself around in a circle. "My long hair feels fab like this, it's so free, just like Olivia's. And look at this pretty flower she has painted on my face."

"Oh my God!" Cassandra said, in a shocked voice. "What the hell is Olivia up to now? And what is she trying to do to my daughter?"

"Don't be angry with Olivia, Mummy," pleaded Rachel. "I asked her to do my hair like this, so it would look just like hers, and to fasten one of her beaded-bands around my head. And I watched Olivia paint a flower on her face, and I asked her to paint me one, on mine too. She says I now look like a Hippy child, and that you would be angry with her when you saw me, looking like this. Anyway I told her not to worry about it, that you wouldn't be, and that's what I've come to tell you. Please, Mummy don't be angry with Olivia, she's so sweet."

"Rachel, Rachel darling, will you slow down please," James said, with a big grin on his face. "You're talking far too fast, and no, I'm not angry with Olivia, for making you look like a little Hippy."

"Well I bloody-well am," Cassandra said angrily. "And I've told Olivia many times before, that my daughter is not a Hippy child. And now I'm just going to have to tell her so again, where is she?"

"No darling, I'll go and talk to her," James replied. "I don't want you and Olivia having an argument over this."

"Well Olivia's Hippy friends are there, and they're moving in. They're all going to live in her back garden, and I promised them I'd help them get their tents put up okay. And I'm going to sleep in their tents with them, tonight," Rachel said.

"What!!!" Cassandra cried out in despair.

"Oh no you're not madam, you won't be sleeping in any bloody tent," James said. "I'd better go and see what's going on at Olivia's."

James went out of his back door into his garden, to see Olivia's Hippy friends, putting up three large tents in her back garden. "Olivia!" He shouted. "You can't set up a fucking 'Hippy-Commune' in your garden, the neighbours will just go mad."

"What the hell are you talking about?" Olivia asked, when James walked over to her.

"Rachel, who now thinks she's a Hippy child, has just told us that your Hippy friends are going to live here in these tents. And she thinks she's going to move in with them. And Cassandra isn't very pleased about all of this, especially with you for doing Rachel's hair, with the band around her head, and painting a flower on the child's face. Just what the hell is going on here Olivia? Would you please like to tell me what you're all up to, and where's Clive? Does he know about this?"

Olivia took a deep sigh and lit a cigarette, feeling that she had a lot of explaining to do. "First," she began, "Your lovely, adorable, Rachel will get me bloody shot. I wish the kid would listen to me when I talk to her. She asked me to do her hair just like mine and paint a flower on her face. I told her, her mummy wouldn't like it, so I said she could look like that for one hour, then I would put her hair back in plaits and wash the flower off her face, because James, it's only put on with make-up. Yes, she agreed to all that, but she obviously didn't tell you it was only for an hour. And no, I'm not setting up a fucking 'Hippy-Commune', as you call it. They bought these tents this morning, and they asked me if they could put them up in my big garden to try them out, and sleep in them tonight. Because tomorrow they are going to find a 'Hippy-Commune' that has started up somewhere in Wales, and stay up there for a week. So James, tell me what's wrong with me letting them stay here in their tents overnight? And yes, Rachel heard Egg jokingly say, if they liked it they might just live here in the tents. She also asked them if she could sleep in a tent with them tonight and they said no, but someone jokingly said to her, ask your mother first. Now, have I explained things clearly to you James, or have you got anymore worries?"

"No," James replied laughing, taking hold of Olivia's hand, and saying. "Come on darling, come and have a coffee with us, and talk to Cassandra, because I'm sure she still thinks your trying to turn her daughter into a Hippie."

"Okay I think I better. I'm just going next door for a coffee," Olivia shouted to her friends. "If Clive comes home from work, please tell him where I am."

"Yes, and please tell Cassandra, that we'll all be over there when the coffee's ready," Lassie shouted back.

***

Over coffee Olivia told Cassandra what she had already explained to James, and that she was honestly, not really, trying at all to turn her daughter into a Hippie child.

But Cassandra asked Olivia, to just be careful with what she says or does in front of Rachel, because the child just worshipped her and the ground she walked on, and that at her age, she was a very impressionable child.

Olivia's reply to Cassandra, was that she understood, and not to worry because she would never hurt Rachel, or try to fill her head with too much rubbish.

"Talking about Rachel," Olivia said, when Rachel came running in through the front door. "Come here kid and let's wash that flower of your face, and put your hair back into plaits."

"Oh! Olivia no, not yet," Rachel whined, beginning to cry, and stamp her foot in protest.

"But you promised me Rachel, that you would only look like that for an hour," Olivia replied.

"Oh daddy!" Rachel cried. "I'm having so much fun with my Hippie friends, and I don't want my hair put back into plaits yet."

"Okay, okay," James replied laughing. "You can stay like that until dinner time."

"Oh! Thank you daddy," Rachel said happily, giving James a hug and a big kiss on his cheek. "By the way, my Hippy friends have sent me to see if you've got the coffee ready yet."

"Yes, let's fill the house once again with bloody Hippies, and do tell them that I really don't mind," Cassandra replied jokingly. "Shep will love that, won't you Shep darling?" The bulldog just grunted a reply. "So tell them all yes, to come on over the coffee's now ready."

They were all sat around drinking coffee and talking, when Clive knocked on the door and walked in, "Hello Clive how was work? Come and have a coffee with us," James said.

"What the hell is going on Olivia? And what are those tents doing in our back-garden?"

"Oh, you tell him Kenny, I'm sick of bloody explaining," Olivia replied.

"I'll tell him, I know what's happening," offered Rachel.

"Rachel, keep out of it, we've all heard your side of the story once," James said.

"Okay daddy," Rachel replied. "But I've not told everyone, all of my Hippy friends, everything yet."

"Rachel darling, please enough?" James told her sternly, this time.

After Kenny had explained to Clive what the tents were doing in his back-garden, and that no, they were not all going to live there in them. That they had set them up in his large, back-garden and were going to sleep there in them only for tonight, 'cause it was suppose to rain heavy later that night, and they would then be able to see if the tents were really water-proofed and would keep the rain out and off them okay. Before they took them to use at the 'Hippy-Commune' with them, where they were going to stay for about a week over in Wales.

"Oh I see, that's alright then. But on first seeing them, my worst fear was that all of you Hippies had decided to move into my bloody-back-garden for the summer-time," Clive replied, with a relieved laugh.

"Oh please don't go thinking stupid things like that Clive," said Olivia. "And if my darling Hippy friends wanted to move in with us, they wouldn't be living in the bloody-back-garden, they'd be living in the house with us."

"Yeah." All of the Hippies agreed.

"Well don't they anyway?" Cassandra asked.

"No we do go home sometimes," Kenny replied.

"Occasionally," stated Egg.

"When we have to, when Olivia kicks us out," added Willie.

Olivia had to protest about not ever wanting her Hippy friends around her, and insisted that they would all be having a party at her house that evening. With James, Cassandra, Diana and David also invited. She also added that Kenny had brought a fab new record by 'Canned Heat', that she thought they would all like to hear.

"Yes that sounds like fun, we'll be there," Cassandra replied. "But I must phone Diana now and ask her to send Andrew home for lunch."

"Ask her to send Antony home for his lunch also," Olivia added. "The boys have been playing with Marcus this morning in his new paddling pool. I bet Diana's ready to have a break from our kids. Oh, and please ask her and Dave to come to our party tonight, around nine-O'clock."

"So you lads will be sleeping in your tents tonight? Instead of on Olivia's floor?" James asked.

"Yes, we'll give her floor a rest tonight," Skippy replied.

"And our couch," Cassandra added laughing. "Shep will be pleased, she won't have to snore so loud tonight in protest."

"Well I've got something that I can arrange even better, for all of my new darling Hippy friends," announced Rachel to everyone. "I suppose you've all seen the lovely Buttercup-field across from Cedars lane? Well the farmer told me, when I asked him, if I could use it to play in and take my friends to play in there with me, that yes, it was okay for me to use it and take my friends in there. And that he doesn't really use my Buttercup-field for anything really at all. Anyway I told the farmer that I would look after it, and make sure no-one left any trash in there at all. And if you Hippies wanted to, you can use my Buttercup-field to put your tents in and camp in there, instead of Olivia's garden and going all the way to Wales, for a camping holiday. And that's what I wanted to tell them all daddy, that it's okay for them to use my Buttercup-field, if they'd like to?"

"Well thank-you very much Rachel darling, and I'm sure all of your new Hippy friends, are so pleased to hear that you will allow them to use your lovely Buttercup-field sometime. Aren't you all?" Cassandra replied, smiling kindly at her daughter, for so much wanting to help and organize her new friends.

"Yeah well thanks Rachel," all the Hippies said to her, with a gentle laugh and a shake of their heads, at this adorable, helpful child.

***

Every six weeks Olivia went with Clive, on his weeklong business trips to London, where they stayed in lovely motels or hotels. During the day Clive visited car company buyers to get orders for his company, while Olivia would stay by herself, and keep busy by shopping and sightseeing around London, or the other towns that they stayed in, close by. One of her favourite places near London was Chelmsford in Essex, and she loved the hotel that they always stayed at there.

In the evenings Clive and Olivia, would drive the buyers, and their wives into London, to have dinner at beautiful top class restaurants. Clive told her that by doing this, and buying them gifts for Christmas, it was one way of ensuring that the buyers would keep giving him orders for his company.

Olivia's son, Antony, would stay with her Parents, or Grandparents, when she went on these trips to London, so she always knew he would be safe and well looked after.

***

On returning from one of their London trips later that summer, they arrived back in time for lunch at her parent's pub, the 'White

Hart', while Olivia's Hippy friends were there having their lunch and a drink.

"This is Vicky, my new girlfriend," Kenny said introducing Vicky to Clive and Olivia, when they went into the Disco-room.

"Yeah I know Vicky, we used to go to school together. But I haven't seen you for ages, what have you been doing with yourself?" Olivia asked her. "And how come you're going with Kenny? What's happened to my Sister Suzanne?"

"Suzanne's going out with Egg now, and Kenny was free, and I've always fancied him, so I grabbed him while I had the chance, before someone else got him," Vicky replied with a laugh. "And I'm working in Sheffield as a Nurse, at the children's hospital, that's why you've not seen me around for a while now."

"Oh yeah, well that explains why I've not seen yu then, I did wonder where you'd got to, and what you were doin," said Olivia.

"Nice choice for a new girlfriend Kenny," Clive said, looking Vicky up and down, and seeing a slim, good looking girl, with long, dark brown hair, and brown eyes.

"Yes I thought so to," Kenny replied putting his arm around Vicky's shoulder.

"Well Nurse Vicky welcome to the crowd then," Olivia said with a smile. "And I'm sure you'll have fun with us crazy lot."

"Are we all meeting down at the 'Marquis of Granby' tonight?" Kenny asked.

"Well we hadn't planned to, we've just got back from a long and tiring, London business trip. Antony's been staying with Olivia's parents and we've just come to pick him up," Clive replied.

"Well I'd like to go to the 'Marquis of Granby' tonight," Olivia said. "Hey Dad," she shouted to her Father, who was serving in the bar, "is it okay if we stay here tonight? So we can go out later, 'cause I don't think I'll be able to arrange a baby sitter at home, at such short notice."

"Yes, I don't see why not, it should be okay with your Mum. And you know I luv to have that little lad staying here with me," Eric replied.

"Okay then we'll stay," Clive said, yawning very loudly. "So if you'll get me some lunch now Olivia dear please, then let me have a few hours sleep, we'll go down to the 'Marquis of Granby' disco tonight."

***

They all had a very good time together that evening, and later when the discotheque closed, Olivia and Clive gave her friends a lift back to Bradwell, and Egg went with them so that he could spend some more time with Suzanne. Kenny and the others promised to come and pick him up later, after they had taken their girlfriends back to the other villages. They told him to wait for them on the bridge.

***

"Olivia, Suzanne, get yourselves up and come down here now!" Eric shouted up the stairs, in a very loud, angry tone of voice, the next morning. "Olivia, Suzanne, get down these bloody stairs right now!" He shouted again.

"What the hell's wrong with him this morning?" Olivia asked, putting her dressing gown on as she came out of her bedroom, at the same time as a sleepy, bleary-eyed Suzanne came from hers.

"God knows," Suzanne replied, in a sleepy voice, before yawning. "He's probably in one of his best Sunday morning moods again."

"Get down here fast you two!" Eric ordered, seeing the girls at the top of the stairs.

"What's wrong Dad? Why are you in such a bad mood so early on a Sunday morning?" Olivia asked.

"I've just had old Mister Bennet up here, and he's told me that the bloody 'Flower Power' car is parked by the entrance to his garden, near the bridge and playing field. And someone has picked all of his prize winning chrysanthemum flowers, and covered the bloody car with them."

"What!" Olivia replied, opening her eyes wide in disbelief.

"Mister Bennet's prize winning chrysanthemums, that he was going to enter into the flower show next week, are all over that bloody-Hippy car down there, and he wants compensating for them."

"Well, why tell us?" Suzanne asked. "We didn't do it."

"That's your bloody-Hippy friends' car, so they must have done it," Eric shouted.

"I don't think so, our friends wouldn't do anything like that," Suzanne replied defensively. "And I don't know what the car is doing here in the village, at this time in the morning."

"Well you'd better contact your bloody-Hippie friends, 'cause they're in a lot of trouble," Eric said. "And Mister Bennet said he's going to get the police."

"Come on Suzanne, we'd better get dressed and go and see the car," Olivia said.

***

Clive went with them, and as they were walking down the hill from the pub, towards the bridge that went over the brook, next to the village playing field. They saw a large, crowd of people gathered there, and a police car arriving.

"Where's the car then?" Olivia asked, pushing her way through the crowd.

"Through there," replied an eight year old, dark-haired child, pointing with his finger in front of him.

They saw the shape of a car at the side of the playing field, in front of Mr. Bennet's garden gate. It was covered all over with brightly coloured chrysanthemums, and children were putting daisies and dandelions on top of them.

"Hey!" Suzanne shouted. "What are you bloody kids doing to the car?"

"It's a flower car," replied a six year old, blonde-haired child. "So we thought we'd give it some real flowers."

"Oh my God, I just don't bloody believe this is happening," Olivia said, in disbelief. "And you can't see the car for the flowers."

"Who does this car belong to then?" Asked the police officer, who had pushed his way through the crowd to have a look.

"It belongs to some friends of ours who live in Dronfield," Olivia replied. "But I don't know what it's doing here, or who covered it in all of these flowers."

"Well, I've just been having a talk to a Mister Bennet, who's very upset about all of this. And he's seriously thinking about pressing charges, against whoever picked his prize chrysanthemums from his garden. He says they've cost him a lot of money and time, planting them, growing them and taking care of them. And he probably would have won a flower show with them next week, as it seems he does with his flowers every year," the police officer said.

"Well I don't suppose he will be winning any flower show, with his chrysanthes this year eh," stated Suzanne.

Kenny, Egg, Bozo and Willie arrived next, pushing their way through the crowd to the car. "What the fuck is going on here?" Kenny asked. "And who's put all these bloody flowers on our car?"

"Let me ask you that?" Said the police officer. "Is this your car?"

"Yes, it's ours," Willie replied.

"Well, what's it doing here? A friend of yours has just told me, that you lads live over in Dronfield," the officer said.

"Yeah we do. And we ran out of petrol last night, so we just pushed our car off the road, thinking it would be safe here in this little village until morning," Kenny replied. "And we've just arrived now with a can of petrol to put in it, and drive it home. But we certainly didn't put any flowers on it, or expect to see anything like this."

"Well we did expect to see some flowers on it," Egg said laughing. "But only the ones that we painted on it last year."

"Who's put all these bloody flowers on it then?" Bozo asked.

"I think these kids will know something about that," Olivia said, pointing at the kids. "And just look at them, they're still putting flowers on the car."

After talking to the children, they admitted that while they were taking their dogs for a walk earlier that morning, they saw the 'Flower Power' car parked there. So they got all of their friends together, to help put flowers on the car. Because they thought the Hippies would be pleased if their car had some real flowers on it.

"You little buggers, come here all of you, I'm guna-smack your backsides!" Kenny said, reaching out to grab hold of one of the children.

"The main thing is Mr. Bennet, are any of you willing to compensate him for the loss of his flowers?" Asked the police officer. Ignoring the slap across the side of the boy's head that an angry, pissed off Kenny inflicted on the child.

"Well I'm sorry, but I can't give the poor bloke anything today," Bozo replied. "Not until I get paid next week."

"Nor me either," added Willie.

"And I'm broke until pay day," Egg said.

"Well don't all look at me!!" Said Kenny. "'Cause even though I'd like to buy the poor bloke a bunch of flowers, to help cheer him up and feel better. I've just paid out for a can of petrol, to get this sodding car of ours back home to Dronfield, and I've just driven everyone over here to pick the thing up."

"I'll see the old man right, for you all, if you like?" Clive said, taking a twenty-pound note from his wallet. "I'll give Mr. Bennet this, and you lads get him a few bottles of beer when the 'White Hart' opens, okay?"

"Thanks a lot Clive," the Hippies each said, not really knowing how to thank Clive, for being there once again to help them out of a mess.

'Yeah I may still not like this bloke that Olivia's married to, but I suppose he can be useful for us sometimes', thought Willie, with a grin on his face.

******

Chapter 20

Olivia was celebrating the end of a wonderful 1968 on 'New-Years-Eve', with her husband, friends and neighbours who had come over to her house to party. David and Diana arrived at their front, door to let the New-Year in for them, after the clocks all over England had struck the hour of midnight, and everyone toasted in 1969, wishing each other 'A-very-Happy-New-Year', before joining hands together and singing 'Auld-Lang-Syne'.

Olivia had spent a very happy year in her new home with her husband and Son, and now felt that her life had at last, finally done a big turn around for her, into happiness. She told everyone how happy she'd been, and was really very, much hoping, that she had many, more years, as happy as 1968 in store to come her way.

She was also looking forward to celebrating her first wedding anniversary, with Clive in a few days time, when he would be taking her out to dinner to a lovely, restaurant somewhere in Sheffield. And a few weeks after that, she was going with her husband on one of his business trips down to London. Clive had told her they would be staying at her favourite, hotel 'The Royal Gardens', in Chelmsford, Essex, and her Grandparents told her they would love to have Antony stay with them for the week that she would be away.

***

Olivia and Clive drove over to Cleethorpes, a couple of weekends later, after their wedding anniversary, to leave Antony there with his Great-Grandparents before their visit to London.

They went to the 'Flamingo Club' on Saturday night to see her friends, then spent a quiet, relaxing day on Sunday, with her Son, Grandparents, and Uncle Brian.

All over England, from the North to the South, the weather had been very bad that weekend, there had been heavy snow storms for two days, and Clive had to dig his car out of a large snowdrift on Monday morning, before they could set off on their long, drive down to Essex.

Olivia's Grandparents, Uncle Brian, and Antony kissed and hugged her good-bye, before she got into the car, to set off on her long, journey.

Her Gran told her to have a good time down there and enjoy herself, and not to worry about Antony, promising her that he would be okay with them.

Her Grandfather asked Clive to drive very carefully, because he had heard on the radio that the roads were very bad, all over England.

"We'll be okay sir," Clive reassured him. "And don't worry, this car that I've got, can go through anything."

They drove along the next street, and Olivia waved good-bye and blew kisses with her hand, to her Cousin Anton, who was just opening the door to his hairdressing salon, for business that morning.

Anton waved back, and shouted, "Bye Olivia and do take care, Please do drive very carefully Clive."

***

After a very long and tiring drive down to the South of England, Clive drove his Jaguar into the car- park of the 'Royal Gardens Hotel', in Chelmsford, Essex.

"Thank-God we're here at last," Olivia said wearily, getting out of the car. "And I didn't enjoy the drive down here at all this time, 'cause I do think you drove too bloody fast in this kind of weather. And Christ, look it's snowing again, they've got as much snow down here as we have up north. Look at it all, it seems like England is buried in the stuff. And I need a good soak in a hot bath and something to eat."

Now laying relaxed and comfortable in a large, warm, bed in their hotel suite, Clive said, "I'll take you over to Karen's in the morning if you like?"

"She's just had a baby recently, hasn't she?"

"Yes a boy, he's about a month old."

"Yeah, I'd like to spend some time with Karen and the baby tomorrow. And then we'll be taking her and Steve out for a meal tomorrow night, right?"

"Yeah, that's what I've arranged."

"Well, now that I'm nice and warm, how about a bit of warm loving from you?" Olivia suggested, snuggling up to Clive, and putting one of her long legs across his body.

"Not tonight Olivia, if you don't mind," Clive replied, before turning over onto his side away from her. "I'm very tired, and we have to be up early in the morning, if I'm going to drive you over to Karen's before I go to work. Goodnight dear."

"Goodnight, you bloody bore," Olivia replied, in a hurtful voice. "And I wish you'd tell me why you seem to have lost interest in me, and why you don't seem to want me anymore."

While she waited for a reply, Clive began to snore softly.

***

Karen, a pretty girl in her early twenties, with shoulder length curly, blonde hair and blue eyes, opened her front, door at eight-thirty the next morning. She was smiling happily and holding her baby in one of her arms. "Come in, it's so good to see you people. I've really been looking forward to you coming over for the day Olivia."

"Hello Karen, me too," Olivia replied, going into the house.

"I won't come in if you don't mind," Clive said, looking at his watch. "I have a meeting with your husband, Steve, at nine o'clock, and I don't want to be late. But I'll see you later tonight Karen."

"Okay Clive, see you later, bye for now," Karen replied, before closing her front door. "Olivia, do you want to hang your coat in the hallway here, and put your boots on the mat over there. I've just bathed the baby and got his bottle ready, and we can have a coffee when I've fed him."

"Okay," Olivia replied, taking her coat off. "Then can I hold the baby, and feed him for you? I just love babies. What's his name and how old is he?"

"Spencer, he's a very good baby, and he's one month old now. Yes you can feed him if you like, while I'll make us some coffee," Karen replied, passing Spencer's feeding bottle to Olivia.

Olivia went into a large, bright lounge, and sat down on a big, comfortable, orange couch to feed Spencer. "He does take his bottle well, and he's a lovely baby. And I love this big new house of yours Karen, when did you move in?"

"About three months ago. We were worried it wouldn't be ready for us by the time the baby was born, but at last it was. We just seemed to get all the curtains up, carpets laid in the rooms, furniture chosen, prepared a nursery, and then I went into labour. It all seemed to be rush, rush, rush, to get everything ready, and the house looking good before Spencer was born. I try to take it easy now, and rest whenever I can. In between feeds Spencer sleeps a lot, and apart from his washing I don't have much cleaning, or tidying to do around the house, because Steve's very tidy, and he will wash dishes for me, if he sees there are any in the sink. And he does what he can to help me."

"That's good of him, and I sometimes wish that Clive would do that for me, but he doesn't. Anyway where would you like for us all, to go and eat tonight Karen?"

"Well, I was thinking about us going to the boat restaurant on the River Thames, do you remember it Olivia? We've been there once before."

"Yeah, we went there in the summertime, and I love to go into London at night. But before we go to eat, let's take a walk down Soho, I haven't been down there since the summer. And after we've eaten I'd like us to drive past Buckingham-Palace, I love to see the Palace lit up at night."

"Yes I don't see why not, it should be a fun evening for us all. And I'm really looking forward to it, because this will be the first time, that I've been into London since Spencer was born."

"Oh is it? Well it'll be good for you to have a fun social evening out then. And Clive's asked me to tell you, that we'd pick you and Steve up at about eight-thirty, is that okay?"

"Yes that's fine, Spencer will be fast-asleep for the night by then, and I have a baby-sitter coming over for eight o'clock. I'll change Spencer's nappy now, and put him in his cot to sleep. I've just got a few of his clothes and nappies to wash, then I'll get us some lunch. Would you like to have a look around the house Olivia? Come on, let me show you, and you tell me what you think of it."

"Well, from what I've seen up to now, I think it's great," Olivia replied, following Karen up the modern, open, wooden staircase to the landing. She saw the baby's bedroom, which was decorated in various shades of blue, and Steve and Karen's bedroom, which was a pretty peach colour, with a lovely brass headboard at the top of the bed. The bathroom was a sunny, lemon colour, the same as the bathroom-suite, with a fluffy, lemon carpet on the floor.

***

Clive later picked Olivia up from Karen's that afternoon, and when they arrived back at the hotel, she lay down on the bed, after taking a couple of tablets for a headache that she felt coming on.

After sleeping for about an hour, she took a hot bath and put her make-up on.

She was getting dressed, in a new, very, short, red skirt and a white, silk blouse, with a page-boy frill, on the front of it and long, frilly, cuffs around the end of the selves, and a red, waistcoat that matched her skirt. When Clive said, "Hurry up will you Olivia, or we're going to be late."

"I'm nearly ready," she replied, whilst standing in front of a large mirror in the bedroom, and brushing her long, dark hair. "Do you like this outfit I bought last week Clive? Don't you think that I really look good in it?"

"Yes Olivia, you look very nice dear, but will you please hurry up," Clive replied, hardly giving her a glancing look, as he walked restlessly up and down the bedroom, smoking a cigarette and looking at his watch.

She pulled on her long white go-go-boots that came up over her knees, before putting on her warm, thick, blue, nylon fun-fur coat, and picking up her pretty silver, open-toed-and-sling-backed-shoes, and her small matching silver handbag.

"Are you ready now at last Olivia? Because if we don't hurry up were going to be bloody-late, and I hate being late for appointments with customers," Clive said impatiently, walking out of their hotel room and waiting for her to follow, before he could lock the door, to the room.

"Yes I am now," Olivia replied with a smile, and mentally checking that she'd got everything with her, including her lipstick in her silver-purse, for this very, enjoyable night out that she was looking forward to, with her lovely, friend Karen and her husband Steve. "But this is not a business meeting that your going to, we're going out for a nice relaxing fun dinner, and I'm sure Steve and Karen won't be annoyed if we're a few minutes late. So stop getting your knickers in a twist Clive."

When they were outside in the Hotel car-park, getting into Clive's Jaguar, it had begun to snow heavily again that evening, it was also very cold with a nasty, bitter, wind blowing, making the roads very icy, slick and slippery.

***

"I wish you would slow down a bit, please Clive," Olivia said, in a pleading tone of voice, feeling that Clive was now driving far too fast, for the dreadful road conditions, and that he should not be overtaking the other cars so impatiently. "And I've told you before, that you've been driving to fast in this kind of weather."

"It's already eight-fifteen now and we said we'd be there at eight-thirty," Clive replied angrily, while overtaking another car, and pointing to the clock, underneath his speedometer.

He put his car into a higher gear and sped down a long, open, two-laned-road, coming up close behind a line of European style eighteen-wheeler trucks that blocked his way and made him slow down.

Clive was becoming very agitated now because he felt his car had come to a very slow crawl behind all of these trucks, that were happily following one-another at a safe reasonable speed and distance.

"Oh fuck this," said Clive, gritting his teeth, and pulling out from behind the trucks, onto the opposite side of the road, pressing his foot down harder on the accelerator.

He began to drive very fast past the trucks, as he was overtaking them, and the men driving the trucks began to slow down and make wide spaces between their convoy, so that this big car that was passing them, had room to pull in between them.

The second truck from the front, of the ones that he was overtaking, began to flash its headlights at Clive, when he saw the big, bright, headlights of another truck coming in the opposite direction, towards the car. *'Fucking pull in you stupid bastard, you'll never make it.'* The driver shouted, when he saw the oncoming headlights getting closer to the car.

"For God's sake Clive, will you please pull in?" Olivia shouted at him, in a frightened voice. "There's another big truck coming towards us, can't you bloody see it."

"Don't worry, I'll pull over in time before we hit it," Clive replied, in a smug tone of voice, before pressing his foot down harder on the accelerator pedal, to overtake the last truck in the lane of traffic, that he now should be driving in.

"No you fucking won't! It's to fucking close to us now! Can't you fucking see it????" Olivia screamed out, in a terrified tone of voice, now beginning to feel the glaring heat from the big truck's headlights, that were nearly on top of her. "NO! PLEASE! NO! NO! NO!!!!" She screamed out even louder, while digging her long nails of all of the fingers on one hand, into her small silver handbag, and pushing her feet down very, hard on the floor of the car, willing it to stop, as she turned her lovely, face to one side, trying to save it by covering it with her other hand, as the very large, very heavy, eighteen-wheeled truck, hit their car head on, and seemed to swallow it up wholly, before it came to a stop.

When she felt all of these tons of steel and metal crashing down on her, and all around her, just enveloping the whole of her body. Olivia's fight to save herself was now over, and completely gone, as she passed out, into a dark, spinning, quiet world, with a bright light shining and guiding her along, to the end of a tunnel, where she could easily reach it.

***

All the truck drivers that Clive had passed, saw the bad accident happen when the car and the oncoming truck collided head on, with nearly all of the car disappearing underneath it. Most of them took a big sigh, or sucked in their breath, while making the sign of a cross in the air in front of them, as they passed the car all smash up, and crumbled underneath the front, of the large truck. Believing the occupants of the car must be dead, they continued driving on into the night, feeling there was nothing that they could now do to help, or save, the dead people.

Ted, a trucker in his late thirties, the driver of the truck who had been flashing his headlights and shouting for the driver of the car to pull over, did stop. He pulled his truck over onto the hard shoulder at the side of the road, hoping one of the other truckers had called for the police and an ambulance. Ted really didn't know what he would be able to do for the people in the car, or how he could help them, because he felt that they must surely be dead by now, if not from the direct impact. But he felt the driver of the other truck, with the car underneath it, was probably in a state of shock and could use some other trucker's support. Ted stopped his truck and turned the engine off before climbing down from the drivers-cab.

Ron, the driver of the smashed truck turned his engine off and jumped down from his cab shaking with shock and fear, as he walked over to Ted. "I daren't look, 'cause I know they must be dead," he said to Ted.

Ted lit two cigarettes giving one to Ron, who gladly took it, inhaling the smoke from the cigarette deeply.

"Why did he do it? I can't believe it, he just drove straight into me," Ron said, shaking his head and looking at the crushed car underneath his truck, when Ted shone a flashlight on the wreckage.

"I could see two people, but they both must be dead, no one could live through this. Oh-God! Please help them?" Ron cried out, running to the side of the road and vomiting, due to the shock of seeing the mangled car entangled and crushed underneath his truck, knowing there were still people in there that he couldn't get out or help to save.

"I can hear the police sirens now," Ted said, thankful that someone had called them. "They're going to have to get some sort of tow-truck to lift the truck off the car, so they can get those people out of the car."

Two police cars came screeching to a halt with their sirens blaring and lights on the top of their cars flashing.

"I'll radio for a special tow truck," said one police officer, after looking at the crushed car underneath the truck.

"And ask for three ambulances to come as well," said Ted.

"I think there's only two people in the car, not three," Ron replied.

"Yes, but you're very shook up," Ted said. "I think you should see a doctor."

It wasn't to long before the tow-truck arrived at the accident scene, and its crane was soon hitched up to lift the front of the truck off the car.

***

Steve and Karen could see all the flashing lights and hear the noise of the sirens, coming from the police cars and ambulances, when they approached the scene of the accident in their own car. They had come to look for Clive and Olivia because they were well over an hour late in picking them up to go out for dinner. And after repeatedly calling the Hotel to be put through to their room, with no reply, they had a bad feeling that something must have happened to them.

When the police officer, who was stopping all the traffic on both sides of the road, flagged them down, Steve wound down his car window to ask the officer what had happened.

"There's been a very bad accident, between a truck and a car Sir. So I'm afraid we can't let you through until we've got the people out of the car," the officer told him.

"What make off car is it officer?" Steve asked.

"I don't know for sure sir, but I think it's a Jaguar, why?"

"Oh no," moaned Steve. "I bet it's our friends that we've been waiting for, to go out for dinner with."

"Well if you think you would know who these people are in the car, sir, would you be good enough to pull your car off to the side of the road please. And tell us if you can identify them when we get them out of their car. And it looks as if they're bringing someone out of the car now sir."

Clive, with his chest covered in blood, was being laid on a stretcher by the ambulance men. When he saw Karen and Steve walking towards him, he raised his hand giving the thumbs up sign to them, to let them know he was okay, saying with a slight, laugh in his voice, "Well I've really done it this time, haven't I?"

"Thank God you're still alive," Steve said very concerned, and wondering if Clive was being so joyful, about this serious, car smash, due to the shock he must be in.

"Oh don't worry about me Steve, I'll be okay once they've patched me up at the hospital. But it looks like I'll have to get myself a new car though."

"Where's Olivia? Is she badly hurt? Is she still in the car?" Karen asked anxiously, with fear in her voice.

"I don't really know about her, and yes I think she might still be in the car. But don't worry about her she'll be okay once they get her out," Clive replied, seeming totally unconcerned, about whether his wife was dead or alive.

"You've got to get Olivia out of the car, someone please help her," Karen shouted out in desperation, to anyone who would listen to her.

"We've just called in for the fire-brigade to come and help us," Replied Shawn, one of the police officers who was stood at the side of the wrecked, vehicle. "We can't get the door open on her side of the car to get into her yet. And look there's her foot stuck up in front off the truck window. It looks as if she may have lost her leg in there."

"Do you know if she's still alive, at all?" Asked Steve, with a lump in his throat and tears stinging the back of his eyes. As he could see the foot of Olivia's white-go-go-boot, shoved out from the bottom of the car somewhere, and reaching straight up, pointing to the front of the truck window. Wondering if her leg was still attached to the foot that he was looking at.

"We don't know yet, or if she's lost her leg. And I'm surprised he was still alive and talking, after a bad smash like this. But I'm going to try and find out if she is still alive," Shawn replied, looking into the car and seeing a girl laying there, covered in small fragments of glass, and blood all over her face, body and hands.

Shawn took a small hand mirror out of his police uniform, jacket pocket, and using his fingers he gently removed some of the glass from around Olivia's nose and mouth. He placed the small mirror underneath her nose, to see if she was still breathing. After what seemed like an eternity to Shawn, a faint mark appeared on the mirror, as Olivia slightly breathed on it. "She's alive, yes everyone it's a bloody-miracle this, but she's still alive, but only just," he shouted happily. "Quickly bring me the oxygen mask, and let me put it on her, lets help her to keep her breathing."

Shawn was holding the oxygen mask over Olivia's face, when the firemen arrived and began to cut off the mangled, crushed car door at the side of her.

"Let me see if she's lost her leg," Shawn said, to the firemen when they had cut the door off the car. He looked into the car and saw the dashboard lying on her legs, pelvis and lower body up to her stomach. He put his hand onto the top of her leg and began to feel down and around it to see if it was still attached to her, or severed somewhere. "I don't believe it," he shouted to everyone in a happier voice, "she's still got her leg, it's still there attached to her. Here someone hold the oxygen mask on her, while I try and unwind her foot and leg back. Her foots gone through the floor of the car and is wrapped around the engine and ended up in front of the truck window. It's a bloody-miracle that her leg's still on, don't let's lose it for her now."

After another hour Olivia, was at last freed from the mangled wreck of the car.

"Oh my God, look at her," Karen shouted out crying, when she saw Olivia being lifted out of the car, and carefully laid on a stretcher by the ambulance men, before being put inside of the ambulance. "What a hell of a mess she's in, and I couldn't see any of her face for all of the blood and glass. Will the doctors be able to save her life Steve?"

"I don't know Karen, but I bloody hope so. Or it will be Clive that's killed her at such a very young age, 'cause she's not very old is she? Still a teenager I think. Yes we'll always have him to thank for all of this, if she doesn't make it, the bastard. 'Cause it's obvious to me what's happened, he was overtaking and didn't pull in, in time, that's why she's just about dead. Come on Karen we'll follow her to the hospital," Steve replied with a deep sigh, putting a comforting arm around a crying, Karen's shoulder.

The police cars roared off into the night with their lights flashing and sirens blaring, in front of the seriously, noisy, red-light flashing, speeding ambulance, that was taking Olivia to the hospital.

******

Chapter 21

"What's wrong Oliver?" Marjorie asked her husband, when she brought him a mug of hot Ovaltine from the kitchen. "You seem to be very restless tonight, and so is our Antony, he's woken up crying a couple of times but he doesn't seem to have a fever."

"I know it's very strange that our little lad is so restless tonight, I thought he'd settled here with us while his Mummy's away. But something seems to be bothering him, is he warm enough? 'Cause it's a cold wintry night outside, and I think it's started to snow again. I thought it was to cold for more snow tonight," an uneasy Oliver replied.

"Yes our Antony's warm enough, 'cause I put him a hot water bottle in his bed, and yes I thought it was going to be a very cold night. You still haven't told me why you seem so restless Oliver, is something bothering you?"

"I don't know what's wrong with me Marjorie, and yes I do feel restless, I'm feeling uneasy about something, but I don't know what it is that's bothering me. I just can't seem to stop thinking about our Olivia, and I don't know why, but I just keep seeing her lovely face in front of me all the time, and I'm wondering if she's trying to tell me something," Oliver replied, before picking the local evening newspaper up, off his knee and trying to concentrate on reading it once again.

The telephone began to ring loudly, in the hallway.

"That was our Brian," Marjorie said, when she came back from answering the telephone. "He phoned to ask me if I'd heard from our Olivia, because he can't stop thinking about her either. I told him I hadn't heard from her yet, and she said she would phone me in the middle of the week."

After watching the late evening news on TV, Oliver went upstairs to bed at eleven o'clock.

***

After a lot of tossing and turning because he was still unable to fall asleep in the early hours of the morning. Oliver decided to get up and make himself a cup of tea, with a drop of Scotch whisky in it, to help him to relax. He could not stop thinking about his Granddaughter, Olivia, and now he was beginning to wonder if something bad could have happened to her, and that she was in danger, but he dreaded to think what could have happened to her. He said a silent, quiet prayer, for her, asking God to be with her, to guide and watch over her.

***

"Hello 'White Hart' Pub," Margaret said, in a sleepy voice, answering the ringing telephone at the side of her bed.

"Hello is this Mrs. Howard?" Asked a voice on the other end of the line.

"Yes it is, why?"

"This is Sister Jarvis speaking, of the Chelmsford General Hospital in Essex. I'm afraid I have some very disturbing news for you and your husband, Mrs. Howard. We have your daughter Olivia here, she has been in a very bad car accident with her husband, and she is in a very critical condition in our intensive care unit."

"Oh No! Oh My God, No!" Margaret screamed, dropping the phone in her shock and panic, while looking at her husband Eric who was awake at the side of her.

"Hello, this is Mister Howard," said a confused Eric, when he picked up the phone that was laying on their bed.

"Mister Howard, this is Sister Jarvis at the Chelmsford General Hospital in Essex. I'm afraid I've just had to tell your wife, that your daughter Olivia, is here in our intensive care unit. She has been in a very bad car accident, and she's in a critical condition."

"Oh! Is she?" Eric replied, in a totally shocked voice. "And what are her injuries Sister?"

"Well I'm sorry to have to tell you, that she arrived at the hospital unconscious, a couple of hours ago. She has a broken foot, a double broken femur, a crushed pelvis, internal bleeding, possible brain damage, and the right side of her face is torn open from the top of her head to under her chin."

"Is she still unconscious?"

"Yes, and we are still trying to stabilize her. Could you and your wife get down here as soon as possible? Because frankly Mister Howard, we don't expect Olivia to live for much longer. I'm afraid it's just a matter of time now."

"We'll be down there as soon as we can. Please try and keep Olivia alive until we get there, Sister Jarvis, please?"

Margaret and Eric had very little sleep for the rest of the night; they kept breaking down in tears and wishing they weren't so far away from their injured daughter. They decided to let their other daughter, Suzanne, continue to sleep, and they would tell her what had happened to her Sister in the morning. Whilst making arrangements between themselves, about who could look after the pub for them while they were away, they began to pack some clothes into a suitcase. Not really knowing what to take or how long they would be in Chelmsford with their daughter, or even if she would be alive when they got there.

***

Their telephone rang early again that morning, and Margaret was afraid to answer it in case it was the hospital with more bad news about Olivia.

"I'll get it," Eric said, lifting up the phone with a shaking hand, and sighed with relief when he heard James' voice on the other end of the line.

"We've just heard about Olivia and Clive," James said. "The police have just been here to check their address. How are you and Margaret getting down to Chelmsford?"

"We're going to drive down."

"Well, I can't let you drive down there by yourself. Christ! I can just imagine the state you two are in, because Cassandra and I are still in shock, after the news the police have just given us. If you could drive yourselves into Sheffield Eric, to my house, then I'll drive you both to Chelmsford myself."

"Well, thank you very much James, that's very good of you, it certainly would be a help."

"I feel it's the least I can do. When will you be setting off?"

"In about an hour, we've just got to arrange for someone to come in, to run the pub for us."

"Okay, I'll see you and Margaret soon."

***

Oliver's doorbell rang at six o'clock that morning, and he opened his door to find a police officer stood there.

"Oh!" Oliver said. "You'd better come in, I've been expecting you for some time now. You've come to tell me about my Granddaughter Olivia, haven't you?"

"Yes," replied the policeman in a surprised tone of voice. "But how did you know?"

"Well I've been thinking about our Olivia all night long, and I've had a bad feeling that something has happened to her."

"Yes, and I'm very sorry to have to inform you, but your Granddaughter Olivia, was in a very bad car accident, with her husband last night. She's in the Chelmsford General Hospital, in critical condition in intensive care. A teddy bear was found in the car, and I've been sent to check that her son, Antony is safely here with you."

"Yes," Oliver replied, sitting down on a chair in the hallway, feeling shaken by what he had just been told. "Her son Antony is safe here with my wife, and I. He's still upstairs asleep at the moment, and he had a very restless night also."

"Oh dear, but it's good to hear that he's safely here with you and your wife, and he wasn't in that car with his mother. And that I can put a report in, that the child is safe with his Great Grandparents. Here is the address and phone number of the hospital, where Olivia is," said the officer, passing Oliver a piece of paper. "And I'm truly very sorry about your Granddaughter being in a car accident, Mr. Howard."

"Thank-you very much," Oliver said, taking the piece of paper from the officer, with a shaking hand. "At least I can now phone the hospital, to find out if she's going to be okay."

"Well if there is anything that we can do, to help you and your wife, with any inquiries at the hospital down there. Please don't hesitate to contact us, down at the station at Clee Road, Mister Howard."

"Okay we will, and thank-you."

******

Chapter 22

Margaret, Eric and James, arrived at the hospital in Chelmsford, Essex, about lunchtime, after a long drive down the M-1-Motorway, from the north of England to the south. They found their way to the intensive-care-unit at the hospital, where they were greeted by Sister Jarvis, who then took them into a room to see Olivia.

Margaret began to cry when she saw her daughter, laying so very still and quiet on a bed there in a coma, with a blood drip attached to one wrist, and a saline drip on the other. Wires from a big machine were attached to her body, and an oxygen mask was over her nose and mouth. A large bandage was wrapped around her head, and her face was cut open all down the right side, and it was still slightly bleeding.

"Oh my God! What a hell of a mess she's in!" James said, gently taking hold of one of Olivia's limp, hands. "And it looks to me, as if she turned her head to the left, before her face hit the windshield."

"Is she still unconscious? And is she in any pain?" Asked Eric. While he was sadly, seriously thinking to himself, *'This is my daughter Olivia, and she is soon going to die. And I don't know what I can do to help or save her. And she left me and is leaving me, her father far to soon.'*

"Yes she is, and we don't know yet if she will ever regain consciousness, because she's had a very severe bang on her head," Sister Jarvis replied. "The doctor's won't even put her broken leg up in a traction yet, because they feel any movement, or adjustment to her body, at this stage, will definitely kill her. We are still trying to stabilize her, and yes we've given her something for any pain that she may be feeling, but we don't think that she will be feeling much, if anything, with her being unconscious. Would you like to see the doctor now? And maybe he can give you more information, about Olivia's chances of living."

"Yes please I do want to see the doctor," Eric replied. "And then I want to go and see the police, and get a report off them, about how this happened."

"Well, knowing Clive, the way I do, I bet he was driving far to bloody fast and overtaking," James stated, as they all walked out of the room, leaving a broken Olivia, alone with the Nurses who were looking after her.

"Do you think so?" Margaret asked.

"Oh yes I'm more than sure of it," James replied. "I've thought for a long time now, that Clive drives far too fast in that bloody big Jaguar of his. And he always seems to think that he owns the bloody road, and that other cars should get out of his way, and let him through."

"Yes, I've always thought that about him, with his driving as well," Eric agreed. "And I remember asking him questions one night, about his age. And what he'd done when he was a younger bloke? And did he ever have any girlfriends, before he met and wanted to marry our Olivia? Well the silly bugger tried to tell me, and get me to believe, that when he was a younger bloke, he used to be a 'Grand-Prix' Racing Driver, so he didn't have time for any girlfriends. As if he thought he could get me to believe that load of bloody rubbish."

"A 'Grand-Prix' racing driver eh! Only in his bloody dreams," James replied, with a sniggering laugh.

"Yeah well it bothers me, that he might have been thinking that he was driving on that bloody 'Brands-Hatch' racing track, that we have here," Eric said, in a concerned tone of voice.

The Doctor on duty at the hospital, who was attending to Olivia, told them that at the moment nothing had really changed yet in Olivia's condition, for them to be able to treat her, with the help that they knew she needed, to help her broken bones repair. But as soon as there was any change in her condition, they would be happy to let them know

***

The Sergeant at the Police station in Chelmsford, whom they next went to visit, was able to tell them in full detail, from a police report that the truck-driver Ted had given to them, of how the accident had happened, and on seeing it happen before his own eyes. And that Clive Lemons, was going to be charged with careless, reckless, dangerous, driving and speeding, due to him trying to overtake too many vehicles at the same time, and if his wife Olivia does die, he will also be charged with manslaughter. The Sergeant also told them that Shawn, the officer who got Olivia out of the car, would be visiting her in hospital, because firstly, Shawn hopes the girl lives, and secondly, when she does regain consciousness, to ask her if she can remember anything at all about the accident, just before it happened.

After Ted's police report was read to them, followed by a lot of talking and agreement about Clive's dangerous driving, and the very serious, accident that he himself had caused, and just about taking his daughters life. Eric was beginning to feel better in himself, after talking with the Police-Sergeant, someone whom he felt could understand his pain. And agreed fully that by law, yes there had to be some kind of justifiable reckoning coming from somewhere, some kind of rightful revenge, soon to be coming Clive's way, after what he had done to his Daughter. Yes some kind of very good, law abiding, rightful revenge, that was well on it's way to Clive, with absolutely no doubt about it.

The Police-Sergeant took them into a big car-park that was behind the police station, for them to see for themselves the remains of Clive's car, which was now impounded there by the Police. And when all three of them walked up, to have a closer look and inspection at the squashed, mangled, metal wreck. Eric, with tears in his eyes now, that were beginning to roll down on to his checks, stated, "How could anyone have come out of that alive?"

Margaret now sobbing as her tears were also running down her checks, looked at and into the car in absolute disbelief, seeing blood and more blood everywhere, as she silently picked up Olivia's silver, shoes, and the silver, handbag that she had been holding onto very, tightly the night before, holding this bag and pair of shoes very close to her. Now thinking that these few things, along with the memories, may now be all that she could have left of her dying daughter, speculating what her thoughts and feelings could have been, before all of this terrifying impact came crashing down around.

"Look at this? Look at these holes in this handbag of hers," said James, with a shudder, taking the small hand-crushed, silver handbag from Margaret. "You can see where Olivia has stuck her nails all the way through this, in absolute fright of what she saw happening right in front of her, before the truck hit their car."

"Oh my God!!! Do you think she'll remember any of this, if she lives?" Eric asked, looking at the hand-bag and shoes, and the heap of twisted metal, with all of the inside of it covered in freshly, dried blood, which was mostly from his Daughter.

"God, I hope not, I really hope that she can't. Because who wants to live through a nightmare episode in life like this, and remember any of it?" James replied, pointing at the smashed up car. " And look at the front of the car, I notice that probably just before he hit the truck, on trying to save himself, Clive must have turned the wheel, so that his passenger sat next to him, took most if not all of the brunt force of the impact. His passenger being Olivia!!! And I'll be very surprised, if hopefully she does live, that her marriage to Clive will last for very long after all of this."

"Oh! And why do you say that?" Margaret asked.

"Because Olivia is somewhere, at this time, that none of us knows about, she is at this moment on the brink of the edge of death, and in between two worlds. And if she is lucky enough and does come back to us, how will she ever be able to forgive, or ever trust again, the man that she loved and married, who's just about taken her life? Yes, the man who's putting her through all that she's going through right now. Yes, I do just have a strong feeling their marriage will be in very serious jeopardy."

"Well I'm not at all bothered about that, she can come home to me and her Mom, if she feels that she can't live with that rotten bastard any more," replied Eric.

"Well let's go back to the hospital to see her again, and here's hoping that there's been some kind of improvement in her condition, since we left her. 'Cause I can't take much more of looking at this wreck of a car, that my Daughter was cut out off last night," Margaret strongly suggested.

***

They had spent another three hours at Olivia's bedside, holding and squeezing her very limp hand, hoping that it would be some kind of sign to her, of letting her know that they were there with her, while they talked to her, trying to will the life back into her, especially when Eric and Margaret kept reassuring her how much they loved and needed her, their Daughter Olivia, in their life's. They were hoping that there would be some kind of response from her. But after trying for hours with no response at all from Olivia, and the Doctors telling them that she was still in a very deep-coma, Eric finally decided that it was time for them all, to get something to eat, and find a hotel to stay in for the night.

"I'm just going to see Clive first before we go. I wonder what his injuries are?" Margaret said. "Are you coming with me Eric?"

"No!" Replied Eric, in a firm resolute angry voice. "Not after what he's done to my daughter, and us still not knowing if she is going to live."

"Are you going to come with me, to see him, James?" Margaret asked, now looking at James.

"No, no, I don't want to see him either," James replied, with a deep sigh. "And I agree with Eric, not after seeing the state Olivia's in. I wonder if he knows, cares or has asked about her?"

Margaret was shown into another room by the Sister, and was told that Clive had lost his spleen, but seemed to be doing alright, much better than his wife was doing. She found him laid in a bed with a heart monitor attached to him.

When Clive saw Margaret come through the door into his room, he acknowledged her, by putting his thumb up to her.

"How are you feeling?" She asked.

"I'm pretty banged up," Clive replied, in a whispered, weak voice. "But I'm sure I'll soon be okay."

"Olivia's very ill, she's very poorly and she's still unconscious."

"Oh, don't worry about Olivia, I'm sure she'll be okay in a few days time."

Margaret just seemed to freeze on the spot, after hearing Clive's, unfeeling, spoken words, wondering how he could be so callous and uncaring towards his wife, as she lay dying?

Had he even asked anyone about Olivia? And how she was? Because she wouldn't be at all surprised if he hadn't.

***

A few weeks later when to everyone's relief, Olivia did at last come out of the coma, which she had been suspended in for some time now. But she had somehow managed to revert herself back into a very, childlike condition. Could this be her inner-self now somehow trying so hard to protect herself? Everyone was wondering. And when life fully did came back into her again, and she began talking, not knowing anything about what she was saying, or where she was at all, she never questioned what she was doing there, or even asking what could have happened to her, to be laid in a Hospital bed, with Nurses and Doctors attending to her. No she really didn't have any idea or any way of knowing who she really was at all, this lovely, long, dark haired, green eyed girl, who was laid there in a hospital bed, with her leg fastened high up, at an angle in a traction. With most of the days feeling that it was now her job in this lifetime, that she now lived in, to scream out as loud as she could in frustration, whilst trying so hard to unfasten this weird, looking contraption, this thing, that was holding her leg up, making it impossible for her to get out of the bed and walk, like she wanted to do. Yes that was her aim in this life now, this very, strange one that she was now living in, to undo her traction to free her leg from it, to try and escape it, to run free again, even if she didn't know where she would run to. But after she would often succeed in undoing it all, and removing the straps, before putting her other leg out of the bed and her foot onto the floor, some Nurse always came from somewhere and stopped her, before she could get away, or would sometimes catch her in the process of trying to undo the traction and stopping her, before she could. Yes hopefully stopping her before her leg, which had a double-broken femur, the reason why it had been put up into traction to mend, and also pulled out of the growing socket, at the top of her leg, to help her crushed pelvis, which couldn't be put into a cast to heal. But she had no idea that these things that she was doing to herself in trying to help herself to escape was having, and the bad effect on the mending process of her broken bones, when her leg would come crashing down onto the bed, traction free. Bringing things to a point of desperation for the poor nurses, when they could not be there with her, all of the time, to see and watch her, in time to stop and prevent her from undoing her traction. Feeling that to help her, save herself from herself, and to get her broken bones to mend and heal, that the best thing for everyone concerned, would be to restrain her hands, to gently tie them to the bed-cot-rails at the side of her bed. But this did make Olivia extremely angry, having her hands tied up, making her scream very, loudly, shout obscenities and spit, at anyone nearby who was close to her, with this of course upsetting the busy caring nurses, who only wanted to help her to recover.

This was how Eric and Margaret found their daughter, on one of their weekend trips to visit her. "Listen," a concerned Margaret said to her husband, when they were walking down the hospital corridor to her room. "I think that's our Olivia we can hear screaming."

"God I hope not, I do hope your wrong, and why would she be screaming anyway? What ever can they be doing to her? They'd better not be hurting her at all, she's been through enough pain already," Eric replied, not knowing what to expect and fearing the worst.

When they opened the door to her room, they were both extremely shocked to see Olivia, sat up in her bed, with her wrists tied to the side of it, seeming to be growling and snarling away just like a Rabid-dog, while spitting everywhere, before throwing back her head, and beginning to howl and scream loudly.

"My God! She just looks like a bloody wild animal," a very shocked Margaret stated.

"Olivia! Olivia! Olivia!" Eric said, in his gentle, but stern, fatherly tone of voice.

Olivia opened her large, green eyes very wide, suddenly recognising her parents immediately as they walked into her room towards her bed. "Daddy! Daddy! Daddy!!" She shouted out, in a monotone voice and now beginning to cry. "Oh Daddy! My Daddy! Where have you been all this time? I've missed you so much Daddy! Please you must never leave me again."

Eric quickly untied Olivia's wrists, from the rails of the bed, where they had been fastened with bandages, before she was able to tightly wrap her arms, around his neck, saying, "Daddy please, please never ever leave me here again, all by myself. Because they hurt me so much."

"Oh do they? Well I'll have to have a word with these people, won't I?" Eric replied, trying to comfort his daughter.

Margaret gently pushed Olivia's long, dark hair back off her face and shoulders, fastening it into a plait at the back of her neck.

Eric held his daughter close to him, trying to comfort her, saying, "Don't worry about anything anymore Olivia, I'm here now so everything is going to be okay. But why were you screaming and howling?"

"I wasn't really daddy, I just wanted my hands to be free, so I can get this damn blasted thing off my leg. And I want you to help me get it off, then I can come home with you, so please take me home with you daddy. 'Cause they keep stopping me from coming home, and I now want to go home with you my mummy and daddy. Have you come here to take me home now? And mummy did you bring me my doll? My lovely 'Bride-Doll' that my Gran and Grandad Howard got me for Christmas."

"Do you know why you are here Olivia? Do you know why you're in a hospital?" Margaret asked.

"No!" Replied Olivia angrily. "No I fucking don't, and I fucking hate it here, and I'm not fucking staying here any longer, 'cause I'm going home now. I know you've come to take me home with you daddy!"

A nurse came into the room and was very pleased to see Eric and Margaret, her Parents there with her.

"How is Olivia doing Nurse?" Eric asked.

"Well, thank God she's come out of her coma," the nurse replied. "But as you can see, she's quite a handful, she has no idea what's happened to her, what her injuries are, or why she's in here."

"Will you stay with her now please nurse?" Eric asked. "Because we want to go and talk with her Doctor, and I don't want her hands tied up again."

"Okay yes, I'll be here to sit with her for a while," the nurse replied.

When Eric and Margaret began to move away from Olivia's bed, she began to cry loudly, shouting and begging for them to stay with her, "Daddy No! No! Please Daddy No! Daddy don't you leave me here again by myself!! Please take me home with you?"

"It's okay Olivia, we're not leaving you. We're just going to see the doctor, and then we're coming straight back here, to be with you again," Eric replied, trying to reassure her. "So please be a good girl

Olivia and no more screaming, 'cause we'll be back soon, I promise you."

"Mister and Mrs. Howard please come in and sit down," Doctor Booth said, when Eric and Margaret knocked on the Doctor's open office door. "I take it you have been to see your daughter Olivia?"

"Yes we have, and we've just left her for a while to come and see you," Eric replied, in a very helpless, sad, tone of voice. "But Doctor Booth, it was a hell of a shock to us both, seeing her in this mental state. What's wrong with her? And how long will she be like this? She's like a wild animal, or something going demented or crazy."

"Yes we had no idea that she was like this, in this state of mind," added Margaret, hopefully wishing that the Doctor would now tell them, not to worry that Olivia will improve and be better tomorrow.

"Well let me try to explain things to you both, in the best way I can," began Doctor Booth, leaning back in his chair, and holding his hands together making a steeple with his fingers. "Now just imagine that we have taken a peach, and put it into a box, and then we seal that box up tightly. Now let us all shake that box around, with the peach inside it for a while. Now we all know and can easily imagine, that the peach we have put into that box is by now, very badly bruised, but we cannot get into that box to see how badly bruised and damaged the peach is, can we? Well I'm sorry to have to tell you both this, but that's how Olivia's brain is at the moment. And over a period of time her brain could repair itself, and she could wake up one day and be perfectly normal again, or she could stay how she is now, for the rest of her life. I'm afraid that's the best and only way, that I can explain and describe the state of Olivia's brain condition, to you both at this moment now. She did have a very, very severe bang to her head, at the point of impact when the truck hit the car. And I'm just hoping that in time, her brain will start to heal itself."

Margaret began crying, when she heard Doctor Booth describe the state Olivia's brain was in.

"And please do come and visit your Daughter, as often as you can," continued Doctor Booth. "As I'm sure it will help her, during her recovery period knowing that you are there for her. And it's a good sign that she recognizes you as her parents, knowing who you both are. Because when her husband Clive, visited her, she didn't know who he was, and she just shouted, screamed and swore at him, telling him to go away, to never come near her again, that he was a horrid man. So I've asked Clive to stay away from her for a while now. I just don't want her getting herself stressed out like that, because it's just not good for her."

"Oh! So he's up and about then, is he?" Eric asked.

"Yes, he's getting around in a wheel chair," Doctor Booth replied. "He's still very weak, but his injuries were not as severe as Olivia's."

"I notice you haven't stitched Olivia's face Doctor," Margaret said.

"No, her face is very badly cut open, but the cuts aren't that deep, they're just very superficial, so her face should heal up by itself over a period of time, and the scars will begin to fade over the years," replied the Doctor. "Now do let me get the nurse to bring you two, a nice hot cup of tea, you've both had a long drive down here from the north, I understand."

"Yes Doctor we have," Eric replied. "And we'll be staying down here now for a few days with her."

***

Going on for a few weeks now, whenever Clive, did feel that it would be okay to visit his wife Olivia, she still did not recognise him, and would always scream and swear at him, until he had left her bedside,

Asking the Nurses, *'To please keep this fucking horrid, evil man away from her.'* And sometimes adding that she knew, *'That he was going to hurt her, that's why he keeps coming to see her.'*

She stayed in this very frightened, confused, childlike, state of mind, for up to six to eight weeks. With her Parents and Uncle Brian now resigning themselves to the fact, that she would never ever recover or be normal in her brain again, and that this is how she would now be, for the rest of her life, always living in this state of a muddled, confused mind forever.

"The only small consolation for us all, somewhere in all of this, is that they, those Doctors and Nurses, haven't cut her lovely, long hair off. And I've always loved that long hair of hers and so does she. So

I've asked the Sister and the Nurses who are looking after her, not to even think about cutting her hair off at all now, because I've bloody warned them all, that if they do, she'll never stop bloody screaming her head off," a very upset Uncle Brian said to the rest of the family one night, after returning home from visiting her in the hospital. Something which he did on numerous occasions, all by himself, when he would often take a drive down to the south of England, from the East-Coast, after finishing his work cooking at the 'Flamingo Night Club' in the early hours of the morning, going to visit his Niece.

******

Chapter 23

A few weeks later the Nurses were handing out breakfast and cups of tea to their patients one morning, when Olivia opened her eyes on another new day there in the Hospital. She sat up in her bed, looking around her, as if she had just awoken from a very, long, deep, sleep like 'Sleeping-Beauty'. "Hello," she said, in her normal tone of voice, to the Nurse who was pouring her tea. "Who are you? And where am I? This looks like a hospital, and what am I doing here?"

The Nurse stood there in shock with her mouth wide open, staring at Olivia, before she then pressed with her finger, an emergency button on the wall at the side of the bed.

Olivia heard a very, loud bell beginning to ring, and a Doctor and Nurses came running over to her. They all stood around her bed, looking at her in amazement.

"I think she may have come back to normal this morning," said the Nurse, who had pressed the bell. "Because she has just spoken to me, in a very ordinary tone of voice, instead of the monotone one, which she has been using."

"Well that's good to know. Hello I'm Doctor Angus. Do you know who you are? And what your name is?" Asked the Doctor.

"Yes, of course I know who I am, I'm Olivia. So why are you asking me that?" She replied, in a very what's this all about tone of voice, looking around her. "But I don't understand what I'm doing here? Or where am I? Or who you people are?"

"You're in the 'Chelmsford General Hospital', in Chelmsford, Essex," replied Doctor Angus. "And you've been in a very bad car accident with your husband Clive. You have been very, seriously ill, with very bad injuries from it, including mental problems. But this is a big breakthrough for you and us, for all of us, because you seem to be sounding and getting back to normal now, after a big bang you've had to your head."

"Oh really. Well I do feel okay now, and if you'll take this contraption off my leg, so I can walk, I can go home now. And where's my Dad? Why isn't my Dad here? My Dad will take me home, Dad where are you?" She shouted out, for him.

"Oh no, no Olivia, I'm afraid you can't go home just yet. And this contraption, as you call it, is called a traction. We've put your leg high up in this to help your broken bones mend," Doctor Angus replied, with a laugh. "You have got a double broken femur, a crushed pelvis, and also a broken foot. I'm afraid we can't let you walk, on your foot and leg yet, not until your broken bones have all healed."

"Well how long do I have to stay here then? And when can I see my parents?"

"You'll be here for a few more weeks yet Olivia. But I'll phone your parents soon today, to give them the good news, and I'm sure they'll be down to see you soon. Now do you feel any pain anywhere Olivia?"

"Only here in the side of my hand," she said, looking at and lifting her right hand up, to show to the Doctor where it hurt her.

"I think it's a piece of glass that we didn't get out of your hand, so I'll take that out for you in a few minute," Doctor Angus said, examining the small, solid lump, in her hand, before shining a small torch light into her eyes, to check her pupils.

"Do you remember seeing any of us or the Nurses, that are around your bed now, before today?" Doctor Angus asked.

"No I don't, but should I?" Olivia replied, looking at each of the people, who were stood around her bed, and smiling happily at her, as if now she was seeing them all for the first time.

She did manage to scream her head off, for one last time, loudly enough to wake up the dead, as the injection was put into the side of her hand, around the piece of glass, to numb it, by Nurse Janet. So that the Doctor was able to cut open her hand and remove the piece of glass, hopefully without hurting her.

"Wow look at that? That's a good size piece of glass, that was left in me, wasn't it? And I think I'll just keep this small piece of glass, as a souvenir of being in here, after that car-smash. So have you got a small container I can put this into? So I don't lose it," Olivia said, with a smile at the Doctor. After Doctor Angus removed the piece of glass from the side of her hand, and passed it to her, before stitching her hand up, with six stitches.

***

Over the next few days and weeks, Olivia began to remember other people and things about her life. First of all she remembered that she had a baby Son, called Antony, asking where he was, and did he still remember that she was his mother? And how long had she been away from him? She even remembered that Clive, the nasty evil man, whom she insisted for a long time was kept at a distance, far away from her, was now her husband. *'And why would I want to keep you away from me, if I had been so happily married to you?'* She would often now ask Clive, when he came to visit her in his wheel-chair, dressed in a pair of pyjamas and a warm dressing-gown. Laughingly telling her about the crazy, unnerving times she had put them all through, and not being able to remember at all who he was, or ever being married to him.

But Olivia did not return any of this laughter at all with Clive, over or about any of the things that he told her, that she was supposed to have said or done, because she could not remember them or had any knowledge of saying or doing these things. All of which seemed to frighten her now, as she could never imagine not being in control of herself at all, and not being aware of what she had been doing.

She was now always so very pleased to see her parents and family, and Steve and Karen, whenever they went to visit her.

The recent X-rays that were taken, showed how well her broken bones were healing. And the scars on the side of her face did not now look as open, fierce, or bloody, now that they were beginning to heal-up, by themselves, without having any stitches put in them.

And the only thing that was still hidden, deep, down somewhere inside of herself, that she could gladly still not remember, was the car-smash, happening at all, and all of the intense pain, which she must have then felt during the impact of it, with her bones being broken, the loss of so much blood, and the whole shock of it all, that she would have experienced. Gladly believing what the Doctors told her.

'That they thought that this was probably a very good thing for her, not to be able to remember any of it. And that it was far better for her, that the memory of any of it, was probably by now safely hidden

and locked away from her forever, in her subconscious mind. Never, ever to be retrieved for her again, because she probably would never be able to survive the horror-filled, memory of any of it. Especially the nearly dead state, she was in from all of her injuries, when they first saw her.'

This is what she told the Police-Officer, Shawn, who came to see her most days in the Hospital, and would sit by the side of her bed for hours, in a straight-back chair. Watching slowly as the time passed by from the hours into days and then into weeks, from her being unconscious to the opening of her eyes, through her childhood insanity, to becoming eventually, her normal self once again. Yes Shawn was always there, sitting quietly in a chair, watching her go through all of these different stages of her recovery, knowing that it would be very wrong of him, to question her at all just now, about anything that she may remember about that dreadful car-wreck, caused by her Husband. That Shawn, had hopefully, helped to save and rescue this poor girl from, when she had managed to breath slightly, on the small mirror which he held under her nose, to see if she was dead or still alive. He would just smile at her, when she would see him sat there, on the chair at the side of her bed, and sometimes Olivia, would manage to smile back at him, if she felt strong enough to do so. And she never shouted or screamed at him, like she always seemed to for a long time, whenever her husband Clive, visited her. And Shawn did just always hope, that deep down somewhere inside of her, that he was able to give this sick, almost destroyed, confused, young girl, some feeling of sense and security, when she opened her eyes and often saw him there, sitting at the side of her bed. But never ever protesting his presence there, or asking him, who he was? Or what he was doing there? And finally telling him, very quietly, when he was able to question her, *'That no, she could not, and hopefully would not, ever be able to remember anything about the car-smash happening at all.'*

Which unbeknown to her, pleased her husband Clive very much, as she made this official statement to Shawn, the Police-Officer. Making Clive, now happily thinking and believing, that all and any of the other responsibility, which may have been laid upon his shoulders, by the Chelmsford, Police Officers, about the injuries he had caused to his wife, Olivia, would and could now all be lifted. With no charges at all pending against him, concerning him or his driving.

***

Not too long after Olivia's mental recovery period, now knowing who she was and what had happened to her. Clive was discharged by the Doctors, from the 'Chelmsford Hospital', and he began to stay in a small, clean, comfortable hotel, that was in easy walking distance for him, very close to the Hospital, so that he was able to go and visit, Olivia, each day.

Whenever he saw her though, he would soon begin to complain very, bitterly, to her, about how ill he was feeling, how much pain he was still in, and how dirty and damp the hotel was, and the room that he was renting to stay in. And how it would be so much better for him, and how much he would just love it, if he could possibly go back home to his Mothers. Where he definitely knew that he would be looked after properly, by her, and how he would, be able to get better much, more quicker, with her tender, loving care.

Olivia was eating her breakfast in the Hospital one morning, when Clive arrived early to see her.

He quickly began by telling her, straight away of, '*How ill and sick he felt and the dreadful pain that he had been in the night before, when he was visiting her. And that when he had left her, last-night, he had no other choice but to go back upstairs to see the Nurses and Sister, who were on duty last night on the ward he used to be on. And he went to see them, to see if they would be good enough to give him an injection, for the horrid, pain that he was in and feeling. And that they were so concerned about him and his pain, that they thought that it would be a very, good thing for him, to sleep in a bed, that was free on the ward, after he told them that he had not been sleeping very, well at all, since leaving the hospital. And that last night was the best nights sleep he'd had, since he'd left the Hospital.*'

He also made a point of making it very, clear to Olivia, that he was now absolutely, dreading having to go back to that disgusting, dirty, damp, hotel that he was now having to stay in.

"Are you telling me that you want to get back home to Sheffield then?" Olivia asked, concerned now after listening to his hard done to, sob story.

"Oh yes, I'd really love to go back home to Mothers," he replied with a deep sigh. "But I can't leave you here alone Olivia dear, now can I?"

"It's all right Clive, you can if you feel that it would be best for you to go home. And don't worry about me, 'cause I guess that I'll be all right here," Olivia replied, beginning to feel sorry for Clive now.

"Really, do you mean that Dear?" He asked, with a big smile appearing on his face, as he felt his spirits lifting.

"Yes, you go on home, I'll be okay. It will be better for you anyway, to have your Mum look after you, and help you to get better. It will be better for you staying with your parents, then I won't be feeling so guilty about you having to stay in a damp Hotel room, 'cause that can't be any good for you, feeling cold all the time. And I always thought that the Hotels were so good around here?"

"Yes they usually are, but the one I'm staying in near the Hospital, so that I can come and see you, and be with you, it isn't a very good one at all. But I guess it's just the luck of the draw."

"Well couldn't you find another one? A better one to stay in somewhere else?"

"No all the other hotels near here, are full, 'cause I've checked them all out."

"Well you get off home then Clive, as I've told you I'll be okay here."

"Oh thank-you, thank-you so much Olivia my Darling, it's so good of you to be so understanding," he said excitedly, while kissing her on the top of her forehead. "And I promise I'll get my Father to drive me down, to see you in a couple of weeks time, when I'm feeling a little better."

"Yeah I hope that you will,"

After kissing her once again on the top of her forehead, Clive then eagerly left Olivia's hospital bedside, without giving her a second thought or glance. He telephoned for a taxi to take him to the nearest train station, to get a train back home to Sheffield, to go and stay with his Parents.

***

One month later on Easter Sunday, Olivia felt sure that Clive would definitely come down to see her, but he never did show up. Her Uncle Brian arrived instead, at about eleven thirty that morning, with Easter Eggs for her, from her Grandparents, her Parents, her Sister and him.

"This is a lovely surprise Uncle Brian," Olivia said happily. "And I'm so pleased to see you."

"Yeah I hoped you would be luv. And you're looking so much better than the last time I saw you," Brian told her, giving her a big hug and a kiss. "And there's another lovely surprise on its way for you."

"Thanks and what? What else have you brought for me?"

"Nothing, no it's nothing else that I've brought for you."

"Well what is it?"

"Oh, you'll see, just be patient, and it should be here soon."

"What? Oh come on tell me what this surprise is? Is it Clive? Is Clive coming to see me?" She asked hopefully.

"Oh no, it's not him. And I'm not telling you, or it won't be a surprise anymore, will it? But it should be here anytime now," he said, looking at his watch.

Olivia, now very curiously, looked towards the doorway of her Hospital room, wondering what to expect, when she suddenly saw Kenny Dee and Vicky appear at the door to her room, carrying with them a large Easter Egg.

"Kenny and Vicky," she shouted out in delight, as they both walked into her room, and put their arms around her, hugging and kissing her. "Oh what a wonderful surprise this is, my Hippy friends coming to see me, it's so good to see you both, and I was getting scared the other day, that you'd probably all forgotten about me by now."

"Well that's why we drove all the way down here to see you, 'cause we luv and care about you Olivia. And we wanted to see if you were getting any better, 'cause we've heard some horror stories about your injuries and how else you've been. We also wanted to bring you an Easter Egg, 'cause we wanted you to have one for Easter," Kenny replied. "And to tell you we want you, to get yourself better fast now, and come back home to us. Everyone else, all your other Hippy friends, send lots of luv to you, and say to tell you, they're all missing you."

"I passed you people down the road, not too far from the hospital, and I waved to you as I drove past, but I don't think you saw me," Brian said.

"Yeah Vicky saw you, she said I'm sure that's Uncle Brian, that's just passed us and waved," Answered Kenny.

"Yeah well I'll never forget this Easter Sunday, and you people coming to see me, you've all really cheered me up. I was feeling really pissed off 'cause Clive didn't turn up, when I really thought he would have made the effort to come and see me at Easter. Has he been in touch with any of you? Or my other Hippy friends?" Olivia asked Kenny and Vicky eagerly.

"No I've not heard anything from him at all," replied Vicky. "Have you Kenny?"

"No none of us have heard anything from him at all, he's not phoned any of us. We didn't even know that he was back at home in Sheffield, until your Dad told us. And when I've phoned his Mothers to talk to him and see if we can go over to see him, she tells me that he's either sleeping or to ill to have any visitors at all. And he's never phoned me back."

"To ill to have any visitors at all? Well he seemed to be okay, apart from having a bit off pain, before he left here. And I talk with him every night when he phones me here, and he's not told me that he's ill," A confused Olivia stated. "So I wonder what's going on?"

"Eh don't you go worrying yourself about him, he'll be alright with his Mummy looking after him now, won't he?" Brain told her, while winking at Kenny and Vicky.

***

After he had left, Clive never did go back to the hospital in Chelmsford Essex to see his wife Olivia. And whenever he telephoned her, and she would ask him why he wasn't coming back down to see her, as he had promised her. He never failed to always tell her, that his Mother had told him, that he just wasn't strong enough yet, to make that long journey back down there to see her. So there wasn't very much that Olivia, felt that she was able to do, to change the situation.

Her Uncle Brian and Parents drove down to the Hospital, to visit her on most weekends now, feeling that she was alone and must be feeling quite lost, without any of her family members down there with her. When visiting her, they often brought with them her Sister Suzanne, and Son Antony to see her.

Steve and Karen invited Olivia's parents to be guests at their home, because they had a spare bedroom, which they said they would be welcome to use. This very, kind offer was helpful to Margaret and Eric, who eagerly took them up on it, by often staying at their home with them. And soon became very, good friends with Steve and Karen, during their stays with them, over this sad period of time, of their life's, during their visits to see Olivia.

***

After a stay of just over three months in the hospital, the X-rays showed that Olivia's bones were now finally mended. So when the traction was removed from her leg, to everyone's amazement she began walking around very, normally and strongly, without even a hint of a limp, which the Doctors expected her to have, due to her Pelvis that had been broken in many parts. So of course the Orthopaedic Doctor and everyone else were so very pleased with her healing process.

A week later the Doctor told her that he was very pleased with the marvellous, and miraculous complete recovery, that she has made, and that he felt comfortable in telling her, that she could now go back to her home in Sheffield. Of course Olivia was so very happy at this wonderful news, which she felt she had been waiting to hear for a long time now.

******

Chapter 24

Eric and Margaret drove down to Chelmsford, in Essex to bring Olivia, back home from the hospital. But before leaving everyone, in this wonderful, healing place, which was now beginning to feel like a second home to her. A tearful Olivia, gave all the Nurses and Doctors that had cared for her, warm, hugs, while saying, a very, big thank-you to them all, for saving her life and helping her to get better.

Eric and Margaret also said, thank-you to everyone, by shaking their hands firmly and warmly, in their appreciative thanks to them all, telling the Doctors and Nurses, that they would always, be forever thankful to them, for saving their Daughter's life, looking after her and making her well again.

They made the long 200-mile drive back up the M1-Motorway from Chelmsford in Essex, to their home in the 'Hope-Valley'-'Peak-District' of Derbyshire, in their Volvo-estate-car. Making Olivia, very comfortable in the back of it, in a bed that her Father, had made up for her, with sheets, blankets and pillows, in case she wanted to sleep, and two hot, water bottles placed on her feet and legs, to make sure that she was kept very, nice and warm, with lots of cushions for extra padding laid all around her.

Her parents had decided between themselves that Olivia and Clive would be staying at the 'White-Hart' Pub with them, for about a month. In their sensible, thinking and feelings that their daughter was not yet strong enough, to go back to her own home right now, to look after her son alone, or wait on her husband, as he would expect her to do, let alone keep their house clean and do the cooking.

***

When they arrived back in the village of Bradwell, at about nine o'clock that evening, and Eric, her Father lifted Olivia, out of the back of his car, and helped her to walk into his pub, the 'White Hart', she saw her Husband, Clive, her Uncle Brian, her sister Suzanne and lots of her Hippy, friends there, all waiting to celebrate her recovery and welcome her back home to their world.

Her best friend Angela, with tears in her eyes, came rushing over to Olivia, giving her very, warm hugs, and lots of loving kisses on her cheeks, before fastening something on a chain around her neck, while saying to her, "Welcome back my friend, and this is what I've got, especially for you, to keep you safe. It's a 'Saint-Christopher' and you must always wear it, so you'll never be in another car smash again, 'cause it will protect you forever."

"Thanks Angel, this is so kind of you, and I've missed you so much," Olivia replied, hugging her friend warmly. "Yes I've missed you all, my wonderful Hippy friends, and thanks so much for all being here to welcome me home."

The topic of conversation that night, and for many weeks to come, in the pub and around the other pubs, in the village of Bradwell, *'Was the car smash.'* The crash that Clive had caused to happen, that Olivia had been involved in, and the very serious injuries, which she had sustained, with her broken bones and recovery period, of confusion, including her state of mind when she reverted back to childhood, after regaining consciousness, all of which Olivia had no memory, or recollection of at all.

And at last after all these nerve wracking months of anguish, Eric, Margaret, Suzanne and Brian, could now begin to laugh and joke at some of the very, strange, crazy things, that Olivia had said and done while she had been in that confused, state of mind. This was at last a big breakthrough, and very therapeutic for their frayed nerves, which had been stretched very raw and tense to the point of breaking, over the last three months. Because for a long time her family, who had loved, cared, and helped Olivia, through her long, recovery period, felt at one time that they would never, be able to laugh, smile or ever be happy ever again.

Among and during all the relieved merriment of her return to the family, that Clive eagerly joined in with, while at the same time was able to seemingly, very easily detach himself from any blame concerning the car crash, as he laughed and joked about what had happened along with the others. Continually asking everyone if they knew how serious his injuries had been, and still were, and did any of them know that while he was in the hospital, he had died at least, three times, and had to be brought back to life again.

"Oh what a pity Lemons and why did the Doctors bother to waste their bloody time, in bringing you back to us? And what really happened? Couldn't you see the bloody lorry? Wasn't it big enough to see when it was coming at you? Or didn't you bother to wear your sodding glasses that night?" Kenny Dee shouted, to him sarcastically, with a laugh.

When Clive went across to the bar ordering himself another drink, Eric who was stood behind the bar serving the drinks, said in a loud, enough voice intentionally, for everyone else to hear, "I hope you know the police are going to charge you with, careless, reckless, dangerous driving and speeding Clive? And I charge you myself, with just about killing my Daughter. It's just a bloody miracle that our Olivia, has survived, and is now as good as new. And I've got nothing that I will be ever thankful for again, on you coming into my family's life. Even though I thought I was about a year ago, but not anymore, do you understand me?"

"Yes, I know what you must be feeling Eric, it must have been very hard for you and Margaret," Clive replied, while lifting his glass of Scotch to his lips, to take a drink. "And I'm very sorry Eric, about what happened to Olivia, but it wasn't my fault at all, you know? 'Cause I thought I'd told you? I can't remember the accident happening either, any of it, because I think I was also knocked unconscious at the time, when it happened."

"Well I think you're a bloody liar Lemons," Eric said, in a very, angry, firm, tone of voice, while looking Clive straight in the eyes. "Because when you were lifted from the car, you were conscious, and you spoke to Steve and Karen before you were put into the ambulance. And you were also conscious when you arrived at the hospital, because the Doctors told me that you were. And the police report also says you were conscious, when they spoke to you, while you were still in the car. So don't try to bloody lie to me Lemons, I don't want to hear any of it."

Olivia stayed with her parents for about a month, beginning to feel stronger in herself every day during this convalescent period. With all of her Hippy friends, the village people and her neighbours Cassandra, James, Diana and David often coming over to see her at the 'White Hart' pub.

***

Diana invited Olivia over to spend the day at her home with her, in Cedars Lane, in Sheffield. Telling her that if she felt strong enough and up to it, she would help her to clean her own house, so that it would be nice and clean and dust free, ready for her to return to it, when she felt well enough to come back home. Because over the months of being stood empty and unused as a house and home to live in, without any cleaning, the furniture and carpets had just been there gathering lots of dust,

So of course Olivia, eagerly took Diana up on her offer and enjoyed being with her friend and neighbour once again that afternoon, also being back in her own house again, as they both worked very, hard vacuuming, polishing and dusting it, to get it looking nice and clean, just the way Olivia, liked it to look, ready for her to return home to.

The week before she returned to her home, she went over to stay with her Grandparents, in Cleethorpes for a week. Enjoying the lovely, fresh, smell of the salty, sea air, which brought colour to her pale, face and cheeks, when she often took her walks along the beach with her Grandparents small, white, Terrier dog, Bouncer. This was all so very, much like a natural, fresh, air, tonic for her, as she ran into the sea and jumped the waves along the beach, when the tide came in and splashed against the wooden, breakers.

She visited her Aunties and Uncle's who also lived in Cleethorpes, and her cousin Anton, at his 'Hair-Dressing-salon' often. And went to the 'Flamingo Night Club' a few evenings to see her friends there, who were all so very happy to see her looking fit and well again, after the ordeal that they had heard she had been through, from her Uncle Brian.

***

Then finally Olivia decided that it was now time to return to her home in Hunters Lane in Sheffield, to begin her life again there with her Husband, Clive, and her Son Antony. But her very, changed attitude to life now, was that after being so near to a death that she did not even remember, she would always make a point of telling her friends, that she would now always, live her life to the fullest, and enjoy every minute of it from now on because you don't ever know when your number will be up, that you can't plan for it, so you must take your happiness when and while you can and really enjoy it.

And once again very soon after moving back into their home, Clive began to go away on his usual, busy, business trips down to London. Leaving Olivia at home with her son Antony, at these times, as she just did not want to make these London, business trips with him anymore, so he would now go on them alone, with his trips seeming now to become a lot more frequent as time went on.

During Olivia's absence in her neighbourhood for a while, new friendships with other neighbours did begin to grow, and Diana introduced her to Jackie, a new friend she had made whilst Olivia had been in the hospital. Jackie, was a very, good looking girl about the same age as Diana, with black hair and dark blue eyes, who only lived a couple of houses away from Olivia's, and they became instant friends on introduction. Jackie's Husband, Don, had recently started to go away for his company to other cities on business trips now, so instead of sitting at home alone like 'grass-widows', waiting for their Husbands to return, Jackie and Olivia decided to go downtown to the discos, to do some dancing and socializing together.

***

Diana and Jackie were round at Olivia's house having coffee one afternoon, when Kenny Dee arrived with Bozo. Kenny told them that he had recently, decided to become a travelling-DJ, which was a 'Mobile-Disc-Jockey', and had made himself a turntable unit, collected a pile of records, and had started up a business called 'Highway 68', with his Brother Mike as his manager, and he now needed some Go-Go dancers.

"That sounds great," Diana said. "But what's a Mobile-DJ?"

"It's a DJ that goes to different clubs and pubs, and does a show for the night," Kenny replied proudly. "And it's something that's now starting up all over England, and our Mike is getting me bookings at different places, and I want Olivia to help me."

"Me help you? But how can I help ye?" Olivia answered, in a surprised voice.

"By being a Go-Go dancer for me, 'cause I need some dancers," Kenny replied. "And you could be a dancer for me also, if you'd like to be Jackie."

"Me dance for you? But I don't think I can dance good enough for that. Can't you find someone else to do it for you?" Olivia said, feeling that she just hadn't got enough confidence to do this job, which would probably be on a stage, in front of people.

"Yes you can, and I know you can do it, or I wouldn't be asking ye. Just throw your arms around, shake your head and move your body. You'll have lots of bright coloured flashing lights on ye, and I've ordered a stroboscope that will make you look really good, especially with all that lovely, long, dark hair of yours flying around while your dancing," Kenny replied.

"Yeah it sounds as though it could be fun. But why don't you get Vicky to dance for you?"

"Because she can't dance. And she wouldn't want to anyway, 'cause she's to busy Nursing poorly kids, at the Children's Hospital."

"Well I'll have to ask Clive if I can dance for you Kenny. But what about my broken leg? I don't want it to break again?"

"You haven't got a broken leg anymore Olivia remember, it's mended now so stop bloody nursing it. Anyway it will be good exercise for it. And as for Clive, well he's always going off down to London, and leaving you alone here. So well what about you Jackie? Are you gonna dance for me also?"

"Oh no, not me, no definitely not, 'cause I know Don would never agree to it. And I know he'd go bloody mad if he found out I was on a stage, dancing half naked to a room full of men," Jackie replied, with a laugh. "No stick with Olivia, 'cause I'm sure she'll be good at it."

"What records would I dance to then? And what would I wear? And when do you want me to dance for you?" Olivia asked, getting interested in this idea now.

"Well you can choose your own records that you would like to dance to, and I'll leave some here for you today, to practice with. And

I'll need you on Tuesday night, I've got a gig booked with a pub on the Manor estate. So do you think you can be ready to dance for me by then?" Kenny replied.

"Wow Tuesday night, but that's only in a few days time. But yeah go on then, ye I'll do it for you," Olivia agreed, with a big smile on her face. "I'll be your Go-Go dancer Kenny."

"Great I knew you would Olivia, I knew you'd help me to get my new career started," Kenny said, putting his arms around her and giving her a thankful hug. "Now let's get this furniture moved so Bozo can bring my equipment in, and you can start practicing your dancing."

"Are you going to be Kenny's, 'Roadie', Bozo?" Jackie asked him, while pushing a chair out of the way.

"Yeah, I've told him I'd like to be, and I like that title 'Roadie'," Bozo replied with a smile. "I think it suits me."

"I wonder what Clive will say about me being a Go-Go dancer," Olivia said, while watching all the furniture in her lounge being moved, to accommodate Kenny's equipment.

"Don't you start worrying about his bloody approval now, don't you go worrying yourself about him Olivia, 'cause I think you've just made a good decision. And I think you'll enjoy yourself and have lots of fun, I can just imagine you on a stage dancing. And as for Clive, well one day I'll tell you something about him," Jackie replied.

"What?" Olivia asked, in a surprised, interesting voice. "What will you tell me about him? I don't think you even really know him, do you?"

"One day Olivia I'll tell you something about Clive," Jackie said again. "But not yet, 'cause the time isn't right, and you'd be mad at me if I told you now, but I promise you I'll tell you one day though. Now come on, let's look at Kenny's records, and I'll help you to choose some to dance to."

"I'll tell you what Olivia," said Diana, who had been listening to all of this with much, quiet interest. "Get me all your bikinis and shorts together, and I'll get lots of different coloured balls of nylon, and I'll make you make some dancing costumes out of them."

"Oh great Diana thanks so much, that will be a big help," Olivia said, now beginning to dance around the room to a record that Kenny had put on his turntable to play.

***

She just loved her job being a Go-Go dancer; she had so much fun dancing on stages, tables, and in cages at different pubs and clubs around Sheffield, where Kenny had his bookings. The first record she always chose to begin her dancing to was *'Born To Be Wild'*. She just loved to feel the very, loud, vibrant music wrap itself around her, as she moved her body to its beat. It made her feel safe, secure, wild and free, like no one had any control or hold over her. She also loved to see the expression on the men's faces in the audience, to the sexy movements she made with her body, especially when she danced to the records, *'Gimme, Gimme Good Lovin'*, *'Kiss Him good-bye'* and *'Yummy, Yummy, Yummy I've Got Love in My Tummy'*. When she thrust, her pelvis forward at them, moving it up and down, backwards and forwards, she noticed that it seemed to drive the men wild, as they watched her closely, and applauded loudly when she had finished her dancing. During the shows there would always be a crowd of Olivia and Kenny's friends there with them, so it always seemed to be like a big, very, happy party, with Olivia afterwards always inviting everyone back to her house, to continue the wild partying.

Over a period of time, after a lot of partying and drinking and realizing how much fun she could have with the guys of her own age group, different affairs began to subtly, suddenly happen with these other guys, whom she seemed to be able to turn on very easily, sexually. Yes they all seemed to her to be a big part of the fun and games that mattered in her life now, these young, good looking fit guys, whom had no sexual inhibitions whatsoever, and who could now satisfy her much, much more than Clive ever did, or seemed to even want to now.

So it soon became a very well known fact, among Olivia's Hippy friends, whom she seemed to collect more of along her way, *'that she made love, to feel loved.'* That she had a very strong, and strange, feeling inside of her, to feel loved by everyone, because it was something that she now seemed to be missing in her life with Clive, as her marriage began to quickly lose all it's roots of foundation, as it began to fall apart.

Clive never had any objections at all, even in the beginning, to his wife being a Go-Go dancer, and he felt it would give her something to do now, with all the spare time that he felt she had in her life, now that he seemed to always be away from home more often.

As the months went by though, with Olivia's dancing now taking up a very big part of her life, with her and Clive seeming to drift further, apart from each other, going their own separate ways, with both of them pursuing their different interests. Clive, always away on business somewhere now for most of his time, telling her that he felt he had to get more orders for his company, and when returning home, finding that they had nothing in common or to talk about anymore, with not even a very interesting or regular sex life, happening between them.

Her Son Antony was now spending a lot of time with his Grandparents, at the 'White Hart' Pub which he loved, and especially when his Aunty Suzanne took him to the playing-field, to play with the other children there on the swings, roundabout and rocking-horse. Because as Olivia told her Parents, she could not leave her Son at home alone by himself, when she had no one to baby-sit for her, when she went out on her dancing- gigs. Her Parents loved to have Antony with them of course, and were so pleased that at last their Daughter, had found a happy, and fun interesting life, to now enjoy.

Over a period of time though, her Parents did start to begin to worry about her, as she seemed to grow wilder in her ways, with the things she did, and said. But she always told them, as she justified her means to them, by saying, *'Get with it, that she now lived in the 'Age-Of-Aquarius, and this was what everyone was doing, and singing about in the words of the songs on the records.'*

Yes Olivia was very much enjoying, her very happy, wild-child, crazy world, and never thought, or could foresee that anything could ever, possibly, now change it or go wrong with it.

******

Chapter 25

Clive arrived home late, from work one night, while Olivia, was at home relaxing, watching television and her Son Antony, after his evening bath, was upstairs asleep in his bed. "I'm glad you're not out dancing tonight dear," Clive said to her, in a happy tone of voice.

"Oh, and why is that? And how many bloody times do I have to keep telling you, not to call me dear? 'Cause I'm nobody's dear. And what are you so bloody excited about? And where have you been?" Olivia asked.

"Well I have something really important to tell you," replied Clive, lighting up a cigarette as he began walking up and down the Lounge, into the Dining room, inhaling his cigarette very, deeply. "I've been in Liverpool today seeing some of our customers over there. And on the way back a pebble, or a stone, flew up from the road, and broke my car windshield. And when the window went bang as it broke, I suddenly remembered everything about the car accident that we were in. And as I've been telling everyone all-along, I know that it wasn't my fault at all. 'Cause I remembered I was overtaking a big lorry that night, and before I could pull over, there was a big bang, and I suddenly couldn't see anything anymore. And I'm sure that one of the lorry's that I was overtaking, it's tires at the side of my car, threw a stone up that broke my windshield. Also I have to go to court in a couple of weeks time Olivia, and I'm going to plead not guilty to dangerous or any other form of hazardous driving. I'll hire myself a good Barrister to fight my case."

"With what? This story that you've just told me?" Olivia asked, laughing at him. "You must be bloody joking Clive. And if that's what did happen the night of the accident, what took you so bloody long to remember it?"

"Because as I've told you before Olivia dear, I was knocked unconscious and lost my memory. But when the windshield was hit by that stone, and broke it tonight, it brought it all back to me."

"Well good for you Clive dear, but it hasn't brought my memory back, thank God. Anyway I don't want to remember that horrid car smash, or anything about it."

"But Olivia dear, just try and think hard about it will you? And try to remember that night? We were driving down the road overtaking those big lorry's and something went bang," Clive said, clapping his hands together in front of her face, making a very, loud crack, in trying to get her to remember a loud, bang that night, before the car accident happened.

"No! No! No!" Olivia shouted and screamed angrily, pushing Clive's hands away from her face. "Don't do that to me. And I don't care how many bloody times you clap your hands in front of me, I still don't or ever want to remember, that car smash I was in. Anyway what good would it do for you? If I did?"

"Well, you could tell the Judge in court for me, that's what you remember happening, and he would have no choice but to find me innocent of all charges. By the way Olivia, have you still got that small piece of glass, that the Doctor at the hospital took out of your hand?"

"Yes of course I have, it's my horrid souvenir why?"

"Well where is it?"

"I don't know, I've put it away somewhere."

"Well could you find it for me please? Because I think that piece of glass from the windshield, that you had removed from your hand, was the piece that got hit by the stone that night. And I'll get some lab to test it, and they'll find pieces of that stone in the glass. And I think that would be good evidence for my court case, don't you?"

"No! But whatever makes you happy," Olivia replied, looking at Clive very bemused, especially after his dramatic performance, of trying to get her into the same wave length of thinking as him. "Only don't you involve me, in your new found memories and stupid ideas, I don't want any part of them. What happened is now over and done with for me. And I'm enjoying my life now, so don't you go putting a damper on it again, okay!"

***

Clive now began telling everyone he saw, about how he had at last remembered, how and why the car accident had happened. And that he had now hired himself a good Barrister to fight his case in court for him, and that the piece of glass that the Doctor had removed from Olivia's hand, would be the evidence that was needed, to prove his innocence, and to win his court case. But he just wished that Olivia would try harder, to remember why and how the accident had happened. So that she could be a good, witness for him, and he would then have a stronger case to present to the Judge and Jury.

But when Clive told his story to whomever he could get to listen to him, people just seemed to look at him in amazement and total, disbelief before laughing in his face.

As Eric told Clive, *'He thought his story was a pack of bloody lies. Just like the one he had also told everybody about, when one night in the middle of a hot September, the year before he married Olivia. He ran his car off the road into a wall, on his way home from the 'White Hart', saying he had skidded on black-ice. It's the first time I've ever heard of black-ice being on the roads on a warm, summers night.'* "And as I've told you before, no I don't want to hear anymore of your bloody lies. And if you wish to perjure yourself in court, then that's up to you. But don't you dare try and get our Olivia to perjure herself and lie for you, just to save your bloody neck. And are you aware of the penalties for perjury? The Judge can put you into prison for as long as he wants to, if he thinks you are lying to him and committing perjury. So you'd better think about it?"

Eric then began to treat Clive Lemons, with the absolute, contempt that he felt he deserved, and began to wish that his daughter, had never set eyes on this man, had never, ever met him or married him.

James and Cassandra, were having coffee and drinks with Clive and Olivia at their home one evening, when they told Clive that they were shocked and horrified, at the thought of him telling such a fabricated, made up story, like that to a Judge and Jury. And they were also very, surprised that a Barrister would present it to court for him, knowing that it was just a load of bullshit.

"Whatever is happening to our legal system now-a-days? It must be cracking somewhere," James asked.

"Well, I'm paying for a good Barrister," Clive replied confidently.

"Yes we thought you might be. Someone who knows that he hasn't got a cat in hells chance, of winning a case like yours, but likes to make himself some money. But money doesn't talk in our courts. And you always seem to think, that money will buy you everything you want, don't you Clive? That is one of your big problems. And how much do you think it would have cost you? To buy yourself another Olivia, if she had of died?" Cassandra annoyingly, truthfully stated.

***

Clive Lemons stood in the Chelmsford Crown Court on the 9th June 1970, and pleaded not guilty in front of the Judge and Jury, to the police charges brought against him, of careless, speeding, reckless, dangerous driving.

The court case went on for two days, with his Barrister presenting as good a defence for him as possible, using only as evidence the small piece of glass that was taken from Olivia's hand, as his only strong possibility of his innocence.

Olivia had to go into the witness stand on the morning of the second day, but only for a few minutes, to tell the court, that she did not remember anything at all, before, or about, the car accident happening, that nearly took her life.

At four o'clock on the 11th June 1970, the Jury found Clive Lemons guilty of, careless, speeding, reckless and dangerous, driving.

The Judge suspended his Driving-License for twelve months, and fined him One-Thousand-Pounds. Telling Clive, that he was letting him off very lightly this time, because it was his first driving offence, and because of the injuries he and his wife had sustained. Hoping that, that in itself had been a very good lesson to him. But if he appeared in his court again on any other driving charges, he would have no alternative, but to sentence him to a prison-term.

******

Chapter 26

During the twelve months that Clive's Driving-License was suspended, Olivia thought that it would keep him at home with her more, so that she could now try once again to get to know, a little better, the man she had married. But he still travelled away as often as before, on his business, trips to London, hiring someone to drive him down there.

Olivia talked to him whenever she had the chance to, about them both, their lives, and the state of their marriage. But after getting no response or interesting, feedback from Clive at all, she finally resigned herself to the fact, that he was too wrapped up in his own world, to show any concern about their marriage, or them, and would always be away from home on business, whenever and as often as he could.

So she decided that the best thing for her to do now, was to quit any worrying that may have entered her head, about her failing, marriage, and to get on with her own happy, life once again. She still had all of her Hippy friends around her, and her Go-Go dancing job, with Kenny Dee, which she did most nights of the week. And now decided to go to the local Modelling-Agency down-town in the centre of Sheffield, to get herself another fun, job as a photographic model, with Biaba-International.

Her life now seemed to become more like one big, party after another, which she really enjoyed. But over a few years she began to feel that it had no direction, and that she was not going or heading, anywhere with it. So she began to think again, what was it all about?

Clive took her and Antony on a wonderful, holiday to Majorca for two weeks, in the spring of the next year, where they both really, enjoyed themselves together. But on their return home she soon felt again, that there was something missing between them, a large gap, a void, an emptiness, that neither of them could seem to fill. This feeling began to bother Olivia, once again, as she was now growing older, but Clive, didn't even seem to notice, and was quite happy with things plodding along, just the way they were, with no change in his mind for either of them, in their life's.

About six months later Cassandra, gave birth to a lovely, baby girl, and Diana, told Olivia, that she thought that she may also be about three-months pregnant herself.

***

"That's it," Olivia, announced to Jackie and Diana, one afternoon, when they were at Jackie's, having cups of tea with chocolate-biscuits, discussing Cassandra's, lovely, dark haired, blue eyed baby, Lucy. And Diana's, now official, fully, showing pregnancy, with her also hoping for a girl.

"What is it? What are you on about?" Diana asked.

"A baby, I want to have a baby girl," Olivia replied, excitedly at this bright, idea that she'd just had.

"Well, a baby girl, or a boy for that matter, won't save your marriage to Clive, Olivia," Jackie stated. "If it's as bad as you think it is."

"No your right, I know a baby, won't save my marriage," Olivia replied. "But I think it could save me, and I just love babies, and I'd love to have a baby girl. So I think I'll stop taking my pills, and get pregnant."

"You should think about more than not taking your pills Olivia," Diana said concerned. "'Cause if you don't stop your fun times, and sleeping around as you sometimes do. You should think about who you're going to choose to be the baby's Father."

"Oh yes I agree with you on that," Olivia replied, "And I promise, from now on I won't have sex with anyone else, but only with my husband Clive."

"Do you think Clive's capable of becoming a Father then?" Jackie asked, with a snigger in her voice.

"Well I can try and see, can't I?" Olivia replied, dismissing their fears. "And thinking about it now, I'm sure it'll bring Clive and I closer together, with us both having an interest in our new baby."

And when Olivia told Clive that she would now, very soon, like to have a baby. He told her he thought it was a good idea, and he secretly hoped that it could just be the thing, to perhaps calm her, and her life, down a bit. With him now sometimes feeling like her parents, often did, that she was becoming to much of an out of control wild-child, even though she was now 20-years old.

So she now stopped completely, taking her birth control pills, or making love with any other man, staying completely true to Clive. But he was still, always going away every month on business, sometimes for a couple of weeks now. So every time they were together, she did so hope that she would soon become pregnant, but her periods were still without fail, always, arriving on time to the day, that she was due for one.

***

Six months later in the hot, summer of July that year, Clive was away again for one of his usual, business trips, down to London. And Antony was staying at the 'White Hart' pub with his Grandparents for a few days.

Olivia told Diana and Jackie, that she was going with some of her other friends that night, to a disco downtown called the 'Penny-Farthing', because Kenny Dee was the DJ there for that night.

"Well we were going to ask you to come out with us tonight, if you want to," Jackie said. "Diana, Dave, Don and me, are going to the 'Gate-Inn' for a drink."

"Well thanks, but I've already told Kenny and Vicky, and the others that I'll see them at the 'Penny-Farthing'," Olivia replied.

"Well have fun then," Jackie said. "And don't forget Olivia, if you can't be good, be good at it."

"Oh I promise I will be," Olivia replied laughing.

"What?" Diana asked. "What will you be good at?"

"I don't know yet, I've not decided," Olivia answered, still laughing.

***

At the 'Penny-Farthing' that night, Olivia was having fun, drinking and dancing with her friends, and going over to Kenny, telling him how good he was doing, being the DJ there, and telling him what records she'd like to hear played.

When she went back to the bar to join her friends who were there, she saw a good looking man, with black hair, walking towards her. "Hey pretty lady," he said. "What's your name? And can I buy you a drink?"

"Yes okay if you'd like to, and my name is Olivia," she replied.

"Mine's Alex, and what would you like to drink?" He said, taking her hand and leading her, towards another part of the long bar, away from her friends.

"I'll have a Scotch and lemonade please," Olivia replied, looking into his silver grey eyes. "Wow! What unusual coloured eyes you have," She said, when he passed her, her drink.

"Yes I know, all the better to turn you on with, my dear," Alex replied, looking at her intensely.

"Oh Christ no, I can't bloody stand good looking, sweet talking guys, like you, who are so full of bloody confidence. And they think that girls should just fall at their feet. You really piss me off you know," Olivia said, turning to walk away from him.

"Hey, wait a minute Olivia," Alex replied, holding on to her arm. "Please don't go Olivia, I'm not really like that at all. I'm just a lonely guy up from London, whose here in Sheffield on a business trip for a couple of days, and I came to this Disco hoping to find some interesting company for the night."

"Interesting company, or a good lay?" Olivia asked sarcastically.

"Well, that's up to you isn't it?"

"Well, if you can cut the crap, you may find I can be a very interesting person. Now let's dance and tell me, what do you do? And why are you here in Sheffield?"

"I'm into Computers, I'm a Systems Analyst."

"I don't know anything about Computers, and what the hell is a Systems Analyst?"

"It's someone who shows people how to use computers, to help them do their jobs. And I'm visiting a company here in Sheffield, that has just had some computers installed."

"How old are you? And are you married?" Olivia asked, when they went back to the bar to get more drinks, and then sit down at a table.

"I'm twenty-three, and no, I'm not married. I've just got a few girlfriends, but I don't want to get married yet, not for a while. Now, tell me about yourself Olivia, and your life, are you married?"

"Yes, I'm married but I don't seem to see much of my Husband, he always seems to be away on business," Olivia replied with a deep sigh. "I have a small Son, and I'm a Go-Go dancer and a Model."

"Are you happily married Olivia? And do you think you'll stay married?"

"No, I wouldn't say I was happily married. My Husband is twenty years older than me, and at the moment we seem to be worlds apart, just growing more apart. And as for staying with him, I don't feel I really have much choice in the matter, 'cause I spend the money I make with my jobs as fast as I get it. I haven't really got anywhere else to live with my Son, and I don't want to go back home to live with my Parents."

Olivia and Alex had more drinks and dances together, and when the Disco was closing he asked her, if she would like to go back to his hotel with him, and she eagerly agreed.

***

Alex closed and locked his hotel room door, before taking Olivia in his arms and kissing her deeply. He caressed her body while undressing her, and when he removed her panties he stared at her naked body and whispered, "You are so beautiful Olivia." He then began to kiss her body all over, slowly moving down to her soft, mound of womanhood, and gently kissing her love button, which by this time was aching for his touch, as he gently pushed her down onto the bed. The intense feelings now going through Olivia's body, told her that Alex would soon have complete control over her sexually, and she did not want it to end, as she moaned passionately to the feeling of his tongue going inside of her, then back again to her love button. Her body tingled all over with the intense pleasure she was feeling, as she yielded her soft mound to his lips, while opening herself to him without any shame, every nerve in her body was now centered, around his touch. He held her sexually paralyzed and on the edge of orgasm, until an intense climax engulfed her whole body. She then felt his hardness inside of her, moving with her, as he penetrated her with long, smooth thrusts, of his manhood, feeling her body explode with climaxes, and then later feeling his whole body shudder, when he moaned and climaxed with her.

With both of them feeling as though they had at last been to paradise, Olivia lay in Alex's arms and he felt tears slowly, running down her cheeks. "Hey what's wrong?" Alex asked, kissing her tears away. "Don't cry Olivia, what we just had together was so beautiful, please don't spoil it."

"I'm sorry, and your right it was beautiful more than beautiful, no one has ever made love to me like that before, and I will never ever forget tonight or you."

After spending the rest of the night with Alex, and making love with him, until daybreak. Olivia finally told him, that she must now leave.

"No please don't go, I don't want to lose you, not just yet."

"But I'm afraid I must go, I have to."

"Okay then, but only if you feel you must go. But please leave me your phone number, because Olivia, I think I love you, and I will come back into your life one day, I promise."

"That would be nice, very nice," she told him, with a last kiss and a smile, before saying goodbye him.

***

She arrived home at daylight, early the next morning, and although she was very tired, she did not want go to bed to sleep. She was afraid of losing, the memory of Alex, and of the wonderful, night of love they had made, while spending it together, it kept on repeating itself over and over in her mind, and she was hanging on to every treasured, minute of it. She later made herself tea and toast for breakfast, and then played her records as she laid down, on the carpeted, floor of her Lounge, while thinking only of Alex, and her wonderful, night of love, that she had spent with him.

***

Her phone rang at lunchtime; it was Diana saying her and Jackie, where coming over for lunch.

When they arrived, Diana opened a can of soup for them all, while Jackie, cut some slices of bread in half, putting it on a plate.

"Did I tell you," Olivia said, while they were sat in her Dining-room, eating their lunch. "That I've asked Clive if he'll take me to America, 'cause I'm sick of living over here."

"Is that one of your crazy ideas of the moment?" Diana asked.

"No, it's not a crazy idea," Olivia replied. "And you know I asked him to take me to Woodstock a few years ago, but he wouldn't."

"Well, what did he say this time?" Jackie asked, with a smile on her face. "Did you get him to finally agree?"

"No, the bastard didn't," Olivia replied. "He said, in his bloody condescending tone of voice. *'Olivia dear, Woodstock is now over. And the Hippies' dreams in Haight Ashbury, were all just illusions that they were all having, from the different drugs that they were taking. And I would be so afraid of you getting involved with any other communes, like that one of Charles Manson's, that are going on over there.........'*

"But sod him, 'cause one day I just know I'll go to America, I've just got to get there."

"Yeah I'm sure you'll get there one day, if you still feel so strongly about going," Diana agreed.

"Oh, did I tell you my Sister Suzanne, is getting married soon to this terrific man called Rodger," Olivia continued in a happier tone of voice, changing the subject. "I used to go to the same school as him, but he's a lot older than me. And I'm very happy for my Sister, and I think Rodger will be a good husband to her. But I'm pissed off at my friend Angel though. She told me the other night, that she's going to marry this farmer, who I think is bloody ugly and looks just like one of his farm pigs. He's from one of the other villages Grindleford. And I don't know where the hell she found him, or how she got in with him, or how she can possibly luv him, 'cause he's just horrid. I've met him a few times and I can't stand him, and when I think of all the great, good-looking, boyfriends Angel's had, I could bloody shake her. She came over here with him last week, and the bastard had the bloody nerve to ask me out for a date with him, when Angel went upstairs to the bathroom. I couldn't believe it, I just felt like smacking him in the face, so I told him to just piss off, and not to come around here again."

"Well, did you tell Angel that he came on to you, and he's asked you for a date?" Jackie asked.

"No, I just don't know what to do, or how to tell her, and it's probably best if I don't say anything and let her find out about him for herself," Olivia replied. "The trouble is Angel says she's going to marry this Peter Crosby very soon, and I'm so afraid of her getting hurt. I love Angel so much, and she's been my best friend for years, we grew up together, but I have a feeling I won't be seeing her very often now, especially when she's married to that bastard. I have a strong feeling that he'll keep her away from me, in case I tell her about him."

"Well you'll have to do what you think is right, won't you? But I'd bloody tell her, poor girl. She should know what she's getting herself into," Diana said.

"You're sounding very cynical in your old age Diana," Jackie replied.

"Yes, I probably am. Now tell us about last night Olivia? That's if you've got anything interesting to tell us," Diana said.

"Like what?" Olivia asked, with a happy, smile and a twinkle in her eye, lowering her head and looking at the pattern on the carpeted floor.

"Come on don't act coy, tell us did you have a good time at the 'Penny-Farthing'? And did you meet anyone nice?" Jackie asked.

"Yes, I did have a good time, and yes I did meet someone nice, very nice indeed," Olivia replied, with a big, dreamy smile on her face. "In fact, I'd say, I had a terrific time when I met Alex, who could be the very man of my dreams."

Olivia told Diana and Jackie about Alex, and going back to his hotel room with him, after leaving the Disco. And the beautiful love they made together all night, and that on leaving him, he said he would phone her one-day. "But I must go to bed and get some sleep now," Olivia said, stretching and yawning. "I'm just so bloody exhausted, and I'm dancing at some pub for Kenny tonight. And Clive is coming home tomorrow, so I have to try and do some more baby making."

One month later Olivia knew that at last, she was pregnant.

******

Chapter 27

EIGHT MONTHS LATER.

"Mummy, Mummy," five year old Antony shouted, as he came running in through the front, door of his home one tea time. "Is my tea ready yet?"

"Yes it is," Olivia shouted to him, from the kitchen. "It's your favourite meal this evening, tomato sausage, with mashed potatoes and baked beans. Now go and wash your hands before I serve it out."

"Okay Mummy I will," Antony said, running up the stairs to the bathroom, as fast as he could.

"Antony will you stop eating your meal so fast, and putting so much into your mouth," Olivia said, scolding her Son.

"I'm Sorry Mummy but I'm in a hurry, Marcus is waiting for me. And is it okay if I go back to his house when I've finished my tea? 'Cause we're playing a good game of Cowboys and Indians. Aunty Diana says I can go back if it's all right with you. And where's my Daddy? Why isn't he having tea with us? He told me he was going to get me a new Hot Wheels car."

"Oh did he? Well he's in London on one of his business trips for a few days. And yes, you can go back to play with Marcus, if it's okay with your Aunty Diana, but only for another hour. Don't forget you've got school in the morning, so be home by seven thirty for your bath."

"Okay Mummy thanks. And I'll try and be home on time for my bath tonight, I was a bit late home from Marcus's last night wasn't

I?" Antony replied, before putting far to much food into his mouth, eating his tea even faster now, and hoping that his Mommy wasn't noticing.

***

After he had finished his tea Antony, went back around the corner to his Aunty Diana's house in Cedars Lane, to continue playing with his friend Marcus, while Olivia washed, dried and put away the pots in her kitchen.

She then went into the porch and took the local, evening 'Sheffield-Star', newspaper out of the letterbox and going to sit down in a chair to relax in the Lounge, by the side of the gas fire. Now holding the lower part of her back, where she felt a bad, pain beginning to start as her baby, began to kick wildly inside of her. She then opened the folded, newspaper reading the headlines of it.

'Angela Crosby Killed In Tragic Car Crash Late This Afternoon.'
'She Was Five Months Pregnant With Twin Girls And They Died With Her.'

Olivia sat there just staring in disbelief, at the headlines of the newspaper, reading it over and over again and again, aloud to herself. "No! No!" She shouted, "No! There must be some mistake, someone has got this all wrong! It can't be true! Angel can't be dead! She isn't dead!"

Panicking she ran out of the house, taking the newspaper with her, jumping over the small, wall separating the two driveways, and ran into James and Cassandra's house.

James and Cassandra were sat at their dining-room table having their tea, with their Children, when Olivia ran through to them, into their dining room, thrusting the newspaper into James' hand shouting, "It can't be true! There's been some mistake somewhere! Angel isn't dead! She can't be dead! Whoever wrote this is mad, tell them James, tell them they've got the wrong name! And my friend isn't dead!"

With a look of shock on his face, at seeing Olivia in this upset state, James took the newspaper from her hand that she was thrusting at him, and looked at the headlines reading them out aloud, "Angela Crosby Killed In Tragic Car Crash Late This Afternoon."

"Oh my God! Is this the Angela, James and I have met and know? Your old school friend? Oh my God, this is just unbelievable," Cassandra said, in a totally shocked tone of voice.

"Yeah! But someone must have got it wrong, it just can't be my Angel!" Olivia shouted, beginning to cry hard.

"Come on! Shush, shush, shush! This all too much of a shock for you Olivia, and just too much for you to have to deal with right now. But come on please don't go getting yourself too upset Olivia," Cassandra said, getting up from the table and putting her arms around Olivia's shoulders, to try and comfort her. "Try and take it easy now, think of your baby."

James, in a stunned, whispered voice, continued to read from the newspaper in disbelief, "She Was Five Months Pregnant With Twin Girls And They Died With Her. Oh my God no!"

"No! No! It can't be true! Angel! Angel! Where are you? Angel! Angel! Let me see you? Let me know that you're still alive? There's just got to have been some mistake!" Olivia screamed out in a long, deep, soul-searching cry. Before passing out onto the floor with her own baby, kicking wildly inside of her.

"Oh my God, James," Cassandra said, in a very worried voice. "Come and help me to pick Olivia up, and lay her on the couch, she's just passed out."

"Quickly phone for an Ambulance," James said, laying Olivia's limp body on the couch. "I think she's passed out through shock, and her breathing seems to be very shallow. But what a hell of a way to find out, how your best friend has just died, from the headlines in a bloody newspaper."

After phoning for an ambulance and knowing that one was on its way, Cassandra then phoned Diana. "Hello Diana, this is Cassandra, Olivia's friend Angel, died in a very bad car smash this afternoon. Olivia's here but she's passed out through the shock of it all, and I've just called an Ambulance. Have you any idea where her Husband is?"

"What did you just say? That Angela's dead? Oh no! Olivia must be devastated, those two were like twins. How's she doing? Is she breathing okay? Do you want me to come round there?" Diana asked, in a shocked tone of voice. "Antony's here with Marcus, and he told me his Dad's in London on business."

"Well could you keep Antony there with you please and look after him? James and I will go with Olivia, to the hospital. Oh and could you please phone Jackie? And ask her if she will come over to my house, and look after my children for me until we get back?"

"Yes that's no problem Cassandra I'll do that. And please call me from the hospital, to let me know how Olivia is okay?"

"Yes okay, I will, bye for now."

Cassandra hung up the phone, as the Ambulance pulled into her driveway. Cassandra met the two Ambulance-men, at the door and explained to them what had happened. One Ambulance-man went into the house to see Olivia, while the other one went to get the oxygen.

When the oxygen mask was placed over Olivia's, nose and mouth, she opened her eyes and moaned, putting her hand on her stomach. "How do you feel?" One of the Ambulance-men asked.

"It hurts, my stomach hurts."

He placed his hand on Olivia's stomach, to feel for any tightening. "She's in labour," he said. "Let's get a stretcher."

Which hospital are you due to have this baby in?" The other Ambulance-man asked her, after they lifted her onto the stretcher.

"Jessops."

"Okay, Jessops, here we come fast," the Ambulance-man said.

She was being carried out of the house on a stretcher to the Ambulance, when Jackie arrived, and she took hold of Olivia's hand to comfort her, saying, "I'm so sorry to hear of Angela's death, I know you loved her very much, it must have been a hell of a shock to you Olivia, but I hope you'll be okay soon."

Olivia just tried to smile at Jackie, through her tears for Angel.

"Cassandra, you go in the Ambulance with her and I'll follow you in the car," James said.

"Jackie, do you think you could look after my children please? Until we get back? Rachel's going to Brownies and Andrew's going to Cubs, and Jema and Lucy need to be put to bed in an hour," Cassandra quickly asked her, before getting into the Ambulance.

"Yes okay, it's no problem I'll see to the kids for you," Jackie replied. "Oh and by the way has Olivia gone into labour? Diana didn't say that she was in labour, but with a shock like that it could easily bring it on."

"Yes the Ambulance-men have just confirmed that she's gone into labour, and I'm not surprised either with a shock like that," James replied. "But she'll be okay though, they'll look after her at the hospital."

"Oh, I must tell Diana, and promise you'll phone me here when she's had the baby?"

"Yes we will," James replied, going to get into his car.

***

One hour later at 7 PM that evening, on the 14th April 1972, Olivia gave birth to Identical-Twin Girls. Four hours after Angel and her Twin-Baby-Girls had died with her.

***

Later the next day Clive, arrived at the hospital carrying, a large bouquet of flowers and a congratulations on the birth of your Twins, card.

Olivia soon found out the lovely flowers and card were not from Clive at all, but instead they were sent from all the men, who worked at his factory.

"That's very sweet of them all, to send me these flowers and this card. And as you can see, nearly all of my family and friends have sent me cards and flowers. The first lovely bouquet that arrived was from my Aunty Winnie and Uncle Alan, and even your Sister Janet and your Parents have sent me flowers. But I don't see any at all from you Clive."

"I've been too busy to even think about getting you any flowers. My Father phoned me at the hotel down in London, to tell me that you'd had twin girls, and what a shock that was. So I drove straight back up to Sheffield, as fast as I could. And just after calling in at work first, I've come straight here to see you. But where are the babies Olivia?"

"They're in an incubator at the moment. There's nothing wrong with them, but the Doctors have told me that they just want to be on the safe side, and watch them for a few hours before they are brought to my room. A Nurse will take you to see them before you go. Have you heard about Angel's death? And I think it's Angel's babies that

I've just given birth to, how do I know? 'Cause I can just feel it is. And Angel couldn't have her babies 'cause she died, so I've had them for her. Why, oh why did Angel have to die?" Olivia asked, now beginning to cry hard, whilst holding in her hand, the Saint-Christopher-medallion that Angel, had given to her a few years ago, after her own car smash had happened. "She can't be dead, she just can't be, there was just too much life in her for it to be taken away so fast. She will never ever be dead to me, I'll never accept it, and one of my babies will be called Angel."

"Please don't cry Olivia, you'll only make yourself ill," Clive said, putting his arms around her. "And if you think it's Angel's-Babies that you've just had, you'll have to get strong and look after them won't you? Or she won't be very pleased with you, if you let her down, will she?"

"Yes, your right Clive, I must look after Angel's babies for her, but I've got so much pain in my stomach at the moment. And I didn't know I was going to have a Caesarean until the Doctors told me it was a big baby, that I was going to have, and it would be easier for us both, if they put me to sleep for a short while, until I gave birth to it. And when I woke up, the Nurses told me that I had got Identical-Twin Girls. And God what a shock that was."

***

A few days later, Margaret and Suzanne came to visit Olivia, and they were shocked to find her with a saline drip in her arm, and tubes up her nose, going down into her throat, all attached to a machine at the side of her bed.

"Whatever has happened to you?" Margaret asked, in a very, concerned tone of voice, as she kissed her Daughter on the cheek.

"I don't really know. But I'm in a lot of pain due to some air that seems to have got inside of me, during the Caesarean operation," Olivia replied, with difficulty speaking because of the tubes that went up her nose and down her throat. "So the Doctors have put me on this machine, to pump the air out of my stomach."

"Oh my God! How did that happen to you?" Suzanne asked, in a surprised tone of voice. "We had no idea you had a Caesarean section, and were in this state, Clive never told us. And we've brought you lots of fruit and chocolates to eat, and Dad's sent you a bottle of shandy that he's made up for you, and some bags of cheese and onion crisps."

"Well at the moment I can't eat or drink anything, but don't worry about me, I'll be okay soon when all this air is pumped out of me. And the Nurses keep giving me injections every three hours for the pain, because it's so bad. So don't be surprised if I just fall asleep on you, while your talking to me."

"Oh, isn't she's just beautiful!" Margaret said, looking at the baby laying in a crib next to Olivia's bed. "Can I pick her up? And where's the other twin?"

"Yes, please pick her up Mum and hold her," Olivia replied. "Because I haven't held her yet at all myself, I just haven't got the strength to, and the Nurses always come and give her, her bottle. And I haven't seen my other twin yet, she's still in an incubator."

"Well is she okay? And will we be able to go and see her?" Margaret asked.

The door to Olivia's Hospital room was opened wide, and a Nurse wheeled into it another baby crib, saying, "Here you are Olivia, here's your other Baby-Twin-Girl, and she's just as lovely as the other one. She's just come out of the incubator and she wants feeding now, so I'll just get her a bottle."

"Could I feed her please?" Suzanne asked the Nurse hopefully.

"Yes, you can if you want to," the Nurse replied. "But just put this white gown on over your clothes first, please."

"Oh she's just so beautiful," Suzanne said, picking up the other baby and holding her in her arms showing her to Olivia. "She's just like porcelain."

"Yes, she is," Olivia agreed. "But why is her skin so white, and the other twin's is so red?"

"Because they're identical twins," the Nurse replied. Pointing to the twin who was still laid asleep in her crib. "That's twin one, and she took all the red-Corpuscles, and that's why this twin, twin two, is so very white and pale looking."

"Well will my twin number two, be okay? Without any red-Corpuscles?" Olivia asked.

"Oh yes, there's nothing to worry about at all, the Corpuscles will sort themselves out and grow okay, now that they've been born," replied the Nurse.

"I'm going to call twin one, Sarah Marie, and twin two, Angel Tanya," Olivia said, looking at her perfect, baby-twin-girls, as she began to cry. "I know Angel will like those names, and that she's watching over us. Please help me to get better Angel? So that I can look after your babies."

"They're not Angela's babies that you've had, they're your babies," Margaret said to Olivia, with tears in her own eyes. "Your Dad said that he thought you would be having twins, a long time ago, because you were so big during your pregnancy. And didn't you know his Grandmother had twins twice? Your Granddad Oliver is a twin, and you're the first one to have the twins back, into the family since your Great- Grandmother, Elisa Jane, had them."

"Oh is that what you all think?" Olivia replied. "Well if that's so? Where are Angels poor babies then?"

"They probably died with her, Olivia," Suzanne said, while holding her hand and crying with her, over the loss of Angela to them both.

When visiting time was over, Margaret and Suzanne left Olivia and her twins sleeping. But she did not know that Suzanne had wanted to tell her, that she went to Angela's funeral the day before, to say goodbye to her from Olivia, and had a wreath of flowers sent for Angela, from her. Suzanne felt that Olivia was far too ill to be told that Angela was now buried, in the church yard in Bradwell, and she thought that Olivia would think that everyone went to Angela's funeral except her, her best friend. But she knew that in time she would later have to tell her, but not until she felt she was much stronger and better, from the birth of her own Baby-Daughters.

***

About seven days later Olivia, was taken off the stomach pump and saline drip, and when the clips were removed from her stomach the next day, she was allowed to take a most welcomed, bath. She then began to feed and bath her Baby-Twins herself now, and the firm, bonding between them all began to grow, as she felt eager and ready to take them home with her.

The Nursing-Sister of the maternity ward asked Clive, if he could get someone in at their home, to help Olivia take care of her babies. As she told him, it would be too much for her to do all alone, because she had been so very, ill and was still weak, and also had some stitches inside of her, that were still healing. Clive eagerly agreed with the Sister and promised her, that he would gladly take two weeks off from work to stay at home with Olivia, to help her himself, to get everything done, until she felt and got stronger in herself.

***

The morning Clive took Olivia home from the Hospital, they went into the city to shop at 'Mothercare', to buy more nappies, Babygrow-outfits, vests, feeding-bottles and bibs for the twins. She also cancelled the pram that she had already ordered from that store, instead choosing a twin-pram that was on display there.

They then went to a 'Berni Inn Restaurant' for a steak dinner before Clive drove her home, so that she would be there when Antony, her Son, arrived home from school.

"I've just got to go and pick Father up from work now, and take him home," Clive said. "Because his car is in the garage being repaired, but I won't be long."

"Oh, can't someone else from the works take him home?" Olivia asked. "Because I have to feed the twins now, and Antony will want his tea soon, and I'm feeling tired. I could do with your help at the moment Clive."

"No I'm sorry but I've got to see about my Dad getting home first. So I'll phone Jackie and see if she can give you a hand, until I get back, okay?"

Clive had still not returned home by eight o'clock that evening, so Olivia phoned his Parents and found he was still at their house, having drinks with them, to celebrate the birth of the Twins. He arrived home at about ten o'clock that night, and went straight to bed, falling into a deep sleep. While Olivia woke up every three hours, at the first hungry cry of her Twin-Babies, to feed and change them both herself.

***

The next morning with hardly any sleep from the night before, she was up very, early to cook Clive and Antony their normal, routine breakfast of bacon and eggs. And when Antony had left for school, she asked Clive if he would fill a bucket with some warm, water and pour it in the baby-bath, so that she could give the twins their morning bath, before their next feed.

"Can't you wait until I get back, before you bath the babies?" Clive asked.

"No, and get back from where? Get back from what? Where the hell are you going?" Olivia asked, in a surprised tone of voice. "There's a pile of breakfast pots in the kitchen waiting to be washed. And I thought you said that you'd be helping me, with things,"

"I know I did, and the house needs cleaning, but at the moment I have to help my Father out first. He needs a lift into work, his car's not ready yet it's still in the garage."

"I don't fucking believe this," Olivia said, in an angry voice. "Why didn't the old bugger arrange for someone else to take him into work? Or why can't he get a bloody taxi? 'Cause he can sure afford one."

"I'll phone Jackie and see if she can help you again, until I get back."

"No you bloody well won't phone Jackie, she's not my Mrs. Scrubit. I'll manage by myself."

The twins now began to cry for attention, while Olivia was getting their bath ready for them.

"Now look what you've done Olivia," Clive said, in his condescending tone of voice, before he left the house. "You've upset the babies now, and Angel is not going to be very pleased with you for doing that, now is she? And I do wish you wouldn't get yourself so upset and swear at me Olivia, over nothing. And you must know that it's not good for the babies, to hear you shouting and being so angry around them. Now do try and calm down dear, and I'll be back to help you with things later."

"Oh fuck off. Just fuck off will you," Olivia shouted, feeling overwhelmingly loaded down and helpless.

And things only got a lot worse for Olivia, when Clive, did not take the two weeks off work to help her, as he had promised that he would. Instead he always seemed to have an excuse for somewhere to go to, someone that he had to see, or something else that he had to do. He never once helped her to feed, or changed the twins, or even had time to hold them, feeling that was solely, Olivia the Mothers job to do. Along with cleaning the house, washing, ironing, and cooking his meals on time, when he was at home.

She never seemed to have any break, in this daily routine of hers, and she got very, little sleep during the nights, due to still having to give the twins, their feed every three hours. She wasn't eating very often, and most days she could not get herself bathed or dressed, until later in the afternoon, because she was always so busy with things that she still had to do.

Whenever she saw Clive now, they just argued all the time, and when she even, pleaded and cried to him for some help. He just laughed at her, in her time of weakness, telling her. That he didn't know what her problem could be, as he thought she was managing and doing quite well, and okay by herself.

Of course over a period of time, Olivia got herself very, run down, and became very, depressed with being so overloaded with everything. Especially when she found out about her friend, Angel's death, and how it had happened. That she had died in a car-accident that had been very similar to her own, like the one that she was in a few years ago. When Angela's, Husband, Peter, had picked her up from work one afternoon, and he was driving far, too fast, on the wrong side of the road, over-taking another car, when he ran into a bus. And the head on crash with the bus had thrown Angela straight through the car windshield, with all of her body hitting the bus, face and headfirst, and her dying instantly on the impact of it. And her Parents Eileen and Jack not being able to identify their Daughter, Angela, by her once, beautiful, lovely face, because it was so grossly, badly, smashed up, broken and damaged, that she was unrecognizable to anyone, any more. And not being able to attend Angel's, Funeral-Service, to say her last goodbyes to her.

Olivia spent most of her days always crying, with not seeming or wanting to ever stop. On one of their visits to see her and the twins one day, Diana and Jackie decided that it was now time to phone their local, Doctor, asking him to go and see Olivia, because they felt that she now needed some sort of help, from somewhere.

***

After what he had been told, Doctor Hamlin was so pleased that Clive was still there at home, the morning that he arrived, to see, examine and talk with Olivia. And after seeing for himself the completely exhausted, physical, mentally, depressed and emotional state, that she was in. The Doctor felt that he had no other alternative, but to give Clive a choice about his worn out wife, who was on the verge of a very, serious breakdown. And his choice was that if he did not get someone in right away, like the very next day, to take care of all the housework for her, while she just looked after her babies and herself, he would have to put her and the babies into the hospital for a long time, until he felt that she was fully recovered and better.

On hearing how serious the Doctor was about things, Clive agreed straight away to get someone in immediately to help his wife. So he went out and put a card in the local newsagent's window, asking for: -

A CLEANING LADY TO WORK AT OUR HOME FIVE DAYS A WEEK.

A lady in her forties called Mrs. Denton, phoned for an interview later that day, and eagerly took the job immediately, starting the next morning, and also asking Olivia, if she could help her with her babies at all?

This made life much easier for Olivia, who could now devote all of her time to just looking after her baby-twins and herself, while Mrs. Denton happily did all the cleaning of the house, the washing, drying, and ironing of clothes, and even preparing the vegetables that would be cooked that evening for Dinner.

Doctor Hamlin often stopped in at the house, when driving by in his car, just to see how Olivia was doing and if she was beginning to feel any better in herself.

***

Many months later after everything that had happened between them, since the birth of the Baby-Twin-Girls. Clive and Olivia were still arguing most of the time, and they just didn't seem to be able to get along together with each other anymore.

Clive was still travelling away from home on business, and when he was at home he began to go out by himself at nights, and not return home until daylight the next morning. When Olivia, asked him where he had been, he would tell her that he, had just been out with friends, partying with them throughout the night.

Different men began to telephone the house, asking to speak to Clive, and when Olivia told them that Clive was away, and asked who wanted to speak to him, they refused to leave their names and phone numbers, or any messages at all for him. Saying only that they would phone back when he arrived home.

Clive just didn't want to have anything much to do with Olivia, anymore at all over the next few months. And he stopped taking her out to dinner once a week, or even up to the local-pub for a drink, to give her a break in her very busy routine of life, being a full time wife and mother. Their sex life had seemed to become nonexistent between them at all now.

But she was still a young girl at the age of twenty-two, who needed much more in her life, than just the love of her wonderful Children.

******

Chapter 28

Clive was getting himself ready to go out one evening, and when Olivia saw him stood in-front of the mirror in their bedroom, putting 'Brut'-after-shave-lotion all over his freshly shaved face. She thought that this was the right time to ask him, to stay in tonight, to come down stairs and talk with her.

"Stay in tonight for what? And what do you want to talk about?" Clive asked, sitting down in a chair in the Lounge, and lighting up a cigarette, before looking at the time on his watch. "You'd better make this quick because I have an appointment."

"Us and our marriage, that's what I want to talk about. Things just can't go on like this anymore."

"What about our marriage? I don't see anything wrong with it, and what more could you want? You've got a lovely home and two beautiful baby-daughters, a good standard of living. And haven't I've told you often enough, that I still love you? So what more do you want?"

"No you haven't. And I don't think we've got a bloody marriage anymore," Olivia replied, now getting angry, thinking Clive was being very cold and uncooperative. "I think we have a marriage in name only, and I want more than that."

"Don't you think you're expecting a bit too much out of life Olivia dear?"

"No! Not when I only want a husband who loves me, spends time with me, shows me some kindness, and wants to make love to me. Not a bloody man who doesn't see me, and uses our home like it was a fucking hotel, I'm just sick of it. And if you don't love me anymore and want to make love to me, why don't you tell me, instead of keeping me hanging on, and for what?"

"Have you finished now Olivia dear?" Clive asked, in an unconcerned tone of voice, looking at his watch again before standing up and walking towards the door and opening it. "I haven't got time to discuss this now, because as I've already told you, I've got an appointment to keep."

"Will you stop calling me what you call your bloody mother? 'Cause I'm not your bloody old dear. And Clive this is our marriage I want to discuss with you, so please don't go out tonight. Because if you do, I promise, you will never get back in here again. So do you now understand me?"

"Please don't try to threaten me in any way Olivia dear. And don't even bother waiting up for me either, because I'll probably be late getting home tonight," Clive replied, walking out of the front door and closing it behind him.

"That's not a threat, it's a fucking promise you bastard," Olivia shouted, angrily after an uncaring Clive.

The very sad now deep-rooted problem with their marriage, was one that Olivia would never realize or ever be able to comprehend, as it was really solely, Clive's problem. Yes the problem! A fact being totally unbeknown to her, was since she had given birth to the baby-twins, Olivia had changed! Grown-up in herself, got older and went forward in her life, with the responsibility of trying so hard to be a good caring mother to her babies. This change was something that had just come very naturally to her. But it was a change which Clive saw and also felt that he did not like or could cope with, this changed girl a different Olivia! Which frighteningly seemed to take away from him, her once child-like, dependent innocence and helplessness, which he loved to have. No! This newfound confidence, which she had acquired in herself, he did not like it at all! He much preferred the happy-go-lucky, pretty, wild, crazy, laughing, Go-Go-dancing, Hippy, teenage girl that she used to be, whom he felt needed him so much, that he could and would always be able to control. But now with her youth and innocence disappearing so quickly after the birth of her babies, and this aura of seriousness that she seemed to have around her, this only made him now feel so cold and uncaring towards her.

As he just longed for a young girl's youth and vulnerability, which helped to keep him feeling very young and needed, and so joyously youthful in himself.

***

She stayed up until very late that night, waiting for Clive to return home, hoping that there was still a chance to sort out the problems in their marriage. But by three o'clock the next morning, when Clive had still not arrived home, she was beginning to feel very angry with him now, and thought it would be pointless and too late to try and discuss with him, all the good ideas she had had about how they could possibly try to save their marriage. So in her anger she began searching through the kitchen drawers, to find a large roll of masking tape.

She found the tape and after locking all the doors securely, she then sealed the doors by sticking tape all around them, turning the key and taping it into the lock of the back door, knowing that Clive, would then be unable to push the key out and open it with his own key. She checked the front door again making sure that the safety-catch on the Yale-lock was down and in place, so a key could not be inserted into the lock. Feeling satisfied with herself and thinking that Clive would now know that she meant to do business with him, about their failing marriage whether he wanted to or not. But before going upstairs to her bed, she poured herself a glass of Scotch and lemonade and before taking the first drink of it, she raised her glass up saying aloud, *'Now try and get in you bastard.'*

She lay very still in her bed unable to sleep, waiting and listening for Clive, to arrive home.

Finally at daybreak, she heard his car pull up and stop in their Drive-way, heard him get out of the car, closing the door quietly, heard him trying to get his key into the lock on the front door, but after a few tries he gave up. She next heard him trying to get his key into the back door lock, but soon realizing he could not unlock either of the doors at all, Clive got back into his car and drove away.

Olivia smiled to herself before finally falling into a deep, dreamless sleep, before soon having to get up and see to her Children that morning.

***

Clive did not contact Olivia all of that week, but he arrived at her house the following Monday just before midnight, with a tall, blonde haired, blue eyed, well-muscle-built-man, whom she had never seen before.

"What the hell do you want at this time of night?" Olivia asked, when opening the front door.

"I've come to get my clothes," Clive replied, stepping inside the house.

"Not at this bloody time of night you're not, and who the hell is he? Have you brought some big muscle man with you, to try and frighten me?" Olivia asked, before slamming the door shut and locked, in the other man's face.

She then quickly ran passed Clive, who was walking up the stairs, and stood in front of him, at the top of the stairs, on the landing.

"Don't you dare come any bloody further Clive," she said, in a very, threatening tone of voice. "The Children are fast asleep, and I'm not going to let you wake them up, by opening and closing drawers and wardrobes getting your clothes out."

"Stop being so silly, will you Olivia? And just get out of my way dear, or I will have to hit you."

"Not if I fucking hit you first," Olivia replied, punching Clive hard in the face, and laughing as he fell all the way backwards down the stairs. "Now just get the fuck out of here, and don't you dare come back at this time of night again, trying to upset me and my Children."

Clive picked himself up from the bottom of the stairs, holding his bruised and swollen nose and cheek with his hand, and cursing loudly, as he left the house.

Olivia was now shaking when she locked the front door behind him. The drama she had just been through, all seemed to have happened so fast. She looked in on her sleeping children, to see if they had been disturbed at all by what had just happened, but thankfully they slept on undisturbed. Going back downstairs she now began to cry, due to all the emotion that she had just been through, and she telephoned her father, telling him about Clive arriving at this time of night, with one of his big-muscled-friends, to try and frighten her. She also told her father that she had hit Clive, and was afraid now because of the way he had left the house, without his clothes, hurt, and very angry, and that he might decide to come back at any time to get even with her, while she was sleeping.

Eric told her to call the Police, and ask them to stay with her, for some protection for herself and the children, until he arrived there.

A Police-Officer arrived a short time later. And after she had told him exactly what had happened, he made Olivia a cup of tea, thinking she looked pale and very shaken up, after the ordeal her husband had put her through so late at night, and he stayed there with her until her father arrived.

Eric arrived about an hour later staying for the rest of the night at his daughter's home, while Olivia could now sleep very peacefully upstairs in her bed, knowing that her dad was around to protect her, if she needed him. Eric sat waiting in a comfortable, chair facing the window in the Lounge, with the curtains purposely drawn-back so that they were now wide-open, so that he had a very good view into the street, watching every car that passed by his daughters home at this time of night. Oh yes he was more than eagerly waiting and hoping, that Clive Lemons, would dare to and be brave enough to make another appearance tonight, to try and frighten his daughter again, because Eric was more than ready to deal with him this time, to put all of the wrongs that he felt Clive had handed out to his daughter, finely all very right in his book, by settling many now outstanding scores!

***

The next day Olivia telephoned Clive's father, Mr. Lemons, at his home, leaving a message with him to pass on to Clive. That she had packed all of his clothes and personal belongings up, including the families heirloom, the solid, silver cigarette case, engraved with his initials on, into suitcases and bags. And that they were all in the porch-way of the house, waiting for him to come and collect them, at a very reasonable hour during the day. She knew that it was no good complaining to Mr. Lemons, about his wonderful, son-Clive, turning up at the unreasonable time of night, that he had done the night before, knowing that her complaint to his father, about him, would only fall on deaf ears. Because as her dad had often told her about these people *'There's none as deaf, as those who don't want to hear!'*

Mr. Lemons told Olivia, that he would tell Clive to go and pick his things up, and that Clive was now back at home living with his Mother and him again.

'As if I care! And he always was a stupid mummy's boy anyway, so he should be happy now that he's back with mummy!!!! Olivia thought to herself, as she hung up the telephone.

***

A few days later Mrs. Denton, was watching the twins playing with their toys, they were crawling around everywhere now, and had to be watched all of the time or they would be getting into everything.

Olivia was in the kitchen preparing lunch for the twins, before she would be putting them into their high-chairs to feed them.

"Where's Angel got to Mrs. Denton?" Olivia asked, looking around the two rooms as she came out of the kitchen into the dining-room, with their plates of food.

"I don't know, I thought she'd come crawling into the kitchen to you."

"No, she's not with me, I bet she's crawled outside," Olivia said, noticing that the glass-front-door had been left open a bit.

"Oh dear the little monkey, I bet she's just gone crawling outside, I'll go and get her back, I won't be a minute," Mrs. Denton replied, going out of the front door. "No! No! Clive. No! No! Stop!" She screamed out loudly, as Clive drove his Jaguar very fast up the driveway, before his tires came to a screeching halt.

Olivia ran out of the house when she heard Mrs. Denton's screaming, and saw Clive's car stop and him get out of it. "Where's Angel? Where is she?" Olivia shouted to him, in a very frightened voice.

"I don't know where she is," Clive replied, in an unconcerned tone of voice. "I'm not looking after her, so I haven't seen her."

"I'm afraid she's under the car somewhere," said a very, frightened Mrs. Denton, beginning to shake and cry. "I tried to stop him driving over her, and I can't see her now."

"You fucking bastard," Olivia screamed, flying at Clive and punching him hard with her fists. "You've run over my baby Angel, and I'm going to fucking kill you."

James was in his porch talking on the telephone, and seeing all this happen he quickly, dropped his phone, and ran outside. Looking over the small, wall between the two driveways he saw Angel, laying there very, quietly and still underneath the front of the long, bonnet of the car. A wheel was touching her, but it seemed to him that it had not gone over her little body. "Thank God! It's a bloody miracle she's not dead," James said, jumping over the wall, and pulling Angel out from underneath the car. "She's all right Olivia, she's alive and I've got her. Angel's alive she's okay, he didn't run over her."

Olivia was sobbing now while she was still punching Clive, so very, hard with every ounce of muscle that she could find in her body. When James got her to stop and look at Angel, as he passed her baby, to her to hold.

"Oh My-Baby-Angel! Thank God! My Baby's Not Dead! And if she was, I promise you I'd have fucking killed you," she spat at Clive.

"But I've just come to pick my clothes up, and it's not my fault if Olivia can't look after her babies, is it?" Clive said, full of his own importance, in an unconcerned tone of voice. "And I didn't expect you to be beating me up again dear, 'cause I'm getting a bit sick of it."

"No," James replied, glaring very, hard at Clive. "Nothing is ever your fault, is it? Why don't you just get your things and fuck off, Mister fucking Perfect. 'Cause I'm sure Olivia and the twins are much better off without you ever, coming around here again."

James took a crying Olivia, and her twins, into his own house with him. Cassandra, who had also seen what had happened through her window, was shaking while she made them all some strong, coffee.

"I'm going to call your Parents, and ask them to come over here to be with you for a while," James said. "You've had a hell of a shock Olivia, here drink this drop of brandy it will help to calm your nerves a bit."

After James had telephoned Olivia's parents and told them what had happened. Eric asked Margaret and Suzanne, to go over to Olivia's house to be with them without him. "Because if Clive, has hurt that baby in any way, I swear to God, I will kill that bastard with my bare hands," he said.

***

Olivia finally gave her twins their lunch and changed their nappies, and now held them both very closely to her and kissing them, before putting them into their cots for their afternoon sleep.

"I'm ever so sorry Olivia, about what happened," Mrs. Denton said. "I really thought Angel was with you in the kitchen. I never saw her crawl out of the door."

"It wasn't your fault Mrs. Denton," Margaret replied, pouring everyone a cup of tea. "If that bastard Clive, hadn't arrived when he did, driving his bloody car so fast up the driveway, it would never have happened. Let's just thank God that Angel's all right."

"It's not God that we have to thank that Angel's not dead. It's Angela up there that saved her little life," Suzanne said, pointing her finger up into the air.

"Do you think so?" Margaret asked, in a curious voice.

"Yes Suzanne's right, now I come to think about it," Olivia replied. "I also believe Angel saw what was happening, and stopped it before my little Angel was killed. Because James told me that the wheel of Clive's car, was actually touching her, and only God knows why it hadn't gone over her little body. Yes, I will always be forever thankful to Angel for saving my baby's life."

The next day Olivia telephoned Clive at his work, and told him she wanted a divorce as soon as possible.

***

About a week later, after Olivia's phone call to Clive, letters began to arrive from a firm of Solicitors, called Taylor and Wrigley, informing her that they were representing Clive Lemons, and that their Client wanted his Wife, Olivia Lemons, and her Children to vacate the house. And if she failed to do so within a reasonable length of time, the house would be sold, and she and her Children would be evicted from the building.

The following month, amongst the letters from Taylor and Wrigley, she received one saying their Client Clive Lemons, did not believe that he was the biological-father of the twin-girls, Sarah Marie and Angel Tanya. He wanted them to have blood tests to prove if this was so, before he would pay any child-support for them.

When Olivia received this letter from Clive's Solicitor's, she was very upset and just didn't know what to do. She'd already had to ask her father to help her out with money, so that she could buy food to feed her children and herself. And the advice her father gave her, was to stay put with her children inside of her home, and if Lemons wanted them out, then let him come around and try to force them out of their home, while he was there. Adding that he would gladly do Olivia a favour, by phoning Lemons himself, and inviting him round to come and put Olivia and her kids, out onto the street!!!

******

Chapter 29

Kenny Dee, and his Brother Mike, went to see Olivia, one night, after Kenny had finished doing one of his DJ-gig-shows. "What's been happening in your life?" Kenny asked her, after she'd made them a cup of tea. "Why haven't we heard from you for such a long time? What's wrong?"

She told Kenny and Mike, about her and Clive splitting up, and that her marriage to him was now over. Before passing them the letters to read that she had been receiving from Clive's Solicitors; telling them she just didn't know what to do anymore.

"I'm not surprised your marriage to Clive, is now over," Kenny said, after reading the letters. "I've seen it bloody coming for a long time now. Things have never been right, between you two, since that sodding car smash."

"Don't you think so?" Olivia asked.

"Hell no, because after that crash, which he caused remember? You were both on fucking different wavelengths. And for one, he should never have been going away the way he has been, and leaving you here all by yourself for so bloody long. If you hadn't have been dancing for me you'd have gone bloody crazy, sat here all by yourself waiting for Clive to come home again. And for two, I've got my suspicions about him, but I've no proof yet, so I don't think I should say anything. But I seriously do think that he's a bloody homosexual, and I also think that you've served a good purpose for him, being in his life all these years that you now have," Kenny replied.

"Christ is that what you really think? That's all I bloody need," Answered Olivia. "And what do you think Mike?"

"Well, he's certainly too old for you Olivia, and I always thought that he has been," replied Mike. "He's just a bloody old man that's tried hard to hang on to his youth, by marrying you his child bride. And as for these disgusting letters, it seems to me like he wants to play dirty now. So the first thing that you now have to do Olivia, is get yourself a solicitor, 'cause I don't think by law for one minute, that Clive can throw you and the kids out onto the street, as he seems to want to. I don't think the courts would let him."

"Those poor little twinies, it's not bloody fair to them," Kenny said. "Clive's going to try and use them as a weapon against you Olivia, and you've got to bloody stop him. We've got a good solicitor who also does divorce cases, haven't we Mike? Tell her his name will you 'cause I can't think of it right now, 'cause I'm to upset."

"Yes we have," Mike replied, taking a card out of his wallet. "Here this is their card, Webster, Glover and Walker, it's Mr. Webster that you want to see, he'll sort Lemons out for you. Phone him tomorrow and get an appointment, and Kenny, or me, will take you to see him."

"Thanks Mike I will, and lets hope that he can do something for me, to protect my Children and I. Then I might be able to sleep better at nights," Olivia said, looking closely at the names on the Solicitors card. "I'll phone this Mr. Webster tomorrow and let you know when he can see me."

***

Jackie and Diana went around to Olivia's for coffee one afternoon, and Diana brought Lulu, her beautiful, blue eyed, curly, blonde haired, baby daughter. Lulu was six months older than the twins, and they always sat on the floor together, contented, playing with their toys.

Jackie and Diana could see that Olivia was upset, and after reading the letters from Clive's Solicitors they could understand why. "The bastard, how could he do this to you and the kids?" Diana asked.

"Jackie, I remember a long time ago you told me, that you had something to tell me about Clive, and when the time was right, you'd tell me," Olivia said. Hoping she would now hear something to use as her own weapon against Clive, because at the moment she did not have much on him, except his behaviour towards her and the Children.

"Yes I did, so I might as well tell you now," Jackie replied. "Don and I knew Clive Lemons years ago. We used to go to the 'Dove and Crow' pub every, night for a drink with some friends of ours, and at ten o'clock every night, Clive always used to arrive there and join us. He was always by himself, and he didn't know any of us before. He just wormed his way into our crowd by buying us all drinks, and talking to us. We couldn't stand him, he told us all such bare faced lies, and tried to impress us by telling us about the *'private schools that he went to, and his family estate and the company that he owned.'* And when we used to see him walk into the pub we'd all say, *'Oh Christ, he's here again, let's just ignore him, and he might go away.'* Then after we'd all left the 'Dove and Crow', we would go to one of the discos' downtown and Clive would have the bloody cheek to follow us there without being invited, we just couldn't get rid of him. We all thought he was bloody weird, we were even rude to him but he still wouldn't go away. Anyway for a long time we didn't see him anymore and we thought, *'Thank God, he's found someone else to annoy.'* Then, when Don and I moved into our new house here, we saw Clive one day, getting out of his car in your driveway, and we saw you holding your baby boy. Well, Don and I said, *'Oh hell, Clive Lemons has turned up again'* and we thought you Olivia, and baby Antony, were his children. Then when you came out of the hospital after that car crash, Diana introduced you to me, and told me you were his wife. And when you introduced Clive to Don and me, he acted as though he'd never seen us before in his life. Don and I just couldn't believe it, so Don said, *'Well if that's the game Lemons wants to play, it's no skin off my nose, but I wonder what he's got to hide?'*

"Christ that's a hell of a story Jackie, but you know what? I do believe you," Olivia replied, not very surprised. "Did you know about any of this at all, Diana?"

"No I didn't, she never told me that her and Don knew Clive before. You've been keeping very quiet about all of this Jackie," replied Diana, who had been listening with interest. "But I do know that Dave, Don, James and Cassandra can't stand Clive Lemons at all, and just hate to be in his company. We all put up with the bastard, for you Olivia, because you're our friend and we like you, but certainly not him."

"Well I've got something very strange about Lemons to tell you girls, that I've never told anyone before," Olivia began, after she had gotten more coffee for them all, and milk for the Children. "When I started to go out with Clive, he told me that he used to be a Grand Prix racing driver. And that he didn't go into the army after the war, along with his friends, because he was a Secret Agent working for MI5. And that he used to often go to other countries in the world to assassinate people for our government. He also told me that he gave up working for the MI5 just before he married me."

"What!" Diana said, beginning to choke on the coffee she was drinking. "Oh come on Olivia! Surely you didn't believe that pack of bloody lies did you? Come on now!"

"No, I didn't believe him, but at the time I had no proof to call his bluff and him a liar. So I just let it go over my head, but knowing that in time I would find out the truth," Olivia replied. "And also I've just found out recently, that the company he says he owns, isn't his at all, but it belongs to his Father, and Clive just works there for him. Yes, I've had a strong feeling for many years now, that he's been lying over and over to me."

"Yes, he's a real weirdo alright, and I'm sorry that it had to be you, that he got in with Olivia," Jackie replied. "And don't let these bloody threatening letters from his solicitor frighten you either. And as for the twins having a blood test, well if he doesn't think they're his babies, why didn't he throw you out of the house when you were pregnant, and why didn't he have their blood tested when they were born? He's just clutching at straws for something to fight you with Olivia, and don't you bloody well let him get you down, 'cause he's just not worth it."

"No I'll try not to, but it does seem to be," Olivia answered, with a deep sigh. "And I'm going to see a solicitor tomorrow, and try to put a stop to him threatening me."

"And don't forget to take all these letters from his Solicitors to show them to yours," Jackie reminded her.

"Yeah I will," Olivia replied.

"What happened to someone whom you met called Alex?" Diana asked curiously. "Has he ever been in touch with you, since that night? 'Cause from what I remember, I think there's a good chance he could be the twinies Father, don't you Jackie?"

"Yeah I suppose he could," Jackie replied. "And anything's possible with Olivia, but she's still married to Clive and he wanted her to have a baby, so let the fucking bastard pay."

"Oh yes Alex, the man of my dreams," Olivia said thoughtfully. "I sure do remember him, but he's never phoned me like he said he would do, and I don't suppose I'll ever see him again either now."

***

Kenny took Olivia to see Mr. Webster, the Divorce-Solicitor, and she was very pleased with the meeting she had with him. He told her she would not have to move out of the house with her children, unless Clive Lemons found her somewhere else to live, appropriate to what she had been accustomed to living in. He also told her that he had no right to ask for the twins to have a blood test, and that until circumstances changed dramatically for Olivia, Clive would have to pay maintenance for her and her three Children.

***

The next evening James and Cassandra invited Olivia over to have dinner with them. And over brandy and coffee, she told them that when she had first met Clive, how he had wanted her to believe he had been, a Grand Prix racing driver, a Secret Agent with MI5. And how Jackie and Don had known him years ago, and when he met up with them again, he just acted as though he'd never seen them before.

"And I must tell my Dad all this when I see him, he'll just love to hear it all," Olivia said. "Anyway the good news is my Solicitor says, Clive can't have me and the Children thrown out of the house, and he has to pay maintenance for us. So I've stopped worrying about all of that for now."

"I should think that he does have to pay you bloody maintenance," James replied. "After all the hell he's put you through during your marriage to him. I've also got something else to tell you, that you may find interesting about him, I have thought for a long time now that

Clive Lemons is a homosexual. And on a few occasions since he's left you, I've seen him, early on Saturday mornings, sat in his car in the Tesco-car-park, with his blonde haired boyfriend. I'll have to start carrying my camera around with me, and the next time I see him with his boyfriend, I'll take a photograph of them for you. Because I'm sure he's been a closeted homosexual for years now, and he's been hiding behind you all of this time Olivia, to protect his fucking image and the family name, the bastard."

"You are going to have to get yourself a boyfriend Olivia," Cassandra said quickly, not wanting this horrid, disgusting subject, of Olivia's Husband really being a homosexual to continue anymore. "You're still a very good looking, young girl you know? With a whole life still in front of you to live. What's happened to all the old boyfriends you had?"

"Oh, they all seemed to get their girlfriends pregnant at some time or another, and they're all settled down and married now. But I never had anything serious going on with any of them, they were all just good friends of mine and lots of fun to be with," Olivia replied, with a deep sigh. "And there's only one other man that I've had in mind for a long time now, but I've no idea where he is because he lives somewhere down in London."

***

Olivia and her Children went to stay with her Parents in Bradwell, at the 'White Hart' pub for the weekend. Antony and the twins loved being at their Grandparents and seeing their Aunty Suzanne, who was now married to Rodger and living in a cottage up the steep, hill road from the pub. It was a very happy weekend for everyone, with a lot of celebrating going on when Suzanne announced, on Saturday night in the pub, that she and Rodger were going to have a baby. Her doctor had told her, that morning, that she was four months pregnant.

"I'm very happy for our Suzanne and Roger," Olivia said later that evening, while helping her parents to collect the empty glasses, to wash and dry them, and empty and clean the dirty, ashtrays, after the pub had closed and the customers had all gone home. "I hate to put a damper on the night, but I think I ought to tell you both the good news first, that my Solicitor gave me, and then what my friends have told me about Clive."

After Olivia had told her parents everything that she had been told by her friends about him. Her Father took down a fancy, green bottle from one of the shiny, glass shelves, high up behind the bar, and poured out into two small, fancy glasses 'Baileys Irish Cream'.

"Here come and sit down, and try this our Olivia," Eric said. "It's a drink that I've just got in the other week, and tell me if you like it? It's called 'Baileys Irish Cream'. Then I've got something I've wanted to tell you about Clive Lemons, for a long, long time now, but your Mother wouldn't let me tell you before. Is it all right if I tell her now Margaret? Don't you think it's time she knew?"

"Yes," Margaret replied, coming to sit at the bar with Olivia, and Eric passed her a glass of 'Baileys' to sip. "It won't hurt her now, and I think she has a right to know."

"Do you remember when you were in the hospital after the car smash?" Eric began. "When Clive Lemons, told you how ill he felt and how he wanted to go back to Sheffield? Well, when we came down to see you after he'd left, your Mother and I were shocked. We had no idea that you were there all by yourself, and that he'd bloody well left you, and was back at home in Sheffield, because he never phoned us and told us. Anyway the Sister on your ward, asked your Mother and I if we would go and see the Sister, on the ward upstairs where Lemons had been, because she wanted to see us both. And the Sister on Lemons ward told us that she wanted us to protect our Daughter Olivia, from Clive Lemons, the monster that she is married to. Because one night after Clive had visited you, he went up to the ward he used to be on, and told the Sister and Nurses on duty there, *'That he felt very ill, and could he have an injection for the bad pain he was in.'* So the Sister got his Doctor in to examine him, and the Doctor told the Sister and Nurses, that after examining Clive, *'That there was absolutely nothing wrong with the man at all, that he was now healed and perfectly healthy, and he just wanted babying.'* So, the Sister decided to put him in a bed on the ward for the night, and give him an injection. The next morning when Clive woke up, he told the Sister and Nurses, *'That he'd had a very good night's sleep, the best one since he'd left the hospital. And that injection that they gave him had worked wonders for him, it killed the pain and put him to sleep straight away.'* And the Sister told me and your Mother, that that injection that she gave him, '*Was an injection of pure, clear water*'."

"What!!!" Exclaimed Olivia in a shocked, disbelieving voice, but knowing all to well that her Father would never ever lie to her, especially about something as serious as this. "Water!!! He was injected with pure tap water? And it gave him a good nights sleep because he felt so much better after it!!! All thanks to some fucking water!!!!"

"Yes water, an injection of water took away all of his unbearable pain," Eric replied, with a laugh now. "That's what was in that bloody magic injection that Lemons said worked wonders for him, he'd been injected with water. And then the next day he gave you some bloody sob story, about how ill he felt, and would you mind if he went home. He just wanted to get back to his bloody Mother, that's what Clive Lemons wanted Olivia, his bloody Mummy. He didn't care about leaving you, or what had happened to you."

"Yeah well after what I've been hearing about Clive Lemons recently, from my friends, I can so easily believe what you've just told me Dad, without any questions. And the bloody sick stories about him, just seem to get worse," Olivia knowingly replied.

"Well you know I'd never lie to you Olivia," Eric said. "And anyway why should I? You know I've always told you and our Suzanne, to always tell the truth. But that Clive Lemons, all he does is bloody lie, just one lie after another comes out of his mouth, he doesn't even know how to spell the word truth. And after everything I now know about that bastard, I wouldn't piss on him if he were on fire!"

"I'm also going to tell you something else about him, while he was in the hospital," Margaret added, pouring herself and Olivia another drink of the delicious, creamy 'Baileys'. "It's about something else that the Sister thought we ought to know. A black, male-Nurse worked on Clive's ward, and when Clive went for one of his daily baths, he asked this male-Nurse to go with him because he felt so weak. Well when Clive was laying in the bath, he asked this male-Nurse if he would do some sexual favours for him, but the Nurse refused to, and reported this incident to the Sister, telling her, '*That for personal reasons, he refused to help Mr. Lemons take his bath again*'."

"Well can you blame that poor Nurse, after what Clive had probably asked him to do for him? The sad sick bastard," Olivia replied, with a horrid cold shudder running through her body.

"And do you remember those friends you had, who lived near Chelmsford, Steve and Karen?" Eric asked.

"Oh yes, they were just great wonderful people," Olivia replied. "I wrote to them and thanked them for letting you and Mum stay at their house, when you went down to Chelmsford to see me, and I also thanked them for visiting me in the hospital, even when I was crazy for a while. I had a phone call off Karen a few months after she received my letter and she told me, her and Steve had just moved to Birmingham, and that Steve had got a new job there, I think it was with some company like Avon. But I haven't heard from them since."

"Well, before Clive left you at the hospital, he had been complaining to Steve and Karen about the dirty, damp hotel he was staying in," Eric continued. "So when your Mum and I came down to see you, Steve and I decided to go and have a look at this hotel, and we asked to see the room that Clive Lemons had stayed in, and neither the room, nor the hotel, was damp or dirty. It was a small very clean hotel, but there was certainly nothing wrong with it, and Steve said, he just felt that Clive used the hotel as a means to get you to feel sorry for him, so that he could leave you in the hospital and go home to his Mother. Steve also told me, after seeing the hotel, that he'd finished with Clive Lemons now forever. Because he just didn't know how he could go back up to Sheffield, and leave you in that hospital all alone and so far away from your family and friends. That's why Steve, or Karen always came to see you, they didn't turn their backs on you Olivia, so don't you ever think that. Steve and Karen are wonderful people, and they were very good friends to me and your Mother, through that bloody car smash nightmare, I can tell you."

"Oh yes I know they were and always will be wonderful people. And yes, I have been finding out a lot this week, about the man I married but never knew. Everyone else seems to have known him but me, and from what I've been told I feel I could write a book about this Clive Lemons, and a lot of people would know who the book was about when they read it," Olivia replied, before drinking the rest of her delicious 'Baileys'.

******

Chapter 30

For over two years now, Clive Lemons did not have any contact at all, with Olivia, and her Children. He never telephoned her to see how the Children were doing, nor did he send the Twins a birthday card on their very first birthday.

The courts had given Olivia sole custody of the Children, ordering Clive to pay only a very small maintenance for the Children. And to carry on paying for the mortgage on the house, the electric and gas bills, as this was still the Children's home. It was also impossible for Olivia, to go out to work because she had no one to look after her Children for her at all.

She'd had to let Mrs. Denton, the lady who used to clean her house for her, go, because she could not afford to pay her. And most times the maintenance cheques that Clive did send to Olivia bounced at her bank, and sometimes he even failed to send her any cheques or money at all for a few weeks.

During the times when she had no money for food or clothes, for her Children, her Parents Eric and Margaret would always be there to help her out financially, and often took her shopping to buy groceries. She felt she just would not be able to manage at times without her Parents, especially her Fathers, support and help, and she would always feel, very grateful to them both.

She was still always receiving letters from Clive's Solicitors, asking her to find somewhere else to live, because their client wanted to sell his house, but was unable to with them still living there. Olivia was so used to receiving these types of letters by now, over the last few years, that she would just glance at them quickly, before tearing them up and throwing them away saying, '*Fuck You.*'

Most weekends her parents, or Suzanne's husband Rodger, would pick her and the Children up, and drive them to the 'White Hart' pub so she could be with her family. Her Children loved their Grandparents very much and loved to be with them, and they also loved to see their Aunty Suzanne and Uncle Rodger's children, their Cousins, Gary and Elizabeth. Antony was always asking his Mom, if he could go and live at the pub with his Grandparents, because he told her he felt much happier there, as his Granddad always took him fishing and she didn't.

James and Cassandra and their Children went to live down in Bristol, where James became a partner in a large, Estate-Agent-Company.

Jackie and Don had also moved away, they'd bought themselves a Newsagent's-Shop in Sheffield, and they now lived in a large flat above it.

Diana and David still lived in their house in Cedars Lane, and their Daughter Lulu, and the twins were now the very, best of friends. Lulu and the twins played together every day at each other's houses, and the three of them became inseparable, as though they were triplets. Which nearly drove Olivia and Diana crazy, because what Lulu wouldn't do or wear neither would the twins. With one day the twins and Lulu deciding that they wanted to be little boys instead of girls, and they all began to insist on wearing only jeans or corduroy trousers, refusing to wear any of their pretty, little dresses anymore.

Olivia spent all of her days now completely, devoted to her Children, but her night times were very, lonely all by herself, after she had bathed her Children, and they were fast, asleep in their beds. She could never go out at nights, for a break from her everyday routine, because she never had any spare, money, to pay for a baby-sitter, which she would need to look after her Children.

***

Kenny would call in to see her most nights of the week, after his DJ shows, knowing that she got very lonely. They would drink tea, talk and play records, and Kenny, would try to cheer her up, if she was feeling depressed, by getting her to laugh at funny, things which he told her about, that had happened with the punters, who went to hear him, spin his records. But he couldn't stay more than a couple of hours with her, on his visits, because he had to get back home to Dronfield, to Vicky who was now his Wife.

***

One very, windy, rainy afternoon, Diana and Lulu were at Olivia's house, and while the twins and Lulu were sat playing at the dining-room table, making lots of different pies, with their pastry sets. Diana and Olivia were sat in the Lounge, drinking tea and talking. "It's days like this that get me so depressed," Olivia said, looking through the window. "I just hate the rain, and when I've put the kids to bed tonight, I'll just be sat here all by myself, listening to it pour, down and pound against the windows. It makes me feel so depressed and trapped, as if I've got no way out."

"Yes I know what you mean," Diana replied. "And the weather forecast says it will rain all day today but the sun will shine for us tomorrow. And if it does we can take the kids for a walk down to the farm to watch the cows being milked. Don't let yourself get too depressed Olivia, you should be getting your Divorce hopefully, from Clive soon, so let that happy thought keep you going."

"With that happy thought and another Valium tablet, yeah I should get through," Olivia said, with a laugh, swallowing her second Valium tablet that day.

"Are you still taking your sleeping tablets at night?"

"Oh yes. I take tablets to let me sleep, tablets to wake me up, and tablets to get me through the day. And I know I must be addicted to them all by now, but the Doctor always renews my prescriptions. 'Cause I've told him I just don't feel I can go on without my little pills, my little helpers. Maybe if I felt I had more love in my life, I wouldn't need them. Oh give me a man someone. A real man who would hold me and love me and.........."

"Stop! Stop!" Diana interrupted laughing, as Olivia's telephone began to ring. "I can guess what else you want a man to do for you, but for now just answer the phone, while I make us some more tea and get the kids some milk."

"Hello, this is Olivia speaking," she said, when answering her phone.

"Hello pretty lady, remember me? Alex?" Said a voice on the other end of the line.

"Alex! The Alex?" Olivia said, in a shocked and surprised tone of voice, now feeling her heart beginning to beat wildly inside of her. "God it's Alex!" She shouted to Diana, who was walking out of the kitchen, carrying two mugs of tea. "I don't believe it Diana, this is Alex."

"Do you remember me Olivia?" Alex asked. "I know it's been a long time since you saw me, but I told you I'd phone you one day pretty lady, didn't I? And surely you haven't forgot that terrific night we spent together a few years ago? 'Cause I never will."

"No, no, I've not forgotten you, or that terrific night we had. I'm just in shock at hearing your voice again after all this time. Where are you?"

"I'm in Sheffield and I was wondering if I could see you. Can you get out to meet me tonight?"

"No sorry, I can't come to meet you, 'cause I'm separated from my husband now, and I've no one to baby-sit the kids for me. But I can give you my address and you could come here to see my if you like."

Olivia gave Alex her address, and he told her he would see her very soon, with some steaks to cook and a bottle of wine for them to drink.

"Wow!" Olivia said, sitting down in a chair, as Diana passed her a mug of tea. "The man of my dreams is coming to see me very soon, and I just can't believe it. All I know is that my day won't be as depressing, or boring as I thought it would be now, thank-God."

***

Alex arrived a couple of hours later, and gave a very nervous Olivia, a long loving kiss, and told her how much he had missed her, and had always been thinking of her. He fell in love with her Children immediately, and after she told him about Clive, and how he wanted the twins to have their blood tested, because he didn't think that they were his babies.

Alex looked into the twin's green and silver-grey-flecked eyes, and kissed them both on their cheeks saying, "Me neither, when were they born?"

"Nearly Three years ago, April the fourteenth nineteen seventy two, why?" Olivia asked, looking at him.

"Well, I don't need to have the twin's blood tested, to know that they're my babies. And only my babies could have silver-grey in their eyes, no one else's."

***

After dinner Olivia and Alex bathed the Children together, before putting them to bed. And about an hour later when they had finished drinking the rest of their wine, they went upstairs to her bed to spend a very passionate night with each other.

When daylight came she was lying very contented in Alex's arms, when he told her that he was in Sheffield, for an interview for a job, which he was told was his if he wanted it. He also told her that he loved her very much and wanted to marry her, as soon as she got her Divorce from Clive, and that he also wanted to be a Father to her Children.

"Oh yes Alex, I love you very much too, and I would love to marry you. And I'll also find us another house to live in, so we can have a fresh start together as a real family."

***

Alex went back to London that weekend and came back the following week with all of his clothes and belongings, moving in with Olivia and the Children, until they found a house of their own to live in. He began his new job at a computer company called S.C.C. Ultimate Computer and Program Systems, that had just opened in Sheffield.

Olivia and Diana telephoned Estate-Agents, and looked through the newspapers for houses for sale. "What sort of house are you looking for?" Asked Diana.

"I don't really know, just one very different to this," Olivia replied, looking through a local newspaper. "And this one that I've just found here sounds interesting, listen Diana and tell me what you think? 'Private-Sale', For 10,000 Pounds. Terraced-Villa-House, With Three-Large-Bedrooms, Large-Bathroom, Lounge, Separate-Dining-Room And Kitchen. Recently-Modernised, Gas-Central-Heating-In-Every-Room. 48 Crowfield Road, Sheffield 8."

"Yeah that sounds okay. And it will be about three miles away from here, so it won't be to far away for us to get a bus and visit each other. Yeah go on phone the people, and ask them if we can go and look at the house, this afternoon?"

***

Olivia, Diana and the three children, all went in a taxi to see the house at 48 Crowfield Road. The taxi driver turned onto a very, quiet, tree lined street, and began to drive slowly down the road looking for the house number 48. He stopped outside a large, house with the number 48 marked very, clearly on the cream, painted, front, door, with a 'For Sale' sign in the window. "Here you are ladies," he said. "I think this is what you're looking for."

"Great, thanks." Olivia said nervously, looking at the house, through the taxi window.

"Do come in," said a young, tall man, with dark hair, and blue eyes, who answered their knock on the front door.

"Oh! I do like this room," Olivia said immediately, as she walked into a Lounge. "It's so big and bright in here."

"Yes you'll find it is a very big house, it goes high-up and far-back. And my name is John Ellis the owner," the man said, shaking hands with Olivia and Diana. "Now let me show you ladies the rest of the house, I'm sure you'll like it."

As John Ellis took them all on a tour of the house, Olivia fell in love with it immediately, with a feeling inside of herself, telling her that, '*Yes I could definitely live here.*' Every room was very, large and nicely, decorated. "Oh yes I can see myself living here, I just love this house," she said. "Would you mind if I use your phone please John? To ask my Alex, to go and get a mortgage for it for us, from somewhere this afternoon? Because I do want to buy this house. What do you think about it Diana, do you like it?"

"Oh yes I do like it very much, and I could live in this myself, I think it's just great. And it's such a lovely, big house and every room seems so lovely and bright. You know these older houses are always so much bigger, than the ones that we now live in. And I love the way this one has been modernised. Now you go and phone Alex, to get a mortgage for it Olivia."

Olivia phoned Alex at work, and he said he would get on to the 'National Building Society', straight away to get a mortgage for this dream house, which she told him she had found for them all, to be their new home. She also told him that Diana, would baby-sit for them tonight, while she brought him, here to look at the house that they were buying.

That evening, after they had seen the house, Alex told Olivia that he liked it very much and he had arranged everything with the Building Society to get a mortgage to buy it.

***

Clive Lemons' Solicitors wrote to tell Olivia, that their Client had informed them that she could have everything out of the marital home, all the furniture, carpets, curtains and pots and pans as part of the divorce settlement, plus 4000 pounds cash from the sale of his house. Olivia was pleased with what Clive was allowing her to have, because in the beginning of their separation, which now seemed to her to be a hundred, years ago, Clive's Solicitors informed her, that their Client, was not prepared to give her anything at all in terms of a settlement, except the Children.

"Oh, let him keep his fucking money, if it means that much to him," Alex said. "Because apart from a lonely life, and that's all he's got and going to have at his age now. I'm certain he'll never be able to find anyone as beautiful as you again, Olivia. I wonder when he'll begin to realise who and what he's lost? Maybe that's why he's taking so bloody long in letting you have a Divorce. Maybe he doesn't want you or the Children, to have any happiness without him."

"I really don't understand him? And I don't want to fight or argue with Clive, I just want my Divorce so I can get on with my life. And I've even told him that he can Divorce me, if it will help to save his precious family name in Sheffield, but he still won't let me go.

Anyway my Dad has told me that a new Divorce law has been passed recently, and is now in effect, so he has to give me my Divorce in the next few weeks, my Solicitors must tell him."

***

Olivia spent the next month packing things into large cardboard boxes and washing curtains. She had to get some wardrobes for her new house, because the ones in Clive's house were built into the walls of the bedrooms. So one day she decided to try to find a man called Ken Morris, whom Clive had introduced her to some time ago. All she knew about Ken Morris, a man with sandy hair and blue eyes, was that Clive had told her that he was a friend of his, and that he owned flats to rent. He also dealt in selling antique, furniture and paintings, and he owned good Second-Hand-Furniture-Stores all over Sheffield, and he filled them mostly with furniture that he had bought in house clearance sales. She managed to reach Ken Morris at a place called 'The Glory Hole', one of his furniture shops on London road.

"Yes I remember meeting you Olivia," Ken said, when she spoke to him on the phone. "And I've heard for a long time now, that you and Clive are getting divorced, how's it going?"

Olivia told him, that she would have her divorce through from Clive, very soon now. And that she was now looking for some wardrobes and dressing tables, for the house that she was moving into, in a couple of weeks' time, and did he have anything which may suit her?

"I may just have what your looking for then," Ken told her. "I've got a lovely cream bedroom suite, that I brought into one of my shops from a house clearance, that I did last week. When can I pick you up to take you to look at it Olivia?"

"Well I can go to see it tomorrow afternoon, if that's okay with you Ken? 'Cause my Mother is coming over to get my Children in the morning, they're going to stay with her for a few days."

"Well, would you like to have lunch with me tomorrow first Olivia? Then we'll go and see the furniture"

"Yes Ken, I'd love to, that would be nice."

***

During lunch the next day in a country pub restaurant at the 'The Fox House' in Derbyshire, Ken told her that he was not really a friend of Clive's at all, and never had been. He just knew him and spoke to him when he saw him, and that he was very surprised, when Clive found himself a beautiful young girl like Olivia, for his wife. "So now that you know I'm not Clive's friend, I'd like to be yours."

"Yes, I'd like that too. But I think I should tell you Ken, that I'm getting married again very soon, so don't expect anything more than a friendship from me, okay?"

"Okay sure fine, that's no problem with me on that score," Ken replied, secretly wishing he had got together with Olivia, long before now, and long before she had found someone else to marry her.

They left the restaurant later that afternoon in Ken's beautiful blue 'Mercedes Benz' car, and drove to one of his shops, for Olivia to have a look at some of his furniture.

"Oh yeah I do like this and I'll definitely have this set," she said, on seeing a lovely, pair of man and women's matching, cream and edged with gold, Georgian, style wardrobes, and a glass, topped, kidney-shaped cream, dressing table, with a matching set of cream drawers. "And I also want that lovely, big, blanket-box over there, and I can paint it cream to match all of this set." She also chose a highly, polished, single wardrobe, with a small, dressing-table and mirror, attached to the side of it, for the twin's bedroom, and a small, man's wardrobe and dressing-table, for her Son's bedroom. "Yes I'm very pleased with this as good as new furniture, that I've found in your shop Ken, and I'm also happy with the price that you've charged me for it all. And I just know that it will all look so good, when I get it into in my new home."

***

On the 12th March 1975, Olivia got her Divorce from Clive Lemons, and the next week she moved into her new, house with Alex and her Children to begin her new life.

***

Ken Morris brought one of his big furniture vans, and Kenny Dee brought his 'Volkswagen' van to help Olivia move house. Alex went to the house early that morning to let the carpet fitters in, so they could lay new carpets on all the floors.

After everyone had worked so hard together, loading and unloading the vans, with furniture and boxes that they placed into the rooms, they began to get the house looking organized and straightened up.

Vicky was also there to help Olivia, make up the beds, and find towels and soap in the boxes for the bathroom.

Antony and the twins had been upset about having to leave their very good friends Lulu and Marcus that morning, but they soon made new, friends that same, day with the Children who lived on Crowfield Road. The Twins kept telling Olivia and Alex over and over, that they had now, made some other friends, and they had seen a big, park at the end of Crowfield Road, that had swings and slides in it, and their new friends were going to take them there tomorrow.

It had been a very, long, hard, tiring-day for them all, and instead of having to find something to cook for them all, for dinner, Olivia and Alex took the Children out with them, to have dinner at a local Chinese-Restaurant that evening.

***

When Olivia and Alex arrived back from the restaurant, that evening, with the Children. Antony eagerly, went upstairs to his new, large bedroom, which had its own, lovely, thick, carpeted staircase, with a door at the bottom of the stairs, to close it off and make it private. "This is mine twinies, and don't you ever dare come into my bedroom and mess it up. Mum can you get me a lock for my bedroom door please? So I can keep the twinies out of my room," Antony asked.

"Oh, I don't think you need a lock on your bedroom door Antony. Because the twins have got a lovely big bedroom of their own, with a new fluffy pink, fitted carpet on the floor. So why would they want to come into your room?" Olivia replied.

"'Cause they like to snoop that's why, and look into my private things."

"Okay Antony don't worry," Alex said. "I'll get you a lock for your door tomorrow, and I'll fit it on for you by tomorrow-night."

"Do you really think he should have a lock on his door Alex?" Olivia asked, after they had bathed and tucked the twins, up into their beds, in their new, bedroom before kissing them goodnight.

"Yes, if he wants one. I think you've all suffered in your own ways, while you've been waiting for your Divorce Olivia, and if a lock on Antony's door makes him feel a bit more secure, then he can have one. Christ, I'd have wanted one, if I'd had a bedroom like that when I was a kid, It's just like a Penthouse he's got up there."

"I just feel that the Children will be very happy here, now that we've moved into our new home, and I know I will be," Olivia said, taking three bottles of tablets out of her handbag.

"What are you doing now?"

"Come with me and I'll show you," Olivia replied, walking to the bathroom carrying her bottles of tablets. "I won't be needing these anymore," she said, while emptying all of her tablets out of the bottles, into the toilet before flushing them away.

"Are you sure you can manage without them?" Alex asked, when they went back into their bedroom.

"What tablets to put me to sleep? Tablets to wake me up? And tablets to keep me going through the day? Oh yes I know that I can do without them, now that I've got my Divorce from Clive, left his house, and now come to live here," Olivia replied, putting her arms around Alex, and holding him close to her. "And now that I've closed that horrid chapter on my life, I can now go forward in my happy new life, with you Alex. And I promise you to be the best wife you could ever want or have or need in your life. And I love you with all my heart, and will always love you forever and ever. Now I must go and unpack some boxes in the kitchen, so we've got some pots out for our breakfast."

"No, not now you're not pretty lady, that can wait until morning," Alex replied, laying Olivia down on the bed and kissing her deeply while undressing her. "This first night in our new home is just for us two, and nothing else."

***

Everyone woke up early the next day; the Children were so excited to at last be living in their new home. "Your Mummy and I are going into town this morning, to get some gifts for the twins birthday tomorrow," Alex said to Antony. "Will you look after the twins for us please?"

"Yes okay I will, I'll take them down to the park to play on the swings and slide there. And could you get them a birthday gift from me please, 'cause I've got no money. Oh and don't forget the lock for my door, and anything else that you think I might like, eh Mom."

"Yes, yes, yes," the twins were shouting, and jumping up and down excitedly. "It's our birthday tomorrow."

"Can we have a party with our new friends please?" Sarah asked.

"And how old will we be Mummy, six?" Angel asked.

"No," Olivia replied laughing, as she gave the twins a big hug and kiss. "You will both be three tomorrow not six, and yes, you can have a small birthday party with your new friends. Now, I want you to both be good girls for Antony, because your Daddy and I have to go into town to do some shopping this morning."

"Yes we will be good girls, we promise," Sarah replied.

***

When Olivia and Alex arrived in town later that morning, the first things they went to buy were pretty dresses for the twins. They chose the same outfits for both of them, pretty, pink lace party dresses, with matching pink ankle socks. Large, pink and blue, rabbit, pyjama-cases, and teddy-bears each as a gift from Antony, and balloons, streamers, and whistles for their party. "I'd better get a birthday cake for the twins also," Olivia said. "Because I know I won't have time to make them one this year."

"Yes we do need a cake for them," Alex agreed. "And there's something else I want us to get."

"Oh yes, we mustn't forget the lock, that you've promised Antony for his door."

"No, I've not forgotten the lock," Alex replied, kissing Olivia. "But there's something else that you haven't thought about Olivia, which I thought you'd like to have, a wedding ring."

"Oh yes," Olivia said smiling. "I would like a wedding ring, let's find a jeweller's shop. When shall we get married?"

"I was thinking about sometime next month, if you'd like to?"

"Like to," Olivia said, while they were walking through the door of a jewellery shop, on Chapel Walk. "I'd more than like to, I'd love to marry you Alex, so just name the date you have in mind."

"Good morning," said a small, balding, man with glasses, who was stood behind a glass top counter, in the shop. "Can I help you?"

"Yes please I'd like a wedding ring," Olivia replied.

"May I measure your finger Madame," the jeweller said, holding up a bunch of ring measures to measure the size of ring, Olivia would need for her finger. "Have you got a particular type of ring in mind, that you would like to see Madame."

"Yes, I'd like a patterned one in white-gold."

"I think we have a very good selection of white-gold-rings in your size Madame, if you'd care to take a look," the jeweller said, lifting a tray of 24-carat white-gold, patterned wedding rings from underneath the glass top counter.

"Oh, I like this one here," Olivia said, picking out a wide-heart-patterned-ring, and slipping it onto her finger. "And look Alex it fits me perfectly. "

"Yes it does, and it also looks pretty on your finger," Alex replied, kissing the ring on her finger. "We'll take this one. How much is it?"

"Thirty pounds sir," the jeweller replied. "And may I say Madame, you have made a very good choice."

"I'll keep it on if you don't mind Alex, I'd like to wear it now."

"That's fine by me," Alex replied, paying for the ring, and the jeweller handing him the small, red velvet ring box. "Now let's go and get some lunch, 'cause I'm starving."

***

Alex and Olivia arrived home later that afternoon, to find Antony and the twins in the house with one of their new friends. "This is Gary," Antony said. "And he lives in the house with that blue-door, across the road from us. And I've just been showing him my new bedroom and he thinks it's great, he says he wished he had one like it. I've taken the twins to the park and I've given them their lunch. And I know where the shops are now Mum, Gary showed us, they're on Yerdbi-Lane, just off Crowfield Road. There's Sheila's, the 'Beer-Off' where you can get groceries from, and Gary took us into meet Sheila, and told her we'd just come to live round here on Crowfield Road, and she gave us all an ice-cream-cornet."

"Yeah we've had an ice-cream-cornet, from Sheila's," the twins shouted happily.

"And next to Sheila's," Antony continued. "Is the Butchers shop, then a Greengrocers shop, then a Newsagent's, but it's not Jackie and

Don's shop. Next to that is a Clothes shop, then a Fresh-fish shop, then a Fish and Chippy. Then just further down the lane is the School that I'll be going to. And past the School near the main-road, at the bottom of Yerdbi-Lane, is the Doctors that I think you'll be taking us to, when we're poorly. And across from the Doctors is the Chemist. Oh it's just so great around here Mum, and I'm so glad we came here to live in this big house."

"Good I'm pleased that you like everything around here, and it seems that you've had a good look around to see where everything is," Olivia replied.

"Hey Dad, did you remember to get me a lock for my door?"

"Yes I did," Alex replied. "I've got you a chain for it, that I'll fix on the side, and you can slip it over your door handle. We've also bought you a lovely big 'Jaws' mirror, look it's got a woman on it swimming and there's the big shark, and it says 'Jaws' along the bottom."

"Oh thanks this is just great," Antony said excitedly, when Alex passed the mirror to him. "Come on Gary, let's get a hammer and nail, and put this up on the wall in my bedroom."

"Can we come to put the mirror up too?" Sarah asked.

"No twinies you can't, and remember I've told you both, to stay out of my room."

"Don't be to hard on them Antony. And come here my twinies," Olivia said. "Let me show you what Daddy and I have got for you. And are these Children with you your new friends?"

"Yes they are," Angel replied, pulling their friends forward to introduce to their Mother. "This is Andrew and Christopher, they're Brothers and this is Claire their Sister. And they live just one house past ours. And this is Caroline and Julie, who are Sisters. And they live in that other house across from ours. And can they come to our party?"

"Yes they can darling," Olivia replied with a smile, and feeling so pleased to know that her Children liked this new house, and the area where she'd brought them to live. "And we'll have a lovely party for your third-birthday tomorrow twins. And look Daddy and I have got you, this pretty pink birthday cake, with three candles on it."

"Oooh!" The twins both said together smiling, looking at their birthday cake.

***

Olivia and Alex both invited their parents to their wedding that they had planned for the following month. But Olivia's parents turned down their wedding invitation, because they thought that she was rushing into another marriage, far too soon after her divorce from Clive Lemons. And they had wanted her, to wait at least, another twelve months, before she remarried.

Alex's Parents, who lived in Birmingham, had met Olivia and her Children once. But sadly because of their very strong belief in their Catholic-Religion, they did not agree at all with their son, marrying a divorced-woman, who had three children. And Alex's father, who just seemed to be a miserable, French-man, from France, eagerly told Alex, in his broken English accent, "You fool you!!! You do not!!! You never marry girls like Olivia!!!!"

"Oh don't worry about what your dad, thinks or says about me Alex. Because In-Laws and I just don't get on. My first mother-in-Law and father-in-Law, didn't like me, so why should I expect my second lot to like me any better?" Olivia laughingly, told him.

"Well if my Parents had decided to come to our wedding, they would only have come to show their bloody protest, against me marrying you. And I know that would only put a damper on our Wedding-Day for us, so I think it's best if they do stay away," replied Alex.

***

On the day of their Wedding, Olivia wore a lovely, new, matching-outfit, of white, flared, cotton trousers, with a white, cotton-waistcoat, a very wide flared-sleeved, blue and white stripped, nylon shirt, white high heeled shoes, and a white, floppy-wide-brimmed-straw hat.

"You do look so beautiful my very pretty lady, for our wonderful Wedding day," Alex said, coming into their bedroom, wearing a new, grey and black, pinstriped suit, with flared trousers, and a pale grey, shirt with a matching wide tie.

"Yeah well you look good yourself," Olivia said, as he kissed her. "Hey be careful Alex, don't go spoiling my make-up please, 'cause I haven't got time to do it again, before our wedding."

"Okay, but where are the twins?"

"In their bedroom I hope, playing with their toys. I've got them ready in their pink lace dresses, and their long hair is hung down in ringlets, with the sides fastened up in a pink ribbon, at the back. They do look pretty, and I hope they are playing with their dolls and teddy bears, and not their pastry sets or plastacine."

"And Antony's ready, he's waiting downstairs dressed in his suit. James and Cassandra are here, after their long drive up from Bristol. And we're just waiting for Ken."

"Yes you and the Children can get off now down-town, to the Registry-Office with James and Cassandra if you like. Ken should be here anytime now to drive me there, in his beautiful 'Mercedes' of course, because I want to arrive in style. Oh and did I tell you? Ken's told me, he's just afraid I might be making another mistake, getting married again so soon, 'cause he thinks I should have waited a bit longer, until I get to know you a little better."

"Why?" Alex asked laughingly, putting his arms around Olivia. "Does Ken think you should be his wife this time? Instead of mine? And I promise you Olivia, I will make you the best husband you could ever wish for. And no matter what happens during our marriage, whatever problems or hardships we have to go through together, I'll love you always and forever."

"Thanks, and I'll always love you forever Alex. Listen, I think that's Ken's car pulling up now, so we'd better go. Oh! And Kenny, Vicky, Bozo, Diana and Jackie said they'll meet us down at the Registry-Office. And Kenny says we'll all go for a Chinese meal on him, after they've thrown their confetti on us."

On 12th May 1975, Olivia and Alex were married at the Sheffield-Registry-Office, with James and Cassandra, as their witnesses.

******

OLIVIA'S FULL CIRCLE.
PART THREE.
1975 - 1981

Chapter 31

Olivia so much enjoyed and just loved being Alex's wife; she felt that she couldn't be happier with her life and the path that it was now taking. She felt that her, and her family, were now living in a big, safe, happy bubble, and that no one would, or ever could, pop it or break it for them all. Alex seemed like her 'Knight in Shining Armour', and she loved him so much that she felt her heart would burst at times.

She was always busy looking after her Children, cleaning the house, washing and ironing, shopping for groceries, and always had a lovely, hot dinner cooked for her family, when Alex arrived home from work, at about six o'clock.

After the children were bathed and put to bed at night, they would curl up on the couch together to watch television, or have an early night of passionate love making in their bed. Olivia felt she had never been loved like this before, and didn't know how she'd ever managed without Alex in her life. Her world just seemed to revolve around him and the children, and this was all she wanted, nothing more.

Antony was attending the school in Yerdbi-Lane, and the twins were now going every day to a Nursery-school, that had just opened there.

Jackie and Diana often came over to see her, and Diana brought Lulu to see the twins during the school holidays.

***

Twelve months later into her wonderful, happy marriage, late one Thursday night, Kenny Dee called into see Alex and Olivia, after finishing one of his DJ shows. "Where do you go, when you go for a night out by yourself, Alex?" Kenny asked.

"I don't go out by myself," Alex replied. "I wouldn't ever think of going out by myself at night, without Olivia. And when we do we get a baby-sitter in, we go out together downtown for a meal, then sometimes on to a disco. Or we sometimes just go to the pub, up the road for a drink. But why do you ask?"

"Well it's just a feeling I had," Kenny replied laughing. "That you don't get a break at all from Olivia and the kids. God, I know that I need one from Vicky sometimes, or I'd go mad. So I like it when she's doing her nigh-shift nursing, at the Children's Hospital, 'cause then I've got my freedom for a week."

"Just because we've been very happily married for a year, and Alex loves to be with me, doesn't mean he's trapped, you bloody chauvinistic pig Kenny." Olivia replied, not understanding Kenny's concern for Alex to have, what most of the British men called their freedom, as it was a rarity that her Father ever went anywhere without her Mother. "Anyway Alex just hasn't seemed to have made many new friends, since he's been in Sheffield, but he knows he can go out without me if he wants to."

"Aye, and I think Alex must need a break sometimes, from you and the kids Olivia, the poor bloke. We all need a break away from our wives nown-agen, you women can be a bit suffocating at times you know? Can't they Alex?" Kenny said laughingly, teasing Olivia. "Tell you what Alex, I'm doing a show at a disco in Rotherham tomorrow night, at a place called Travesis, that's owned by some big entertainment company in London. So if yu like? I'll come and pick yu up at about seven o'clock tomorrow night, and yu can come for a night out wi-me, 'cause I'm sure you'll enjoy yourself."

"That sounds like an idea, but would you mind if I have a night out with Kenny?" Alex asked Olivia.

"No no, I don't mind at all if you want to have a night out with Kenny," Olivia replied with a smile. "You go, and you never know Alex, you may even enjoy yourself without me. And don't forget if you can't be good, be good at it. But I don't really mean that you know?" She added quickly.

"Thanks Olivia," Alex said, putting his arms around her. "And I think I will go out with you tomorrow night Kenny, for a change, Yes I could use a break. And don't you go thinking about me doing anything, that I shouldn't Olivia, 'cause you know I only have eyes for you."

"Yeah I know Alex, I was only joking with you."

***

It was daylight on Saturday morning Olivia was fast asleep, and not wanting to disturb her, Alex quietly got into their bed at the side of her. But in her deep sleep she was aware of Alex being there, and she wrapped her arms around him, when he turned over onto on his side with his back facing her.

Later that morning at eight o'clock the twins came into their bedroom, asking their Mummy to get up to get them their breakfast. As she got out of bed and put on her dressing gown, she saw Alex's clothes laid in a pile, on the floor at the bottom of their bed. So she picked them up and took them with her into the bathroom, to put them into the clothes' basket to be washed. *That's odd,* she thought, looking at Alex's' clothes as she dropped them into the basket, noticing a smudged, bright pink stain, on the front of his blue shirt.

She then went downstairs and prepared cereal, boiled eggs, toast and milk for the twin's breakfast, and drank her cup of tea while she sat with the twins at the table in the dining room, reading her morning newspaper.

When the twins had finished their breakfast, she went with them into their bedroom to get them dressed, before taking her morning bath.

Alex was still sleeping when she had finished her bath and got dressed; she drew the bedroom curtains back, before going downstairs to make him a coffee.

***

"Wake up sleepy head," Olivia said, gently shaking Alex on the shoulder. "Come on Alex you can't sleep all day, and the twins want you to take them to the park this morning. They're both dressed and waiting for you downstairs. Antony got himself up early this morning, and has gone fishing with his friends."

"Oh God," Alex said, opening his eyes and beginning to sit up in bed. "That sun's bright this morning, and what time is it?"

"It's ten o'clock, and what time did you get home last night?"

"I didn't get home until daylight."

"Daylight!" Olivia repeated, in a surprised voice. "What the hell were you doing until daylight? And did you have a good time?"

"Yeah it was okay, but it got better when Sue and Sue arrived, then I started to have a good time."

"And who the hell are Sue and Sue?" Olivia asked, still holding the mug of hot coffee.

"Well I don't know who had the other Sue, but I know I screwed the one with me."

"You did what!" Olivia said, in a very shocked, surprised voice.

"You heard me, I made it with Sue."

"Oh you did, did you? You fucking bastard!" A shaken, shocked Olivia shouted, throwing the hot coffee into Alex's face. "All this sounds so crazy, and how could you do this to me?"

She then ran from the bedroom, and went into the kitchen to make herself a cup of tea. She was shaking with hurt and rage while lighting a cigarette, feeling that she couldn't think straight anymore, and wondering if she was really, awake or still asleep having a nasty, bad dream.

"Mummy, Mummy," Angel shouted, "Is it okay, if me and Sarah go to Caroline's to play?"

"Yes, it's okay you can go 'cause Daddy is still sleeping," Olivia replied, feeling tears begin to run down her cheeks. "Just don't go anywhere else twinies, without asking me first."

"Okay Mummy we won't," the twins both shouted back.

Olivia took her mug of tea and went to sit in the dining room. She lit another cigarette inhaling the smoke from it deeply. She still didn't want to believe what Alex, had just told her, because that would be so out of character with the Alex, that she knew, the one she loved and had recently, married. There had to be some other reasonable, explanation to this wild statement that he had just made to her she thought.

As she was drinking her tea and angrily smoking her cigarette, suddenly a flash of the colour, pink she saw in front of her, and remembered the bright, pink stain, that she had noticed on Alex's shirt, when she had put his clothes, into the clothes' basket to be washed. "Yes I bet that's sodding lipstick that I saw," she shouted, while running upstairs to the bathroom to get Alex's shirt out of the clothes' basket. She held his blue shirt up, and looking at it closely, she could see that it had bright pink lipstick on the front of it and around the collar. "Yes I'll fucking kill him for this," she shouted angrily, running across the landing and into their bedroom with Alex's shirt.

"What's this on your shirt Alex?" Olivia asked, pushing the shirt into Alex's face.

"What's, what?" Alex asked moodily, now taking the sheets and pillowcases of the bed. "I've got to change the sheets now 'cause they're covered in coffee."

"Oh leave the bloody sheets, and just tell me what's all this pink stuff on your shirt?"

"I think it must be her lipstick, but I was hoping you wouldn't see it."

"So you really did have sex with this Sue then? And afterwards you came home to me, with her fucking pink lipstick all over your shirt! Thinking that I wouldn't notice it? So do you think I'm fucking stupid Alex? Or what?"

"No of course I know you're not stupid. But don't worry about Sue, she was nothing to me really, honestly she was rubbish. She was just some nymphomaniac out on the loose for the night, that needed fucking, and she just laid back there like a sack of potatoes. Anyway it was your friend Kenny, who told me she fancied me like crazy, and could he set it up so she could have my body at the end of the night. The manager of Travesis was away on holiday, so Kenny spoke to the doorman who was in charge of the place, and he said, that after the disco was closed and everyone was gone, we could have a private party 'cause he fancied having the other Sue himself."

"So who did Kenny go with then? Didn't anyone have a Sue lined up waiting for him to fuck?"

"No he didn't get off with anybody. Him and Bozo just packed his records and equipment up, and loaded it into Kenny's van."

"While you and this doorman fucking got it off, with these wonderful Sue's eh? Oh Why? Oh why? Did it have to be you Alex?" Olivia asked, crying and feeling that her heart was now breaking into little pieces. "I really believed that you loved me Alex, and we had a marriage made in heaven. You don't know what you've done to me, to us, how could you have done this to us?"

"I told you Olivia, it was nothing honestly, so don't go getting yourself so upset about it, it's just not worth it. And I'm really very sorry, it was a very stupid thing for me to do. But please don't forget? I still love you Olivia, very much, and I always will do," Alex said, going over to her, and putting his arms around her, and trying to kiss her on the lips.

"No! No! Don't you dare touch me you bastard, and if you really did love me, you wouldn't have made it with that Sue," Olivia screamed, pushing Alex away from her, then slapping him very, hard across his face, before also spitting in his face. "And I don't believe you, that you do love me at all. In fact I don't believe in us, or anything about us anymore." She then tore Alex's blue, shirt up into shreds, while telling him, "This is us Alex, and this is what you have gone and done to us and our marriage, you've just managed to destroy it all in one night, how very good and mightily clever of you. But I promise you this, you'll be sorry for what you've now done to me, yes very sorry, all of you will be so sorry. And what was it you told me, that your father said about me? *You don't marry girls like Olivia.* And no, you shouldn't have Alex, because girls like me are too fucking good for men like you. First of all there was Antony's, Father, who tried to fuck me up, then there was Clive Lemons and now you. God, can my life really get any worse? All because of you fucking stupid self-serving men. Well let me tell you something, I've had enough and it's my turn now, and I'll slowly start to destroy men just like you and enjoy it. And I'm sure I'll have lots of fun doing it, 'cause there are a lot of men like you, out there, just wanting a good time for the night, and not caring who gets hurt because of it."

A destroyed and heartbroken Olivia cried continually, feeling that her recent, happy world had now crumbled and shattered. Yes that wonderful, happy-bubble that she kept herself and her family in, had now been burst by Alex. She was slowly veering to the edge of a nervous-breakdown, as her nerves were now shattered, she couldn't sleep at night, finding it difficult to now sleep at all. She just didn't know how to escape, from this nightmare that she was now living in, as Alex's uncaring words kept repeating themselves over and over inside of her head, when he'd told her that, *'I made it with Sue'*. And because of this, the pain she felt in her heart could not be bigger, or hurt even more, if someone had stuck a knife, straight through it.

***

"What's wrong Olivia? What's happened to you? And you look like hell!" Ken asked, when he went to her house to see her, about a week later.

She made them a cup of tea and sitting at the dining room table, she began to tell Ken what had happened to her marriage, what Alex had done to her, that Friday night he went out with her friend, Kenny. "I just don't understand Alex anymore, or why he had to do this to me. Why he had to screw this girl called Sue, just because she supposedly fancied him, it's all beyond me. And I always thought that we had a wonderful terrific sex life, so why would he want to look or go elsewhere for it. I would never have dreamed of doing anything at all like that to him, to us, or our marriage. Of course I always keep thinking that this Sue must have been much younger than me, better looking, and much sexier than me. All of those insecure thoughts and feelings that all us females must have, when we think that we've lost our man to some other women. What or where did I go wrong Ken? What did I do that was so bad to deserve all of this? Did I give too much of my time to the Children? Or did I not tell him often enough that I loved him? My head just seems to be spinning out of control thinking about all of this, and how I can put it all right, as if none of it had ever happened? But I'm just an emotional wreck now, all thanks to him, and the damage he has done to us and our marriage, the night he fucked another girl. It just doesn't matter to me now anymore, how many times he tells me he's so sorry, and that he'll never do anything like that ever again, and how much he still loves me. I just don't believe him, trust him or will ever want to forgive him. And why the hell should I fucking trust him ever again? And after this I don't even know if Alex has seen or is still seeing her, this fucking slag Sue, who likes to get laid after hours in Discos, 'cause he maybe for all I know or even really care now. What am I supposed to do Ken? Just sit around being his good little wifey? And wait at home until the next time he fancies another bit of fresh on the side? No I don't fucking think so?"

After she had finished telling Ken, about everything that had happened, including her feelings on the matter, she began to cry really hard, and Ken put his arms around her to try and comfort her. "I know you must be feeling heartbroken over all of this Olivia. And I do wish to God that you had listened to me, when I told you that I didn't feel good about you marrying Alex. 'Cause I just had this gut feeling that he wasn't the right one for you, I wish that you had just continued living with him, and that you had never married him, until you got to know him much better. I know that you just wanted to have a happy home, with some security in your life with your children, after what Clive had put you through, the bastard. And when Alex came onto the scene you fell to hard, you fell to fast, and now your paying a big price for it, aren't you? But where do you go from here love? What are your plans for the future? What are you going to do now? If you feel that your marriage is now over?"

"I just don't know what I'm going to do right now Ken. Because my biggest problem is that I still love Alex, but I also hate him just as much. I don't even know what will happen between us now, 'cause I don't feel we have got a marriage left together anymore. Silly me what had I been thinking all this time? It now seems that I was just fooling myself about having a wonderful marriage, that was made in heaven? And my Solicitor, who I've contacted, says that I can't get a divorce yet, until I've been married to Alex for two years. But I don't trust him, or think that I'll ever be able to trust him again, so please roll on two years.

"Yeah its going to be a long time for you to have to wait, is two years," replied Ken.

"So maybe I should get myself a job, to help pass all of that time on. Have some other interest outside of the home in my life, then the two years may pass quicker, yeah I think that would help me. And I've read in the newspaper that they want some cocktail-waitresses, at the Fiesta-Night-Club, you know that big nightclub that's opened downtown. Yeah I'll go and get myself a job at the Fiesta, it should be good working there, and getting to meet all the pop-stars. But first, I've got to get some sleep. I'm so bloody tired I can't remember the last time I had a good nights sleep, or slept through the night, so I can repair myself and shut this nightmare out of my life for a while. Then maybe, I could start getting on with a new life for myself again, ye one that belongs to me only, and not shared with any other man who will only break my heart again!"

"Here I'll give you something to help you sleep," Ken offered, taking a bottle of sleeping tablets out of his jacket pocket, and shaking some out to give to Olivia. "I've just been to the chemist to renew my prescription so I can let you have some of these, take one of them before you go to bed and you'll sleep like a baby, they're strong sleeping tablets so don't take more than one. And phone me if you need to talk at all, or fancy going out for a meal. I'll try and help you to get your life back together on track Olivia, 'cause remember I told you a long time ago, I was your friend."

"Thanks Ken, I know that you will always be my special friend, and thanks for being there for me in my time of need, I'll always be thankful to you for that. And I can't wait to take one of these pills tonight so that I can have a good sleep, I feel as though I could sleep for a week, but I've just about forgotten what sleep is," Olivia said, putting her arms around Ken, to thank him with a loving hug, and a kiss on the side of his cheek.

***

After a couple of months Olivia, was feeling much better and stronger in herself. She was sleeping okay at nights now without the aid of any sleeping tablets. She was still trying to keep her marriage and relationship between her and Alex, seem as normal as it possibly could be, for the sake of and in the eyes of her Children. They also after a period of time, once again got back on track, with the wonderful, very, good sex life, that Alex, and her always used to enjoy so much with each other.

But unbeknown to Alex, she now only made love with him, to once again feel love and be loved, nothing more. She also felt unable to ever give herself to him, completely again, when she made love to feel loved, and that so easily now became her motto. But she often always wondered if Alex really did love her, or even know what he was saying, about that strong, emotional, heart felt, feeling, and did he really know what it was? When he told her over and over again, that he loved her. But no she could not forgive him or ever forget how he had hurt her so much, the man of her dreams, who had so easily destroyed them, taken all those dreams away from her, now making her feel that she would never be able to ever really, love or trust a man again.

And yes this revenge that she had promised Alex, was always simmering, somewhere deep inside of her, but in spite of that her life must go forward again for her now. Because no nothing could or would ever keep her down for very long, as things in life had tried to destroy her before, but when she knew that she had had enough, of what was being dished out to her. The time always came for when she knew, she had to push it away from her, and rise up above it all, just like an avenging Phoenix. Yes rising up and feeling reborn again, like being all new and better, and much stronger after each nasty, experience that she had encountered in her life. Now becoming a much wiser, grown, healed person, as she pushed the past behind her, all the way back behind her, so that she was always able to once again, go forward in her life. But never, ever forgetting about it, or the things that had happened, as they would always be laid away, stored somewhere deep down inside of her!!!

***

The next month Olivia happily, began working as a cocktail-waitress at the Fiesta-Night-Club in Sheffield, the Fiesta was a club that was advertised and known as the best Night-Club-In-Europe.

Alex would arrive home from his job, and she would have the evening meal prepared for her family to sit down and eat, before taking a bath, and getting herself dressed and made up, then going to catch the bus to go to work. Leaving Alex behind to bath the children and put them to bed.

She instantly grew to love and enjoy this job there at the Fiesta, as a cocktail-waitress, which now played a big role in her new life, with making lots of new friends with the other waitress's and people who worked there. The Fiesta was a classy, expensive club, which top-stars appeared in from around Europe and America. She really did enjoy her meetings with the stars such as 'The Four Tops', 'Jimmy Ruffin', 'The Supremes', 'The Drifters', 'The Foundations', 'Frankie Valli and The Four Seasons', plus many more famous singers, pop-groups and Comedians. She would usually meet up with them backstage, when she took drinks for them into their dressing-rooms, and was often invited to their parties which they would hold in their dressing-rooms after their shows. Where she was always lucky enough to get signed, autographs on their photos from these stars, to take home for her Children, who would take them to school to show all of their friends.

Most of the punters who visited the club tipped Olivia generously, when she brought them their orders of drinks to their tables, and often opened bottles of champagne for parties of people celebrating special events in their life's, like Job-Promotions, Birthdays, Wedding-Anniversaries, Engagements, etc, etc, etc.

Also sometimes at the end of the night the other waitresses and staff who worked there, would all meet up and party, in the downstairs-disco, when they had removed the glasses and ashtrays from the tables, in the upstairs cabaret room where they worked.

Often she would not arrive home until five o'clock in the morning, and Alex would ask her where she'd been, and what she'd been doing. *"Oh nothing you need to know about,"* she would say to him, with a smile on her face, whilst laying in his arms. *"Just having some fun with the pop-stars, who are in town for the week."*

For over twelve months she had begun to live her life in the fast-lane now, and was enjoying every minute of it. Telling Alex, her Sister, her parents, and Diana only a quarter of what she now did in her exciting life, believing that they really wouldn't understand her at all, or what she ever did, so she would just tell them, *"You would really have to work in these night-clubs, to know and appreciate the scene there. It's just a totally different world from the one you all live in, and are used to."*

***

One evening when the Children were in bed, Olivia and Alex were sat in their Lounge together, having a glass of wine while watching television. When Alex began to tell her about a job, that he'd seen in the newspaper, with a company down in London, who were advertising for a Computer-Systems-Analyst, and he had applied for the position. He then asked her if she minded him taking the job, if it was offered to him.

"No, why should I? And I don't really care what job you take, or where you go to work. Only don't ever expect me to go and live down in London, 'cause remember I'm a northern girl."

"What's happened to us Olivia? We used to be so close, and over the last twelve months, ever since you started working at the Fiesta-night-club, I feel I've been slowly losing you. And I feel you've put a barrier up between us two Olivia, Why?"

"Why?" She replied, looking at Alex in amazement, with her big, green eyes. "Why? How dare you ever ask me why? I thought you'd know why, after what you did to me."

"Yes I know that I hurt you once, and I'm very sorry about that night, and always will be. And yes you were right, there is no excuse for what I did that night, I must have had too much to drink, or just been out of my fucking mind. But I've tried to make it up to you Olivia, and I thought I had by now, but I'm beginning to feel that I'm banging my head on a brick wall, trying to make things right with you. I love you very much Olivia, and I don't know what to do next. Don't you love me anymore?"

"Oh yes," she replied, when Alex put his arms around her. "In my own sad, sick way I suppose that I do still love you very much, and I always will. But I can't get over how you hurt me so much, and I won't give you another chance to do it again. Anyway I don't feel that I've evened the score up between us yet, so maybe it would be best if you took this other job, and we separated for a while. Or at least until I've got this deep sad hurt and revenge out of my system. Maybe that's the problem, you've not given me enough space to heal yet. And when and if I do ever heal, who knows maybe I could give us another try sometime."

"Once again I'm so sorry about that night, and I'll always love you forever Olivia," Alex said, holding her very close to him.

"Yes you may love me for now, but how do you know you won't find someone else to love, just as much? Anyway I don't want you to feel tied down to me anymore. I would much rather you went out into this big wide world, all by yourself for a while, and find out what and who you really do want, for the rest of your life. Before making any other commitment with me, and then screwing everything up again."

Two months later Alex moved away to begin his new job in London.

******

Chapter 32

Olivia was waiting for a bus, at the bus stop just around the corner from Crowfield Road one morning, when a tall, good-looking, slim-girl, with blonde hair, came running around the corner and up to the bus stop. "Oh Thank God I've not missed the bloody bus," she said, to Olivia out of breath.

"Hello you," Olivia replied, whilst looking at this girl, that she recognized. "And aren't you the girl, who always looks through my window when you pass my house. I was hoping I'd meet you one day to ask you why you do that?"

"Hello I'm Cindy, and you're the Mother of those adorable twin girls, aren't you? And yes I do always look through your window when I go past your house, because you have a big mirror hung on your wall, that faces the window, and when I pass your house on my way to the bus stop, I look through the window into your mirror to see if my hair is okay."

"Oh, so that's why your always looking through my window is it?" Olivia said laughingly. "Well Cindy, my name's Olivia, and do you live on Crowfield Road?"

"Yes, about six houses up from you on the opposite side of the road."

The blue and white double-decker bus arrived, Olivia and Cindy got on, paid their fare, then went up the winding metal-stairs of the bus, and sat-down together in a seat up there.

"What are you going into town for?" Olivia asked.

"I'm going for a job interview at the 'Mandy-G-Modelling-Agency', to see if I can get a job there doing modelling and promotion work, 'cause I'm bloody sick of my Mum getting on my case about me not having a job."

"You shouldn't have a problem getting a job as a model. You're tall, good looking, and those big, baby blue eyes of yours should do it for you."

"Do you think so?" Cindy asked, flicking her lovely, honey-blonde, soft, curly hair, back off her shoulders. "I had my hair styled like Farrah Fawcett last week, you know? Like her off 'Charlie's Angels'. So maybe that'll help me?"

"Yeah I'm sure it will, but you look more like Goldie Hawn than Farrah Fawcett. I used to work for a modelling agency in Sheffield years ago, but I think that one has closed down now. It used to be called Bebas."

"What do you mean, years ago?" Cindy asked, offering Olivia a cigarette. "You don't look that old, how old are you Olivia?"

"Twenty-seven, how old did you think I was? And how old are you?"

"I thought you were about my age, twenty four. Are you married?"

"Yes, only I don't feel like it. I've been married twice but my present husband Alex, is working and living down in London now, we're having a trial separation. I have three children, the twins you seem to know and a son Antony who, a couple of weeks ago, decided that he would be happier living with my parents at their pub in Bradwell. 'Cause his Granddad has lots of money and takes him fishing most days. And Antony caught himself a trout in the village brook the other day. Anyway I've let him go to live over there with them, and I don't mind as long as the kid is happy, and I've told him he can come back to live with his Mummy whenever he wants to. So there's just me and my twinies living in that big house now."

"Oh kids I don't think that I'll bother having any of them myself, I think they can be to much trouble. Anyway have you got a spare room to let then? I'm just asking in case my Mum throws me out, 'cause she's always fucking threatening to. Especially when my boyfriend Glyn stayed with me the other night, and the bitch came into my room the next morning, and saw us in bed together. She nearly had a bloody-shit-fit. Anyway she's now told me, that if I don't get a job this month she's throwing me out. I'll be about an hour in this interview," Cindy said, standing up when the bus was coming to her stop. "When you've done your shopping can you meet me outside the 'Crazy Daisy' in High Street? And we'll get some lunch there?"

"Okay yes I will, so I'll see you later, and good luck with the job," Olivia replied.

"Thanks and keep your fingers crossed for me that I get it, or I'll have to find somewhere else to sleep tonight."

***

"Hi Olivia I've got it," Cindy shouted, before running across the road, to Olivia, who was waiting outside of the 'Crazy Daisy' for her. "I'm so glad you've waited for me, and I've got a job as a model, oh I feel so happy. Look it says on this food board that the food special for today, is chicken and chips, lets go and get some and I'm ready for a drink."

They both walked down the wide stone steps, and through the large, brown, wooden door into the 'Crazy Daisy' club.

"This place is big I've never been in here before," Olivia said, looking around her. "It looks like the inside of a castle dungeon, with it's large flag-stoned floor, big wooden tables, and candle-shaped, wall lights and these big round candle chandeliers. It's certainly bigger inside than it looks from the outside."

"Yes, it does seem like a big underground dungeon. And the food is good here, it's all freshly cooked. Look, this is the dining area here."

They both sat down on a long, wooden bench, at one of the long, wooden tables across from the bar.

"There aren't many people in though," Olivia said. "That DJ is playing records to an empty room."

"No, it doesn't get very busy at lunch-time, except on Saturdays and holidays. But it's packed at night and the music's always good."

"I just love this record 'Grease', and John Travolta's new film, 'Grease', is playing at the Odeon. Shall we go and see it tomorrow?" Olivia asked.

"Yeah I think John Travolta is just gorgeous, and yeah we'll go and see it tomorrow afternoon if you like. We won't get in at night to see it, 'cause people will be queuing for miles to see that film."

A tall, good-looking, broad shouldered, west-Indian-man, with short-black-tight-curly-hair and dark brown eyes, came over to the table, where Olivia and Cindy were sat talking. "Hi Cindy," he said. "Can I get you ladies a drink and something to eat?"

"Hi Winston," Cindy replied. "This is my friend Olivia, who I've met today and we've decided we'll have two Bacardi and Coke's and chicken and chips twice."

"Hi Olivia," Winston said, smiling at her, while offering his hand for her to shake. "I'm very pleased to meet you, I've not seen you in here before have I?"

"No you haven't, I've not been in this terrific dungeon place before. But Cindy dragged me in here today, I think this is one of her favourite haunts. But I've not been to any of the discos or clubs around town for a long time now, 'cause I've been working nearly every night at the 'Fiesta-night-club. But now my husband and I are separated, I've had to quit for lack of a baby-sitter."

"I bet you've met some great pop-stars while working at the Fiesta," Winston stated.

"Oh yeah lots of them," Olivia replied. "And I've made good friends with some of them to, most are just terrific people, especially the Drifters."

"What! Do you know the Drifters?" Cindy asked, when Winston went to get their drinks and give their food order to the kitchen.

"Yes, I know the Drifters and their band that comes with them from America. They're just great, terrific people. The next time they come to town to play at the Fiesta, we'll go to see them and I'll introduce you to them all after their show."

"Oh great, I can't wait to meet them, I've always been a great fan of the Drifters."

"So tell me about Winston, how do you know him? He's a big good-looking guy, who's his girlfriend? Or is he married?" Olivia asked, sounding curious.

"Yes, he certainly seemed very interested in you Olivia, I saw the way he was looking at you, and I wondered if you'd noticed. Well, as I suppose you've guessed he's Jamaican, he's from Kingston in Jamaica and has lived in England for quite a few years now. He works here as bouncer, doorman, odd job man, and under manager. He's about six foot-five tall, he's thirty-two and I don't think he's married, I've never seen him with a girl in here. A friend of mine asked him, one night, if he'd like to spend the night with her, 'cause her parents were away, and he turned her down and she cried. I think Winston's life is very private, I see his Jamaican friends in here most nights. And later on, about two o'clock, when it closes here, they all go up to the red-light-area to a 'Shubeem', to drink and gamble. Oh, and he drives a big brown Jaguar car. Dez is coming over to our table, he'll tell you about Winston. Hi Dez, I want you to meet Olivia."

"Hi Olivia," said Dez, with a lovely, big infectious smile that showed off his beautiful, white teeth.

"Hi," Olivia replied. "You look like an advert for a toothpaste company when you smile, did you know you have a set of lovely, even white teeth?"

"Do you think so, lovely lady?" Dez asked laughing. "I suppose it's 'cause my skin's black, it shows my teeth up nice and white, so I just walk around smiling, don't I Cindy?"

"Yeah you do, especially when you're tryin to impress someone. You're from Jamaica aren't you Dez?" Cindy asked. "Can you tell Olivia anything about Winston? 'Cause she's interested to know?"

"So, you want to know about the head of Sheffield and South-Yorkshire's Black Mafia, Pass-Tru, do you Olivia?" Dez asked, with his lovely smile. "Well, I didn't know him in Jamaica, he's older than me, but I know him from here. And he's a great guy, and a friend of mine thank God, 'cause he can be fucking dangerous if he wants to be. So I must warn you, anyone in their right mind doesn't cross Winston, or they end up very sorry later."

"Sounds like a man I could get along with very easily," Olivia replied. "My feelings about people are the same. Does he have a girlfriend? Or is he married? And why did you call him Pass-Tru? I thought his name was Winston."

"No, he's not married, as for girlfriends I don't know but I suppose so, but I've never seen him with anyone in particular, he seems to be a very private person. And that's his nick-name Pass-Tru, that's what most of us guys call him, 'cause he just passes through our life's and stops only for a short while, to see what's happenin, what we're doin and if we've got any problems, or want anyone seein to," replied Dez. "Now can I get you ladies another drink?"

When Dez brought Olivia and Cindy another drink, over to their table. Olivia asked him about a 'Shubeem' and what they were.

"A 'Shubeem', is a big house that's owned by a West-Indian-guy, and they open it up for parties and illegal gambling of cards, dominoes, and craps. They make money on the side by selling liquor, mostly West-Indian-Rum, but they have to be careful 'cause they don't have a gaming or liquor license, they are selling it illegally. Often the cops raid these houses and stop the parties. We don't call it a 'Shubeem', that's the African word for them, but you honkies also call them that. We West-Indians call them 'The Blues', and reggae music is played in them continually."

"They sound like fun, we'll have to visit one, won't we Cindy?"

"No, no," said Dez, his lovely smile now leaving his face, as it turned very, serious looking. "They're not places for ladies like you to visit, and you must never go to them alone. They're up the Square in the red-light-area of Sheffield, where the prostitutes walk the streets, and then go into these 'Blues-Houses' to give the money they've made to their pimps. There's a lot of West-Indian pimps at the 'Blues', who can be dangerous guys for their hookers, if their girls don't make enough money for the night, they beat them up. And if the pimps got their hands on you, Cindy and Olivia, they'd think they'd struck gold. So stay away from the 'Blues' for your own safety."

"Yeah I guess your right Dez," Cindy replied. "But I'd love to go to a 'Shu… I mean a 'Blues House' one day, they sound like another world. But I wonder when our fucking 'Yorkshire-Ripper' is going to strike up there, in the red-light-area. And if I were a hooker working in the red-light-area, I'd be terrified of getting into these stranger's cars. No one knows what the 'Yorkshire-Ripper' looks like, do they? And I feel sure he'll come to Sheffield and kill one of our girls sometime, 'cause he seems to be killing prostitutes everywhere else now in South-Yorkshire, except Sheffield."

"Yes," Olivia agreed, lighting a cigarette. "How many has the bastard killed up to now? About nine or ten, he's killed girls in Leeds, Halifax, Preston and Bradford. I think Manchester and Sheffield will soon be on his list, it gives me the bloody creeps."

"I know," Dez replied, with a grim look on his face. "That guy, whoever he is, is fucking evil, I've also heard that when he's killed his victims, he then mutilates their bodies. I just wish the cops would catch this bastard, or better still I wish I could catch him, I'd break every fucking bone in his body. You girls just be careful who you talk to and mix with in the clubs, and don't go off somewhere with any men from out of town."

"No we promise we won't," Cindy and Olivia both replied, before saying good-bye to Dez, and begin to make their way through the large, club to leave the 'Crazy Daisy', until Winston shouted, "Hey Olivia, can I see you for a moment please."

Olivia went over to the other bar, across from the dance floor, to see what Winston wanted and he asked her where she was going?

"I've got to get home, my twins will be home from school soon, and they're not latch key kids. I always like to be home for them when they get back from school."

"Oh, you've got twins have you?"

"Yes, five year old identical twin girls."

"I heard you say you're separated from your husband Olivia. Is there any chance I can see you sometime."

"Yes, if you want to," Olivia replied, taking a book of matches out of her black, bag, and writing her telephone number down on the inside of it, before passing it to him. "Here's my phone number, and only give me a bell if you're not married, and if you are don't bother. 'Cause I don't want to hang around with frustrated married men. I've got one of my own somewhere, probably out there sowing his wild oats."

"Thanks," Winston said laughing, as he took the book of matches off her, looking at the phone number. "And no, I'm not married, I live with my Aunty. You're a very outspoken person Olivia, and I like that. I'll phone you sometime if that's okay with you."

"It must be, or I wouldn't have given you my phone number, would I? And I might just let you make a short stop in my life, if you want to pass by sometime, Pass-Tru," Olivia replied, before leaving him, giving him a wink with her right, eye, to let him know she knew, where he was coming from.

Cindy went back with Olivia to her house to have a coffee, and told her she wasn't seeing her boyfriend, Glyn, that night. So if Olivia wasn't doing anything either, she'd got a bottle of wine she'd bring over, and they could play records and have some girl talk. Olivia told Cindy that would be okay. And that the twins were off school the next day, so they'd take them along with them, to see the film 'Grease' tomorrow afternoon.

"Sure," replied Cindy. "I don't mind being with kids, as long as their someone else's, 'cause I don't really like kids, some of them can be brats. But your twinies are good kids aren't they?"

"Yes my twinies are very good kids," Olivia stated proudly.

******

Chapter 33

Winston phoned Olivia about two weeks later, to say he wasn't working that night, so would she like to go out with him. She told him that she wouldn't be able to get a baby-sitter for the night, so would he like to come over to her place. Winston agreed and arrived at her house about ten o'clock that evening, with a bottle of Scotch for them both to drink.

"I hope Scotch is okay for you Olivia?" Winston asked, pouring it into two glasses. "I forgot to ask what you drink."

"Bacardi and Coke, or Scotch and lemonade, either will do," Olivia replied, going into the kitchen to get a bottle of lemonade, to add to her drink.

"Oh yeah," Winston replied, passing her a drink, and sitting down in a comfy chair. "You were drinking Bacardi and Coke in the 'Crazy Daisy' weren't you, I forgot what it was you were drinking then. Where are your twins?"

"In bed of course," Olivia answered in a surprised voice, before putting the 'Saturday Night Fever' album on her stereo to play. "Where did you think they'd be at this time of night? My children don't run around until midnight, they have a set bedtime. So after they've had their tea, they have a bath and are in bed by eight o'clock. They're only five years old and they need their sleep at night, they're growing kids. Hey, I hope you don't mind my sort of music Winston?"

"No," he replied, with a laugh. "The DJ's play this honky music in the 'Crazy Daisy' all the time, and I expect you like this John Travolta also."

"Oh yes, the new guy on the disco scene with the polyester look, he's great looking. I like that dimple in his chin and would love to kiss it, and I also love his dancing. I've seen his 'Saturday Night Fever' film five times, and Cindy and I took the twins to see his new film 'Grease' last week."

"Do you like ganja?" Winston asked, as he began to sprinkle seeds that looked like grass seeds, onto the top of some tobacco, laid on two, white, cigarette papers, that he began to roll into a big, long joint.

"What's ganja? I've smoked grass before, but I've not heard it called ganja."

"That's the West-Indian term for it," Winston replied, lighting the joint he'd just rolled and passing it to Olivia, telling her to have a toke, and getting her another drink.

"Wow! This is good stuff," she said, drawing on the joint before passing it back to him, she inhaled the smoke deeply, letting it come down her nose. "I've never smoked stuff as good as this before, what is it?"

"Senseamillion, it's good stuff this, and I thought you'd like it. Are you going to get a divorce from your husband Olivia?"

"No, not at the moment," she replied, sitting on the floor and laying back to rest her head on the couch. "I feel lovely and relaxed now, can I have another toke of that beautiful stuff, please?"

She took a few more long, tokes of the joint and inhaled it deeply, while she told Winston, that her and her husband Alex, were still in love with each other, but they didn't seem to be able to live together anymore. So they were having a trial separation, while he was working and living down in London somewhere and probably sewing his wild oats with someone else. She also told him that, yes she did have affairs with other men occasionally. Because she was a normal, healthy girl who needed her share of sex. But that she had no intentions of ever, getting involved with anyone, or falling in love again, because she was sick of being hurt by men. So she had now turned the tables around on them, and she used men the same way they used women. "So Winston my dear, we can be friends if you like or want to be. But don't go falling in love with me, or even talk about love, I just don't need that in my life, 'cause love doesn't play a part in the rules of my game. I just don't need it or want it, 'cause when I make love then I can feel loved, and that's just fine by me."

"You're certainly a very unusual, good looking girl Olivia," Winston replied, pouring them both another drink. "And I feel that you have no intentions, of ever letting anyone get inside of your heart. If you've got one of course? A heart I mean."

"Oh yes believe me, I do have a heart. But it's buried very deep inside of me, and only shows itself for my children. And it doesn't beat for men like you Winston, that I pick up in clubs, who think they can use me."

"I don't want to use, or hurt you Olivia, but I would like to try and understand you, and get to know you better, if I can?"

"Maybe," was her reply. "Maybe."

Winston then sat down on the floor close to Olivia, and began to kiss her deeply, and caress her body as he unzipped her tight jeans. She tried to maintain a very, cool outward composure, but was filled with a burning, longing desire, deep inside herself for Winston. Thrilling him with her own arousing deep kisses, and caressing his very manly body. Winston's physical desire for Olivia began to burn inside of him like a fever, when she pressed her now naked body against his hardness, sending shivers of excitement through him. His hand moved from her swelling, breasts to stroke her womanhood, finding her love button that he began to gently, caress until it exploded, with a strong climax, now making Olivia, just ache for his manliness as she surrendered herself to him. He entered her gently, and began to move slowly inside of her, as she opened her thighs, wider to Winston, so that she could feel all of his hardness fully, inside of her, and they began to move together as one. The climaxes Olivia felt were so intense, she wanted to scream out loudly, while digging her long, finger-nails into his back, she then felt his body begin to shudder, as he finally climaxed with her, in a moaning noise.

They lay together on the floor wrapped in each other's arms. Olivia now feeling very, satisfied and good in herself, knowing that she had been able to give Winston, this hunk of a man, so much sexual satisfaction and pleasure.

She just smiled at him when he kissed her and said, "You're just a terrific lover."

***

Winston began to spend a lot of his free time with Olivia, now feeling that he must see her whenever he could. He introduced her to Jake and Allan, his two very close West-Indian-friends, who were also from Jamaica. Jake and Allan owned their own 'Motor Body Repair And Spray' garage-shop, called 'STOCK and INKS' just a few miles outside the city centre of Sheffield. They liked Olivia when they first met her, and they soon became good friends of hers.

Some nights during the week when she could manage to get a baby-sitter, to look after her twins, and Winston wasn't working. She told him that she'd like to see and visit the 'Shubeems', the 'Blues-Houses' that the West-Indians called them, with most of them being located around the 'Red-light-area' of Sheffield, so he would take her up there with him to visit these places.

Winston, often frequented these large, 'Blues-Houses' just to relax listening to the 'Reggae-Music' that was always playing continually in them. He would socialize at the unlicensed bar, buying a strong, Rum drink, and discuss business when meeting up with his close, West-Indian-friends, whom he had know for many years now, some of them from way back, when they had all lived in Kingston, Jamaica.

Sometimes during these 'Blues' nights Winston, would disappear for a while, walking down a long, dark hallway, towards the back of the house, and going through a door which had the sign in bold letters on it saying- 'PRIVATE', into a closed, private, illegal-gambling room. Small, wooden, round, or square tables, with stools or chairs around them, were set up in these rooms, with serious, faced men, sat around these tables, playing card-games and exchanging money. The atmosphere in these gambling rooms, only seemed to lift in a happy, frame of spirit, when Winston, used to enter laughing and cracking, jokes with everyone who greeted him, loudly shouting, "Pass-Tru-man, were-u-bin? Wi-not se-u-fu-long-tim-now?" Pass-Tru of course usually had a few, winning hands with his card games, leaving these private rooms very happily, while placing money into his wallet. Some evenings they would also go for a drive over to the 'Blues- Houses' in Bradford and Huddersfield, to see his other West-Indian-friends, who lived over there.

Olivia found these 'Blues-Houses' that she visited very interesting, and the people who frequented these places were different, very cool, only slightly friendly, and very wary of someone like her, whom they'd never seen at the 'Blues' before. Of course it was exiting for her to get a glimpse, into what most of everyday, society did not even know about, or would ever really accept and would probably refer to these places, as the seedier side of life.

And as she observed, some of the white, women she saw at the 'Blues-Houses', they really surprised her. As they seemed to be what she thought were old, prostitutes, looking about fifty or sixty years of age, always wearing heavy, make-up and wigs, to hopefully make themselves look younger, hoping to make some money for the night. "Very sad, but they've got no chance," she stated to Winston, shaking her head from side to side and pushing her long, hair, back over her shoulders. "Who are these dirty old bags trying to kid, they look like fucking dirty rats, that have just crawled out of the sewer to feast. Yes how very sad it all is, for these poor old ladies."

She also saw the pretty, young girls about seventeen and eighteen years of age, coming into these 'Blues-Houses', and taking all of their money out of their purses, and handing it over to their mean, looking pimps. These pimps were always looking around for someone new to work for them, and of course always had their eye on Winston's, classy, looking lady, Olivia. Who to them, looked as though she had just walked out of a 'Vogue' fashion magazine. They often greedily, wondered as they discussed with each other, doing their hi-fives and rubbing their hands together, just how much money she would be able to make for them each night, working out there on the streets, oh if only they could get her to work for them. But deep down from what they knew and had heard about Olivia, whom they all felt was a squeaky-clean-high-class-snob, who always smelt of some lovely, expensive perfume, that they had never smelt on anyone before, and couldn't put a name to it, that wonderful smell of hers. When she sometimes walked passed them, with her head held high, speaking to or even communicating with just a nod of her head, to a chosen few of the people in the room. These pimps, deep down also knew that she was far to smart and above doing their kind of work, and being controlled by them. So they just watched her, from a distance and fantasised whether Winston, could ever, did ever, or would ever, be able to control her.

"Yeah I'd luv-tu-wrap all dat long hair a-ers, around er-neck, an-pull on it a litt-al tight sometime. And I wonder who's got de-control a-dare sex life in bed, Pass-Tru or Olivia?" One of the pimps muttered nastily, but loudly enough for Olivia, to hear him as she walked by them all.

"Why both of us, is the answer to your troubling question. And why does our sex life seem to bother you so much? Is yours so fucking boring? And please for your own sake, don't ever touch my hair," Olivia replied, while turning around to glare at him, with a warning look in her large, green eyes.

***

They left a 'Blues-House' in the red-light-area of Sheffield, one night, in the early, hours of the morning. And were walking across the road to Winston's Jaguar, when Olivia saw a girl lying on the pavement near his car, screaming in pain. "God Winston, what's wrong with that girl? Let's see if she's okay."

"No leave her alone. Her pimp has probably beat her up man, and you don't get involved."

"What do you mean, don't get involved?" Olivia asked, walking over to the girl, to see if she could help her. "Christ, look at her face Winston, it's covered in blood and her arm looks as though it's broken."

"Leave her, or you'll have her pimp after you. You shouldn't get involved with these hookers Olivia, 'cause I don't."

"Fuck off Pass-Tru, and don't piss me off," Olivia shouted back to Winston, in a very angry voice. "This poor girl is badly hurt and she needs help, she needs an ambulance, now go and phone one for her, Winston. You don't have to say who you are, just give them the name of the street here."

Winston got into his car angrily, slamming the door closed, before driving away. While Olivia held the dark haired girl, in her arms, trying to comfort and soothe her, as she cried in pain. "You will be okay soon," Olivia, gently told her. "The ambulance is on its way. What's your name? And what's happened to you?"

"My name is Janice, and my pimp has beat me up 'cause I've not made enough money for him for the night. But I've told him I don't get into the cars with every man who stops me, if I don't like the look of them, 'cause I'm scared of meeting the Yorkshire Ripper. 'Cause he murders girls like me, and then he cuts up our bodies, and I don't want to have to die like that"

"Yes I agree with you. But you know Janice, if you want to do this kind of work, you don't have to walk the streets in fear of your life every night, scared of meeting the Yorkshire Ripper. And you don't need to have a pimp either, you could clean up your act and become a call girl, and work for yourself from your home. "

"Do you think so?"

"Oh I'm sure so, then you wouldn't have to go through this ordeal again, or be controlled by these fucking evil men called pimps, so think about it. And listen hear that siren? It sounds like the ambulance is here. Is there anyone you'd like me to contact for you? To be with you?"

"No thanks," Janice replied, when the ambulance pulled up at the side of her. "And thank you, Winston's girl, whoever you are, I'll be okay now. And I'll think seriously about what you've said to me, giving up walking the streets. I just wish I didn't love my pimp as much as I do, but he's also my boyfriend."

How very sad. And how do these young girls get so involved? And taken over by these fucking people who just use them? Olivia thought, as the ambulance drove off to the hospital with Janice.

After the ambulance had left, Olivia saw Winston's car parked farther up the street, she walked up to it, opened the door and got in. "You waited for me then," she said, slamming the car door shut, before Winston drove off. "You didn't have to wait for me you know, I could have made my own way home, and no I'm not afraid of Janice's fucking heartless pimp, even if you are Winston."

"Man," Winston replied with a laugh, and started to drive his Jaguar faster. "You certainly have some guts, or maybe you're just fucking stupid. For one, no, I'm not afraid of the pimps, they keep away from me 'cause they know I've no time for them. Two, no one, not even the pimps, would ever hurt, or touch you Olivia, 'cause they all know you're my girl. Three, you just don't get involved with these hookers. Whatever their problems are, whatever goes on between them and their pimps, is their business, it's got nothing to do with us. These girls aren't like you, you know, you're worlds apart and they all know what they're doing, and you could never change them or their way of life. And four, I don't know if I've told you before Olivia, but I do love you."

"Oh Christ Winston! That's all I fucking need right now. And don't you ever go thinking that I'm fucking stupid, just because I thought someone could use my help. But please will you just take me home, I've got blood all over my clothes off poor Janice. And right now I just need to take a nice hot bath."

***

The affair between Olivia and Winston became very intense over the next two years. And her twin daughters, Sarah and Angel, loved Winston and began to feel that he was like a second Father to them, in the absence of their own, Alex.

Winston adored Sarah and Angel, as though they were his own children, even though they never called him Daddy, because Olivia felt there was no need to bestow on him, this burden of a title. He often bought them gifts, and ice-creams when the ice-cream van came onto the street. And the twins would also get him to buy ice-creams for their friends, who loved to see Winston and looked up to him as their friendly, gentle giant. Often, when the children who lived on Crowfield Road saw Winston's car arrive outside Olivia's house, they would run out of their houses just to talk to him, and loved to do hi-fives with him, against his large hand. These young children all felt very, safe and secure being around him, assuring each other that if they ever got beat up, by their enemies at school, Winston would take care of these bullying, nasty kids for them.

Olivia would sometimes allow Winston to stay over at her home with her, but only for a few nights of the week, always making it very clear to him, that this could never or would ever be on a permanent basis. Their lovemaking was of course always, wonderful very, exciting and passionate, and finally she even admitted to Winston, and herself, that she did now have some feelings for him, that you might just call love. She also made it very, clear to him though, that she still did not want any other deeper, involvement between them, in their relationship. Because she felt she would still be unable, to deal with another full, time commitment in her life, especially when Winston began to ask her, to live with him and become his wife.

But she still felt that after all the heartache she'd had and been through, concerning the other men that she had thought would be permanent in her life. No man could or ever would, still be able to love her completely. Although she felt that Winston was trying so hard, to get her to believe that he did truly, love her, she was still scared that something would pop the latest, happy, safe bubble, that she was now beginning to allow herself to live in.

Alex still kept in touch with Olivia and the twins, he phoned her often, wrote her letters and would come up from London, to visit her at weekends, whenever he could. Alex now also knew about Winston being in her life, but he also knew that there was nothing, that he could do about this, knowing that if he told her, he did not like the situation, she may stop having anything to do with him at all anymore. But this did not stop Alex, from still loving her so very much, and his greatest fear, was now losing her completely to Winston. So he would always be racking his brain for new, ideas on how to win her back to him again.

Olivia still liked to see Alex sometimes, and cherished the memories of the life and love, that she felt they had once, happily, both shared together. But she could never admit to still being in love with him now, because she was still always holding onto the hurt and pain, that he had once caused her and put her through. Even though sometimes she felt that it would be easier, to just forgive him. But she knew that she would never be able to forget, so what was the point in her forgiving?

Yes she now felt that she was on a happy, merry go-round of fun, and that she was at last in control of everything, in her own life. Which she now seemed to play just like some board-game, that needed no commitments from herself. And these feelings gave her the attitude of an ultimate, girl-power-player, that the game was all hers, making her feel that she was very, much in control of her own happiness!!

******

Chapter 34

"Who can that be?" Olivia said to Cindy, who was sat in her Dining-room with her drinking coffee, when they heard someone knocking on Olivia's back door, one lunch time.

"Ello, I'm Danny yur new milkman," said a man, with blue eyes and a blonde haired crew cut, who was stood on Olivia's back doorstep.

"Oh, you are, are you?" Olivia replied, to the good looking man, with a very, cute smile on his face, who had his hands, deep into the pockets of his dark, blue, work overalls, jingling money.

"Dus-tha want tu-pay mi this week?" He asked, in his very broad Sheffield accent.

"Yes, and what did you say your name was? Danny. Well Danny, I pay my milk bill every week. So come in, will you? How much is it two pounds and something? No wonder I'm always broke. Oh, this is my friend Cindy," Olivia said, when Danny went into her Kitchen, before then walking into her Dining- room.

"Aye, I've seen er-be-fur," Danny said, with a big grin on his face. "I deliver er Mum's milk as well, an Cindy, yu-du look bloody rough in a morning."

"You cheeky bugger," Cindy replied, flicking her curly, blonde hair, back off her shoulders. "How the fuck dare you say that about me? And when have you seen me in the morning?"

"I see yu in-yur kitchen, through't window," Danny replied, with a laugh. "No don't tek-it seriously luv, I'm only joking, yu-look very good int-mornings. Better than that fucking old witch that lives across ru-ed from-ere, I just can't be du-in-wi-er. As I put-er milk ont-doorstep every morning, she op-ens-er bloody- du-or, just as I bend down, tu-see that I always leave-er two bottles. She gis-mi-t-bloody creeps she-dus. I've just been tu-er-ouse now tu-be paid, an she always bloody tells me-ow much she knows she owes me, she won't ever let me tell er."

"Would you like a coffee Danny? I'm making another one for Cindy and I."

"No thanks, I don't like coffee, but I'll ave a cup a tea wi two sugars in-it please," Danny replied laughing.

"Okay, I'll make you tea then Danny. You're very outspoken aren't you? I like that, and are you always joking, grinning and laughing? And what's a bright smart guy like you, doing working as a milkman?"

"Well I feel tis-only way tu-be-wi people, is straight, then thee know were thee are wi-yu. Don't thee? An yeah, I'm al-us bloody laughing an joking, 'cause who wants tu be bloody miserable? Life's tu bloody short tu mope around. An I'm a milkman 'cause I've just cum-out-at-army, bout a month ago, an I needed a job ant money's good."

"How long were you in the army for?" Cindy asked, while drinking her coffee.

"Bout four years now. It's good int-army, I really enjoyed it. I've been all ove-rt world, an ave been fighting bloody IRA, in Belfast fur a couple a years. Shoving fucking razor blades in-tu rubber bullets before I fired em, that made the fuckers jump."

"What made you leave the army, Danny? If you thought it was so good?" Olivia asked.

"Well, I didn't want tu-leave. I'd been training wit S.A.S. an-wer about tu-join-em, went wife, Gayle, ad a baby. So I ad-tu decide whether tu divorce our Gayle an forget our baby, or give up S.A.S. 'cause yu can't belong tu that if yur married, in case yu get caught. So I decided I do luv Gayle an our baby, so I give it all up an came-ome. Now I'm trying tu-fit back in-tu civvy life."

"What's the S.A.S.?" Cindy asked.

"Are yu as dumb as yu're blonde?" Danny asked laughing. "Yu must ave-eard-et S.A.S? I thought everyone in England ad."

"It's the Special Air Services," Olivia replied. "Is that right Danny?"

"Yeah," Danny answered. "But I'm not gun-ner bother explaining tu Cindy what thee do, she'll probably find out when she's older. So are yu as dumb as yu're blonde? Cause yu do sound it."

"Oh piss off," Cindy replied, in a hurt tone of voice. "And stop fucking picking on me, what am I suppose to know about the fucking army?"

"Aye, I will an I suppose yur-right," Danny said, with a big grin on his face. "I'm guing-tu-pub now tu get me some liquid lunch."

"What the hell's a liquid lunch?" Olivia asked.

"Beer," Danny replied with a laugh, before saying good-bye.

Danny and Olivia soon became very good friends; she just loved his happy, honest, personality, including his jokes. He would always arrive at Olivia's house with her milk, at eight-thirty every morning, when she was getting the twins ready for school. He would often bring the twins, orange juice, chocolate milk and yogurts, and Olivia would ask him how much they were. "Don't worry about it," he would always say with a laugh. "I'll add it to someone else's milk bill." He would always have a hot, cup of tea with two sugars in it, and give the twins ten pence each, just before they left for school, telling them not to buy any bubble gum, but to get themselves a' Kit-Kat' or a 'Blue-Ribbon' to eat with their morning school milk.

Sarah and Angel also liked Danny very much, because he was always teasing them, and telling them jokes. So that the twins would always set off for school every morning, laughing and trying to remember the latest joke that Danny had just told them, so that they could repeat it to their friends.

He invited Olivia and the twins to his home one day on 'Upper-Valley-Road', to meet his wife Gayle. Who was a lovely, tall, brown eyed girl with dark hair, and his beautiful, six-month-old blonde, haired baby son, called Dean.

***

Danny arrived one morning with the milk at Olivia's, house, the same time as Winston, and when she was about to introduce the two of them, she found out that they did already know each other. "But how come?" She asked.

"Well, wen-me-an-sum-a-me friends came ome-on leave," Danny replied. "We always went tut 'Crazy Daisy' in our army fatigues, an I would knock-ont-dour at Daisy wen-it were full. An I'd ask fur Pass-Tru here, an he'd used-tu let us in."

"Yeah I did eh," Winston agreed laughing. "I'd always let them in man 'cause I knew they were okay guys. And if any fights broke out, I would leave it to Danny and his friends to sort it out for me, so I could carry on drinking at the bar with my friends."

"Du-yu remember that night tu-ther year Winston? Went Daisy were closing ant people wunt bloody leave? An-yu-were-aving a bit a trouble getting em-tu-finish their drinks? So I-elped-yu-tu ger-em out?" Danny asked, with a big grin on his face.

"Oh yeah, I've not forgotten that night," Winston replied laughing.

"Why, what did Danny do?" Asked Olivia, who was really interested in their reminiscing conversation."

"Well I just dropped a small tear-gas-grenade," Danny replied laughing. "An that soon cleared bloody place out."

"Oh yeah it sure did, I've never seen everybody move so bloody fast before," Winston added laughing.

Olivia's window cleaner Jeff arrived next, to get some fresh, water in his bucket, to clean Olivia's windows. While he was stood at the Kitchen-door, waiting for her to fill his bucket, he saw Winston and Danny, inside and they all began talking and laughing with each other.

"Come in man," Winston shouted to Jeff.

"Oh it seems that you all know each other," Olivia said, while making another pot of tea for them all.

"Oh yeah we do," Danny replied smiling, "Jeff ere, used tu-be a bouncer at 'Crazy Daisy', that's how we know each other."

***

"What's up-we-yu this morning, Olivia?" Danny asked, putting her milk into the fridge, before pouring himself a cup of tea.

"I'll tell you when the twins have gone to school, Danny, I don't want to discuss any of this in front of them," she replied. Looking very unhappy and glum, as she closed the morning newspaper that she had been reading, before she began to brush the twins, long, hair and put it up into ponytails for them.

"Ere yu are twinies," Danny said, taking two silver ten-pence coins out of his blue, overall pockets, and passing them to the twins. "An remember no bubble gum, or I won't gi-yu anymore money."

"Thank you Danny," Sarah replied. "And we never buy bubble gum with our money at all, do we Angel?"

"Oh no," Angel replied. "'Cause if we did and you found out Danny, we know you won't give us anymore ten-P's. So we always get Kit-Kat's, or Blue Ribbon chocolate biscuits from Sheila's, on our way to school."

"That's good girls. Now off yu-gu-tu school 'cause yu don't want tu be late. An remember what I've told yu both, don't gu-talking-tu any strangers."

"No we won't," the twins both replied, before kissing their Mummy goodbye and leaving their house for school.

"You spoil my kids," Olivia said, after the twins had left.

"Aye," Danny replied. "Someone's got tu, an they haven't got their Dad ere-tu-spoil-em, an I luv kids, especially those twinies. You're bringing em-up good Olivia. An our Gayle and Dean luv tu-see-em, they're a pleasure tu-ave around our-ouse. An our Gayle says their ever-su-good-wi-our Dean. Now, why are yu-so-down-int-dumps this morning?"

"There's a big article in the newspaper, this morning, about the 'Yorkshire Ripper'," she said, showing Danny the newspaper. "And I'm bloody terrified, 'cause he's killed twelve girls up to now, I think it says four more have survived his attacks. But it's not only prostitutes that he's killing now, it's also ordinary girls out walking their dogs, or going home from work. The police just don't seem to be able to catch this maniac, he's always one step in front of them. He's killed in Leeds, Halifax, Preston, Bradford, Manchester and Huddersfield, and I feel sure he's going to come to Sheffield and kill someone here. Because he's now sent a letter to some cop over here saying, 'Sheffield will not be missed, next on his list'. Do you know Danny? If I've run out of cigarettes at night, I daren't walk down to Sheila's now to get myself another pack, 'cause I'm so scared. Especially with that park of ours being at the bottom of our road. And No one knows what this guy looks, or talks like, we've only been told he has a Newcastle accent. So if Cindy and I meet any guys, in the Discos or clubs, with that accent, we just get well away from them. But who the hell knows if he's a 'Jordy' or not? Or if the 'Jordy' accent is really his? Or what his accent is like?"

"Yeah I know how-yu feel, 'cause every woman I talk tu-now is fucking, terrified of meeting the 'Yorkshire Ripper', an-yu-all-ave a good reason to be. I won't even let our Gayle gu-tu see er Mother at night, by erself. Allt-police in Sheffield are working overtime looking fort Ripper, especially int 'red-light-area'. An most of us men are-ont look out fur-im also, I wish I could find't bastard, 'cause I'd fucking castrate im, among other things. But fur-now I'll teach yu what I've been teaching our Gayle, some Aikido, just int case yu-av-tu defend thee-sen."

"What the hell's Aikido?"

"It's what I learnt int army, an now I teach it one night a week in a school up our way in Sheffield. It's unarmed combat, ow-tu defend yurself, an kill, wi-yur hands an feet. It's very effective. An you'll be able tu defend yurself if yur attacked be anyone Olivia. So I'll come around here about one o'clock on Saturday, when I've finished wi-me milk, money collection, an we'll move some-at furniture in this room out-at-way, an yur lessons will begin. Then I'll go an get mi-sen some liquid lunch afore pub closes."

"Hey, that's great Danny," she replied, with a smile on her face. " And I'm very eager to learn this Aikido that you call it."

"Well, I think yu'll feel a lot safer when yu know sum on it."

"Yeah I'm sure I will," she replied.

******

Chapter 35

Olivia was lying in her back garden sunbathing, one hot, sunny morning in July, when she heard the telephone inside of her house start ringing.

"Hi, Olivia speaking," she said, after running into the hallway of her house to answer the phone.

"Hi Olivia, it's Winston. What are your plans for today? I was thinking of coming over to see you in about an hour."

"Well I'm going out to see Jake and Allan, at their garage in a couple of hours, and I've got to take a bath and get myself ready yet. But I'm just getting some sunshine on my white body this morning, and I'm pleased to tell you I'm slowly turning brown. Here's hoping that by the end of the summer, I'll be more your colour Winston, lovely and dark."

"Yeah keep trying hard then," he replied, with a laugh. "But people my colour get a lot of problems."

"Well I don't know why, 'cause I've always said black is beautiful Winston. Anyway I must go, 'cause I want to get some of those great fish and chips for lunch, from that chippy next door to the garage."

"Okay then, and I'll come down and pick you up at their garage at about five o'clock, so wait for me until I get there. See ya later."

***

When Olivia arrived at Jake and Allan's, 'Stock And Inks Body Repair And Spray Garage', they were very pleased to see her. Two of Jake's younger Brothers, Bob and Paul, had now also started working there, and they were helping to spray-paint the cars. "We'll break for lunch now if you like, 'cause it's 1 o'clock," Jake said, looking at his watch. "Paul, will you go to the chippy and get fish and chips for us all? 'Cause I know Olivia likes the fish and chips we get here."

"Yeah I sure do, and can I have some mushy-peas with mine please?" Olivia said, getting some money out of her purse.

"No put your money away Olivia, have lunch on us today. Wow, it's too hot to work," Allan said, cleaning off his hands with some gel and a large rag before washing them. "And I think I'll just go across to the pub and get us some cans of lager to drink. Your looking lovely and brown Olivia, have you been sunbathing?"

"Yes I have," she replied. Pleased someone had noticed that her skin was turning darker, as she put her arm next to Allan's to compare colour. "I've still a long way to go before I'll be as dark as you guys though, but I'm trying hard. And I keep hoping that some of Winston's colour will rub off on me sometime. He says he will be down here around five o'clock, to give me a lift home. So I hope you guys can put up with me until then."

"Of course we can, we luv to see you Olivia. And you've picked a good day to come and see us, 'cause we're not very busy today," Jake said, with a smile. "And where are the twins? Why didn't you bring them with you? Now that the kids are all off school, for their holidays."

"Oh they're over at my Parents pub the 'White Hart', with their brother Antony. And my Dad is taking them all over to Cleethorpes this weekend, to see their Great-Grandparents and Uncle Brian. My Uncle Brian has opened his own restaurant in Grimsby, that's just outside of Cleethorpes. And he's bought himself a lovely baby Lion-cub from the Cleethorpes zoo, he's called her Ester. And Uncle Brian is always taking her to his restaurant to show her off to his customers. And the twins and Antony want to see the Lion-cub, so my Dad is taking them over to see her."

"I'm surprised you aren't going to see the Lion-cub Olivia," Jake said with a laugh. "'Cause I thought you luved animals more than people, don't yu?"

"Yeah your very right there Jake, I do love animals very much, and so much more than a lot of the shitty people that I've met in my life," Olivia agreed, with a big smile. "And my Dad asked me if I wanted to go with them? But I told him I'll go with him next time.

'Cause I don't know what it is that's wrong with me of late, I just can't put my finger on it. But for a few days now I've had this uneasy feeling in the pit of my stomach, like there's something brewing something's in the air, something bad is going to happen to me. And I just can't work it out what it could possibly be, or what could go wrong in my life now. So maybe it's just my imagination going crazy or working overtime," she said, while shrugging her shoulders, as if trying to dismiss this uneasy feeling that she kept having inside of herself.

"Well is everything going okay between you and Pass-Tru? Are you both still so in luv with each other?" Paul asked with a laugh, passing Olivia her fish, chips and peas. "Or are you two beginning to have some problems now?"

"No not really everything seems to be fine between us, we do have our little spats with each other at times, but not very often, but doesn't everybody have spats about something? No I don't think that there's any problem there with Pass-Tru. And I hope you've put lots of salt and vinegar on these fish and chips for me Paul?"

"Oh yes I have plenty, try them."

"Hmmm they're so good," she mumbled, when taking a bite of the fish.

Olivia spent the rest of the afternoon sitting, on a chair soaking up the hot sunshine outside of the garage, drinking from a can of 'Lager' that Allan had given to her. Only Jake seemed to be working, while Allan, Paul and Bob were stood idly around, talking laughing and joking with her.

"Oh-oh I think were going to have a storm," Bob said, when the sunshine suddenly disappeared behind a big, black cloud, and they began to hear thunder rumbling, in the distance.

"God, I hope not," Olivia replied. "I've not got a jacket with me and I'm only wearing these jeans and a T-shirt, and they won't keep me very dry, or warm, if it rains."

"We'd better go inside the garage," Paul said, as it began to start raining heavily, with direct over-head thunder and lightning. "Yeah it's definitely a bad storm that's blown in, and the sky's turned pitch-black now."

"God I wouldn't have come out, if I'd have known we were going to have a storm today. Especially one as bad as this, 'cause I just hate thunderstorm," Olivia said. Watching the heavy, rain bouncing off the ground, as they were all now stood inside of the garage, by the door watching the storm. "It's five-thirty now but Winston hasn't arrived yet," she continued, whilst looking at the time on her watch. "And I've got to get home 'cause I'm feeling cold, now that the heat's gone. This rain has sure cooled things down a lot."

"Here, this will help to keep you a bit warmer," Allan said, putting his jacket around her shoulders. "And we're clearing up now, then we're all going for a drink, and I'll drive you home afterwards if Winston doesn't show up. So don't worry Olivia you'll be okay."

The Garage was locked up for the night, before they all went to the 'Talbot Arms' pub at six o'clock that evening to have a drink.

***

"I can't understand why Winston hasn't arrived," Olivia said. "He definitely told me he'd come to the garage at five, so I'd got to wait for him there."

"Oh just relax and enjoy your drink Olivia, don't worry yourself about him," Paul replied laughing. "'Cause I'm not bothered about Pass-Tru not being here and watching us, so that we don't get too close to you. I don't know if you know this Olivia? But he hates it when you spend too much time alone with us, he's afraid of losing you to one of us."

"No I didn't know that, I thought he knew that we were all just very good friends?"

"Well, he knows where we always come for a drink after work," Jake added. "And he must know that you'd still be with us Olivia, if he still wants to come and pick you up."

"Well, he's got about another half hour," Allan said, with a laugh. "Then I'm going, and I'll give Paul and Olivia a lift home. But for now, let's get another round of drinks in."

Later Olivia gave Jake and Bob a hug and a kiss good-bye, they thanked her for going to see them, and told her she must come and see them again very soon. Bob put his arms around her waist and looked into her eyes deeply saying, "I want you to look after yourself

Olivia, to take great care and be careful, I don't want anything bad to ever happen to you, because I care about you."

Thanks Bob," she replied, kissing him on the cheek. "Thanks for caring about me, and I promise I will be careful in life."

***

"Well we know whose car that is, don't we?" Allan said. As they were driving down a quiet, tree lined street.

"Whose car where?" Olivia asked, while she was sat in the front seat of Allan's car.

"That one back there, that we've just passed," Paul replied. "It's Pass-Tru's-Jag, didn't you see it?"

"No I didn't," Olivia said in a very, surprised voice, turning around in her seat to look through the back window of the car. "The bastard, that is his car outside that pub, and what the hell's he doing there? When he asked me to wait with you guys 'cause he was going to come and pick me up. Stop the car Allan, I'm going to find him and find out what he's up to."

"No Olivia," Allan said, coming to a halt-sign at the end of the road. "Pass-Tru's probably on some business."

"Well, I'll soon bloody find out who he's in that pub having a drink with, business or not," she replied, opening the door of Allan's car, to get out.

"No, no Olivia, leave it!" Allan said, trying to grab hold of her arm, to stop her from getting out of his car. "Please, Olivia don't go, you'll probably see Pass-Tru later tonight."

"I want to see what he's up to, and why he didn't come to pick me up," she replied, getting out of Allan's car and slamming the door closed, shouting. "Don't worry I'll be okay, I promise."

She walked back up the quiet, tree-lined street to Winston's car that was parked outside a small pub called the 'Black Cat'. *'I wonder who he's in there having a drink with. Maybe he is doing business with someone, like Allan says. So I'll just sit in his car and wait, then it will be a nice surprise for him, when he comes out of the pub and sees me,'* she thought.

She got into Winston's unlocked car and sat in the front passenger seat, thinking. *'I wonder how long he's going to be? Maybe I should have gone into the pub to him.'* She picked up a newspaper that she saw laid on the back seat of his car, and began to look through its pages.

She then slowly turned her head towards the pub doorway, and saw Winston coming out of the pub with a girl. A girl, who had very long blonde hair, was dressed in brown corduroy jeans, and a blue and white chequered shirt, holding Winston's hand.

In the surprised, shock of what she was now seeing, she dropped the newspaper that she had been looking at, and just sat there inside the car, staring at them both in total disbelief.

Winston looked back at Olivia, and did not acknowledge her in any way, acting as if he did not know her, or had ever seen her before in his life.

The blonde haired girl, let go of his hand and ran to the car, banging her fists on the window of it, while screaming and shouting at Olivia, in a very, broad, thick Sheffield accent, "What tha-fuck are-tha- doin in our fucking car? I'm gun-a kick yur fucking ead in, when I ger-old a yu!"

Olivia just sat there in the car dumbfounded, staring at Winston and this very loud girl, in total amazement and shock. She felt unable to understand, respond, or even speak about what she was now seeing before her very own eyes, what was happening before her, in front of her. The only other feeling that she was now beginning to have and be aware of, was that she just shouldn't be here, there in this place or sat in this car at all!!!

The girl then angrily, opened the driver's-side of the door to the car, and got in. While Winston slowly opened the back-door of the car, and sat himself in the backseat. "What's yur name an what the fuck are-yu doin in Winston's car?" The girl shouted nastily, now she was sitting in the drivers seat of the car, next to Olivia, and really glaring at her.

"Well please do excuse me, you two," Olivia replied. Still reeling with confusion, but beginning to think faster now, as she realized that this girl had just given her, her cue to be able to exit out of this bad, ugly, situation of a mess, that she had now gotten herself into. "Er-a my name's Olivia, and I'm a good friend of Jake and Allan's. And I've been to their garage this afternoon to see them, and I was going home but I got lost. Anyway I ended up on this street trying to find my way to the main road, so I could get a bus into town, when I saw Winston's car parked outside this pub. And I thought, maybe he would be good enough to give me a lift into the city centre. So I just got into his car and sat waiting for him to come out of the pub, but I'm sorry I seem to have picked a bad time, haven't I? 'Cause I didn't know that he was in there with anyone. Anyway who are you?" She curiously asked the girl.

"I'm Brenda," the girl replied. "And I'm Winston's common-law-wife of eight years. But ow the fuck du- yu know Winston?"

"Yes very common and I'll certainly not take that one away from you dear," Olivia replied smugly, to the girl, before saying. "And I don't really know him, Winston at all. I've only met him at Jake and Allan's a couple of the times when I've been there, that's all."

"But I've never met you, or have ever seen you before in my life man," said Winston, who was sitting in the back seat of the car.

"Oh no you haven't? Have you not? Well I don't need this, or anymore of your fucking lies Winston! So fuck you!" Olivia shouted, turning around now and glaring hard at him. "You stupid bastard, I just gave you a fucking way to save yourself, in front of Brenda's eyes, your sad wife of eight years. But you just fucking blew it man, so you just sort your own fucking messy life out, and leave me out of it."

She opened the car door, and got out, slamming the door shut very, hard behind her. Walking down the street still, feeling very, shocked, stunned, and confused. She just wanted to find a bus somewhere to take her home, where she could shut this nightmare out of her world.

"Hey yu! Olivia! Cum-ear! I'm still guner kick yur fucking ead in," Brenda shouted, running down the street, after Olivia. "Yu lied tu me. Yu do know Winston, don't yu?"

"Oh yes I do know him, but not as well as I thought, " Olivia replied, in a loud angry voice. As she now stopped walking down the street, and turned around to face Brenda. "But I just want to make something very clear to you Brenda, not you, nor anyone else, is going to kick my fucking head in, or do anything else to me. So just piss off, for your own sake. Okay?"

"But tell me, ow-du-yu know Winston?" Brenda asked, in a much calmer, voice now, feeling defeated after what Olivia had just said to her. "Please tell me, ave-yu-ad an affair wi-im?"

"Yes I have, and we've been having an affair for over two years now. But I didn't know about you Brenda, his common-law-wife of eight years, I had no idea. He told me he lived with his Aunty and I just accepted it. Stupid me for not questioning why a good looking guy like him, didn't have a regular girlfriend or a wife. But Brenda, how come you didn't know about me? Where did you think that Winston was, all of the nights that he wasn't in your bed? Because, Brenda darling, I'm sorry to have to tell you this, but he was in my bed with me."

"Oh was he? So tell me ow-old are yu Olivia? Where du-ye live? An are yu a hooker? An does Winston luv you?"

"No I'm not a fucking hooker, and please don't insult me! And I'm twenty-nine years old. But how can Winston love me after the way he's lied to me, or you Brenda for that matter? Does he love you also? As well as lie to you? Or maybe he just loves us both! And how old are you?"

"I'm twenty-three. And yeah I thought Winston luved me, I really did, 'cause we've been together for years now."

"Well, you're still very young Brenda, and you've still got time to learn as you find out about men. But as for me, I'm sick of fucking learning and the lessons never seem to end," Olivia said, feeling very sad and still confused.

The girls were stood talking very, calmly & civilly together, beginning to feel some compassion for each other now, as they both began to realize, that they had both been used and deceived by Winston. As they were walking towards the main road still discussing the situation, Winston suddenly appeared from somewhere around the next corner, shouting at them both and demanding to know what they had been telling each other, afraid of the stories that they may have been swapping about him

Olivia thought that this or any other questions from him, about what they may be discussing, did not deserve any answers from her at all. Instead she just gave him one of her, *'Who the fuck do you think you are man?'* green-eyed stares, before walking away, leaving him and Brenda, shouting, slapping and fist-fighting with each other in the street.

When crossing the road of the main-highway that she had now reached, a bus pulled up at a bus-stop that was right in front of her, as though it had appeared suddenly from nowhere, but just there for her, waiting for her to get on it, pay for her fare, and take her home.

***

She arrived home just before nightfall, feeling very cold and began to shiver whilst closing and locking the front, door to her home. She switched the lamps on in the lounge, drew the curtains closed, lit the gas fire, and poured herself a strong, drink of 'Scotch', before going upstairs to run herself a hot, bath.

She was laid there with her eyes closed, soaking herself in her lovely, hot, bubble-bath, feeling hurt, and still in shock about everything that had happened, everything that had been revealed to her and discovered that afternoon. When she heard the telephone in her bedroom start to ring. *'No! No more Winston! Just leave me alone!'* She said out aloud, as warm tears now began to run down her cheeks, as the phone continued ringing. *'Please, please just leave me alone you bastard; you're just like all the rest of them. And I won't have or take anymore heartache from anymore of you fucking men.'*

She lay in her hot, bath crying for about an hour. But her tears began to stop when she got out of the bath and dried herself with a large, pink, bath towel, then using her deodorant and dusting-powder on her body, before putting on her dressing gown.

She then went downstairs to pour herself another drink, taking the phone off the hook when she passed it in the hallway. She put the record 'Emotions' on her stereo to play, listening to the words of the song while she was drinking her 'Scotch', feeling exhausted and now needing a good night's sleep after the ordeal that she had been through earlier.

She took a sleeping tablet before going upstairs to bed, and soon drifted off into a deep, sleep while seriously thinking, *'YES WINSTON, I WILL GET MY REVENGE ON YOU, AND THIS I DO PROMISE!!'*

******

Chapter 36

She was awoken from her very, deep sleep, at around lunchtime the next day, by the sound of someone banging loudly, on her front door, and shouting her name. As she opened her eyes, realizing that it was Cindy's voice which she could hear. She got herself out of bed, put on her dressing gown, and went downstairs to open the door to let her in. Saying, "Oh thank-God it's only you banging on my door Cindy."

"Why? And what the hell is happening Olivia? I've been trying to phone you all morning, but your phone is always engaged. And Alex has phoned me 'cause he can't get through to you either, and he's so worried. So I told him that I'd come down to see if you're okay. Oh and Alex has asked me, to ask you, to give him a bell at work. What's wrong Olivia? Why is your phone off the hook?"

"Because I took it off that's why," Olivia replied. Going into the kitchen to make her and Cindy a cup of tea, before they went to sit down in her Dining-room at the Dining-table.

"God, did I have a fucking hell of a day, yesterday Cindy. I would just like to think that it was all a bad dream that I've had. But now I'm awake I'm realizing that it really did all happened. And I can't understand why Winston lied or did any of this to me, it's still all so confusing."

She then continued to tell Cindy, about how yesterday, she had met Brenda, Winston's common-law-wife of eight years. While Cindy sat there in disbelief with her mouth wide open, before saying, "Oh my God, the fucking bastard. And I'm so sorry Olivia, but I had no idea about her. But why the hell didn't he tell you himself about this fucking Brenda? Whom he's been living with, what seems to be for years now?"

"God-knows why he didn't tell me about her. And I suppose he thought I'd never find out about her. And as I've told Brenda, I was stupid enough to believe his fucking shit story, about him living with a fucking Aunty of his," Olivia replied angrily, as she lit another cigarette. "And I also believe that the stupid bastard underestimated me, yes he very much underestimated me. But he's going to be in for a fucking big shock and surprise, 'cause it's my turn to start playing bloody dirty tricks now. And when I'm finished I don't think that he'd try to ever underestimate me again."

"Oh come on Olivia, surely you don't want to see the fucking bastard ever again after all this? But do tell me what she's like? This Brenda?" Cindy said, now sounding very curious. "Is she good looking at all?"

"Well no not really she isn't good looking at all, now I come to think of her." Olivia replied, with a laugh. "She's quite ugly really, she's got blue eyes that really bulge out of her eye sockets. A small mouth with very thin lines for lips, and very, long-thin-straggly blonde hair, that looks as though the colour came out of a bottle. She's very common really, and has no finesse about her whatsoever, and she speaks with a dreadful, low life Sheffield accent."

"Oh Christ, she sounds bloody awful. And I wonder what the hell Winston saw in her for eight years? He must have thought he'd struck gold when he met you Olivia, 'cause you know everyone thinks your just a classy lady and beautiful. And even Winston thinks that about you, how do I know? 'Cause he's told me often enough, and he's always thanking me for introducing you to him," said Cindy, while helping herself to one of Olivia's cigarettes, from the pack that was laid open on the table. "But what are you going to do now? Apart from hating the bastard forever, 'cause, I guess you've now had your heart broken once again by him? The prick. And honestly Olivia, I'd no idea about this fucking Brenda of his. Well for Gods-sake you know that I'd have told you, if I'd have known anything."

"Yes I'm hurting a bit 'cause I'm feeling very deceived, but I won't stay like this for much longer Cindy. Because after what Alex did to me years ago, I vowed I would never go through any of that heartache again, 'cause I thought it would just about finish me. And over the years I'm pleased to say that I've hardened my heart. Yes stupid me I have to admit I did, and guess I still do love Winston, 'cause when you do grow to love someone, the love that you have for them, doesn't suddenly die, when you've found out something bad about them. But the most important thing is that I love myself, even more than I could love him, so that's why my life isn't once again going to be shattered. Because I believe that if you do love and respect yourself, you can get through pretty much anything unscathed. Anyway the more I think about it all, I'm more shocked and angry than hurt. And it's now time I got a bit of revenge on him," Olivia replied, before going into the kitchen to make them both some more tea. "And it seems that any close relationship that I've had with any man, always seems to go tits up at some time for me, and turns into a love-hate relationship in the end. So I've now decided I'm just going to use men even more from now on, and my affairs with them will just be one nighter's, no more and nothing else. 'Cause I certainly don't want anymore Winston's or Alex's or Lemons like my first husband, in my life. But the trouble is Cindy, I always seem to need men in my life; I must be just a glutton for punishment. And I'm still going to need them for my game of revenge. And you know what I always say to you Cindy? I don't ever get mad, instead I just get even."

"So what are you going to do to Winston then? What have you got in store for him?"

"Well I've been warned that he can be a very dangerous guy, the head of the Black-Mafia. So I think it's in your best interest if I don't tell you anything that I plan on doing to him Cindy. Then you won't be involved, and it would be pointless for him to come looking for you, when he's trying to find out who it is that's after him. Yes, I have got something good in mind for Winston, that will have him running scared around Sheffield and the other towns and cities, that he sometimes goes to. And I think it will teach him never to underestimate or fool around with me ever again!! Also," she continued with a revengeful looking smile on her face. "Don't ever forget Cindy, pay-back is a fucking bitch!!!!"

Cindy later left Olivia's house saying, that she was going downtown to see Dez and the rest of the crowd at the 'Crazy Daisy'.

She was eager to ask them if they knew anything about Winston's wife, Brenda? And she would then be going back to Olivia's that night, with a bottle of wine and hopefully some more interesting gossip about Winston, that she had been able to pick up from other people that knew him. So they would be having an evening of drinking wine, playing records and having some very, serious girl talk.

***

Olivia phoned Alex at work telling him, that she hadn't been feeling well at all, so that's why she hadn't wanted to talk with anyone, making that the reason being why she had taken the telephone off the hook.

Alex asked her if he could come and see her the next evening, because he wanted to ask her about something very important. She told him that would be okay, and that she would love to see him again. She put the phone down and smiled thinking, *'Alex always seems to be around to come to my emotional rescue.'*

She then got out her typewriter that she hadn't used for years, and a 'Jamaican' newspaper that Winston had forgotten he'd left at her house a few months ago.

She began looking through the 'Jamaican' newspaper, and smiled to herself as ideas came into her head, before going into her Kitchen to get a pair of scissors out of a drawer. She then cut out of the 'Jamaican' newspaper, two large advertisements that said, 'FLY AIR JAMAICA' and had pictures of aeroplanes on them. The next piece she cut out of the newspaper, was a large section of 'JOB- VACANCIES IN KINGSTON.' And the last piece that she cut out was 'HOUSES FOR SALE AND FOR RENT IN KINGSTON, JAMAICA.'

She put paper into her typewriter, and typed out on it in capital-letters, 'GET OUT OF ENGLAND FOR YOUR OWN SAFETY!!!!' This was then put with the first 'FLY AIR JAMAICA' advertisement, into an envelope, which she sealed, before typing Winston's name and address on the front of it. The next piece she typed out, to go with the descriptions of 'JOB VACANCIES IN KINGSTON', was, 'JOBS WILL STILL BE AVAILABLE WHEN YOU ARRIVE!!!!!' She typed Winston's name on the next envelope, and addressed it to him, at Jake and Allan's garage. The third note she typed out, to go with the notice of 'HOUSES FOR SALE AND FOR RENT IN

KINGSTON, JAMAICA', said, 'SLEEPING BAG, OR BLANKET, WILL BE LENT TO YOU, UNTIL YOU CAN AFFORD TO RENT/ BUY A HOUSE!!!!!' This envelope she addressed to Winston's own address. The last note that she typed out, to go with the 'FLY AIR JAMAICA' advert, said, 'GOOD-BYE. HAVE A GOOD TRIP AND ALWAYS WATCH YOUR BACK MAN!!!! NEVER COME BACK TO ENGLAND, OR YOU WILL HAVE TO DIE!!!!!' This envelope was addressed to Winston where he worked at the 'Crazy Daisy'.

Olivia then put her typewriter away and the envelopes into a drawer of her white dresser thinking- *'Yes Winston revenge is a lot sweeter than honey, and when you start receiving those letters, you'll just fucking shit! And pay-back is such a wonderful bitch! Why? Because it always makes me feel so much better!!'*

***

Alex arrived at Olivia's house, at nine-thirty the next evening, taking her out for a meal to a Chinese- restaurant down town in Sheffield. Whilst they were eating their delicious Chinese food and drinking wine, she asked him, what it was he wanted to ask her about?

"I'm going to America on a business trip, the middle of next week Olivia, and I've got some vacation leave owed to me, so I've booked into the hotel for four weeks. And I would like to know if you'd like to come with me, to have that honeymoon that we've never had before? I know you've always wanted to go to America Olivia, so what do you think of my idea?"

"What do I think about it? I just can't believe it," she replied excitedly, with a smile. "Oh Alex, I'd just love to go to America with you, it would be like a dream come true for me. Where are we going to?"

"Miami, Florida." Alex replied, pouring more wine into their glasses and holding her hand. "We'll be staying at the 'Caesars' Hotel, on Collins Avenue in Miami Beach."

"I can't wait to go, and I want to start packing straight away, so come on Alex, let's go home. Oh and I've got to phone my Mum and Dad and see if they will have the twins for me, while I'm gone, when do we fly there?"

"Next Wednesday lunch time at twelve o'clock, from Heathrow airport," Alex replied, kissing her hand. "I was hoping I could at last make you happy Olivia, 'cause I do love you so very much. I've got to go up to Manchester on business this Monday, and I was hoping I could spend the weekend with you? If you haven't got any other plans? Then I could drive from here on Monday morning."

"Yeah I'd love you to stay for the weekend with me Alex, and if you don't mind I've got a favour to ask you to do for me? There's a couple of letters I'd like you to post for me in Manchester, and another one in London when you get back there. I will post the last one myself, from 'Heathrow' airport. Please don't ask me any questions about them, the letters, Alex, 'cause believe me, I do know what I'm doing."

"Okay my love," Alex agreed. "If you say so."

***

Margaret, Olivia's Mother, came to see her on Sunday, agreeing to have the twins stay with her and Eric, while Olivia went to America with Alex. "But," Margaret said to Alex, after asking him to come into the Dining-room, where she could speak to him alone. "I don't think you know what you're doing to Olivia, by taking her over to America, because she's always had a fascination for the place and the people there. And I know that when she's been over there and comes back home, she will never be able to settle in England again. Your just making a rod for your own back Alex, I hope you realize that? And thank God she's leaving the twins with me, or I know she wouldn't ever come back at all. But I know she loves the twins too much to desert them, so I can be sure that I'll see her back here in four weeks time!"

******

Chapter 37

The following Wednesday, on the 24th July 1980, Olivia flew with Alex from Heathrow Airport, on a jumbo jet aeroplane to Miami, Florida, feeling that she was now on her way to a paradise.

Their room at the 'Caesars' Hotel on Collins Avenue was big and bright, with two large double beds, with matching bedside tables, and a cream, coloured telephone on one of them. They unpacked their suitcases the evening they arrived, and hung their clothes in a large, fitted wardrobe that was the length of one wall. Olivia put her hairbrush, cosmetics and perfumes, on the top of a low, long, dresser with a large, mirror above it. The room was lit by four large table lamps with cream lampshades, placed around the room. Off to one side of the room, near the doorway to the entrance of the room, was a lovely sized bathroom, with a shower built into the bath. At one end of the room in front of large, sliding, glass doors were two couches, with a matching chair, facing a television set with a tape deck underneath it. At the side of the television set was a refrigerator with an icebox. Through the glass doors was a balcony with chairs for them to sit on, looking out onto Miami-beach and the ocean. "Oh I just love this room, and the view of the beach and the ocean," Olivia said, walking out onto the balcony. "And I feel that I could stay here forever."

"Well it may not be forever, but just enjoy yourself while we're here," Alex replied, following her out onto the balcony, and wrapping his arms around her waist, kissing her lovingly on the neck.

***

Alex had to attend to only four days of business meetings. And for the remainder of the next four weeks they spent all of their time together. Swimming in the ocean and sunbathing on the beach in the mornings. Later on they would swim in the hotel pool, drying off in the very, hot sunshine, while having drinks from the poolside bar. At lunch time they would go out walking around Miami, looking at all of the lovely, different stores. And pick up a whole, freshly barbecued-chicken and French fries, which they would take back to their hotel room to eat. After lunch they would make passionate, love with each other, before going back out to the beach. Later on after they had finished their swimming and sunbathing for the day. They would go back to their hotel-room and shower together, before getting dressed to go out to different, restaurants around Miami-Beach for dinner in the evenings.

They went on tour-bus-trips that left from the 'Caesar's Hotel', to visit 'Disney World' in Orlando for two days, and had their photographs taken with Mickey and Minnie Mouse, Pluto and Donald Duck. Olivia did wish that her twins, Sarah and Angel were there with her, to meet these wonderful Disney characters. They saw the 'Epcot-Center' being built, and vowed they would come back to visit it one year when it had opened.

They visited the 'Kennedy-Space-Center', that is situated in the Florida Everglades, and was full of wild life including large alligators. They saw the building where the 'Space-Shuttle' was being built, and went into the control rooms where previous 'NASA'-space-rockets had been launched from over the years.

On their visit to the 'Indian-Reservation', they talked to many of the red-skinned-Indians whom they found to be friendly people, and they felt very honoured when the 'Chief' came over to talk to them, asking them with interest about their strange accents, and where they came from and where they lived. The 'Chief' told them that the 'Florida-Everglades' belongs to the red-Indians who came from many different tribes. Who had found their way there many years ago, when escaping from the white-man, and the reservations that the white-man, wanted to put the Indians on to live. He told them his tribe of Everglade-Indians had never signed a peace treaty with the white-man, but not to worry as they had no intentions of going to war with the white-man, even though he did steal their country from them. He invited them to watch him wrestle with a large, live alligator, and showed them one of his fingers that an alligator had bitten in half a few years ago, when he had been wrestling with it. They went for a ride on a very fast air-boat through the lush, dense, very, green Everglades, and when the boat stopped in the grassy waters they saw large, snakes that were wrapped around a few of the trees. And alligators lifted their heads up out of the water, to have a look at them. So it was understandable when the Indian who drove the air-boat, kept telling everyone to keep their hands out of the water for their own safety.

They went for an interesting evening out on the 'Jungle-Queen' paddle-steam-boat, leaving from 'Fort-Lauderdale', passing many, beautiful, millionaire's homes which had their yachts anchored in the water near their homes.

They made friends with Rick, an ex-Vietnam-war-veteran, who worked at the reception desk in the 'Caesar's' hotel. Rick was pleased to take these very interesting British-people, that he had made friends with, to his lovely home to meet his beautiful wife Jocelyn, and his six children, three-boys and three-girls. Olivia immediately fell in love with the lovely, big house that Rick and Jocelyn lived in, which had a big in-ground swimming pool, in their back garden. Rick and Jocelyn often invited them over to their house for dinner, before taking them out in Rick's beautiful, big, black Cadillac-car, to visit other places in Miami, like Coconut Grove, and the clubs around there, to discotheques in the other luxury, hotels, and to a 'Bob-Marley' concert.

Olivia and Alex's bodies were now a very dark brown, from all the sunbathing they were doing each day. They also drank gallons of lovely, fresh Florida orange juice that was full of vitamin-C, which they bought from a local supermarket, called 'Pantry-Pride'. They were now both feeling very, relaxed, happy and healthy, with Olivia feeling once again that she was very, much in love with Alex, and on the honeymoon that had been worth waiting for. She did give Winston an occasional thought, wondering if he might be missing her, and hoping by now that he'd received all of the letters that she had addressed to him.

Yes America was everything she thought and dreamed that it would be. And she soon fell in love with the way of life there. All the lovely, big houses that the people lived in, with their large, outdoor swimming pools. The big cars that they drove on the lovely, wide, straight highways. The very, big supermarkets where they did their grocery shopping, which had lots of different foods that she'd never seen or heard of before. The way the groceries were always packed into large, brown paper bags, and then passed to you by someone who always said with a smile, 'Have a good day now.' The lovely, clean restaurants that served over-filled plates of food, especially any meal that came with French fries. And the coffee cup that never emptied because it was always being topped-up or refilled by your waitress, but you were only charged for the price of one coffee. The spotlessly clean toilets that were called rest-rooms. The confident, definite, but laid back attitude of the North Americans, who were not afraid to express in the words they chose to use, the way they felt about things and life.

For four weeks life was just wonderful for Olivia and she did not want it to ever end, this beautiful lifestyle which she had come to know and love in Miami with Alex. It was the kind of lifestyle that she now knew she wanted to have, and felt that the only thing now needed to make her stay here complete, was her children.

The only thing that could have put a damper on this life in paradise, if they had allowed it to, was the political refugees and prisoners who arrived on the Miami-beaches from Cuba, after Castro had thrown them out of their own country. These people who seemed to arrive by the hundreds every day, throwing their drugs in large, wrapped parcels over-board from their small, un-seaworthy boats. Were now being housed temporally, in the 'Orange Bowl' football stadium, and in tent-cities at intersections underneath the large, Miami freeways.

After Alex, and Olivia's first two weeks stay in Miami Beach the crime-wave increased tremendously and tourists were warned not to take their late night walks on the beach by the ocean anymore, as girls were now being raped by Cuban men who held sharp knives to their throats. This sad news soon stopped Alex and Olivia's romantic moonlight, late night strolls on the beach, which they loved to take by the side of the ocean. So instead they would now lay in each other's arms on one of the beds watching a late night movie.

Towards the end of their stay in Miami when she was reading the Florida newspapers, Olivia began to notice articles that were now being written in these newspapers. To warn Americans about a new, sexually transmitted disease that had recently been found. The signs of symptoms of this disease, were red, blotchy, weeping, open sores, that looked like cold sores, around the genital areas of males and females. And the scientists had not yet found a cure for this disease, which was later called 'Herpes.' She decided to take these newspapers with this interesting information home with her to England. To forewarn her friends back there about this new, sexually transmitted disease that the Americans had now got to deal with. Never for one minute thinking or believing that it would ever reach the shores of England, which was at least three thousand miles away from America.

***

At the end of their wonderful four weeks vacation, they glumly, packed their suitcases before leaving their beautiful hotel room with heavy hearts, to go to the airport to get the plane which would fly them back home to England again. Olivia cried for most of the journey home on the plane, because she really didn't want to leave America, and the wonderful life she had found there. And she kept telling Alex, that America had turned out to be, just like everything that she'd ever dreamed that it could be, and she so much wanted to go back with her children to live there. "Please don't cry Olivia? But I do know how you feel," Alex said, with a lump in his throat as he held her in his arms. "I know you love America, and I'll try to take you and the kids back there to live one day, I promise you."

That evening when the plane had taken off from the Miami-airport, it flew through the night, arriving back at Heathrow Airport in London the next morning. They were now both very tired and just exhausted after the long, train journey which took them up to the north of England, back to their home in Sheffield, arriving back in the late afternoon of that day. So they just dumped their suitcases in the hallway, before going straight upstairs to bed, to try and catch up on some sleep with them both now starting to feel the jet-lag, with the five-hour time difference between the two countries.

***

They didn't have much to say to each other when they awoke the next day, as they were both lost in their own wonderful, memories of their life's in another world, in another country, for the past four weeks. That had now disappeared in the short time of just a plane ride. They both felt as if they had lived out a marvellous fantasy, but now it was gone and seemed so far out of their reach.

Alex left for London, to go back to his home and job down there, later that evening. And Olivia had an early night, hoping that she would soon be able to catch up on the time difference and get over her jet-lag feeling. To then get on with her life once again back in 'Jolly-Old-England'.

Her Mother and Sister Suzanne were coming over the next afternoon, to bring the twins back home to her, and she was looking forward to seeing her family once again, and giving them the lovely, gifts that she had brought back for them all.

******

Chapter 38

The following morning Winston, brazenly, opened Olivia's back, door with his own key, walking into her Kitchen, where she was stood making herself some tea. "Wow your almost black," he said, referring to the colour of her skin. "Cindy told me you'd gone to Miami, Florida, with Alex. Did you have a good time? Did you like America? And was it how you expected it to be? It looks as though the weather was nice and hot, and you did a lot of sunbathing Olivia, you're a lovely colour, you're nearly as black as me."

"Yes I know I have gone very dark," she replied coolly, taking her mug of tea into the lounge, to sit by the window in there where she could feel the heat of the sun on her face. "Yes we've had a terrific time in Miami, there was a heat wave while we were there. And I just love America and especially the way of life over there, now that I've seen it. And I feel I will miss it all very much, now that I'm here back home," she finished with a deep sigh. "Anyway what do you want? What are you doin here?"

"I wanted to see you, I've missed you. And did you miss me at all, Olivia? While you were with Alex over there?"

"No not really, no not at all Winston," she replied, giving him one of her hard, uncaring, unfeeling, cold, green-eyed looks. "But how could you expect me to, when I was in America enjoying myself with Alex my husband? But do tell me Winston? How have you been getting on without me? And how is your dear wife Brenda? Has she forgiven you at all yet?"

"You fucking snobby bitch Olivia," he replied with a laugh. "You always come through anything okay in the end don't you? You must have got luck on your side. And when your parents made you girl they certainly broke the mould afterwards, didn't they? I came to see you, the week after you found out about Brenda, to ask you to marry me. But then I found out you'd pissed off to America with your fucking husband. So how do you think I felt Olivia? I love you and I was prepared to give up Brenda for you."

"What give up poor Brenda for me? Oh Winston how can you be so fucking heartless? And I can't marry you 'cause I'm already married, remember? So please don't try doing me any favours. Anyway it would break Brenda's heart if you left her for me, poor girl. You know that I'm too much competition for her. And where the hell did you find her in the first place? Some fucking garbage dump? And don't you ever call me a fucking snob Winston. I may be many things, a bitch yes, a first class bitch and bloody good at it, if I have to be, but I've never been a snob. That's if you know what one is?"

"I've been receiving some very nasty letters while you've been away Olivia, and I keep thinking someone is after me, following me everywhere I go. I keep looking man, but I have no idea who it is."

"Is that why you look so tired? Are those letters keeping you awake at night? Poor Winston you must tell me about them," she said with a smile. Putting the 'After The Love Has Gone' record on her stereo to play, as Winston told her all about the letters that he had received, and where they were delivered to.

"I think they are more like threats on my life man," he said, in a concerned tone of voice. "But I can't think who it is that's trying to get me."

"Well Winston dear, who else have you been upsetting and pissing off, apart from me?" She asked, while changing the record to *'I Will Survive'*, and turning the volume up very loud, hoping that Winston would hear the message in the words.

"No I haven't upset anyone recently, apart from you."

"Well, it must be me then who sent those letters to you Winston. And listen to the words on this song, 'cause I think they must have been written just for assholes like you," she said, in a very American accent. Now I've got to take my bath, because my children are coming home this afternoon. So Pass-Tru I think you've stayed around long enough in my life now, to find out all about me, and it's now time for you to move on. Like just fuck off, close the door on your way out, and don't forget to leave your key."

Olivia walked out of the lounge, leaving Winston sat there looking after her in disbelief. She went upstairs to her bathroom and turned the taps on to fill the bath. She was pouring bubble-bath into the running bath water, when Winston walked into the bathroom grinning.

"Oh haven't you gone yet? You don't believe that I sent those letters to you, do you Winston?" She asked, turning off the bath-taps, then taking off her long towelling dressing gown revealing her lovely, naked, dark brown body to him, before stepping into her bubble-bath, and lying down to soak.

"There were four letters that you should have received, two were posted to you from Manchester, and two more were sent from London. I really do hope they had you running fucking scared Winston, while I was away enjoying myself. 'Cause you deserved to be running scared. And don't you ever play your fucking sad sick games with me ever again. Because do remember this man, play with me and your just playing with fire, and I'll do something even worse to you next time. Oh and don't bother trying to give me any boring explanation, for what you did to me, 'cause I'm not really interested. Anyway there's no need for you to come around here, because I'm going away again in a couple of days time, for a few weeks. I'm taking the twins to see their Great-Grandparents, Uncle Brian and his Lion-cub Ester, and other family members who live over in Cleethorpes."

"Oh are you? Well if that's what you'd rather do than hear me out, go. But Olivia I really didn't mean to hurt you in any way honestly," he replied, now beginning to feel very defeated.

"Oh really."

"And maybe when you get back from spending some time with your family and your twinies, you'll be in a better mood to listen to me, and to talk to. 'Cause your kids do seem to be able to bring out the better side of you Olivia."

"Oh just go, fuck off will you. And I don't even know why I'm allowing you into my home, or even bothering to talk to you anymore. But I did want you to know who'd been sending you those nasty scary letters."

"Okay then, so bye for now. And please, don't drown in your bath water?"

"No not bye for now, it's goodbye for ever Winston. And I promise you, you couldn't be lucky enough for me to drown, 'cause I'm a pretty good swimmer. Now go on get out of here before I get angry."

***

She just fell in love with her immediately, Ester the four months old Lion-cub, when she met her, at her Uncle Brian's restaurant in Grimsby. "Oh, she's just adorable," she said, wrapping her arms around Ester and hugging and kissing her. "Oh I want one Uncle Brian, and you know that I'd love it and look after it."

"Yes I knew you'd fall in love with Ester and wouldn't be afraid of her Olivia, because you've always loved animals," Uncle Brian replied, giving Ester a large sirloin steak to eat, that he got from his restaurant's kitchen refrigerator. "When you were a baby, you'd crawl out of the back door of your Grandma and Granddad's hotel, and we'd find you asleep in the big kennel with you Gran's Golden-Labrador-Bonnie, and her six puppies. Even as a baby you loved animals and had no fear of them, and Bonnie thought you were one of her pups, so she'd let you curl up with them and go to sleep. We've got photos of you as a baby asleep with Bonnie and her puppies in the kennel."

"Yeah Gran showed me them the other year. And don't we all look so sweet the puppies and me curled up asleep together? And how does our Suzanne get on with Ester?"

"Okay, but she doesn't make a fuss of her the way you're doing. She's stroked her once or twice but that's enough for our Suzanne, 'cause Esters a Lion and Suzanne's afraid of her roaring, or biting her."

"Well I'm not afraid of her," Olivia said, holding Ester close to her and kissing her on the nose. "Has she got any Sisters?"

"Yes but I'm afraid you can't have a Lion-Cub Olivia, because you can't keep one in your house, there's a law against it. Ester lives at the zoo and I visit her everyday, and I bring her in my car down to the restaurant. She's so tame because she's been used to humans from when she was first born, her Mother died and I used to bottle feed her, and nurse her to sleep. She was going to be sold to another zoo, but I got so attached to her I just couldn't bear the thought of losing her, so I bought her myself. I paid the zoo owner, who's a friend of mine, 600-pounds for her and I also pay the zoo for her food. Her full name is Esterrel, that's the name of my restaurant, and she's called Ester for short. When she gets to be about six months old, I don't know if I'll still be able to bring her out of the zoo, to the restaurant. The police have told me it all depends on how tame she still is. I've also got a beautiful guard dog that lives at the zoo, called Bandit. You'd love him Olivia, he's crossed with a wolf and looks just like a wolf. Now he does bloody terrify our Suzanne when he's growled at her."

***

Olivia was spending a very happy time with the twins, at her Grandparents. And with being so busy and short of staff, most evenings she offered to work for her Uncle Brian, in his restaurant the 'Esterrel'. Making friends with the waitresses and other staff who worked there. Elaine, who washed dishes and made coffee in one of the other kitchens at the restaurant, was a lady in her late fifties who also told people their fortunes, by reading ordinary playing cards that they would shuffle and cut into packs of three.

Olivia and Elaine became friends on their first meeting, and later in the week Elaine asked her if she would like to have her fortune told, by her reading of the cards. Olivia thought that this would be fun, and eagerly agreed, and was pleased when she cut her cards, that Elaine, could see things that had happened in her past. She also told her that she could see two men who figured prominently in her life, who both loved her very much. One was her husband, and the other was a man who was afraid of losing her over some upset, or problem they'd recently had between them. The future cards, which Olivia had cut, began to tell her of a very big removal that would be coming into her life. And that she and her family would move from the house, which they were now living in, and go very, far away, across a lot of water to live at the other side of it. This removal that was seen for her, in the cards, also said that it would be filled with happiness, brightness, love, and lots of money. But these fortune-telling cards had Olivia very confused, as she told Elaine that she had no intentions or plans of moving house just yet. But in time she would like to go and live where she'd just been for a holiday, over in America.

"Well this removal is on its way to you, and will be here and happening very soon. Because that's what I see," Elaine definitely told her.

She asked Elaine if it was possible for her, to be able to read Alex's cards, even though he wasn't there? And Elaine's reply was yes, if Olivia thought hard about Alex in her mind, and could picture his face as she shuffled and cut the cards into three.

"Oh yes this is all clear for Alex," Elaine said, reading his cards. "The cards tell me that Alex is very much in love with his wife, and he is trying to win her back. His greatest fear is losing her to another man. He will come to visit you at your house one day, bringing papers with him concerning another job. These papers concerning this other job, will have been given to him by someone, who has brought them across a lot of water from another county. His future is also filled with a big move in his life very soon, and love brightness happiness and money."

"Oh is it?" Olivia said, staring at the playing cards laid out on the table in front of her, and not being able to see anything but pictures of Kings, Queens, Diamonds, Spades and numbers on the cards. Wondering how Elaine could possibly see people's fortunes on them, or in them. "I don't know what to think," she said, laughing out loud now. "'Cause I just can't see how you can see anyone's fortune in these cards Elaine. If they were 'Tarot-cards' maybe yes, I could believe what you could see in then. But with these playing cards I really don't think so. Anyway as far as I know Alex is very happy with the job he's already got. And he's not said anything to me about looking for another one."

"How's it going then?" Brian asked, bringing Olivia a drink into the kitchen. "Has Elaine read your cards yet?"

"Yes she has and I'm very confused, I don't know what to think, or if I should believe anything that she says she can see."

"Well what Elaine sees when she reads people's cards for them, all usually comes true," Brian said confidently, supporting anything which Elaine may have seen for Olivia, in her coming future. "But don't go worrying about anything that she's told you, 'cause what will be, will be."

"Okay then I'll try not to think about any of it. But Elaine's also told me she saw a car accident happening around me. And I really don't want to be in another one of those Uncle Brian."

"Yes I saw a car accident," Elaine agreed. "But I don't think that it's you that will be in it Olivia, because as I told you. I saw a car, police, an ambulance and someone hurt, but I didn't see a hospital, or a hospital bed. Or you laid in one."

"Oh God this sounds all too scary to me, and I'm not happy with what you've seen Elaine," Olivia said with a shudder.

"Now come on? Don't you go worrying about being in another car accident Olivia," Uncle Brian told her, trying to dismiss her fears. "And can I get you a drink now Elaine? 'Cause we'll be closing the restaurant up soon, and I'll give you a lift home."

***

At midnight that night Brian was giving Elaine a ride home in his car, and as they were approaching some traffic-lights at the intersection of the road, just before reaching the street to turn off to her house. They passed an accident on the opposite side of the road from them, which had just happened between a car and a motorbike. Looking through the car window as they drove by it, they could see a motorbike turned over onto it's side, and the driver of the motorbike lying in front of the wheels of the car, with the police and an ambulance just arriving there at the scene. "That's your accident that Elaine saw happening in your cards, Olivia," Brian said, pointing through the car window at the side of it. "And look? There's the car, someone hurt, the police and an ambulance."

"Yes," agreed Elaine, who was sitting in the back seat of Brian's car, looking through the side window at the accident. "I'd definitely say that's the accident that I saw for you Olivia, and remember the cards said that you wouldn't see a hospital or a hospital bed at all?"

"Wow! My god you're both right you know," Olivia said, in amazement. "And I'm now beginning to believe those cards that you read Elaine. I wonder what else that you saw coming to me will also happen?"

"Well just try to remember what I saw in your cards? And let me know if anything else does come true for you, 'cause I'll also be interested to see if it does," was Elaine's reply.

***

After they had taken Elaine home, Olivia and Brian went back to her Grandparents home and decided to have a Scotch and lemonade night-cap drink. "I'm very pleased for you and your restaurant, Uncle Brian, it's a great place you've bought, and the business is good. You've been busy every lunch time and evening."

"Yes, I'm pleased with it, but it was difficult at first, and I had a lot of problems with Sandra."

"Who's Sandra?"

"Oh, didn't your Mum and Dad tell you? Well, obviously not. Do you remember Portuguese Manuel, one of the waiters who used to work at the 'Flamingo-Club? And Sandra that lovely blonde girl he got pregnant and married? Well I bought the restaurant off Portuguese Manuel, didn't you know?"

"No, I'd no idea Manuel owned a restaurant," replied a surprised Olivia, lighting a cigarette. "The last time I saw him he'd bought a green grocers shop, and he told me Sandra was expecting their second baby."

"Well Portuguese Manuel used to be a very good friend of mine Olivia. Don't you remember? I went with him to Portugal one year to meet his parents, and you asked me to bring you back a long string of onions from Portugal, to hang up in your kitchen. It was soon after you married that Clive Lemons."

"Oh yes, and that was a long time ago," she replied, with a laugh. "But I do remember those onions that I hung up in my kitchen, anyone who came to my house had to see my Portuguese onions. I also remember Manuel and Sandra being very happily married."

"Aye, well not for long. Manuel loved Sandra very much, and she had two boys to him. But he was also very, very jealous, and he gave her a hell of a time, if he thought she was looking at another man. Anyway he bought this restaurant, and soon afterwards they split up and got a divorce. And Sandra went back home to live with her parents, taking the boys with her. Manuel had visitation rights to see his boys of course, and he took them out at weekends. Anyway I bought the restaurant off him, and a week later after he'd sold it to me, bloody Portuguese Manuel took his boys out for the day and never brought them back home again. He fucked off to Portugal with them, and hasn't been seen since. Well Sandra was convinced I knew something about this, and she kept asking me about it. Like when had Manuel told me that he was going to steal his sons and take them out of the country? Then she got a bloody subpoena on me, and I had to go to court before a judge, and tell him what I knew. That I didn't know anything, and Manuel hadn't said anything to me about kidnapping his boys and leaving the country, so I told the judge that. But it bloody unnerved me I can tell you. And to this day I know Sandra doesn't believe me, and every time I see the fucking bitch she says to me, in her fucking whining voice *'Brian, are you going to tell me where my children are?'* But honestly Olivia, I'd no idea what Portuguese Manuel was up to."

"Yes Uncle Brian," she replied, pouring them another drink. "I really do believe you, anyway I think if you'd have known what Manuel was up to, you'd have told Sandra about what he planned on doing."

"Yes probably."

"Anyway why would someone tell anybody, that they planned on kidnapping their own kids? And I didn't know that you could kidnap your own kids. How can you if the kids are yours and belong to you?"

"No I didn't either, but I've found out that by law, if one Parent has got custody of them, and the other Parent takes them out of the country, to live with them in another one, it's classed as kidnapping."

***

After a couple of weeks Brian told Olivia that he would drive her and the twins back to Sheffield, when they were ready to go home, because he wanted to visit some friends of his who lived there.

She kissed her Grandparent's good-bye and discussed with them the possibility of seeing them later in the year, at Christmas at her parents' pub.

Just before leaving Cleethorpes, Brian took her to the zoo so she could say good-bye to Ester. She did this with tears in her eyes, as she hugged and kissed Ester good-bye, afraid of what the cub's future would be. And dreading the thought of her having to spend the rest of her life in a cage, making her unsociable, nasty and viscous, just as lions are expected to be. Oh how she wished, that it were possible for her to take this beautiful, friendly, loving, cuddly, Lion-Cub-Ester, home with her, to look after her.

******

Chapter 39

A few nights later after Olivia, had returned home from her Grandparents, and the twins were asleep in their beds, she was sitting in the lounge having a drink, while watching a boring, television program. Yawning and looking at her watch she saw that the time was now 10:30, and thought about having an early night, when she heard someone knocking on her front door. On opening the door, she saw Winston stood there smiling, dressed very, smartly in his white-suit, black, shirt and large black, wide brimmed hat.

"Hi," he said, before walking past Olivia, and going into her lounge. As he passed her, she noticed that he was also wearing his thick, gold chain necklace with its matching, gold bracelet. She could also smell his lovely, expensive, 'Channel' after-shave lotion, which Winston, knew Olivia loved the smell of. She also noticed he was holding two records in his hand.

"And hi to you Winston, how yu doin?" She asked in surprise, before closing the door after him and watching him walk across the room, to go and pour himself a drink of 'Scotch', from one of her decanters.

"I'm fine," he replied, quickly knocking back his 'Scotch' before pouring himself another one. "No I'm not, I'm not at all fine, not really. I've been missing you like crazy Olivia, and I've come around to see you, and I hope we can talk about things? But first I want you to listen to these records I've brought you, 'cause the words on them say it all a lot better than I can. So I'm going to play them for you, and I want you to listen hard, 'cause they're from me to you, every word of them. Let me pour you another drink while I play the records. Then I want us to talk about our problems."

"Our problems? Don't you mean the problems that you alone have caused for me? And us?"

He turned the volume of the television down, before putting on the first record '*Working My Way Back To You Girl*'. "Now please listen to these words?" He said. "'Cause I know you do listen to the words on records, as well as the beat."

Olivia lit herself a cigarette while listening to the words on this record, and kept looking at Winston who was sat in a chair across from her. As she was hearing, '*I'm working my way back to you girl, with a burning love inside. And I'm so sorry for acting that way for so long.*' "Umm," she said, when the record had finished playing. "What are you trying to tell me Winston? That because you love me, you're so sorry, and that I should forgive you and take you back? Well I don't think so!" She said stubbornly. Feeling that right now, she would have to dig her heels in, so that he knew she was being very, definite about the way that she was now feeling.

"Shush!! Don't say anything yet Olivia, before you listen to the other record, and this one is also from me to you." He replied, putting on, '*Let's Go Round Again*'.

She sat quietly in her chair, drinking her drink, smoking another cigarette, and looking at Winston while listening to the words of the song. '*Let's go round again? Maybe we'll turn back the hands of time.*'

It was very silent in the room when the record had finished playing, while they were sat alone together, just looking and staring at each other, with so much love in their eyes. But Olivia was now afraid, to admit to the love that she still felt in her heart for Winston. Because she now also thought, that he was, just like the other men that she had had in her life. And no matter how much love she gave to someone, nothing lasted forever. And like the others, he had hurt her, by taking her for a big, ride on the wings of his love, fooled her, tricked her, deceived her and used her. And she had now vowed to herself, that neither he, nor anyone else, would ever do it to her again. So she was now trying to figure out a way to explain to him, how to understand her reasoning's of why, things could never be the same between them, like they were before.

"So you, who I've told to keep away from me forever, must have a lot to say for yourself I feel, with coming around here, to probably just grovel and make a bigger fool of yourself than you already have done. And for starters are you trying to tell me that you really do mean all of those words on those songs?" She said with a very, deep sigh.

"Yes I really do Olivia, every word," he replied, with a loving smile.

"Okay then I just may believe you in time, but you have got to prove those words to me. And first you must write on the record labels if you do mean them."

"Okay then I will, if that's what it will take to get you to believe me," he replied. Taking a pen from the inside of his jacket pocket, when Olivia passed the records to him. "Will- *'From Winston to Olivia, with all of my heart.'* Be okay?"

"Yes I guess it will do for a start. And I've got a record that I want to play for you also. Then we must do some very serious talking about us two. Yes I know we can say a lot to each other through the songs on records, if we have a problem putting our feelings into our own words. But there's a lot that we both have to say, and explain about ourself's. Especially you Winston, 'cause there's a lot about you that I don't really understand."

Olivia put on the record for him to listen to the words of, *'Don't Make Waves'*. And poured them both another drink. "So what was your sick game then Winston? Why didn't you tell me about Brenda, your wife of many years? And how long did you think you could keep your sad sick secret from me?"

"Well first of all just let me make something very clear! Brenda is not my wife, she never has been or ever will be. She's just my long time girlfriend. It's her who sees herself as and wants to think of herself as, my common-law-wife, as she calls it. But in my way of thinking she can't be my wife unless I legally marry her. And I wanted to tell you all about her many times now. But I always put it off because I was so scared of losing you Olivia. I always had this deep feeling that you would just finish with me, and hate me forever if you found out about her. And I just didn't want that to happen at all."

"What you mean hate you like I do now?" She replied, looking at him very hard as she lit herself another cigarette, and not intending to make his explanation easy for him at all.

Do you remember when our affair first started? What seems like years ago to me now. Well you made all of the rules about it Olivia, and remember they were all your rules about our affair? Not any of my rules at all, on how it would go, only just yours. And the first rule was, you wouldn't see me if I was married, had a girlfriend or involved with anyone. Rule number two, absolutely no falling in love whatsoever. You made it very clear to me, that you didn't want me to love you, only sexually. As you told me that you had no intentions of ever loving me, or anyone else. Oh yes Olivia everything was fine for me in the beginning, because I told you that I wouldn't fall in love with you. So I didn't think that it mattered that you didn't know about my girlfriend Brenda. But I fancied you like mad, and I thought you were just great when we made love. But you had made it clear that I must enjoy you while I could, 'cause you wouldn't be with me for very long. Then look what happened to us? We did end up falling in love with each other, even though we both tried so hard not to feel it, or admit to it. But in the end our feelings for each other became so strong, that we had no choice but to tell each other how we felt. And by then our affair had become so very intense, and I just didn't want to lose you at all. And you would have just finished with me straight away, if I'd have mentioned Brenda to you. The girlfriend that by the time that you met her, I was ready to tell her that it was all over between me and her. Yes your timing was all so wrong when you found out about her, 'cause the week after that she would have been out of my life. And I'm sorry about the shock that it must have all been for you."

"Oh you are, are you? Well that's nice to know that you might just care about my feelings. And yes you're right Winston, they were all my rules that were made only by me, to protect myself. And I guess that they always will be, my rules. And I guess that I got burned by you too, when I decided to play with you eh? 'Cause that's only what I was doing with you in the beginning. So where do we go from here? Is it really over for us both now? After what happened? After what I found out about you?"

"Well I was hoping that it wouldn't be, 'cause I do still love you very much Olivia. And I would very much like to marry you. So will you marry me?"

"No I can't marry you Winston because I'm still married. But no I don't really want to finish with you either, 'cause yes I do still love you. And I think it was brave of you to come around to see me tonight, and explain things along with your apologies. When you've known for a long time now that I just wanted to kill you. And no I'm not sorry about those letters either, I'm still glad that they had you running scared. But there are going to be some big changes in my life now, because I can feel it. So don't think that because you want to marry me? That you can put me in a cage and throw away the key, thinking it will keep me closer to you, because it won't, it would just push me further away from you. I've still got to have my freedom, and some space now, even more for a while, that's very important to me. And I've got to be able to do whatever I want, and be accountable to no one but myself, for wherever life takes me okay? Because I feel that whatever all you men have done to me, you've never felt guilty or accountable to me for any of your actions. Now do you understand me clearly Winston?"

"Yeah kind of," he replied, pulling Olivia up from her chair and holding her close to him, while kissing her neck and ears. "And I have a feeling there will be some more new rules now, for me and anyone else, including Alex. You must have your freedom and feel free, but as long as I think you love me also Olivia, I can accept that. Because I just think that you have a lot of hate for men buried deep down inside of you somewhere that started a long time ago, years before you met me. And you've got to get rid of it sometime or somewhere, before you can or ever will settle down again with any one man. And I'm so sorry I hurt you Olivia, I really didn't mean to, but you sure got your own back on me with those letters, they had me running scared for a while. Now do you want me to finish with Brenda? Get her out of my life? Would that help you at all?"

"No it's okay, I don't feel that she's any threat to me. And I do like the idea of me being the other woman for a change, being someone else's bit on the side. I think it could be fun and very exciting, and then you'll also know not to be able to expect any commitment from me, if I'm just your bit on the side. And will you still love me tomorrow? No don't answer that one 'cause I really don't care if you don't," she said, laughing with a mischievous, twinkle in her eye. "Now just hold me, and love me all over Winston."

They then began to make love with the same, fierce, loving, passion that only those two could have for each other.

Much later after their wonderful, passionate, love making together was finished, Olivia rolled out of his arms to light herself a cigarette, whilst Winston chose '*Your Fabulous Babe*' from her record collection putting it on to play. He then laid down next to her, holding her lovingly in his arms whilst saying, "This is just for you Olivia and this is how I've always felt about you, just listen to the words."

He also began to realize that Olivia needed plenty of space in her life now, and that she did not want him to be so clinging or attentive towards her. So with loving and respecting her wishes, he did try not to go around to her home, to see, or contact her, as often as he used to. He also found that she wasn't as eager to go for nights out with him, to the places that he thought that she enjoyed visiting, like the 'Blues-Houses'.

She still kept her days very, busy when her twins went off to school in the mornings. She often went into town to do some shopping, and meet up with Dez, Cindy, and her other friends, in one of the pubs in the city-centre for lunch.

As the months passed by her though, she began to feel that most of her nights were very, lonely and empty now. Especially after the twins had eaten their evening meal, had their bath and were tucked up in bed fast-asleep.

***

Her friend Cindy had been round for the evening, and they had drunk a bottle of wine, played records and had lots of important, girl talk. But Olivia was all by herself once again now, as she stood looking out of her window in the lounge, into the empty, dark, street outside, whilst listening to the record, '*Gimme, Gimme, a Man After Midnight*'. '*This is just how I feel most nights, and these words could have been written for me*', she thought, singing along with the words on the record.

She decided, after the song had finished, that the next evening she would get a baby-sitter in, and go out to start having some fun of her own.

******

Chapter 40

"Yes of course I'll come with you," said Cindy, talking with Olivia on the telephone the next day. "I've been telling you for ages now, that you should go out at night. And Isaac's opened a new club downtown called the 'New York Bar', we'll go there if you like, I've heard it's a great place. And Dez and the rest of his crowd have also started going there. And I've also heard that Dez has got a share in the place."

"Right then, we'll go. I'll get my baby-sitter to stay the night, 'cause it'll be late when I get back. Now I've got to find some clothes to wear."

"Oh, wear a pair of your lovely tight shiny trousers Olivia, you look great in them, and you've got some lovely tops to wear with them, for mix and match. And do you think I could borrow your shiny pink pair of trousers please?"

"Yeah if you want to," Olivia replied, with a laugh. "And I'll see you around ten o'clock tonight."

***

Later that evening Olivia bathed, and took an hour to carefully apply her make-up. Her eye-shadow was dark grey with a touch of gold under her black, pencil lined eyebrows. *'My green eyes look as I like them to, lovely and big'*, she thought, looking at her reflection in her dressing-table-mirror.

She removed her dressing gown, and picked up the pair of shiny, gold-trousers that she had laid out on the bed. She put them on pulling the zipper up on the front of them before breathing out. She looked into the full, length-mirror on the wall at the side of her dressing-table, very pleased to see that her trousers fitted her like a second, skin, showing off her lovely, slim, shapely figure. The top she wore, to match the trousers, was black, loose and sleeveless, low cut with a large, round gathered, collar with gold thread spun through it. She pulled it down from her shoulders, then pulled one side up over her left, shoulder. *Yes, that's it, that looks good, one side pulled down off my shoulder, and the other side just covering my shoulder*, she thought before fastening a thin, gold belt around her waist, and adjusting the top to fall in large, gathers on her hips underneath the belt.

Cindy arrived in Olivia's bedroom saying, "Are you ready Olivia? Oh! You look great, you really do."

"Yes, I think I do. And I'm going to wear my black fitted, three and a half-inch-heeled suede boots, with this outfit."

"They'll look good, but won't the heels on them be too high for dancing in?"

"No, I feel okay dancing in those boots."

Olivia then brushed her lovely-very-long-shiny-hair, sprayed her neck and arms with 'CHARLES-OF-THE-RITZ' perfume-spray, and put her cigarettes into a pretty, very much treasured, cigarette-case, which her once, but now dead, best friend Angel, had bought her for her nineteenth birthday gift. She put this with her lipstick, hairbrush and money, into her small, black suede, shoulder bag, before getting her black suede jacket out of the wardrobe.

"Well I'm feeling all lovely and ready now," she said, to Cindy, who was zipping up on herself, a pair of Olivia's pink trousers.

"Yeah so am I now," Cindy replied, with a smile. "And these trousers fit just like a second skin, don't they? And I can bend down and sit okay in them, how come?"

"It's because they're made with a new type of very stretch elastic, they move on you attached to your body, and don't feel tight or restrict your movements."

"Magic. Now let's call a taxi, if you're ready to go. It's about ten thirty now, we should get to the 'New York Bar' for about eleven, I always think that's a good time to arrive, about eleven or eleven-thirty."

Olivia told her baby-sitter Barbara, who was seventeen years old, that one of the beds in the large bedroom upstairs, had been made up for her to sleep in. "The twins are fast asleep now, and I don't know what time I will get back. So just make yourself at home, there's pop and food in the fridge if you feel hungry, and crisps in one of the kitchen cupboards. I'll take the phone off the hook and make sure both the doors are locked and don't let anyone in. Do you think you'll be okay?"

"Yes I'm sure I will, and I'm looking forward to my evening sitting for the twins," replied Barbara, who was laid on the couch watching the TV. "Now you go and have yourself a boogie night Olivia, you know everything will be okay here with me."

***

Cindy paid the taxi fare when they reached the 'New York Bar', and they went in through a door and down a carpeted staircase to the cloakroom at the bottom.

They were greeted by a blonde-haired, broad, shouldered very, tall bouncer, wearing a dark, blue suit, white shirt, and dark-blue-bow-tie, "Good evening ladies, can I take your coats for you? And here's your cloakroom tickets," he said, passing them numbered tickets as he took their jackets from them

"Thanks, and what's your name?" Olivia asked.

"Keith. And we love to see good looking ladies like you two come to the 'New York Bar'."

"Well Keith I don't know about the rest of the ladies who'll be coming to the club tonight, but you've got two very beautiful ones, with us two here tonight," Cindy replied smiling sweetly, sounding so very narcissistic as she passed him her jacket.

They walked through a door into the club, and up some steps to one side that went into a small, bar with stools placed around the front of it, and low tables and chairs on the floor in front of it and around the bar. Before them was a dance floor with a mirrored wall in front of it, and up a few steps across from them, were more low tables and chairs and another small bar with a restaurant to one side of it, facing the dance floor. The DJ was playing records from the *'Off The Wall'* album, and coloured lights were flashing on the people who were dancing. Olivia and Cindy sat on the stools at the bar waiting to be served, and watching the people dancing.

"Look who's here," shouted Dez, with a happy smile on his face walking over to Olivia and Cindy, with a crowd of guys following him. "My two lovely ladies Cindy and Olivia. And you do look very beautiful tonight Olivia," Dez complimented her, gently kissing her on the cheek. "Now let me buy you ladies a drink, what will you have?"

"Yeah we've just got here, and it seems as though you've been waiting for us to arrive Dez, so you can buy us our first drink. We'll have 'Campari' and orange juice please," Cindy replied. "Is that okay for you Olivia?"

"Yes, 'Campari' and orange juice is fine, I want lots of ice in mine though."

"I've not seen you down here before, Olivia," Dez said, with a smile. "But Cindy did mention to me that you might be coming here. Where's Winston tonight? How come he's let you out by yourself? Or is he coming down here later?"

"Ssh," Olivia replied, putting her hand on Dez's shoulder and her finger up to his lips. "Don't spoil my night by talking about Winston. Come on let's dance, I love this record, *'Stomp'*."

After dancing to a few more records, Olivia and Dez went back to join their crowd at the bar. "I do like this place very much," Olivia said. "It's not too big, it seems more like a small, private club, and everyone is so friendly."

"Yeah it is," Dez replied, getting Olivia another 'Campari' and orange juice. "This is the way Isaac and I have tried to make it. A very cliquish crowd come here, mostly West-Indian guys, who all seem to know each other. It's for the older crowd here, and there are never any fights, 'cause the kids aren't allowed in. They still go to Isaac's other big disco the Kaleidoscope, and there are always plenty of fights there between the black and white guys."

"There was a bad fight over at the Kaleidoscope last week, eh Dez. Did you tell Olivia about it?" Asked Joey, who was stood next to Dez.

"No Joey I didn't," Dez replied, with a laugh. "So why don't you tell her? As I'm sure she'd like to hear about that one."

"Well it was like this," began Joey. "There we all were, this big crowd of us, at the Kaleidoscope one night, and it was very hot. So most of us were stood outside the club in the large entrance by the doorway, trying to cool down. Well it seems the white guys, weren't having much luck scoring in the club that night, with many of the girls. It was the black guys who seemed to be in luck in getting all the girls. So a lot of the white guys got pissed off and left. Anyway, there was us guys, stood by the doorway minding our business trying to cool off from the heat, when this white dude walks out of the club carrying a pint-glass in his hand. He looked at us all, broke the glass against the wall, then smashed it into Andy's face, and walked off leaving Andy's face pouring in blood."

"My God! Are things getting as bad as that out there in the Discos now?" Olivia said, in a horrified tone of voice. "So what did you do to help poor Andy?"

"We were all putting cloths on his face," Joey continued. "And someone called an ambulance to take him to the hospital. It seems the glass cut into his tear duct, they told us at the hospital later."

"Poor sod, how's he doin? Is he okay now?" Olivia asked concerned. "And where does Dez come into all of this?"

"Oh yeah thank-God, Andy seems to be doin okay now," Joey replied. "The hospital stitched his tear duct back in, kept him in for a couple of days, and we all visited him. We also told him that Dez got the fucking bastard, who'd put the glass into his face. 'Cause, while we were all seeing to Andy, trying to stop the bleeding that was coming from God-knows where on his face. Dez ran after the white-dude who had done this, and he saw to him. So the next thing we know, we see Dez walking back to the entrance of the Disco, with his shirt all covered in blood, a big smile on his face, and he puts both of his thumbs up and says to us all *'That fucking honkey will never touch a black man again'*. So we all asked him why? And where was he? And Dez tells us *'Behind the club somewhere laying in the fucking daffodils'*."

"Good for you Dez," Olivia said approvingly, as she gave Dez a loving hug. "It really served that guy right what you did to him, he just fucking asked for it."

"Well you know me Olivia," replied Dez, with one of his lovely, big, infectious smiles that showed of his lovely, even, white teeth. "I always believe in an eye for an eye. Now come on my lovely lady let's go and dance. Hey you guys save our seats at the bar here, 'cause it's starting to get very busy in here tonight."

After Dez and Olivia had danced to some of the records, that the DJ was playing. They went back to sit at the bar, before Dez soon excused himself, noticing that he had just seen his Cousin, Alisha across at the other bar. Alisha was a model who had just got back from doing a modelling job down in London, and he wanted to hear how she had made out, and if she'd managed to contact some business, friends of his down there. "I'll see you later Olivia, I'll just be over there at the other bar talking to my cousin."

"Yeah okay Dez," Olivia replied smiling. "I can see a good looking Jamaican guy watching me, and when you go I'm sure I'll get to know him."

***

"Hi, I hear your name is Olivia, mine's Nathan, and I've been watching you for some time. Are you with Dez?"

"No," Olivia replied, with a smile. "Dez and I are just very good friends."

Just then another guy appeared at Nathan's side saying, "Be careful Nathan, this is Pass-Tru's girl Olivia, and I've known that for a long time. How come Pass-Tru's let beautiful Olivia out by herself tonight? Does he know you're here?"

"What's your name?" Olivia asked, glaring at him.

"Chuck, and I'm a friend of Pass-Tru's. Have been for a long time now."

"Well Chuck, Winston, or Pass-Tru, as you call him, sure has a poor taste in choosing people as friends, if you're one of them. And just let me make something very clear to you, no I'm not Pass-Tru's girl as you put it, I'm nobody's girl, I'm just me, myself, I, Olivia. Now if you'll excuse us? Nathan and I are going to dance."

"Okay then if that's how you put it, go and have some fun together you two. Because I know that Nathan will, 'cause he's got the hots for you," Chuck replied laughing. "Have you met Brenda yet Olivia? Does she know about you and Winston?"

"Oh just fuck off you prick," Olivia replied, pushing Chuck out of her way when passing him to go and dance. "Who is that jerk?" She asked Nathan.

"Oh he's okay, he's a friend of mine, he just likes to have a joke, he's harmless enough really, you'd like him if you got to know him."

"I doubt it."

After dancing Nathan took hold of Olivia's hand, leading her through the crowd back to the bar saying, "It's hot come on let's get a drink, I'll introduce you to the rest of the guys. We usually come here on Wednesdays and Thursdays, so if ever you come down here on either of those nights we'll be here."

Nathan introduced her to a few of the other guys who seemed to be with his crowd of friends, Gary, Jack, Arts, Eddie, Roger, Graham, Ken, Joe, Len, Mike and Frank.

"Hi Olivia it's good to meet you," they all told her

"Are all you guys from the West-Indies?" Olivia asked, when Nathan passed her a 'Campari' and orange juice.

"Yes," replied Chuck. "I'm from Montego Bay, where the men like to make love to beautiful women like you Olivia, and get you to reach sexual heights that you've never known before." He then began to whisper into her ear, about how he would make love to her, if he had the chance to. He then waited for her reply, hoping that he'd managed to arouse her sexual interest in him.

Olivia sipped her 'Campari' and juice slowly, through the pink, straw, whilst calmly, listening to Chuck, and the sexual favours that he had in store for her. All of the other guys in their party, were watching her, and waiting eagerly to hear her reply, to the things that they knew Chuck, would be saying to her. She then said, loud enough above the music, so all of the rest of his crowd of friends could hear. "Chuck do be very careful, because I would just suck you up and blow you out in little bubbles."

All of the other guys just fell about laughing on hearing her reply, while she and Nathan went to dance, and she asked him if he would like to go back to her place for coffee.

"Coffee?" Nathan asked, with a raised eyebrow.

"Well coffee and good music for starters," she replied, with a smile. And if you enjoy that, who knows what you might get to enjoy next?"

"Oh yes well I'm game for what might come next, after the coffee," Nathan eagerly answered, while wrapping his arms around Olivia. "Let's go and finish our drinks, then we'll go if you like."

When they went back to the bar Chuck, and the other guys were all still laughing and joking. As Chuck put his arm around Olivia, telling her that they all thought she was a terrific lady, and good fun to be with, and they hoped to see her down at the 'New York Bar' again. "There aren't many ladies with your sense of humour Olivia. Most girls before now have been very offended, when I've told them how I'd like to make love to them. And we really must get together and try it sometime."

"Sure, and I guess that you've had your face slapped a few times Chuck, if that's how you've told all of the other ladies, how you'd like to make love to them. But it all sounds very perverted decadent and exciting to me, if you can perform or do anything like that," was her reply. "Nathan just wait for me for a few minutes over by the door will you please? I'm just going to find my friend Cindy and tell her that I'm leaving. Good night you guys, and I'll see you again sometime."

Olivia found Cindy in the ladies' room, cutting a couple of lines of cocaine on a small mirror. "Oh Olivia are you leaving already? I've got myself this great guy called Stew tonight, and I'm going back to his place soon. Here try a line of this, it's good stuff, Stew gave it to me."

"Okay I'll just do a couple of lines then I'm leaving with Nathan," she replied, taking the small straw that Cindy passed to her. "I bet this Stew of yours is a white guy."

"Yes he is. I don't know why, but I never seem to have your luck Olivia with the West-Indians-guys. I always seem to end up with a white guy, but how did you know that Stew was white?"

"Because the white guys always do coke and the black guys do Ganja, that's how I know. Bye for now Cindy, I'm going. Be good, and if you can't be good, be good at it."

"Yeah I promise I will."

"Bye for now, and I'll give a bell tomorrow."

"Yeah call me around lunch time."

***

When Nathan was leaving Olivia's bed at daylight the next morning, he asked her, "Can I have your phone number please? And can I give you a bell sometime soon?"

"No don't call me, why? 'Cause I don't want you to. It was just sex that we had, nothing more, so don't get involved with me and don't fall in love with me. And don't spoil what we just had for a few hours, you've got your life and I've got mine. I'll see you down at the club most weeks, and we'll just be friends when we meet again, okay?"

"If that's the way you want it to be then Olivia, okay but that's your choice and not mine. And it's a pity, 'cause I really do like you a lot."

Nathan kissed Olivia good-bye and left her sleeping for a few more hours. She was feeling no regrets about the night of sexual passion that she had shared with him.

***

Olivia began to go to the 'New York Bar' every Wednesday and Thursday nights, usually by herself or with Cindy, when she didn't have a date.

Her new crowd of friends, Nathan, Chuck, Gary, Jack, Arts, Eddie, Roger and Joe, Len, Mike, Frank, Graham and Ken were always at the club eagerly waiting for her to arrive, because they all had such good, fun together. With each one of these men secretly, hoping that Olivia would choose him, to spend the night with her. This crowd of men were by now very, infatuated with Olivia, who became their dream girl, with each one of them wishing she would somehow, calm down, stop playing the field and choose just one of them to become her steady boyfriend. But the ones who had been stupidly, brave enough, to ask her to go steady with them only, had heard the hateful, nasty tongue-lashing other side to her, when it would be revealed what her true feelings were towards men. Then afterwards she'd become very, cool towards these fools for quite a few weeks, safely keeping them at a distance, as far away from her as she could. Especially the guy called Chuck, who thought that he was the perfect match for her, and could make her world perfect, if she would only let him into it some more. But no this only made her put a bigger, barrier up against him, with never asking him if he would like to spend the night with her again.

She also kept the personal side of her life, very private from these men that she dated and socialized with in the club. None of them really knew if she was married or still going with Winston, because when asked, she would tell them, that it was none of their business.

Yes she was having herself just a wonderful time, treating all of these men just like toys, for her to play with, and then throwing them away, when she was bored with them. It was a game she now played, which was her game only, feeling that it helped her to now get back at the men who had hurt her over the years. She always did think and feel that it wasn't her fault, if these new toys in her life got hurt, because she didn't believe men could have any true, loving feelings at all. Not strong, loving, emotional feelings like her and all of the other females in the world, who had been hurt by men. She thought that she was being a lot fairer to men though, than they themselves were and had been to females. Always making it very, clear to all of them, never to ask for her phone number; because she didn't want them to phone her, they must never get involved with her in any emotional way. And lastly never mention that taboo word of love! Because they must never, ever, fall in love with her, as she had no love for any of them at all to ever give back. And why should she? When she was now of the opinion, that nothing lasts forever! No she would just see them all down at the club, and party with them if she felt like doing so.

But little did Olivia think, know or realize, that with these harmless games that she was now playing. She was giving these men a good challenge in their life's, that most men like to have but very, rarely got. As now unbeknown to her, her game quickly turned into a game of the hunter and the hunted. With her soon becoming the girl in their life's, that they all wanted but felt that they could never really have, just all for themselves.

She still left most of her Friday nights free to see Winston, who liked to come around to spend the evening with her. And she made no secret about letting him know where she went to on Wednesday and Thursday nights, and the fun and laughter that she always enjoyed and had, while partying and dancing. And when asked by Winston, her reply was always, yes some guy would probably spend the night with her if she wanted him to. Her attitude towards Winston now seemed to be, so what the hell can you do about it or anything I do in my life anyway? But she never would or wanted to see, the hurt and painful looking expression that showed in Winston's eyes, when he played the record for her, hoping that she was listening to the words of, 'Who Were You With In The Moonlight'.

Yes it did seem to make life a lot easier for her, to believe that Winston didn't really care about who she saw, who she was with, or what she did in her life anymore. Feeling that he couldn't possibly be hurt by her playful actions. Even though he was one of the very, few people who were allowed to tell her, that he loved her. And deep down somewhere inside of her, she always knew that he would!!!

******

Chapter 41

Would you like to do some promotion work with me during the day? For the agency that I work with?" Cindy asked Olivia, one day. "Because my agency is always looking out for new promotion girls. And we could work together doing promotions for make-up, hair shampoo, hair colours and conditioners. Our main bases to work from will be the large shops downtown."

"Yes sure it sounds like fun. So you make me an appointment to see your boss? And I'll ask him how many hours he wants me to work? And what he's prepared to pay me?"

She took the job doing promotion work with Cindy, and they worked together mainly in large chemists and department stores in the heart of Sheffield's city-centre.

They were doing promotion work for a new, name-brand of hair-colour, 'Claira' one afternoon. While it was pouring with rain outside, and the inside of the shop was very quiet. "This is so boring," Olivia said, giving a deep sigh. "We've not seen or spoken to any shoppers for over an hour."

"I know, but who wants to be out shopping in this kinda weather? I'm just seeing people coming in to get out of the rain, or to dry off. No one's interested in looking at fucking hair colours."

"So where did you go last night Cindy? And who were you with?"

"I'm still seeing Stew, that guy who I met at the 'New York Bar'. And I went over to his place last night."

"Did you spend the night with him? And was it good?"

"Yeah I stayed the night with him, because he's good in the sack. And that's why I'm still going with him."

"I see, God I'm so tired I can't stop yawning," Olivia replied, covering her mouth with her hand, so no one would see her big yawn. And really I'm nearly falling asleep stood here. I was out at the 'New York Bar' last night, so you can imagine how much sleep I got afterwards, before I had to get up and get the twins off to school this morning. Then take my bath get ready and come into work. So if you don't mind? I think I'll go home Cindy, to get myself some sleep. I'm sure you can manage by yourself for the next couple of hours. And if you do suddenly get a rush of customers interested in new hair-colours, and you need some help, then give me a bell."

"Yes, you go and get some shut-eye beauty sleep then. I'm gonna go to the restaurant to have a coffee and a cigarette, and talk to some of the other staff, who are on their breaks."

"Okay, bye. Don't work too hard, and I'll see you at nine o'clock tomorrow morning," Olivia replied, leaving Cindy holding the boxes of hair-colourings and discount coupons for it.

***

Olivia put her umbrella up on going out of the store into the pouring, rain. And was suddenly splashed by the water from a roadside puddle, by a big Daimler car, while she was standing at the side of the road waiting to cross over to get her bus home. "You fucking dirty bastard, that's all I needed," she shouted to the driver of the car, when the water soaked her pink, corduroy trousers and bare feet in her high-heeled shoes.

The driver of the Daimler car stopped a few feet away from Olivia, before backing up to her. A good looking man, who looked to be in his fifties with blue, eyes and black and silver greying hair, wearing a very, expensive looking dark, blue suit. Stopped his car in front of her, before winding down his window to talk to her, in a very, well-spoken southern, accent. "Excuse me my dear, did you shout something to me?"

"Yes you bet I fucking did, and I hope you heard me," she replied angrily. "Just look at what you've done to my clothes with your bloody big car? Can't you see the large puddles at the side of the road? Or do you always make a point of driving through them and splashing people? Is that your idea of fun on a rainy day Mister?"

The man looked at Olivia's wet feet and trousers in surprise before saying, "I'm really very sorry, my dear, I had no idea that I'd splashed you with my tires. So please do let me help you? I'm on my way to the Grovernor Hotel where I'm staying. Let's get you dried off there, and your trousers cleaned, then let me buy you a drink or a hot coffee or something. I really am so very sorry about this, so do accept my apologies, please?"

He opened his car door on the passenger side, for Olivia to get in, before driving off with her to the big, expensive hotel in the city-centre, that he was staying in.

She got out of his car in the car-park of the hotel, before going with him in the elevator up to his hotel suite, still feeling very angry at this man.

"My name is Peter," he said. Closing the door of his suite and throwing his keys onto a table. "And your name is?"

"Olivia, and just look at the mud and dirty water on my trousers."

"Yes I'm sorry, they do seem to be in an awful mess, don't they? Would you like to go into the Bathroom and take them off? Then I can get the hotel to send them out to be cleaned. There's a bathrobe in the Bathroom that you can put on until your trousers are returned."

"Okay that seems like a good idea, and I'll take a shower while I'm in the Bathroom. But what if those dirty marks won't come off my trousers?"

"Oh, I'm sure they will," Peter said, taking his wallet out of the inside pocket of his suit. "But here's fifty pounds Olivia, is that enough for you to buy yourself a new pair of those trousers? Now let me order you a drink while you take your shower, and would you like something to eat? While your waiting for your trousers?"

"Yes please that would be nice. I'll have a fillet-steak, mushrooms chips and coffee, and a 'Campari' and orange juice. Oh and have my steak cooked medium rare please?" She replied smiling, while walking into the Bathroom.

Olivia put the fifty-pounds, which was in two, twenty and one ten pound notes, into her purse, before passing the trousers to Peter, around the Bathroom door. Then taking a lovely, long hot shower, soaping her body all over, with the lovely, smelling toilet-soap. She pulled the shower, curtain back stepping out of the shower, picking up off a towel-rail, a large, white, bath towel to dry herself with. Before covering her body all over, in Peter's expensive, smelling, talcum-powder, that was stood at the side of the wash basin. She then put on, to cover her naked body, a large, dark blue bathrobe, that was hanging behind the bathroom door. And coming out of the bathroom, saw an assortment of bright, silver tureens, placed on a large dining table.

"The food and drink have just arrived," Peter said, lifting the lids of the tureens. "Come and sit down to eat something my dear, I bet you're hungry. I also ordered this bottle of 'Asti Spumanti' wine for us. I hope you like it? The hotel has sent your trousers out to be cleaned, and it won't be to long before they're sent back."

Olivia laid a white, cloth-napkin across her knees, before she began to eat her delicious, fillet-steak, fresh, mushrooms and French-fries, drink her 'Campari' and juice and sip the wine, from the wine glass, that Peter had poured it into. "Thanks this food is really good."

"Yes I'm pleased to see that you're enjoying it. You've got beautiful, large, green, eyes Olivia, in fact you are a very, beautiful, looking girl."

"Ye I guess it was just your lucky day, eh Peter, to splash me with all of that dirty water, that your car went through? Instead of some dirty old bag-lady with a mouth full of bad, or false, teeth. Or a blind-man, or a cripple, or a paraplegic eh, that you'd offered to clean up?" She replied laughing. "And yes I know that I've got a lovely name and lovely green eyes. I get the green eyes and my name, from my Grandfather, who's called Oliver. So where are you from Peter? And why are you in town?"

"I'm from Sussex and I own a couple of companies down there. And I come up to Sheffield about twice a month on business."

***

About an hour later, when Olivia had finished eating her delicious meal and was lighting a cigarette. There was a soft, gentle knock on the hotel room door. The bellboy was stood there, delivering Olivia's pink, corduroy trousers back, now all freshly, cleaned and pressed. "Oh they've come out great, all lovely and clean," she said, when pulling the polythene bag, off her trousers and looking at them, before heading for the bathroom to put them back on.

"Don't go yet Olivia please," Peter said, putting his hand onto her arm.

"But why not? I don't think that I owe you anything, do I?"

"No you don't owe me anything at all Olivia. It's just that I like you very much. And as you've said, yes it must be my lucky day, to have splashed your clothes with my car. And it would be just a very wonderful complete day for me, if I could make love to you before you go. Because Olivia, I think that you are not only beautiful, but also a very sexy lady. Even when you did get angry with me, when I splashed your clothes. That's why I offered to invite you up to my room and get them cleaned up for you."

"But I'm not a hooker or a prostitute Peter. So I think that you must have got the wrong impression of me."

"But I didn't think that you were Olivia. I had no thoughts of you being a hooker at all."

"So for splashing me, getting my clothes and me wet, and then getting me a fucking drink and a meal, and getting me to wait here with you until my jeans come back fucking clean, you now expect me to blow your fucking mind in bed for nothing? Well Peter just think again will you? Because no fucking way will I do that for nothing, because I would never sell myself so cheap. Got it? Understand me?"

"Yes Olivia I do understand you very well," Peter replied smiling, and taking money out of his wallet. So if it's okay with you? I'll give you seventy pounds, to go and buy yourself a few clothes or shoes, or what ever else that you'd like to treat yourself to, because I just wouldn't dream of putting you into the same class as a prostitute. So please say you'll stay with me for a little longer Olivia."

"So that's the only reason that you had on your mind, when you invited me to your room isn't it Peter? 'Cause you hoped that I'd have sex with you? Okay, but let's make it one-hundred-pounds, for me to go and get myself a few new clothes and some shoes. And then I think that you've got yourself, a very good deal."

"Yes I'm prepared to pay that price for a beautiful lady like you Olivia, although it is a little expensive," Peter agreed, taking one-hundred-pounds out of his wallet in notes of twenties, and handing it over to her. "I don't usually carry this amount of cash around on me that I've got today, because when I purchase something, I always ask if I can pay with my credit card 'American-Express'. "

"Yes well I don't care how fast you go Peter, it's still going to cost you one-hundred-pounds," she replied quickly, wondering if he would get her sense of humour. And come on Peter, don't go worrying now about the thought of me being too expensive for you? Or you're just not going to enjoy me blowing your mind for you. Are you?" She added, before counting the money and stuffing into the pocket, of her pink, corduroy, jeans, then kissing him.

***

After an hour, which Olivia had decided was all Peter was going to have, of her time in his bed. All Peter wanted to do with the rest of his day was now sleep. Because after making love with someone as experienced as her, of course just sexually, blew his mind, leaving him feeling spent, drained and weak. She was for Peter something that he had never, ever, known before, in his sexual history. So he was very, eager to fondly praise her, by telling her, what a wonderful, terrific lover she was. And that he had never been made love to before, as excitingly as that by anyone else, even his wife. So would she please give him her phone number? And would she be good enough to have dinner at the hotel with him? The next time that he was in Sheffield on business.

"Maybe," she replied, now getting herself dressed. "For a price though, 'cause I wouldn't dream of selling myself cheap to anyone for anything."

"Oh of course my dear, of course. And after what you just did for me lady, Peter now understands you very well."

"Good then we may just have a deal," she replied, passing Peter, her phone number which she had written on a small, piece of paper for him, before leaving his room and blowing him a kiss goodbye with her hand.

After closing the door of his suite behind her, she lent back against the wall in the hallway, laughing out loudly, to herself, and saying. *'Talk about easy money and the things I get myself into. I must tell Cindy about this one; 'cause I know that she'll just love it.'*

***

"Oh my God! Shit! No! I forgot!" Olivia said, in a panicky voice now to Don, a long time friend of hers, for many years, who was laying at the side of her in bed, at ten o'clock that morning. "I think that must be Winston banging on my door, in fact I'm sure it's him. We are supposed to be going out this morning and I forgot. So you stay here Don, and please don't come downstairs until I've talked my way out of this one. 'Cause I've got a feeling that he may be angry with me."

"Hi Winston, I'm sorry I forgot we were going out today, and I slept in," she said to Winston, opening her door to him, in her dressing gown.

"Forgot! Slept in! What the hell are you talking about man? We made definite arrangements, when I phoned you yesterday, that I'd take you shopping this morning. And we'd meet Jake and Allan in the pub at lunch time," Winston replied. As he walked into the lounge noticing an empty, wine bottle, two used wine, glasses, a bunch of car keys, an ashtray full of ash and cigarette ends, and a packet of 'Marlboro' cigarettes, all on the coffee table.

"So if you'd like to go and make yourself a tea or a coffee Winston? I'll be ready in about half an hour. I'll just go and take a quick bath, and I won't be long," she said. While wondering how she could get Don, out of the house, without Winston knowing that he was there, still upstairs in her bed.

"No thanks I don't want a coffee, but just a minute I don't want you to go anywhere yet," he said. Now going over to the coffee table, and picking up the packet of 'Marlboro' cigarettes, while looking at the large, ashtray on the table, that was full of cigarette ends. "Whose are these cigarettes Olivia?"

"Well they're mine of course, who else's could they be?" She replied defiantly, not wanting to be interrogated.

"But you don't smoke this brand of cigs Olivia, you smoke 'Benson and Hedges'."

"Yes I know I usually do, don't I?" She replied with a laugh. "But I ran out of cigarettes late last night, and I had to get some from the machine down the road, and all it had in it were 'Marlboro', so I had no choice really, did I?"

"Oh I see," Winston said, his voice beginning to sound even, louder now, as he looked at her, very disbelievingly. "And on the way back home you thought you'd pick up a bottle of wine? And you also thought it would be a very good idea, to drink it out of two glasses."

"Well ye I guess so, because the first glass that I poured the wine into, had a nasty crack in the side of it. And I thought that it might break, you see?"

"Yes what a very quick clever explanation, you've suddenly just come up with Olivia. But I know that it's just fucking bullshit that you're giving me. And whose are these car keys here?" He said, pointing at them on the table. "Don't tell me? Let me guess. You found them on the way back home? Along with that red sports car that's parked outside of your house. So don't try lying to me anymore Olivia, because I'm not quite the fool, that you seem to think or hope that I am. And that's your friend Don's sports car, that's parked outside isn't it? And he's obviously home on leave, from his radio operators job at sea, and he's still here upstairs' in your bed. Isn't he? You know what Olivia? You're beginning to slip up aren't you? With the little games that you've been playing with your different men? And your not playing them as well as you think you are, 'cause, you've just been caught out, by me. Now go and get that fucking Don, out of your bed and out of this house right now. Then go and scrub yourself well all over, while your take your quick bath."

"Now just a fucking minute Winston, who the hell do you think you're talking to?" She shouted, now stupidly feeling that she had backed herself into a tight corner, with allowing Don to stay the whole night with her. After telling and promising Winston that there would never, be anyone else with her, when he came around to see her. And she now felt that she needed a quick, escape from all of this, just to keep her pride and save face. As she began to angrily ask, "So tell me who the fuck do you think you are Winston? You're not my fucking Husband, you're not my fucking boyfriend. You're just some fucking Mandingo stud, who likes to have me as his bit on the side remember? Because your still living with your fucking stupid sad wife Brenda. But you love to have sex with me, 'cause I just blow your fucking mind. And also remember this you bastard?" She snarled at him, very nastily. "It's none of your fucking business, who I go to bed with, or how much time I spend with someone else. And you know that Don is a very good friend of mine, and has been for years now. A lot longer than I've known you. And it's also none of your fucking business, when Don and I get together, go out together, or fuck together. So just fucking butt out of my life, and piss off will you Winston? Because I'm not going out with you today, or ever again, got it?"

Winston very, angrily walked across the room, and pushed her up against the wall, holding her there with his hand on her chest, near the bottom of her neck, but so close to her throat, that he could easily, choke her. While looking deeply, into her green eyes saying, "You know, I'm beginning to get a little sick and tired of you, your other men, and your stupid sex games Olivia? And yeah I've put up with all of these other men that you seem to need and want in your life, for some time now. Haven't I? Because I thought it was some kind of sick demon revenge that was inside of you that you had to get rid of. And I hoped it would very soon leave you and go. But instead as the fucking months go by, you're just becoming more like a high-class tramp. And I just don't know how much more of this I can take? I accept your husband Alex in your life, I know that I have to, and don't have much choice about the times that he wants to spend his weekends with you. But I remember that I told you girl, a long time ago, that I don't and won't, accept Don in your life. And I can't work out what magic that guy waves over you, or what's so fucking special about him. But you always seem to have a place in your heart and your bed, for him, whenever he comes back home to Sheffield. Don't you? And we are going out together this morning Olivia, so don't argue with me anymore about not going. Now go and take your bath and get that fucking Don out of here, or I'll throw him through the fucking bedroom window, so the choice is yours."

She was now beginning to feel that she really had no choice, but to do what Winston had told her to do. After his angry outburst towards her, which she thought could possibly turn very, violent at some point, if she angrily pushed him away from her. Which could also cause a lot of trouble for Don, who would surely also get hurt. So instead of physically fighting with Winston, she just silently, glared, very hard back at him, until he stopped holding her up against the wall and she was then able to run up the stairs, to the Bathroom to take her bath.

After taking her bath she got dressed quickly, and went downstairs with Don following her, walking into the lounge to face an angry, Winston. "Hi Winston," Don said, in a friendly, confident tone of voice. "I'm sorry about this, but I didn't know that you two had made arrangements, to go out this morning. I hope my being here hasn't upset any of your plans at all."

"Don," Winston replied, nodding to him. "Just let me ask you this man? Why is it that every time you come home from your job at sea? You have to come to see Olivia? Haven't you got any other girlfriends in Sheffield? Who you can go and fucking visit?"

"Oh yes I have a few," Don replied, with a smile, putting his arm around her shoulders. "But Olivia is very special to me, we're very good friends, and I've always been very fond of her. Now where are my car keys?"

Olivia, and Don, began to search the room for his car keys, while Winston, just lent against the wall watching them and looking bemused.

After about five minutes of searching for them everywhere, Don said, "That's very strange Olivia, because I'm sure that I left them here, on the coffee table last night."

"Well I can't find them anywhere Don. And I don't know where else to look for them, in this room," she replied.

"Are these your keys Don?" Winston asked laughingly, holding the keys up in his hand and shaking them.

"Winston you bastard, you had them all the time," Olivia said. "Now will you please give them back to Don."

He passed Don his car keys over to him, while saying, "And if I ever see that fucking red sports car of yours, parked outside Olivia's house again, I promise you this Don, I'll slash your fucking tires just for starters, before I then smash the fucking windows in it. Do you understand me Don?"

"Yes okay Winston, I've got your message. We'll just have to be more careful next time, won't we Olivia?" Don replied defiantly, winking at her, while taking his keys from Winston's hand.

With Olivia just silently glaring at Winston.

***

Whilst they were driving into town, they were having a very, nasty argument. With her telling him, how much she hated him and never wanted to see him again.

"Oh please just shut up will you Olivia? Until you know what it is you're talking about? And who and what it is you want in this life. 'Cause until you can decide that, I promise you that I will always be around, because I love you. But God-knows why? 'Cause your nothing but heartache and trouble for me of late."

"Well why don't you just finish with me then? Just stop seeing me anymore? 'Cause I don't fucking care if I never see you at all ever again. Why make yourself so unhappy with having me in your life? What are you now Winston? A fucking masochist or what?"

"Will you shut up and just listen to this record that's playing on the radio? 'Cause the words on it are just from me to you. And the first record shop that I come to, I'm going to stop to buy you a record of it. Just so you won't forget what it is, that I'm trying to say to you, and tell you." He then turned the volume on his car radio up very loudly, as the song *'Him, Him, Him. What's She Going To Do About Him?'* began to play.

After listening to these words on the song, she turned to look at Winston, saying "Yeah well, you've got no chance of me, or you, ever stopping me from seeing 'HIM'- Don, or any one else for that matter. Anyway what the fuck is wrong with you Winston? I thought that you liked and went along with these, wild crazy decadent hedonistic times, that we're now living in, and all enjoying in the swinging 70's? With everybody having so much fun, fucking and enjoying each other so much? So come on go with it? And what about this big blonde lady? That someone saw you out with last week? So don't you go trying to get me to believe? That I'm the only other bit on the side for you? 'Cause I do know that that's not at all true."

******

Chapter 42

One cold and rainy November morning, after unfolding her daily, newspaper and laying it out on the Dining-room table, to read the headlines on the top of the page, Olivia said, "Oh my God, no not another one!"

On hearing these words as he came into the kitchen through the back door, carrying two bottles of milk, and putting them into her fridge. Danny asked, "What's up?

"There's been another 'Ripper-Murder' over in Leeds," she replied, in a very sad tone of voice.

"Ye I know, I eard about it ont news early this morning. But I've not see-nt newspaper yet, let's ave a look."

"It says, that this victim was a twenty year old Leeds University student, the poor girl. And the last girl he murdered, was another young twenty year old student, who lived in Bradford. And the one before her was a young nineteen year old building society clerk, who was just on her way home from work, when he found her, and killed her. It now seems to me, that the fucking 'Yorkshire-Ripper' is now killing any girl he feels like, not just prostitutes."

"Ye I know he is, well that's what he seems to be doin now. Killing any girl that he comes across," Danny agreed, reading the newspaper. "And it'll be Sheffield next, I can just feel it. Unless e's-bin-ere already, ant bodies ant been found yet. E's just some fucking maniac who ates women, an gets off on killing 'em. I just wish I could findt prick, I'd save police, an our courts, a lot a money, an when I've finished wi-'im, e'd be very fucking appy to die."

"Yes Danny he probably is a woman hater, and I guess you could also call me a man hater. But I don't go around killing men.

"Aye only in bed eh, I hear Olivia," Danny replied, with a laugh. "This is-is seventeenth victim an thirteen of 'em are now dead. Just yu be very careful Olivia, where yu-gu-to an who yu talk to. An don't gu picking up any strange blokes, or yu could be sorry. Do yu-ant twins want tu-cum down tu-our ouse-on Sunday fer-tha dinner?"

"Thanks for asking me Danny," she replied, going into the kitchen to make some tea. "But no thanks, not this weekend, because Alex is coming up from London to see me, and I've not seen him for a few months now. I think he's probably coming to tell me that he wants a divorce and I suppose that I'll tell him, that yes he can have one, if he pays for it. Then we'll make love for the last time together, before he leaves, and then we'll never see each other again."

"Yea I suppose that's ow-it'll-gu, if he's cuming tu ask yu for a fucking divorce.

***

Alex arrived that Friday evening, to spend the weekend with Olivia, bringing her a large, box of 'Black Magic' chocolates, and a bunch of beautiful red roses, telling her how much he loved her and had been missing her.

Although their lovemaking was still very exciting for them both, Alex felt that she was now keeping him at a distance from her, after their wonderful night of passion.

So the next day during their breakfast he felt that he had to ask her, why? What was wrong? Why did he feel that she was suddenly, being so cold to him? "So what have I done so wrong to upset you now Olivia?"

"Oh nothing that I can think off recently," she replied, sounding very uninterested in his question.

"But I feel that there must be some reason, why you seem to be cold now towards me?"

"Oh I didn't think that I was being so distant from you. But I guess that it could be, that I'd just like to be back in Miami Florida with you again, instead of here in this house of horrors, waiting for you to ask me for a divorce."

"No I've no intentions of asking you for a divorce. And why do you call this house, a house of horrors?

"Well that's what it became here with you, where our marriage all seemed to fall apart for us here. By what you did of course. Oh why did you have to go and fuck that slag that night Alex? When we were so happy and in love? With so much going for us, in our new home," she replied with a deep sigh. While taking hold of his hand, and looking sadly into his eyes.

"I know I'm sorry, but what can I do about what's already happened? And it was a long time ago now I thought. Anyway you should be getting over all of that by now. Don't you think?"

"What!" She replied pulling her hand away from his. "I don't fucking believe what you've just said to me. And I suppose that your now going to tell me, that it was all my fault why you did it eh? That I made you do it?"

The telephone in the hallway began to ring, and Olivia went to answer it, while Alex watched her writing something down on the note pad next to the telephone.

"Who was that?" He asked, when she came back into the Dining room.

"Oh it was just a friend."

"You have a lot of friends and acquaintances now, that you've made at the 'New York Bar', haven't you?"

"Yes I do and they're all great fun people," she replied smiling, lighting a cigarette. "What's wrong Alex? Don't tell me that you're becoming jealous of my friends now?"

"No I'm not jealous of them, just very scared of you falling in love with someone else. I love you very much, and I just don't know what I can now do for you, to win you back. Because since we arrived back from that wonderful time we had together in Miami. I feel like I'm just banging my head on a brick wall, with you at times now-a-days, while I'm still hoping so much, for us to be together again. Like we were in the beginning, living together, happily married, and it could and would work again, 'cause I would make sure that it does. But I'm beginning to now wonder what's the point, 'cause you seem to have drifted further away from me, with whatever you are doing now, in your times of fun."

"Oh stop it, will you Alex? I do still love you, but?"

"But what?"

"I just feel that little bit safer in myself, still keeping you at a distance. You hurt me so much once before remember, and I'm not going to let you ever hurt me again, it was too painful. Over the years I've tried to forgive and forget, but I still remember what you did to me, when you were all I lived for. And you see Alex, it takes me a long time to forgive, but I never forget. And don't go worrying about losing me to any other guy, I just know that will never happen, 'cause I'll never love anyone else again, I promise. These other guys in my life that you know about, are just friends."

"Even Winston?" Alex asked, in a concerned tone of voice.

"Yes, even Winston, 'cause he's also filled his book with me, as you all do. Anyway I'm going to take my bath now, do you want to join me?"

Alex finished his coffee before following Olivia up to the bathroom. Looking at what she had written on the note-pad by the telephone, when passing it in the hallway. Seeing, Room 268, 8:30 PM. Monday, written on the pad, and he smiled to himself shaking his head when he read it.

***

Laying in the other end of the large, bath that was filled with hot water and bubbles, resting his head, in between the taps. He asked, "Do all hookers hate men Olivia?"

"What?" She replied, while she lay soaking in the bubbles of the bath, opening her large, green eyes to look at Alex.

"I asked you, do all hookers hate men?"

"Well how the hell would I know? What a very strange question to ask me! And what the hell would I know about Hookers, or their sodding feelings? But yeah, I guess girls that feel they've been used and hurt by men, do hate men, well most of them anyway. And I guess they feel that most of you stupid men are also there for the taking and using. Then it evens the score up doesn't it?"

"And is that how you now feel about men Olivia?"

"Yes I fucking do," she replied, in an angry tone of voice. Now vigorously, rubbing soap all over her legs. "I guess that I do enjoy surviving that way, and it's none of your fucking business Alex. So stop asking me questions and trying to get into my head. And maybe it's best if you go back to London this afternoon. You've had what you came here for haven't you?"

"Wow I can't understand why you think I only come to see you, for a good time in bed Olivia, and now to ask for a divorce. It's not any of those things at all. I wanted to see you because I love you. I've also brought a record with me and I feel the lyrics could have been written just for you. And when we go downstairs I'm going to play it, and I want you to listen to the words."

"Oh another fucking record to hear the words of. That's all I seem to be doing now-a-days, getting the message," she replied with a laugh. "Sure, I'll listen to your stupid record. Why not I listen to Winston's, and I'm starting to get quite a good collection of them."

They both finished bathing and dressing, and went downstairs.

***

Olivia poured herself a 'Dry-Martini' to drink, while Alex went outside to his car, to get the record he had brought for her.

"Listen to the words on this please?" He said, putting the record on her stereo to play, *'How Could This Go Wrong'*, "Because I feel that it's a very sad story, that could have been written about you Olivia. And I'd like to know? If you think that you could tell me? Where it will all end? 'Cause I do think that you've got, so many lovers holding on to you. Quiet a lot in fact! And while you've still got them all hanging on to you, just for a good time! Well you'll never be free or be able to decide what it is that you really want for yourself!"

"Yes, well thank you very much, for your well thought out caring opinion Alex. Like as if I really do fucking need it," she replied. Beginning to dance to the record now, and the only words that she could, or would, hear in it, was the chorus of.... *'How could this go wrong, so many lovers holding on. How could this go wrong, it's what she needed all along.'*

"Yes this is a good disco record to dance to," she said, going to pour Alex a 'Dry-Martini' for him to also have a drink, while he put the record on again to play.

"I like good disco records, and I'll keep this one if you don't mind? Thanks Alex. Now why don't you stay with me again tonight, and drive back down to London tomorrow? Because I'm not planning on going out at all tonight. So yeah, come on Alex, let's have some fun together today, okay? Just you and me, Please?" She asked, kissing him.

"Yes you are still my wife, so I'd very much like to stay," he replied, pulling Olivia over to him to sit on his knee.

With the fun that she now had in store for them, he just wished that she would slow herself down a bit, and listen to all of the words in this song. But also knowing that he couldn't get, or would be able to ever get, his now very head-strong, man-hating, wife Olivia, to do anything that she did not want to do!!!

***

Olivia and her twins spent the Christmas of 1980 with her parents, son Antony, Grandparents, and Uncle Brian, at her parents' pub, the 'White Hart' in the small, Derbyshire village of Bradwell. She enjoyed being with her family very, much. Especially at Christmas time, and everyone had brought lots of gifts for each other. With the twins having so many toys that 'Father-Christmas' had brought for them, they didn't know which to play with first. Their new baby-dolls that needed feeding, sitting them in the lovely, new high-chairs, before changing then, washing the dolls nappies, that their babies came with. Or the selection of different, Children's games and jigsaw puzzles etc. etc. etc.

A few days after Christmas day, before the pub was opened for the evening customers, Olivia and her Uncle Brian, were sat at a table in the 'Tap-room', having a drink together and talking about different things. When she asked him how Ester, his pet Lion-Cub, was doing, and how old she was. "I bet she's really grown and getting very big now. Is she still as gentle and tame? I must come over and see her again soon."

"Oh don't tell me you don't know what's happened to Ester?" Brian replied, his eyes filling up with tears. "She's gone! Didn't your Mum and Dad tell you? She's gone! Been taken from me!"

"Gone where? Taken where?" Olivia asked, in a surprised tone of voice. "What do you mean she's gone? She didn't escape from the Zoo, did she?"

"No she didn't escape from the fucking zoo, but I wish that she had done," Brian replied, starting to really cry now for the loss of

Ester, his Lion-Cub. "It would be about a six weeks ago now, when I went to the zoo to pick her up, like I did just every day, and bringing her down to the restaurant. But when I got there I couldn't find her anywhere, she wasn't in her cage, she was missing. So I went to ask the Zoo-manager Chris, where Ester my Lion-Cub had gone? Had someone taken her out for a walk? Because some of the people who work at the zoo with the animals, often used to put her on a leash and take her out, walking around the zoo, meeting people there. Anyway, when I asked Chris the manager, where she was? He told me that, Ester became very sick during the night, and they had to take her to the vets. And that's where she is now, but she'd be okay, 'cause the vet had given her some medication, and we can have her back in a few days time. But the vet had told them, that he didn't want me to go and see her, because it might upset her recovery. Anyway Olivia, I eventually found out that Ester wasn't sick at all, and had never been to the bloody vets. The fucking Zoo-people, had fucking sold her to someone else. And I can't find out who to, who's got her or where she is. I've nearly had a fucking nervous breakdown over losing Ester, I love her so much. Anyway I'm now in the process of suing those fucking Zoo-people, who sold her to me. And pocketed the six hundred-pounds between them, that I paid for her. And I've still got the receipt they gave me, when I gave them the money, to prove that she is mine."

Olivia felt the tears running down her own cheeks, as she listened to her Uncle Brian's story, telling her what had happened to his Lion-Cub. She could still see Ester's sweet, pretty face, in her mind's eye, who would now be living in a cage, at some other zoo somewhere. Just looked and stared at, through the bars of a cage, and kept as a wild, viscous animal, that she would now be portrayed as, for the rest of her life. Never ever being let out, held, nursed, hugged, loved, kissed, or being or feeling ever free again. "Yeah I hope that Ester turns vicious and attacks and mauls everyone," she said. Crying hard herself now, for what she could see as poor Ester's future, and getting up and going behind the bar to get Uncle Brian and herself a large drink.

"God so do I, I hope she fucking attacks someone and makes a mess of them. Do you know Olivia? I will never get over the loss of her, she was my baby, and I dream about her every night. And I honestly believe and feel, that she must be missing me, and wondering where I've gone to. Don't you think?" Brian asked, sobbing heartbrokenly now for his precious Lion-Cub, Ester.

"Oh-God yes I'm sure she's missing you very much, and probably was pining for you a lot. Shit the fucking nasty things that people do to animals, it just makes my blood boil. And I do hope something very bad happens to those Zoo-people, who took Ester away from you, and ruined her life!!! Here uncle Brian, get this double 'Scotch' down you? 'Cause I'm sure you do need it!!"

******

Chapter 43

Friday night the 2nd January 1981, Winston arrived at Olivia's home just before midnight, while she was lying on the couch in her dressing gown, watching a movie on television. "Hi, what are you doing here? I thought you were going up to the 'Square' gambling tonight," she said, when Winston walked into the lounge and poured himself a drink.

"Yeah I was," he replied, with a laugh. "But a fight started in another room at the 'Blues', some guy got hurt, and the cops arrived, so I left to go on to another 'Blues'. But you can't fucking move for cops up the 'Square' now, and around the Broomhill area. Something else must have also happened around there, for so many cops to be checking things out. And you know what I think about fucking cops! So I just got the hell away from any mess that might be going down."

"Well haven't you any idea why there's so many cops around that area, at this time of night Winston? Obviously something bad must have happened. Has anyone been murdered? Or do you think there's any chance someone has caught the 'Yorkshire-Ripper' up there?"

"I don't know, I've no fucking idea what's going on man. I only know it's swarming with cops up there. Anyway are you watching this film Olivia? Or can I play some records? And I think I'll stay here with you tonight, to wish you a very happy new year."

"To wish me? Or give me something, to remind me of what I've been missing in bed with you?" She sarcastically asked him.

"Hey come on get real Olivia? And don't say nasty things like that to me. 'Cause this is the first time I've seen you, since you've been away for Christmas. And I thought you'd be pleased to see me?

Did you have a good Christmas with your family? And did you miss me?"

"Miss you…" She began to reply. As Winston with a laugh in his voice, began to say with her, "But how could I miss you? When I was with my family?"

"Yes thanks I did have a good Christmas, and it was fun being with my family. And the twins had lots of presents, so they won't need any more toys until next Christmas. The upsetting thing though was when I talked with my Uncle Brian, he told me that the zoo where he kept his Lion-Cub Ester, have sold her to someone else. And as you can guess he's really very upset and feels that he'll never get over the loss of Ester, he loves her so very much. And I've got a good idea of how he's suffering, 'cause I fell in love with Ester when I met her, she's just a lovely gentle friendly Lion-Cub."

"Oh, well does your uncle Brian know who's got her? Who the zoo has sold her to?"

"No not yet why?"

"Well let me know when he finds out where Ester is? And I'll take Dez and some other guys with me, to get her back for your Uncle okay?"

"You would? Well thanks and I'll contact my Uncle Brian and let him know. Then he'll be thinking all is not lost, that he might be seeing Ester again very soon."

***

The Headlines in the Sheffield Evening Newspaper on Monday 5th January 1981

'RIPPER: MAN ARRESTED IN SHEFFIELD'.

A thirty-five year old married man will appear in court later this afternoon, facing charges arising from the five-year manhunt, for the thirteen time killer, the 'YORKSHIRE-RIPPER'.

Peter Sutcliffe, a long distance lorry driver from Bradford, is the man who was arrested in Sheffield this weekend, by two policemen on vice-squad-patrol in the vicinity of Broomhill, very close to the city's 'Red-Light-Area'. Mr. Sutcliffe's arrest came on late Friday night, the 2nd of January, after police checked the license plates of a car that he was driving, a Rover-V8-Saloon, and found that the plates were and had been stolen.

He was found sat in his Rover-car talking with a prostitute, who was luckily unhurt. Seventeen women have crossed the path of the 'YORKSHIRE-RIPPER' as he has held Britain in a five-year reign of terror -- 13 of his victims have been murdered!

"Thank God he's been caught," said Cindy, who had gone to see Olivia, to ask her if she'd heard the good news? About the 'RIPPER' being caught. "Is there a photo of him in the newspaper?"

"No there isn't," Olivia replied, passing the newspaper to Cindy, to read for herself the article about 'Peter Sutcliffe'. "But if we watch the news on television around tea-time tonight, we'll see him on there I'm sure. I'm so so glad that the bastard's been caught at last, but I feel that it was just some good luck, for the vice cops up there. 'Cause if those cops hadn't thought to check the license plate number of that Rover car he was in, that girl with him would have been found dead somewhere the next day. And I guess Winston now knows, why all the cops were in the 'Red-Light-Area' on Friday night."

"Well I say, good for Sheffield and our cops," Cindy said, with a deep sigh of relief. "Us girls will all feel a lot fucking safer now, thank God. 'Cause this guy had me scared for many years."

***

On the six o'clock evening news on the TV that evening they saw the man. A handcuffed 'Peter Sutcliffe' who had dark, brown hair, a dark, brown moustache and a beard, showing dark, ringed circles underneath his eyes, being helped out of a police car, before being led into the court house, by two very, well built, big, police officers.

"So that's the bastard who's murdered all those girls? Well he looks so fucking ugly, I know I would never have had anything to do with someone who looks like him. But do you think he looks like a murderer Olivia?"

"Tell me Cindy what does a murderer look like? 'Cause I wouldn't know one if I fell over one, and neither would you. So just think about it? Anyway remember this? What my Dad told me today, *'That there will always be another bloke to take the place of this 'YORKSHIRE-RIPPER'. So don't go feeling so safe!'*"

******

Chapter 44

"Hi Alex," Olivia said, answering her telephone one evening and hearing Alex's voice on the other end of the line. "Yes, I am going out tonight. No sorry but I don't think it's such a good idea, you coming to see me tomorrow, 'cause I'm busy. And no never mind with what or who with. Remember you've got your life and I've got mine okay. Anyway I want you to listen to me Alex, because I've been doing some serious thinking, and I'm sure you'll agree. I've got an appointment with my solicitor next week, and I'm giving you a divorce! Because it's not fair of me to keep you hanging on, the way I have been doin all of these years, until I can make my mind up whether I want to live with you again or not. And if I'm honest with myself, I think that I'm beginning to realize that for a while now. I'm starting to become something that I could never imagine being, or ever wanted to be, just a-run-around-lover! I don't really know when and where, my solo social life, turned into this? Maybe I just got lost somewhere along the way, in these very hedonistic times of the 70s. And I'm sorry to have to tell you this Alex, but I'm having a good time enjoying myself, 'cause there's no involvement with anyone, so no one gets hurt. And I don't know when I'll decide to stop all of this fun that I'm having and calm down. So it's just not fair at all to you Alex, 'cause you don't need a wife like that, like me! I do still love you Alex, and because of that love, I'm prepared to set you free from me, so that you can now seriously find the sort of girl to love, who could make you happy and be the kind of wife that you need want, or dream about. Because honestly I don't feel that I could be that sort of girl for you anymore Alex, yes I tried to be for you once a long time ago, remember? But it didn't work out for us, did it? So good-bye Alex and take care of yourself."

"No Olivia no! Please don't give up on the love that we still have and feel for each other? We can still work something out together, so please just try to let yourself give me another chance?"

"No I'm sorry Alex, but I know it's just far to late for that. Anyway I've got to go now bye."

Alex was left with the empty dial tone signal ringing in his ear, when Olivia said goodbye to him, and hung up her phone. *'I have to and will win her back somewhere somehow, but where do I start?'* Were Alex's last thoughts, before he hung up his phone, and went out to the pub for a drink.

After replacing the receiver of her telephone, she went upstairs to her Bathroom to take a lovely, hot, bubble bath. Before making her face up and dressing in one of her sexy 'Disco' outfits, to go out downtown for a 'Boggy-Night' at the 'New-York-Bar'.

***

On her arrival at the 'New-York-Bar' a few hours later, the record *'Don't Stop Till You Get Enough'*, was playing very, loudly with lots of people dancing to it on the dance floor. Through the crowd of people stood around the bars, she spotted Dez talking to his Cousin Alisha, a top fashion model, Dez blew a kiss with his hand over to her, and Alisha smiled and waved. Olivia smiled and waved back to them both, before walking over to the bar that was in front of the dance floor. She joined her other friends there, who were smiling and greeted her warmly, looking as though they had been waiting and expecting her to arrive at anytime soon.

"Hi guys," she said to all of them, with a big smile.

"You've arrived later than usual tonight," Chuck said to her with a smile, checking his watch. "And are we going to have some fun together much later on Olivia?"

"I doubt it Chuck. 'Cause if I want to have a good time in bed with someone tonight, I know that it won't be with you. Okay?" She replied, as Nathan passed her a tall, glass of 'Campari' and orange juice.

"Thanks Nathan," she said to him, taking the drink from his hand.

"And you're looking very lovely and beautiful tonight Olivia," Arts said, smiling at her while admiring her figure. "And I love those tight trousers that you wear, they really show off your terrific figure. But tell me? Who helps to pour you into them?"

"Just me, I pour myself into them alone," she replied, sipping her drink through a straw.

"Oh don't bother, you're just wasting your time, giving 'Ms.-Lovely' here compliments Art. I think she gives them to herself all day," Chuck said with a laugh. Before whispering into her ear, "Where do you go to my lovely, when you're alone in your bed?"

"That's for me to know and for you to wonder about," she replied laughing. "Now who's going to dance with me? I love this Abba record."

***

Olivia, Gary and Nathan, all went to dance for a while, then went back to the bar to get more drinks. She lent herself back against the wall, next to the end of the bar, looking around at everyone in the club. The coloured lights over the dance floor were flashing on everyone, as they were dancing to the loud music, and she began to notice a tall, good-looking man, with black hair and blue eyes, stood to one side of the dance floor watching her.

"Yeah do you see him, that guy over there? He's been staring at you for ages now, and he's a good looking white guy," Chuck asked, with a laugh. "So do you feel like doing some coke tonight Olivia? And would you like all of us black guys to leave you alone? So he can come over and talk to you. 'Cause I think he's trying to decide which one of us you're with."

She just smiled at what Chuck said to her, while still, leaning against the wall, feeling relaxed, listening to the music, sipping her drink through a straw, and staring back at the man, who was looking at her flirtingly.

A record then began to play that Olivia, knew she had heard somewhere before, but couldn't think where. It had a long instrumental disco-beat at the beginning of it, and as the lyrics began to start, she just smiled to herself. Remembering now that it was the record that Alex, had brought for her a few months ago. She hadn't really listened to many if any of the words on the record before, only the chorus. But now she did begin to listen to the lyrics, and even heard the first few lines as the song began with, *'Dancing, romancing, but no second chancing, nothing more. She comes alone, every night on her own, looking for romance. She stands there watching, while everyone's touched. She takes a chance, standing there, waiting anticipating. How could this go wrong? So many lovers holding on.'*

She listened even harder, when the words to this song went on about, *'A man who is on the make and is watching a girl. The girl will give him sex but nothing more, because that's what she needed all along, and how the man will tell the girl he loves her, but will have someone new the next night and that's just fine by her.'*

Oh God no! Olivia was now beginning to think, as she closed her eyes, letting the beat of the song wrap itself around her, and the words that were being sung, whirl around inside of her head. *'This record has a definite story to it, just like Alex told me it did. And yes it could be all about me. And it has no ending to it, because this is all the girl is wanting and doing night after night! And probably month after month, and year after year! And she's just like me, going nowhere! Because yes I can get my man! Any man that I usually want! And all I want them for is sex! Nothing more! But where is it all going to end for me? Because I'm so afraid of love and loving anyone. But I guess that deep down inside of me, I know that it's something that I need so badly!! But I now realize that I won't find it, especially in this way of life!!!'*

She next heard a voice very, close to her, as someone spoke, and she opened her eyes, to see the man who had been looking at her, now stood in front of her smiling. "Would you like to dance?" He asked.

"No. No thanks." She replied, looking around the room and seeing so many of her lovers who were holding on. *'Holding on for what?'* She thought, *'Me??? No I don't think so! Not me, myself, I! Just a good time in bed with me tonight! If they get lucky! And I'm fucking stupid enough, to ask any one of them, knowing that they'll tell me that they love me, before they leave me, because that's what they always do! But God I don't need this fucking shit anymore! I've got to find something different in my life! And I've got to get myself out of here, out of this place right now!'* She then pushed the man away from her, who was still standing in front of her, saying something that she couldn't or even wanted to hear.

She next turned towards the bar, picking her hand-bag up off it, and quickly ran from the club without bothering to say goodbye to anyone, grabbing her coat from the checkout as she passed it, and finding herself a taxi outside to take her home.

***

On arriving home she found the twelve-inch-record that Alex, had left for her, and now noticed that he had written something, across the sleeve of it saying, *'Olivia's record. With love from Alex. Please listen.'*

She put the record on her 'Stereo-System' to play, playing it a few times over and over again, and really listened to the lyrics of it, much more intensely now, and the strong message that she could hear in it for herself, while laying on her couch crying.

She laid there crying for a few hours, and finally beginning to realize how much Alex, really did love her. And how he knew her, much, better than she really, did know herself, and how he wanted to try and save her, from herself. She was now beginning to realize that her game of destruction against men, was leading her nowhere fast, and for a long time it had been achieving her nothing. Only more men who were using her, just like she used them. So in the end no one could win, as it was a no win game that she now realized that she had been playing, on this her never ending roller-coaster, merry-go-round of fun.

Both Alex and Winston, have probably been very hurt by me and what I've been doing to them, with how I've been living my life, for so long! But what can I do about it all now? Because it was their own faults, as they both hurt me first. Anyway they shouldn't play with fire like me, or I'll burn them. But they probably enjoyed themselves, playing my game. So the best thing for me to do now is to set them both free, and get away from here. Go and live somewhere else to start my life again, yes I'll even get out of this country. I'll go and live over in America. Yes, that's what I'll do, go and live in America. I'll write to my friends over there in Miami, Florida, and see if the twins and I can go stay with them, until I get myself a job and somewhere to live. And if I find I don't like living in Miami, I'll move on to California.

With these thoughts and plans for her future, now fixed firmly in her mind, she fell asleep on the couch, for just a few hours before daylight came.

***

Winston went to see Olivia a few days later, and of course she was eager to tell him of her decision and plans, to go with her children and live in America. "I've written a letter to my friends, Rick and Jocelyn in Miami, asking them if they would be good enough to let us stay with them for a while, until I find myself a job and somewhere to live. And if the reply from them is yes, I'm then going to see my solicitor and get my divorce. So Alex will be completely free of me to get on with his own life."

"All of this to me, sounds as though you've really made your mind up, and are prepared to burn your bridges Olivia," Winston replied in amazement, after listening to her plans for her future.

"Oh yes I've been doing a lot of thinking and planning, and will burn my bridges if I have to," she defiantly said.

"But what about us? Are you going to leave me as well?"

"Oh please stop it will you Winston? Your beginning to sound like a bloody sad record, and don't worry I know that you'll survive without me."

"But I think I've told you before, that my parents are living over in America, in a place called 'Long Island', in New York. So I can go over to live in America with you, we could meet up there when you've got yourself somewhere to live, in your new life in Miami. So what do you think Olivia? 'Cause it sounds like a really good idea to me?"

"No, no Winston, oh no! You've got it all wrong, my plans when leaving don't include you. When I go I leave my past behind me, which does include you. And I want to make myself very clear so will you listen to me please? When I leave here, I will go alone with my children, to start a new life in America, a new beginning. I feel there's a lot more for me still in this life of mine, than just men and records. And when I do leave England Winston, I leave us, you and me. Winston and Olivia will be over and finished forever. But don't look so sad about it all. Because I'll always have the good happy memories, of what we had and our wonderful love for each other, and I can live with that. Can't you Winston?" She replied, in a very definite tone of voice.

"But I don't know, I thought that we'd be together forever," He replied nervously, beginning to feel a little insecure as he lit a cigarette, inhaling the smoke from it deeply.

"Forever? Us two stay together forever? But don't you realize that forever is a very long time Winston? And I never thought about us being together for as long as that, and I thought what we had between us, was just great fun for us both."

"Yeah I guess I really must admit, that I shouldn't be surprised at anything you say or do anymore eh Olivia? Especially after you found out about Brenda, even though I told you that I would finish with her, so it could be just you and me."

"Oh please do stop Winston? Don't go there at all? It's over it's finished."

"You know something? I always thought you were a very different girl; one on your own, and after you were made they broke the mould, 'cause I know of no one else like you. But deep down Olivia, I always hoped that it would be us two together, someday somewhere along the line. I always thought that the strong wonderful love that we have for each other, could never die. But it obviously has died for you somewhere eh? And you never told me."

"For Gods-sake stop it, will you Winston? Just please, please stop? And no, it's not my fault if you've always had these fucking delusions of grandeur about us two, because I never have. And stop trying to make me feel so bloody guilty, about wanting to do something else with my life. And if you do love me Winston, you'd try and understand me, and let me be free to go forward with my life, with no regrets. And aren't you forgetting something? Your names Pass-Tru, remember? Meaning just passing through, not Mr. Stay-around-for-ever."

"Okay all right Olivia," he said, putting both of his hands up into the air dismissively, walking towards the door. "If that's what you want to do? Then go, do what the fuck you want to, 'cause no one can ever get you to change your fucking mind, can they? Not even me? But don't you ever forget Olivia, I'll always love you, wherever you go."

"Yeah thanks Winston, I promise you that I'll always remember that," she shouted to him, just before he closed the door behind him.

******

Chapter 45

After about two weeks later, Olivia received a letter with American, postage stamps on it, from her friends in Miami, Florida, Rick and Jocelyn. It was a lovely written, friendly letter, telling her that her and her twin-Daughters, could go to stay with them, at their home in Miami, when she arrived over there, going to live in America. And they would be very, happy to help her find a job. They were looking forward to seeing her again, and to meeting her twin-Daughters, and would she let them know the date and time that she would be arriving in America, so that they could meet her at the Airport.

"Oh this is just great," she said out loud excitedly, holding the letter close to her. "I knew that these guys were my friends, and would be able to help me. And this is now the door to the opening of my plans for a new life. So I can now start to put things into action."

***

Three months later one Friday morning, after she had seen her twins off to school, Olivia went back to bed. She'd had a very, restless sleep the night before, and was still very tired, so she soon fell into a deep sleep, sleeping soundly until lunchtime.

When she woke up she stretched out in her bed, feeling very rested but confused, as she lay there for a while remembering the dream that she'd just awoken from. She sat up and lit a cigarette, laying her head back against the pillows, thinking about the dream she'd just had of Alex. Not understanding why she would be dreaming about him at all, with not seeing or hearing from him, for many many months now. But in this dream he had told her, that he was coming to see her about something very, important. But she couldn't think what it could be about, because she hadn't told Alex yet about her plans to go and live in America. She could still vividly remember the clothes that he was wearing in the dream, a red and black chequered, shirt with blue jeans. And he even knew that she was going into town this afternoon to do some shopping and meet with her friends to go for a drink.

Later while taking her bath, and getting ready to go out, she began to wonder if she'd had an omen.

***

At 5:30 that afternoon, the twins had eaten their evening meal, and were sitting on the couch in the lounge, watching children's programs on television. While Olivia was lying on the floor in front of the gas-fire dozing off to sleep, when she heard the front, door open and someone come into the lounge.

"Daddy! Oh Daddy, you've come to see us!" Sarah and Angel happily shouted together.

Olivia opened her eyes and saw Alex, giving the twins' hugs and kisses, and telling them how much he had missed his twinies. He was also wearing the same chequered, shirt and jeans that she'd seen him in, in her dream,

"Hi Olivia," Alex said, smiling at her.

"Hi Alex," she replied, very calmly. "I've been expecting you. You've come to see me about something important, that you want to discuss with me, haven't you?"

"Yes I have," he replied, in a very surprised voice. "But how did you know? And how come you aren't surprised to see me after all this time?"

"Let's just say that I may have had an omen this morning, telling me that you were coming to see me," she replied, smiling at Alex and getting up off the floor. "I was just sleeping, but let's go into the Dining-room to talk, and I'll make us some coffee. While the twins finish watching their TV program."

Alex followed Olivia into the Dining-room and sat at the table, while Olivia went into the kitchen to make their coffee.

"You have to tell me what you've come to see me about Alex, I can't stand the suspense any longer," she said. Coming back into the Dining-room carrying two hot mugs of coffee, and putting them down on the table. "Is it about the divorce? As I guess you know by now, that I'm divorcing you?"

"Yes, I know you are," he replied, while taking some papers out of his brief case, and putting them onto the table. "But I've come to ask you not to divorce me? I've just accepted a job offer to go and work in Canada. And I want you and the kids, to go with me to live there, because I love you so much Olivia, and I would like us all to go and start a new life there, together."

Olivia sipped her hot, coffee and lit a cigarette, while trying to stay very, calm, cool, and in control of this situation, as she began to feel her heart begin to start beating rapidly inside of her. While thinking, *This moment is just like something out of a fairy tale, suddenly Alex, my 'knight-in-shinning-armour', has just appeared in my life once again. To try and make everything right for me, by wanting to pick me up and whisk me away to a much better life and times.*

Alex got up and walked over, putting his arms around her, kissing her and saying, "I'm sorry if this is all to much of a shock for you Olivia. But I love you so much, that I just couldn't sneak off to go and work in Canada, without giving you the chance to consider coming with me. To somewhere where I feel that we could begin our marriage all over again, a complete new start for both of us together. So please think very hard about this move and new start for us Olivia? And do say that you'll come with me?"

She put her arms around Alex holding him close to her. Saying, "You know? I knew you were coming to see me about something important, but I had no idea that it was as important as this. And yes Alex, I still do love you very much. And I have this strong feeling deep inside of me, that it would be the right and best thing for me to do, to go and live with you in Canada, for us to start again there. So I can be a very good wife to you, like I've always really wanted to be. So yes Alex I'd love to go and live in Canada with you."

Alex kissed Olivia holding her very close to him, feeling that the love that they always had between them, would now begin to grow much stronger. "Come on let's go and ask the twins, if they'd like to go and live in Canada with us?"

"Oh yes and I'm sure they'll want to. But just let me ask you something first Alex? Those papers that you've put here on the table, are they about your job in Canada? And were they given to you by a person who had come over to England from Canada?"

"Yes a Canadian guy brought them over from Canada with him," Alex answered, in a surprised tone of voice. "And he gave them to me after the interview that I had with him, the other week. But why do you ask?"

"Elaine's fortune telling cards were right then," she said smiling to herself. "And so was my omen that I had this morning, telling me that you were coming to see me about something important, because you're also wearing the same shirt and jeans that I saw you in, in my dream."

***

Over the next few months Olivia was very busy with her life. The first thing she eagerly did was go to see her Solicitor, to stop her divorce proceedings to Alex going through. Contacted her son Antony, to ask him if he would like to go with them, to live over in Canada? With of course Antony eagerly agreeing to go and live with them over there. She wrote a letter to her friends Rick and Jocelyn in Miami, Florida, America. Very happily telling them that her and Alex had had a reconciliation, and were going to live in Canada, with Alex getting himself a job over there. She put their house on 'Crowfield Road' up for sale, and soon found a buyer for it. She sold most of their furniture, all of the curtains and the electric appliances that they were not taking with them. And lastly saying good-bye to all of her friends and broken hearted relatives, that she would be leaving behind her. Of course during their tearful farewells with each other, most of them asked her not to go and live so very, far away, in case they never, ever saw her again. But she promised everyone that she would come back to see them again one day, if in time after a few years, they hadn't forgotten her, like she thought that they might, and promised to send everyone a card every Christmas.

***

Olivia, Alex and their three children, eagerly took Danny and Gayle's very, generous offer up, for them all to go to their home to stay there overnight, for their last night in Sheffield, before they would leave the City by train, early the next morning, on their way to go and live in Canada.

"It will be bett-ur than spendin yur last night in Sheffield England, in a hotel room, wondering if yu've made rate choice in-yur life tu-leave-ear, Olivia," Danny told her. "Anyway our Gayle, as already made them spare beds up fort kids int-one-at bedrooms. An you an Alex will be okay sleeping on our big couch, int Lounge eh? An our Gayle, seys to tell thee, that she's cooking a luvly big dinner fur-us all. An we can ave a party afterwards for yur last night ear-in Sheffield, so it should be fun. But what I'd like to know afour yu leave England though? Is what about yu-an Winston? Is it finished an all over wi-yu two now? Or will it continue elsewhere, like in Canada?"

"Well I guess you could now say, Winston was my bit on the side, until I decided to have my husband back. And you guys do that sort of thing all the time, don't you? So why can't us girls also do it?" Olivia sassily replied with a laugh.

***

Early one very, warm August morning at six o'clock, Olivia, Alex and their Children, all kissed and said their last, good-byes, to Danny and Gayle, and their little son Dean. Thanking them both very, much for letting them spend their last night in Sheffield, England, at their home. "I know I'll never be lucky enough to have another friend, or milkman like you, over in Canada, Danny," Olivia said, with tears in her eyes, and her arms wrapped around Danny, holding him very, close to her. "And once again thanks for everything, including your wonderful friendship Danny. And I'll never ever forget you, I promise."

"No I should bloody ope not," Danny replied, with a laugh. "An don't forget bout that Aikido that I've taught yu. An ear's-sum-ut else that I want yu to take wi-yu, int memory a-me. It's mi 'Riot-Baton' that I used in Northern Ireland when I wer fighting IRA. An all those pieces knocked out ot-wood-ear, art-teeth I've knocked out, ov blokes ova-thear, look?" He said pointing to all of the dents in the very thick, wooden 'Riot-Baton', that the teeth marks had made, when he was passing it to her. On taking from him, this very, much treasured, leaving gift from Danny, to take to Canada with her, she was looking at the teeth marks on it, which Danny was pointing out, when she quickly noticed that he had written around all of the 'Baton' in blue pen, '*To Olivia, I hope "u" ave plenty of fun, as I did. Luv Danny. XXXXXX*'

"Oh thanks Danny, and I promise that I'll treasure this always, because I know this 'Riot-Baton' was very special to you."

"Yeah it wer, so do look after it okay? Now cum on, yur taxi's ear-an-yu don't want tu miss yur train an plane. An just remember tu come back an see us sum time."

On Wednesday the 26th August 1981, as the 'Air Canada' aeroplane lifted up off the runway at 'Heathrow' Airport, Olivia looked down through the plane's window and said a silent good-bye to England and all her friends. She was now going three thousand miles away to live in Canada, where she felt she would, and could be, a good, loving, caring wife to Alex, her husband, the man she now knew that she could and would love forever!

******

OLIVIA'S FULL CIRCLE.
PART FOUR.
1981 - 1987

Chapter 46

Olivia and her family, found life in North America, all wonderfully, fresh, and so very, excitingly different, to what they had ever been used to before, with a new start and beginning for all of them to enjoy together. They went live in the province of Quebec, and loved to see and visit their beautiful, big, cosmopolitan city of Montreal, that was surrounded by the water of the St. Lawrence River. They also enjoyed meeting and being with the French Canadian people who lived there, whose French culture and influence had now taken a very, strong hold in the province of Quebec.

They rented a just recently built, brand new, large, condominium to live in for a few years, thinking that it would be foolish for them, to rush into buying a house to settle into as their home, until they had got to know the areas around Montreal, much better, and where they would all feel comfortable living.

The people who moved into the condominium below them, a few weeks later, were the newly, married couple, Charlene and Serge, whom they became instant friends with. And just maybe by coincidence, they found that they all loved to share together, the same, happy, crazy, sometimes off the wall, sense of humour. These two new, French Canadian friends of theirs, made them all very, welcome into their Canadian world.

Serge, a small, plumpish, large muscled man, with dark hair and blue eyes in his late thirties, was a 'Truck-Driver'. His driving route took him to the other Provinces all over Canada, and often across the 'American-Border-Line', through 'Customs' there, who sometimes felt in the mood to give the Canadian-Trucker's a hard time, by asking them lots of questions and really searching the inside of their trucks, before allowing them to go forward into America, to deliver their goods to different, companies in different States across there.

So when Serge arrived home after his sometimes, difficult, long, hauls as they were called, often driving a haulage the distance of at least three-thousand-miles there, and then back again, in a week. Serge insisted on really needing to wind down on his arrival home, before going out again on his next 'Trucking' trip. So he always insisted on inviting Alex and Olivia to come downstairs to join him, in his own condominium, in his drinking and partying, with playing his pop-music very, loud to help him to unwind, and having a few, good drinks of the American-Bourbon 'Jack Daniels', which he very, much felt that he needed. While talking and laughing about some of the funny, or scary, experiences, that he'd encountered along his way. And not forgetting to mention the country of England, a place that he said he would like to go and visit one day. And eventually, after a few hours of socializing and unwinding, he would wander off into his bedroom, and fall into a very, deep, dreamless sleep, on these return home trips of his.

Charlene a small, lady, with bright, blue eyes and blonde hair, in her middle twenties, eagerly, took Olivia under her wing. Showing her around Montreal and the Suburbs of it, even the out of the way, very, uninhabited countryside. Also taking her shopping to the best, and cheapest, 'Supermarkets' to buy her groceries. The best value for money 'Furniture-Stores' and places like 'Wal-Mart' and 'Zellers' to choose any curtains, pots, pans or clothes that her family needed. And very, happily shared lots of North-American girl talk over coffee with her, mostly telling her about the way of life that the men and women had over there, and the things that they did. Leaving Olivia thinking, that the women in England and Europe, were far more liberated, than the North American women were. But she had no intentions of changing anything about her European status, or what she thought and believed in, just to fit in, so that she could be just like most of the other North-American ladies.

Charlene also introduced Olivia, Alex and their children, to her Parents and Brothers and Sisters, whom often invited them over to their houses for supper, making them all feel very, welcome on these visits to their homes. With Charlene's Father, Joe, wanting to spend a lot of his time on these occasions, just reminiscing to Olivia, about the towns and city's in the England, that he still and would always remember, when he was over there with the Canadian Forces during the 'Second-World-War'.

These lovely, friendly, Canadian people who welcomed Olivia, and her family, into their way of organized, settled, loving, family life, all helped her to easily, settle into her new, way of life and role in Canada. And to quickly get over any homesickness that she may, occasionally feel, for her family and friends that she had left behind her, back in England.

Alex soon settled very, easily into his new, 'Computer-Programming-Analyst's' job, in Montreal. And instantly made good, friends with Serge, whom he admired very, much for the hard, working job that he thought he did, in being a long, haul 'Trucker', moving goods across North America, just to keep the countries on the move.

Sarah and Angel, who were now ten-years old, loved their new school and the friends that they made there. And soon began to learn to speak the Quebecois-French language, which was taught in the schools of Quebec, soon making them both become bilingual, with being able to speak French as good as their own English language.

Antony who was now a teenager, began to talk with a North American accent, as soon as he stepped off the plane in Canada, sounding as though he had been born there. He soon got himself a job in a local Supermarket 'A&P' Stacking shelves, helping to fill the trunks of customers cars with their groceries, collecting shopping-carts that were left outside, and taking them back into the store. Soon making friends and socializing with a crowd of 'French-Canadian' teenagers who also worked there.

Yes Olivia soon began feeling that she had definitely, made the right choice in coming over to live in Canada with Alex. With their relationship growing much, deeper and stronger over the years, filled with lots of love, passion and understanding for each other, than it ever had been or could have become back home in England. She was also very, aware that her lifestyle had changed, somewhat, dramatically and drastically, but all for the better, from the sex, drugs and rock-an-roll one, that she had been so falsely, leading and living, but had thankfully left back behind her in England.

***

They eagerly moved into their new home, in the summer of 1984 after finally finding their dream, house to buy out in the countryside, in a town and place called by a very, French sounding and spelling name of 'Ile-Perrot', about twenty miles away from the city of Montreal. It was a large house, with Four-Bedrooms, a Lounge, Dining-Room, Kitchen, Two-Bathrooms, a very large Carpeted-Basement, with a built-in liquor-bar along one wall, and a big Fireplace at the front of the room. The garden at the back of the house was the size of a football field, with an in-ground swimming pool in the middle of it.

Antony, who by this time, after a lot of job changes, had got himself a good, job as a 'Sheet-Metal' worker, and now lived by himself, in a small, rented apartment. Telling Olivia and Alex, that he much preferred living by himself than with them, because this was where he could have all his friends around, anytime he wanted to see them. And hold his parties, playing his loud, Heavy-Metal-Music, all weekend long if he wanted to, with no complaints from either of them. He also wanted to have some privacy alone, with his girlfriend, Shawna, a very pretty, petite girl, with shoulder length dark brown hair, and green eyes. Who, after only a few meetings with, he had started dating seriously.

But Antony was four-years older than Shawna, which did not please Olivia, at all, warning him, and describing their relationship, by telling him, *'That Shawna, was nothing more than just a high-school kid, out looking for a bit of fun, and some puppy-love to play with, in between her homework and school.'*

As she got to know her better, Olivia grew to like Shawna, thinking that in time she would be good for Antony, who could sometimes be very irresponsible.

Her greatest fear though, for the relationship between Antony, and Shawna, was the age difference that would always be there, and could sometime in the future become a problem between them. And the possibility of another, sad, history repeating itself again sometime over, in this next generation, with her Son, whom she never wanted to be hurt by anyone, in anyway. And over the years, Olivia felt confident in often saying to them both. *'Please be very careful you two! Because we don't want anymore baby Antony's around just yet. Not until you're a lot older than you are now Shawna. Because I don't want to see another young girl's life nearly ruined, by her getting pregnant while she's still so very young. And although you may not think it, you've got a lot of growing and learning to do and go through in your life's yet. And in the end, when you get older, you and Antony may decide to go your separate ways in a few years time.'*

But Shawna always insisted to Olivia, that she didn't have to worry. That she wouldn't be having any babies for a long, long time yet, because her career came first. And Antony was still like a baby himself sometimes, and took enough looking after.

When Shawna reached the age of eighteen, she had finished her college education, and got herself a very good job, working with a firm of accountants in Montreal. With the relationship between her and Antony still going along very strong. And Alex always telling them both, that they already acted like an old married couple, the way they often, argued and shouted at each other.

******

Chapter 47

Over the years Olivia and Alex met and made a lot of new friends. And in the lovely, hot days of summer, from May up until September, they would often invite these friends over to their home in 'Ile-Perrot' on weekends, to barbecued suppers, and swimming-pool-parties.

One of these friends was Ivan, a twenty-six year old, Electronics-Computer-Engineer, who worked for the same company as Alex. And over a period of time they got to know each other much better, becoming very, good friends. Especially during their business trips away together, visiting other countries in the world, often Venezuela. To advise companies over there about Computers and the best kind of 'Software' for them to use.

When Olivia first met Ivan, she thought it was a Greek-God who had just walked through her front door, as she shook hands with a six foot five inch tall, brown, eyed blonde, haired very, broad shouldered, firm muscled, good looking guy. So on becoming instant, friends from their first meeting, he was always invited to the parties given by Olivia and Alex, and he usually stayed over for the weekends there in their home. He especially loved to party if Antony and Shawna were over, because then the parties would go on until daylight, with everyone laughing, and having so much fun. Yes they all seemed to work hard, and play hard in their life's, and really enjoyed, unwinding and relaxing at the weekends, from Friday nights until late Sunday afternoons.

Ivan soon began to fit in and feel just like one of the members of this family, especially when the twins Sarah and Angel, told him that they had decided to adopt him as their second big Brother. Which he loved the thought of, because as he told them, he hadn't got any Sisters of his own, only a much, younger Brother.

Over the years everyone soon began jokingly, referring to and calling Ivan, 'The Bolshevik'. Once he had told them all, that his parents, who now lived in Vancouver, instead of Montreal, where his brother and himself had been born and brought up, were Russian. And that his Grandparents had come over from the Ukraine, as farmers' years ago, to start a new, life over here living in Canada.

Luckily Ivan had the same as all of these friends of his, a very good, crazy, off the wall sense of humour. Telling them all that he had to have that around them, just to survive. And no he never took any offence at all from any of them, by being referred to, or called 'The Bolshevik Man', by this very, outspoken new family of his. Even when Alex, who would sometimes, as Olivia thought, rudely refer to him as the 'Donkey Dork', the nickname that he had been given by the other men at work.

***

After Christmas Ivan finally brought with him to their house one evening, one of his many but his all time favourite, girlfriend, Sherrie, to meet Alex, Olivia, Antony, Shawna and the twins. Sherrie, who lived about a six hours drive away from Montreal, in the great metropolis, Toronto, had been seeing Ivan for about three years now. She was twenty-three years old, five-feet-six-inches tall, with lovely, soft, wavy, shoulder length red hair, and large blue eyes. A fun and easy, going party, type of girl, who liked, and got on very well, with Ivan's friends, whom she had heard so much about before meeting them. "Yes you guys this new family of his, are all Ivan talks about, when we get together," Sherrie told them. "Especially you Olivia, it seems to me that you're his dream girl."

"Yeah, I guess that could be so, eh Ivan?" Olivia replied, with a laugh winking at him. "But don't worry about it Sherrie. 'Cause Ivan's just a big boy-toy, and the only man I want in my life now-a-days is my wonderful hubby Alex. So your boy-toy will always be safe around me, we're just very good friends."

"I like to think of Olivia as my big Sister, and I think she's just one great lady," Ivan said, putting his arm around Olivia's shoulder, hugging her closely to him. "Hey you guys, do you like shooting?" He continued, pouring himself and Sherrie, a Rye and Coke to drink.

"Yeah people, I wouldn't mind shooting some of them, 'cause that seems to be what you North Americans are into, when you feel like doin it." Antony replied laughing. "But I don't know, I've never tried it before."

"What shooting people? Well you never know we might enjoy it." Alex said, joining in with this conversation and laughter.

"No not fucking people, you stupid fucking limies." Ivan replied, also laughing. "Guns, have any of you ever done any target shooting with guns?"

"Yeah but only at fairgrounds, to win teddy bears for Olivia, and the twins, why?" Asked Alex.

"Well I've got a country cottage up in the Laurentians, it's about a two-hours drive away from here, and it's got lots of land to it," Ivan continued. "And I don't know if I've told you all before? But I'm an avid gun collector. And I was wondering if you guys would like to spend a weekend at the cottage with me and Sherrie? We could party out there, and do some target shooting with some of my guns, and have some fun out in the snow, riding the Snowmobiles, that I've got a couple of."

"What you've got two Snowmobiles? Well I think that's a bit greedy Ivan, 'cause I haven't got one myself yet." Answered Antony.

"No neither have I," added Alex.

"Shush you two. And yes Ivan if you've got a country cottage, that we could all go to visit? I'd like to go there, and doing some target shooting should be fun," Shawna replied. "It sounds like it could be a great fun weekend, what do you think Olivia?"

"Yes definitely I'm all for it. When can we go?" Olivia asked. "And have you got a rocket launcher Ivan? 'Cause those things just fascinate me, I'd love to fire a rocket launcher, I just love those big crazy guns."

"Oh sorry but no, no, no Olivia, you will not be firing anything like a rocket launcher," Ivan replied laughingly, while shaking his head. "You girls will only get to shoot with something like a 22 calibre rifle. My big guns, like the Fie/Spas, 12 gauge, pump action, shotgun, or the 308 calibre M-60 assault rifle, would break your wrists in half with their recoil."

"What's a recoil? And can't we leave the recoil behind?" Shawna asked, making all the men laugh loudly, due to her ignorance of guns and what recoil is.

"A recoil is the way the gun jumps back at you when you fire it," Ivan replied seriously, feeling sorry for Shawna and her ignorance with guns and how they work. "It's also called a kickback, and it would be too powerful and dangerous, for you girls to hold on to any of the big guns and fire them, without you getting hurt."

"Have you got many guns then Ivan?" Antony asked.

"Yeah just a few," Ivan replied with a smile. "So let's all go over to my cottage next weekend, and you can see for yourselves."

"Okay then that's a date," the others all agreed.

"You people have no idea how lucky you are, to be invited to Ivan's cottage, and to shoot his guns, because he never ever lets anyone go out there. And he's only ever taken me to his cottage twice before, in all the years that I've known him. And I've not been allowed to touch any of his guns yet," Sherrie said.

"Yeah, well I guess Ivan likes you to touch and play, with his other gun when you're there with him, eh Sherrie?" Alex asked with a laugh.

"Of course that's right Alex, but how did you guess that?" Ivan asked laughing, while pouring himself another drink.

***

After a two-hour drive the following Saturday evening, they all arrived at Ivan's cottage at six o'clock. They were all surprised by the size of this country cottage, with it having three Bedrooms, a very, large, Living-room, with a big, stone fireplace built along one wall, and off to one side of the Living-room, was a Kitchen with pretty curtains hung at the windows.

"Oh this is just great and it seems to be out in the middle of nowhere, I just love places like this. And who built it?" Olivia asked.

"My Grandfather built it for our family, many years ago. But I'm the only one who ever comes here now. I've put the electric heating on, and I'll get a fire going with some logs in the fireplace, so it'll soon get warm in here. Have you brought the bottle of 'Rye' and some Cokes' Olivia? 'Cause I think we could all use a drink, before we go down to the village and get something to eat at the restaurant there."

"Why doesn't water come out of any of these taps? And where's the bathroom?" Shawna asked, turning the dry, running taps on at the sink in the kitchen.

"Oh yes well don't worry about that Shawna, I forgot to tell you guys. I'm afraid there's no plumbing fitted into the cottage yet," Ivan replied, in a fake sorry tone of voice. "But that's no problem, 'cause I can get water from the well that's just outside in the back. And the toilet when you need it, is in that little hut at the bottom of the garden. It's really just a big hole in the ground, but I've put a toilet seat on it. And after you've used it, you throw sawdust that's in the big container next to it, into the hole, to cover anything that you've done."

"You're bloody joking us, aren't you?" Shawna asked, in a shocked tone of voice. "I'm not going to sit in a fucking hole when I want to pee, never, no way. It's okay for you guys, you can go out there and just pee in the snow. But Olivia and I can't."

"It's not a hole in the ground that you'll have to sit in Shawna. It's got a proper toilet seat, that Ivan said he's put on it," Sherrie said, with a laugh. "It's just that you can't flush it like a proper toilet afterwards. So you throw sawdust down it and everything eventually goes into the ground. It's not that bad really, come on I'll show you."

"Ugh," Shawna replied, with a shudder. "And where do we then was our hands? And where do we take our shower in the morning? I suppose we will have to have a strip wash from a bowl of water eh?"

Yes I can arrange that for you girls, I'll even give you a strip wash myself if you like Shawna," Ivan happily jokingly answered.

"Yeah and I can help you bath the girls Ivan, no problem," Alex added, with a laugh.

"Get out of here Alex, I can manage to wash myself," Olivia replied, smiling at him.

"Yes well come on? Let's go and get our supper down in the village, where we can discuss and decide who's going to wash who," Ivan said.

"Yeah in your fucking dreams Ivan," Shawna replied.

***

After eating a good meal for supper, they all returned in their cars from the restaurant, which was about a mile away from the cottage. Ivan was pouring everyone drinks, while they were all sat around the brightly, burning log fire getting warm, as the temperature had now dropped to thirty-below-zero outside. "Have you got some good music on those tapes you've brought, Olivia?" Ivan asked. "There's a ghetto-blaster stood on the table over there, you can play the tapes on that."

"Oh, have you brought that tape with '*I Want Your Sex*'?" Asked Shawna. "I love that song, which tape is it on?"

"I've recorded it on a few of my tapes," Olivia replied, passing the bag of tapes across to Shawna. "You'll just have to find which one it's on. Can I see your gun collection now Ivan? Where is it? Where do you keep them?"

"Ah yes, my gun collection," Ivan said, clapping his hands together, after passing everyone their drinks of 'Rye' and coke. "I guess that's why you've come here, to see my gun collection eh? I keep the guns in my Bedroom, so come on then I'll show them to you."

They all went into Ivan's Bedroom and saw, along the length of one wall, a large, glass-showcase with locks on it, filled with different, guns. Ivan took a key out of his trouser pocket, before going over and unfastening the locks. He then opened wide, the glass doors of the showcase, so his friends could see all of his beautiful, collection of guns.

"Wow! Just look at all those fucking guns?" Antony said, in an amazed tone of voice, before going over to have a closer look at the guns. So what are you Ivan, another fucking Rambo? I think you must be with all this collection, I've never seen anything like it before in my life, except in movies of course. And how long did it take you to get this lot?"

"I started my collection about ten years ago. I take after my Father who's also an avid gun collector. But he's not helped me at all with my collection of guns, I got all these myself," Ivan replied. Feeling very proud of himself, as he began lifting his guns out of the showcase, and passing them over to Antony and Alex for a closer inspection. "And no, I'm not a fucking Rambo. Although sometimes

I'd so much like to be, with all the fucking shit that's going on in the world today."

"How many guns have you got here?" Asked Alex, taking a gun off him. "'Cause it all looks very impressive."

"Impressive or intimidating," Ivan replied laughing. "I've got about twenty guns, and here, this is a Rambo gun Antony, a 308 calibre M-60 assault rifle. And this is a Dessert Eagle, a 44 magnum, semi-automatic pistol with a 6 inch barrel, this is a combat weapon. This is a very lethal weapon Alex, that you might like to shoot, a Model 92F Beretta, a 15 shot semi-automatic military hand gun."

"Have you got the ammunition for all these guns, Ivan? And who's your gun supplier?" Alex asked.

"Yes, the ammunition is in that big chest of drawers over there," Ivan replied, pointing to some drawers in the room. "And I've got two sources where I get my guns from. One is a small, back street, gun shop in Montreal, and the other is Isaac, a big, black market, gun dealer, that I know down in the 'States."

"Pass me that gun there please, 'cause I fancy shooting that one," Shawna said, pointing to one of the guns still in the showcase.

"Yes, you can look at it, but no way will I let you fire it," Ivan replied, passing Shawna the gun she was pointing to. "That's a 'Dirty Harry' gun, a Smith and Wesson, Model 29, 44 magnum, a double action revolver, with an 8 inch barrel and a very strong, deadly, nasty recoil. I've got a 22 calibre rifle, and a Ruger 22, semi-automatic pistol, that you girls can use safely, and maybe my Uzi 9 millimetre submachine gun, if you feel you could hold onto the gun, when you fire it, we'll have to see."

"I'm still waiting to see a rocket-launcher," Olivia said. "I don't suppose you've got one of them eh?"

"A rocket-launcher eh! Yeah I know you are Olivia," Ivan replied, putting his arm around her. "I'll show you one later, I promise. Now let's all go and get another drink and just relax, it's party time remember!"

"Okay then if you promise to show me one later on," Olivia said, believing him. "And I want Alex to take a photograph of me holding that gun there, what is it?"

"What this one?" Ivan replied, taking a gun out of the showcase, and passing it to Olivia. "This is the Fie/Spas, 12 gauge, semi-automatic shotgun, that they use in the 'Miami Vice' television show. Here girls, all of you grab a gun, and let Alex take your photos with them. Have you got your camera ready Alex? The girls are going to pose like Rambo's' for you."

***

For the next few hours they drank beers, 'Rye' and Cokes, popped corn on the stove, roasted chestnuts and marshmallows around the log fire, talked, laughed danced and sang, 'I want your Aids' to the song, 'I Want Your Sex', every time it played on one of the tapes. With Olivia telling everyone that she felt, that it was now a sign of the times. Because when she left England a few years ago, no one knew about, or had heard of, AIDS or Herpes. "But if you pick anyone up for the night, in a club or a bar nowadays, you've no idea what bizarre sexual diseases they've got. And most people seem to have something they unknowingly pass on, so it must be hell out there for the young and single people of today, who don't have a monogamous relationship."

"Listen to the great moralist here talking," Alex said, giving Olivia a loving tender kiss. "You've really changed your way of thinking, over the years, I'm pleased to say."

"Well God I should hope that I have. And I like to give advice to people, about how dangerous it is out there now."

***

"Well you guys I've got to get some fresh air, it's so bloody hot in here now that log fires really got going. Come on let's all go out for a walk in the snow. And I'm going to wear those snowshoes, that I saw hanging up on the wall outside the cottage," Alex said, going towards the back door just after midnight.

The weather seemed to have turned warmer outside, as they were all walking through the very, deep snow, with a large, round, full moon, shinning brightly up in the clear, unclouded sky. The moon was reflecting against the undisturbed, untouched by anything, brilliant, white snow, making everything very visible. "Will you stop throwing snow at me, Shawna," Antony said. "Unless you want a snowball fight."

"It's difficult to have a snowball fight with this Canadian snow," Alex said, trying hard to form and make a snowball with his hands. "The snow over here is far too dry, it just won't stick together, your snows more like soap flakes Ivan."

"Ivan what's that gun you're carrying? And what are you going to shoot with it?" Olivia asked, when they had been walking for about a mile, through fields full of snow.

"I'm going to show you something soon, that I think you'll like," Ivan replied, pointing his finger at something in the distance. "Can you all see that '75 Chevy Nova car, that I've dumped about three hundred yards away over there? That used to be a great car of mine, but it finally died, and there's nothing else I can do for it anymore, but cremate it now, poor thing. So all stand back and watch this."

Ivan aimed his M203, a 223-calibre M16 assault rifle, with a 40-millimetre grenade launcher, at the old abandoned, Chevy Nova car and fired. Suddenly the whole car was blown to pieces and it became a huge ball of bright, flames, burning brightly in the distance.

"Wow! Look at that!" Everyone exclaimed, as they stood watching the car explode into very, large, bright flames.

"That's really something that I've only seen happen in movies," Olivia said.

"That Olivia is what you've been wanting to see," Ivan replied proudly. "This is a rocket launcher that I've just fired. I hope now you will realize how deadly these guns can be, and you will have some respect for them, when we're target shooting with them tomorrow. 'Cause I hope you can now appreciate that they're not toys to play cowboys and Indians with, as I think that's what most of you Brits would like to do."

They just stood there silently for a while watching the burning car. While listening to Ivan, seriously, lecturing them all, about his greatest fears, of their innocence and lack of respect towards his guns. And the simple fact that they, could so easily hurt, wound or kill someone, if the guns were dangerously, fooled around with.

***

The next morning, after they had all been to the restaurant and had a bacon and egg breakfast, they spent most of that day until it began to go dusk, target shooting with some of Ivan's guns, and going for rides on his snow-mobiles through the snow. Olivia was pleased with herself when she hit four bull's eyes, on the target board that was pinned up for her on one of the trees.

"I think that's great," she said, now firing a 22-calibre rifle at some cans in the snow. "I've never fired a gun, or even held one, in my life before, and I got bulls eye. So just you all watch me make the tomato juice explode out of these cans. And this is what I call, having good fun in the snow, over in 'The-Great- White-North'. It's sure different to winter time in England, which I always hated, because I always got so cold and wet in the snow over there."

******

Chapter 48

"Could you pick Shawna up, at the metro station tonight at seven-thirty please?" Olivia asked Alex, when talking to him on the telephone at his work.

"Okay, but don't you mean Shawna and Antony?"

"No, Antony's working tonight, so he's not coming over until tomorrow. Shawna's bringing her friend Hollie, over with her for the weekend, and from what Shawna's told me about this Hollie, it seems that she's been having a rough time with this guy she's been living with. He's a drug dealer and he's been beating her up badly. And Shawna feels Hollie could do with a break, so she's bringing her here for the weekend to get some space and to think about things."

"I see, I see, but don't you go getting yourself too involved in this Hollie's sad life, will you? And when are Ivan and Sherrie coming over?"

"Tomorrow, their plan is to come over here tomorrow, 'cause it's party time tomorrow night, not tonight. So we'll just send out for some pizza for us four for supper tonight, have a few drinks and get an early night for a change. The twins are going to a friends house for a sleep over party, so it'll be pretty quiet around the house tonight without them around."

"Yeah it sure will be without them and all their friends at our place, but that's okay no problem. And I'll see you at about eight o'clock tonight then, after I've picked Shawna and her friend up. Love you and bye for now."

"And I love you to Alex, see yu later."

***

"Hi Olivia, I'm pleased to meet you. And it's so good of you to let me come over for the weekend, I needed to get away. And I love your dogs, what are they black Labradors?" Hollie said, shaking hands with Olivia, before stroking and making a fuss of her dogs.

"Yes they are, I seem to be collecting black Labradors, they're my favourite dog and I've got four up to now," Olivia replied, with a laugh. "So if your violent, drug dealing boyfriend, comes around here looking for you Hollie, I'll set my dogs on him okay."

"Yes please do," Hollie replied with a smile, feeling safe in this house that she had come to stay in for the weekend.

"Olivia I want you to talk to this girl. 'Cause she's just crazy getting in with a guy like that. And I don't know what the attraction was to him? 'Cause he's not even good looking, but he sure seems to have Hollie hooked on him and wrapped around his finger. And she's also very scared of him," Shawna said. Walking into the kitchen with a bottle of 'Rye', and putting it down on the Kitchen table. "I've brought a bottle with me tonight Olivia, so I hope you've made lots of ice. I'll just go downstairs and get some glasses from behind the bar."

"And I'll order a large, all dressed pizza for us," Alex said. Picking up the receiver of the telephone that was mounted on the kitchen wall. "I'm starving, how about you guys?"

"Yes, I'm pretty hungry too, I only had a yogurt for lunch," Hollie replied.

"What do you expect me to say to Hollie then?" Olivia asked Shawna, looking at Hollie, a very, tall, blue, eyed, blonde, haired, slim, good-looking girl. "I don't even know this boyfriend of hers, or how long she's been living with him. In fact what's it got to do with me? I can't see that it's any of my business."

"Yes on that your right," Alex said with a laugh. "If Hollie's boyfriend beats her up, more fool her for letting him. And I can't see what Olivia can do about it, or help her?"

"Oh you shut the fuck up Alex, Hollie needs some good advice, not your opinion, so don't you start preaching to her. Here's your drink, get a few of these down you and you might mellow out, eh Olivia?" Shawna said, in a very, bossy slightly, laughing tone of voice, passing Alex his drink, and wanting him to know, that the situation of Hollie, was now definitely in her hands.

"Okay but I'm only trying to help," replied Alex, taking his drink.

"So are you still seeing, or living with this guy Hollie?" Olivia asked. "And why does he beat up on you?"

"He doesn't anymore 'cause I've finished with him and left him last weekend, and I've moved back in with my parents for now. But I've heard he wants me back 'cause he still loves me. And if I don't go back to him, he'll probably come looking for me, and find me. And when he does he'll beat me up again for leaving him. And when I was still with him, if he didn't get paid for any of his drug-dealing, he always fucking took it out on me, and used me as a punching bag," Hollie replied, with a deep, sad sigh.

"Oh really! He sounds just like the kind of guy I could get on with. I just love guys like him," Olivia said sarcastically. "And from what you've just told me. It sounds to me as though this fucking assole, just wants to own and control you, not love you. 'Cause if he really did love you Hollie, no matter what his problems are, or what you do or say to him, he wouldn't ever hit you, ever. You're still a very young, good-looking girl Hollie, and if you do really want my advice? You'll keep away from him and assoles like him, and find yourself a guy who knows what the word love means. Now come on stop worrying and have a drink and relax. I'm sure he won't find you out here, so you're quite safe for the weekend. Oh Alex, that's the doorbell can you get the pizza please?"

***

At ten o'clock that night the telephone began to ring, and after Alex answered the phone, he passed it to Shawna saying, "This is for you, and guess who?"

"Hi Antony I thought you were working tonight?" Shawna said. "What, you're on a break? Well what are you calling for, just to check up on me? And I told you I was coming over to your Mom's tonight, and yes Hollie's here with me. No, Ivan and Sherrie aren't coming over until tomorrow night, so you're not missing anything. Oh we're just all having a quiet night here, we're sat in the kitchen talking and having a few drinks. No don't sign off from work Antony! And stop being a baby! Alex says he'll pick you up tomorrow afternoon when you've had some sleep. Yes I know that you want to be with us, but you've got to work tonight. So look I'll see you tomorrow, bye now Antony. Ugh God!" Screamed Shawna, hanging up the kitchen telephone. "That Son of yours Olivia is really something, and sometimes he really pisses me off, he's just like a fucking baby. He says he's missing all of us, and thinks that he should be here with us tonight. So he can't really concentrate on the work that he's suppose to be doin. But his fucking problem is that, he's just terrified of missing something we may all be doin, eh! He says he thought we might be having a party tonight, with it being Friday night."

"Here Shawna have another drink and calm yourself down, don't let Antony upset you so much, just 'cause he's pissed off about having to work tonight." Alex said, pouring her another drink.

"Yeah I know your right Alex. It's just that he makes me so fucking angry," Shawna replied, sipping her drink through a straw. "I just wish your Son would grow up one day Olivia. Maybe you and your parents spoiled him too much when he was a kid. Don't you think that you all probably did spoil him too much?"

"Hey please leave me out of this Shawna?" Olivia said with a laugh, passing her glass to Alex for a refill. "All of this is between you and Antony, not me. And yes maybe the little brat did get spoiled rotten as a kid, but by my Father not me, I didn't spoil him."

***

Two hours later into the night, the kitchen telephone began to ring again, and Alex answered it saying, "Hello, yes just a minute. Shawna it's for you again, and guess who?"

"Yes and what is it now? Still checking up on me?" Shawna asked, rather annoyed when she spoke into the phone. "You did what? I don't fucking believe this! What it was an accident that you had? Sure right! You fucking liar! And hold on I'll have to ask him. Alex, Antony says he's just cut his finger open on a machine at work, and the boss is now sending him home. But he's got to go to the hospital first to get his finger stitched up, 'cause the cuts pretty deep. And he wants to know if you'll go and pick him up from the hospital in Montreal? And then bring him over here?"

"No sorry but no can do! 'Cause I'm not going out driving the car tonight, because I've been drinking too much. So tell him that I'll pick him up from his apartment tomorrow as we arranged, after I've been into work for the morning. And tell him to go home and get some sleep, after he's been to the hospital," Alex replied.

Shawna repeated back to Antony, everything that Alex, had just said to her. Adding that she was sure, that a couple of stitches in his finger, wouldn't fucking kill him. After all he'd have a nice boo-boo to show everyone for about a week, when he needed sympathy from people. But he wouldn't be getting any from her at all, as she felt, that he'd cut his finger on purpose, so he could get off work and come over to stay at his Mothers. "I've had it with him," Shawna shouted, banging the phone down hard, into its holder on the wall. "Antony's just gone and fucked up royally. Why does he do these things Olivia? I mean it's so fucking obvious he's cut his finger on purpose, and he now wants me to believe it was an accident."

"Well I do know Antony loves to have attention," Hollie replied with a laugh. "But I wouldn't have thought he'd be stupid enough, to go and cut his finger on a machine. 'Cause I think that's kinda dangerous, because he could have lost his hand trying to make a small cut on himself."

"I wish he'd have cut his fucking hand off," Shawna said angrily, pouring everyone another drink. "So what do you think of your adorable Son now Olivia? Surely you don't agree with this fucking clever trick that he's pulled tonight? Do you?"

"God no of course I don't. And like Hollie says, it could have turned out to be very dangerous for him, cutting himself." Replied Olivia, who was sat in the Kitchen listening to opinions about her Son. "I never would have thought he'd be stupid enough to purposely cut himself on a machine at work. But I have a strong feeling that Antony takes after his Father in many ways, and there's not much that I can do about that, 'cause it's in his genes. He even looks the image of his Father, from what I can remember of him, even though it's so long ago since I've seen the guy. So don't start havin a go at me, about Antony, Shawna. I've done all I could for the kid, and I still do so. But if he's turned out to be a baddy, blame his Father, don't blame me, I only tried to do my best for him."

"Okay yeah you're probably right, but where the hell is Antony's fucking Father?" Shawna asked.

"Well how the hell would I know?" Olivia replied.

"I think he went to live somewhere in Australia," stated Alex. "That's where Olivia told me where he'd taken off to. But she didn't tell me why eh, did you Olivia?"

"Oh didn't I? Well I thought I'd told you that he fancied a job working over there, shearing sheep for a living," Olivia replied, with a laugh and a shrug of her shoulders.

"Oh he likes sheep then does he?" Alex said winking at Olivia. "So do you think he lives on a sheep farm somewhere out in the wilderness? 'Cause that's where these sheep farms are in the middle of nowhere, with no civilization close to them at all."

"Well, let's find this fucking assole then wherever he is, or whatever fucking sheep farm he's shearing fucking sheep on. And remind him and tell him, about his baby Son Antony, whom he left behind him years ago now. Come on Olivia, let's give him a call? Lets find out whereabouts he is living in Australia?" Shawna said.

"No! No! No! For Gods-sake No! I don't want to find him, and why should I after all these years? Anyway how the hell do I know where he's living in Australia? Olivia replied, in a very definite tone of voice. Now beginning to have a strange, nervous, feeling in the pit of her stomach. "It must be twenty years since I last saw, or spoke to him, and he may even be dead now. But whatever, I'm sure he won't remember me, or his Son Antony, after all this time. So just forget about this crazy idea of yours Shawna."

"No I won't, I can't, " Shawna answered, now really getting into wanting to know Antony's Father, and where he was living.

"Well I don't know if you know this? But Australia is a fucking big continent. So I'd be surprised if you could find anyone over there, unless you'd got an address for them," Alex said with a laugh. "And I don't think that you'll ever find the guy, it'll be just like searching for a needle in a haystack. What do you think Hollie?"

"Christ, I don't bloody know. I don't know much about Australia, only that it's a very big country like our own. And don't they have a lot of poisonous snakes over there?" Hollie replied. "And can you even remember this guy's name Olivia?"

"Yes of course I can, his name is Stan," replied Olivia.

Let's get the phone book out then, and let's try and find him," Shawna said eagerly.

"Do you all really think that we should?" Olivia asked. Now feeling that for some unknown reason she should try to find Stan, the Father of Antony.

"Well here's the phonebook," Shawna said, laying the telephone directory on the kitchen table in front of Olivia.

"But that's a Montreal phone book, not Australian, so how will that help us?" Hollie said laughing.

"Okay then, all shush up please now everyone if you want me to try and find him? I'll need some quiet time, while I concentrate for a while, if I'm going to be able to try and do this," Olivia said, putting a finger up to her lips.

She opened up the Bell telephone directory, finding the page with areas listed for the country of Australia. Picking up a pen, while trying to focus and concentrate very hard on Stan, trying to tune into him, and what he used to look like when she knew him, so many years ago. Where he may or could be, living in the enormously vast country of Australia. With a red, marking pen she began to search through the three columns of areas listed for places in Australia, putting a pen line through them as she read out the names of, "Adelaide, no he's not there, Brisbane, no, not there, Canberra, no, not there, Newcastle, no, I don't feel he's there either." On the third column she circled Sydney, and closed her eyes, as she felt a very, strong sensation, in the inside of her whole being, that was now feeling very, positive and telling her something that felt like a yes! "Yes this is where Stan is probably living. I think I've found it," she said confidently to the others, who were sat around the Kitchen, laughing, talking and drinking. Forgetting now all about what they had asked Olivia to do.

"Found what? And what are you doing looking in that phone book?" Alex asked, while still laughing at the joke Shawna had just told him.

"Will you all stop laughing and just listen to me? I think that I've found the place in Australia where Antony's father, Stan is living," Olivia slowly replied. "'Cause I can feel it inside of me, that he's here living in Sydney. So I'm going to now call the operator and ask for his phone number over there."

She gave Stan's surname to the operator over in Sydney Australia, and was told that, there was only one listing for the name of 'Brummly' and the number was, Sydney 136-354-6021. Her hand was shaking as she wrote the number down on a note pad, before hanging up the phone.

"Did you get his number then?" Shawna asked.

"Yes I did, I've got it, but I want Alex to call him and see if it is him, if I've got the right Stan Brummly, because I just can't do it."

"Yeah okay I don't mind, I can call him for you if you like," Alex said laughing, while thinking that it was all such a big joke, that his wife could have possibly found this Father of her Son, so easily over there in Australia. "But don't be surprised if it's not the right guy you've tracked down! So give me the guys name and I'll try this number for you. But if it is him, what shall I say to him?"

"I don't know, I just don't know," Olivia replied. Now not really believing herself that it could be him, because he would have been so very, easy to find. "But just go ahead and find out if it is him first? And if it is, then I guess pass the phone to me, so I can talk with him, okay?"

"Okay!" The phone in Australia rang for a short while, before Alex said, "Hi is that Stan? Oh it is? Well you don't know me, my name is Alex, and I'm calling from Montreal, in Canada. Do you by any chance know or remember a girl called Olivia Howard, from Bradwell in England? You do, well that's good 'cause so do I. And she's here with me, stood at the side of me, and would you like to speak to her?" Alex then passed the telephone to Olivia, smiling at her and saying, "Yes it is him, it's Stan. God knows how! But you've found the right one Olivia. Yes after all these years you've managed to find Stan, and he wants to talk to you. So while your talking to him, I'll make you another drink, a strong one, because I think you'll need one after all of this."

"Thanks Alex, and I love you very much," Olivia said gratefully, with tears starting in her eyes now, as her shaking, hand took hold of the telephone, that Alex passed to her.

"Hi, Stan, this is Olivia, had you just about forgotten me, after all these years?"

"Hello Olivia," replied Stan, in a shaky, surprised voice "No I haven't forgotten you at all, and I never could do, I loved you very much once, remember?"

"Well, before I carry on talking to this guy called Stan. Who I'm sorry to say doesn't sound at all like the Stan that I remember, because you've got a dreadful Australian accent. Just let me check with you first, to see if you are the right Stan? And not just some jerk who's having fun talking to me on the phone, because you really could be anyone. So tell me something that you know about me okay? Something that can get me to believe that you were the Stan that I once did know?"

"I remember that you a have a Sister called Suzanne. And she used to go out with my best friend Ian. But most importantly, we had a baby Son named Antony. How is our Son Olivia? He must be a grown lad, in his twenties by now."

"Oh my-God it is you! God I can't believe it!" Olivia replied, nearly dropping the telephone as her hand began to shake violently, and tears started to run down her cheeks. "So it really is you Stan, the guy that I used to love, when I was a very young girl eh! Oh it's been such a long time now. So tell me how are you doin? Tell me things about yourself? Are you married? Have you got any kids?" There were so many questions to ask him, after all these years, it seemed difficult for her to know where to start, except of course with the polite, easy, simple, non-intrusive ones.

Stan went on to tell Olivia, that he was married and had two boys. That he was homesick for Bradwell, for a very, long time when he arrived in Australia. And that it took him many many, years to get over her, because of the love he felt for her, for such a long time. Always thinking that he could never go on, or ever live without her, ever being once again in his life. But he eventually made it by himself, he had no choice, he had to, or he would have died! They talked on the phone together for about forty-five-minutes, with them somehow trying to turn back the clock, with the hands of time, trying to get to know each other once again, before they felt that they must say their good-byes to each other for now. With Stan promising her very, sincerely that he would be phoning her, on Sunday morning from his home. Olivia was unable to say goodbye to this long, lost, love of hers from years ago, and hang her phone up, before Shawna, on hearing Olivia's goodbye to Stan, eagerly grabbed the phone off her, very insistently, demanding that she have her talk with Antony's Father, wanting to ask him some questions of her own!

Olivia left everyone talking in the Kitchen, while she slipped, quietly away, going into the bathroom, closing the door behind her, as she now began to cry very hard, but for what, she had no idea, as her whole body was now violently, shaking.

"Olivia, what's wrong?" Hollie asked, knocking on the Bathroom door before entering and seeing Olivia, stood there crying her eyes out. "Oh my God, I think you've gone into shock, that's why you're shaking so hard, so much, let me go and get you a sweater from your bedroom. And how long has it been since you've spoken to Antony's Father? Is it about twenty years now? Yeah it's no wonder you're in such shock after all this time. But you must feel Olivia, after you found him so easily tonight, that it was just meant to be, that for some reason, you had to find Stan again. Don't you think so?"

"Maybe, but I can't think why? And now I'm beginning to think that I should have just let sleeping-dogs-lie. Now that thought does make more sense to me!"

******

Chapter 49

Olivia awoke from a heavy, deep, dream filled sleep, at eleven o'clock the next morning. She couldn't understand why she had been dreaming about a hospital, and screaming and crying out, for a small baby that somehow was hers. But she couldn't hold this baby, because it was dead, and she was trying to find Stan. *That was a very strange dream for me to have, when the baby I had to Stan, is now twenty-one years old and very much alive. I must have had too much to drink last night*, she thought, switching on the radio in her bedroom, before going into the kitchen to make herself a coffee.

She opened the door to let her dogs go outside into the back, garden, before getting the Saturday morning newspaper from the mailbox that was hanging on the wall outside the front door. She then went back into her bedroom to read the newspaper and drink her coffee, trying to wake herself up enough to give Alex, a call at work, to see what time he would be home this afternoon. She really missed Alex when he had to go into work on the weekends, instead of being at home with her.

She lay on her stomach on the top of the bed, drinking her coffee, and flipping through the pages of the newspaper, lighting herself a cigarette as the song *'Papa Don't Preach'*, began to play on the radio. She began singing along with the words of the song before suddenly stopping, and sitting up on the bed with a horrified, look of remembrance and realisation on her face. "So that's why my dream was about a baby, it was my baby," she said out loud to herself. Beginning to cry now, as at last she finally remembered after all the years of denial, a secret that had been buried so deep, inside of her for so long. Yes the secret! That secret! The one that she should by now have forgotten forever! "You bastard, you fucking bastard!" She screamed out. "I was so stupidly fucking nice to you, when I spoke to you last night. When you fucking pissed off to Australia all those years ago, leaving me bare foot and pregnant once again! And you must have known that I was pregnant when you left me. Well there's only one way to find out."

She got Stan's phone number that she had put into her bedside table drawer, and put a call through to Australia.

The phone rang for a long time before it was answered in a very sleepy voice, by a woman with an Australian accent saying, "Hello."

"Hi this is Olivia calling from Canada, and I want to speak to Stan please," Olivia said.

"Oh hello Olivia, this is Sandy, Stan's wife, and I'm afraid Stan's asleep. It's the early hours of the morning here Olivia, so we're all still asleep."

"Oh really! Sleeping is he? How dare he? Well Sandy I don't really care what the fuck Stan is doing right now, I want to talk to him, okay! And let me just make something very clear to you lady. I'm not in any kinda mood to start taking any bullshit off anybody," Olivia replied, in a very angry definite tone of voice

"Okay love if you really insist that you must talk to him now? And I suppose this does sound like something really important. But just hold on a minute will you? I'll have to go and wake him up," Sandy replied, with a deep sigh."

After a while Olivia heard Stan's voice on the other end of the line saying, "Hello Olivia, I didn't expect to hear from you again so soon, had you forgotten I'm phoning you on Sunday?"

"Oh Stan darling did I wake you up? Oh I'm so sorry," Olivia replied, in a very, sweet but nasty tone of voice. Now feeling this fresh, raw, anger that was burning deep down inside her, all for him. "No I take that back, I'm not fucking sorry for waking you up, or for anything that I may do, or say to you. You fucking tow-rag, slime bag. When you fucked off to Australia all those years ago, did you know that I was pregnant again? Yes you left me with your second baby growing inside of me. And do you know what happened to the poor little thing? My parents made me have a back street abortion done, by some Aunty of ours when I was five months pregnant. And in some hospital in Manchester England, I gave birth to our second baby-Son who was dead. Yes Stan our poor little baby-Son, whom I never got the chance to hold and love, was born to me dead. And because of you leaving me, that is a secret that I've had to keep hidden, buried deep inside of me for all of these years. Yes to the point that the secret had to die and go wherever our poor little baby went. And another secret that I've had along with our dead Baby-Boy, is one that I will now share with you, and only you. So do think of yourself as being very privileged Stan, with me sharing my secret with no one else but you. I secretly gave our Son a name, yes I named him, and his name was Oliver! So do you like the name I chose for our Son? Would you have agreed with his name being Oliver? Oh I do hope so?"

She then began to cry very, hard now remembering as though it had happened to her, only yesterday, as she began reliving everything in gory, detail very, vividly, the ordeal of twenty years ago, when she lost her dead baby-Son, Oliver. And what had happened to her afterwards, because he had been born dead!

There was a long, silence on the other end of the telephone line, between Canada and Australia, before Stan slightly coughed, then said in a very, sad unhappy, tone of voice, "I'm so sorry Olivia, I really am so very very sorry. But I'd no idea that you were pregnant again, with my baby. And if I'd have known, I would never have left you ever. I would definitely have married you right away, because I loved you so very much. Don't you remember how much I loved you? And I'm so sorry that I hurt you and what you went through, having to lose our baby Son Oliver, and yes I do like the name Oliver, that you chose for him. And once again Olivia please do believe me, I'm so very sorry and I had no idea that you were having our second baby. But you know all of this happened such a long time ago now, so please, come on don't cry about it so much after all this time?"

"Don't you be so fucking condescendingly patronizing, or fucking sorry for me at all Stan, because you weren't back then, all those years ago. You were so fucking busy running away to save yourself, finding a new life, while I was left holding the baby, the Son of ours who did live. So I don't really need any of your fucking sympathy for me now, I got by without it then, so I sure will get by without it now.

Even though after all these years, I've sadly remembered our poor Oliver," Olivia shouted at him, down the phone line, still crying hard from the memories of her baby-boy, that she could now see in her mind's eye, laying there all pink and perfect, lifeless and dead, with his small, eyes tightly, closed, in the bottom of that hospital bedpan. "I was never ever allowed to feel anything, or shed a tear to cry for my baby, all those fucking years ago, but now no one has the power to stop me. And you never saw him Stan, so you've got nothing to remember have you? But I do, and now I've remembered him I will never forget him. He was a very small perfectly formed little boy, who never had a chance in this lifetime with me his Mother, and wherever he is now? I just hope that he's very happy. And where the fuck were you when I really, really needed you so badly Stan? You'd taken off to bloody Australia, to start a new life for yourself, and to sow a few more wild oats no doubt. And tell me? How many girls have you got pregnant over there? 'Cause the Stan that I remember couldn't go without sex for very long. You bastard, you nearly destroyed me and my life, but what the hell did you care? You were just out for yourself and why would you have rushed into marrying me suddenly? Because I was having our second baby? I already had our first, and we were supposed to be married soon after he was born, but instead what did you do? You started drinking heavily, you got drunk every fucking night, you gave up your job, and you started hitting me. And you say you loved me Stan? Bullshit, cut the crap, you didn't know how to love me, only fuck me, and you didn't know how to do that very well. And the last time that I saw you, you nearly killed me, you were strangling me until I passed out, and when I came to you were gone, just vanished into thin air. And this is the first time that I've had any contact with you, after all those years. But do tell me Stan? Because I'd just love to know, how long did it really take you to get over me? The Olivia that you loved so much? Before you met and married Sandy? Did you get her pregnant too? Is that why you married her? Yes one of my biggest mistakes in life Stan, was loving you, because I certainly feel that I paid a fucking high price for it. And starting with you Stan, my battle with men went on for many many years. But thank God for my husband Alex, who asked me to come to live in North America with him, and yes I do know that

Alex loves me very much. Anyway I'm so upset and worn out after everything that I've had to say and tell you, but I think I've got some of the pain hurt and anger out of me, so I'm going to say goodbye to you Stan. And yes you can still call me tomorrow if you want to, but I won't care if you don't! So goodbye."

Olivia hung up her telephone, feeling very drained after all that emotional, pain, that she had finally let go out of herself, the pain that had been hidden, very, deep inside her for many, years now. She laid her head down on her pillow, crying and thinking of the baby that died, her dead baby laying in the bottom of the hospital bedpan; the Son she was never allowed to love or feel anything for, all because Stan had left her.

***

An hour later she answered the ringing telephone that was on the night table at the side of her bed, hoping that it would be Alex, to say he was on his way home. "Hi Olivia it's Ivan, what's happening? Is the pool party still on tonight? And it sounds as if you've got a cold."

"Oh yes," she replied, wiping her tears and blowing her nose on a tissue. "I'd forgot about the party tonight, I must go to the liquor store and get some more Rye in. I don't think we will be around the swimming pool tonight though, 'cause it's very hot today and the forecast is for a bad thunderstorm tonight."

"Okay we'll just have a house party instead then. But Olivia what's wrong? You sound kinda strange, and you're talking in a monotone voice. What's happened are you sick? Have you got allergies a cold or flu?"

"No not any of those things at all, just some very bad memories that I'm trying to deal with. And don't want to talk or discuss with anyone."

"Hey come on Olivia, this is Ivan your best friend, that your talking to. And I'm realizing now that you're very upset, and I want you to tell me about it. Who's upset you? Alex? And where is he? 'Cause I want to talk to the guy if he's upset my big Sister."

"No! No! It's not poor Alex, he doesn't know anything about me being upset. And he's had to go into work this morning, and he's not back yet. It's something that happened in my life many years ago now, that I didn't really deal with then, I just tried to survive and get through it all, past it. But after contacting someone, I've let all the bad memories come flooding back into my life, which seem to be haunting me now, they are so very painful, but I'll be okay soon. And it's my own fault, I shouldn't have contacted Antony's Father in Australia after all these years. And I'm sure you've heard the expression, 'Let-Sleeping-Dogs-Lie'. Well that's exactly what I should have done. Anyway I must go and take my shower now, 'cause I want to go to the liquor-store. And I'll see you and Sherry around seven or eight o'clock tonight, so bye for now Ivan."

"Okay then for now, but I expect you to tell me what's upset you, when I see you later on. Bye for now."

Shawna and Holly had both taken their showers, and were putting the leashes on the dogs to take them out for a walk, when Olivia came out of her bedroom. "I won't be long," she said, going down the hallway to the bathroom. "When you girls get back from walking the dogs, we'll go to the liquor store. And then get burgers and fries for lunch from the restaurant across the street. I think Alex is going to cook us one of his spaghetti dishes for supper tonight."

***

When they were walking up the road to the liquor store, Shawna kept looking at Olivia, and asked her if she was going to tell them why she was crying.

"I can't, I just can't, I don't want to talk about it. Anyway I wouldn't know where to begin to tell you," Olivia replied.

"Is it something about that Stan? Some bad memories eh?" Hollie asked.

Olivia just bit into her bottom, lip hard and nodded her head.

After she had bought a large bottle of 'Rye' at the liquor store, they went across the road to sit at a table, outside the restaurant there. While Hollie went inside to get food for just her and Shawna, when Olivia had told them she couldn't eat anything.

While they were eating their lunch, Shawna opened a large, bottle of wine-cooler, passing it to Olivia to have a drink, saying, "We can see you're very upset Olivia, 'cause you can't stop crying, don't you think it would help if you told us about it?"

"You seemed to be okay when you went to bed last night, after you got over the shock of talking to Stan again. What's happened since then?" Hollie said.

"Yeah you guys were very good and supportive to me last night, and I guess I ought to tell you what's wrong. But now we're in this day and age, what year are we in now 1987? I don't think that you'll be able to understand why I am so upset, about something that happened to me many years ago, when life was so very different back then for everyone, in the year of 1967," Olivia replied through her tears, as she began to tell Holly and Shawna, about the abortion that she had, when Stan left her years ago. And how she had made herself forget about it for all these years, until after she'd spoken to Stan again last night. And the dream that she'd had about everything, and the song, 'Papa Don't Preach'. How all of this had somehow managed to jog her memory. And she now felt that she could not stop reliving it all again, what had happened all those years ago, because it had been so wrong of her to have forgotten about her dead baby for so long.

"My God Olivia, you must have been through hell," Shawna said, putting her arms around Olivia to comfort her, when she had finished telling them both her story.

"You see way back in that time, I had no choice, no choice at all," Olivia cried.

"It seems that it must have been a fucking nightmare for you, life back then. And I thought I had fucking problems," replied Hollie.

"Oh I'll be okay soon," Olivia said, wiping her tears away with the back of her hand, and trying to smile. "I got through it then, and I'm sure that I'll get through the memories of it this time. I've got to get back to the house now 'cause the twins, Alex and Antony will be home, and I don't want them to know about any of this okay!"

"Well I think your wrong, you should tell Alex about everything Olivia," Shawna advised her, when they were walking back home. "Alex should know about this, and I'm sure he'll understand and give you some comfort and the support that you need to get over it. Because he loves you very much, remember?"

***

Later on in the evening, after Ivan and Sherrie had arrived, there was a bad thunderstorm outside and it was raining very, heavily, while everyone was sitting in the dining room, drinking, laughing, joking, and listening to tapes, while watching the storm with the thunder and lightning, through the large, glass, patio doors. "You were certainly right about the weather forecast tonight Olivia," Ivan said. "So tell me what else is new? You're not your usual, happy, bubbly self tonight, and I've noticed that every time the record, 'Papa Don't Preach', plays on one of those tapes, your eyes fill with tears and you go to the washroom. So are you going to tell me what it's all about Olivia? I've also noticed you've only had one drink tonight, here let me get you another one."

"No thanks I don't feel like drinking much tonight. And I don't feel too happy, so I guess that's why I'm not my usually bubbly self, eh!" Olivia sullenly replied.

"Okay so you're not feeling too happy, and are you going to tell me what's making you so sad? What's upsetting you then eh? 'Cause I'm sick of asking you what's wrong and getting no answer," Ivan said, pouring himself another 'Rye' and Coke. "Hey Alex, do you know what's wrong with Olivia tonight? Has she told you about anything?"

"No I've no idea what's upset her," Alex replied. "I've been asking her, but she just won't tell me what's wrong."

"Look you guys, just can it for now will you? And I might tell you later, if you really want to know. And I'm sorry if I'm spoiling the party for you, I didn't realize it was so important to you all, that I must always be so fucking happy and bubbly," Olivia said, in an irritated tone of voice

"Hey Ivan, have you seen Antony's boo-boo on his finger?" Shawna said laughing, and trying to change the subject. "He tried to cut his hand off on a machine at work last night, so he could get off work and come over here to his Mommy's. But he only managed to cut his finger, and he's got three stitches in it. Go on show Ivan your stitches in your poor little finger Antony?"

"You can be such a nasty bitch at times Shawna," Antony replied angrily, glaring at her, while showing Ivan his cut finger, with the three stitches in it. "I've told you a hundred times, that I did not do this on purpose, it was a fucking accident, believe me."

"Sure, of course we all believe you," Hollie laughingly agreed, as they were all looking at Antony's stitched up finger.

***

In the early hours of the morning at about three o'clock, the twins were asleep in their beds, and Antony had told everyone, that he was sorry to be such a party pooper, but he was going to have to go to bed, so please could they turn the music down.

Hollie said she would sleep on the large, couch downstairs, so Ivan and Sherrie would be able to stay for the night, in the other guest room. "Would you be good enough to make a pot of coffee Alex?" Ivan asked, when they went into the kitchen, to wash their glasses out in the sink. "Because I don't think we should turn in yet, until we've talked to Olivia, I think she's in the washroom crying again. And I seem to think that she's crying about something very serious, over something that happened in her life, a long time ago, and she's having a job dealing with it now."

"Come here Olivia and tell me what's wrong," Alex said, going to her and putting his arms around her, when she came out of the bathroom. "You know that I love you very much don't you? And you can tell me anything? Now what's been upsetting you so much today? Is it Stan?"

"Oh Alex, I love you very much to," Olivia replied, wrapping her arms around him and resting her head on his chest, while still crying. "Just hold me please. But I'm sorry I really can't tell you what I'm so upset about, you could never understand any of it. So just be there for me please Alex?"

"Well I'll tell him what's upsetting you, if you won't Olivia," Shawna said angrily, taking the coffee mugs out of the cupboard, and banging them down on the kitchen counter. "Alex won't hate you or pass judgement on you, and neither will Ivan. And I've told you, you did nothing wrong at all Olivia. You really didn't have any choice over the life of that baby of yours, the choice was made for you by the adults. And you were nothing more than just a young kid, who was trying to survive, after that fucking assole Stan left you."

Olivia began to cry, as her mind once again reached back to twenty years ago in her life. As she began to tell them, how Stan had tried to strangle her, during an argument that they were having, before he then left her, going to live in Australia, leaving her pregnant again. And the abortion she went through, when her parents found out that she was having another baby. Her baby boy that was born dead, in the Manchester hospital. The nasty, Indian doctor who for whatever reason hated her so much, that she scraped her womb out, with her long, red painted, finger nails, without first giving her an anaesthetic.

When Olivia had finished telling everyone her long detailed story of the nightmare she had been reliving over and over in her mind that day, she fell into Alex's arms holding on to him so tightly, as big, sobs, racked through her whole, body, while she cried.

Alex held her very, close to him, stroking her head softly, feeling tears starting in his own eyes, now he was aware of all the pain, hurt and suffering that his wife had buried deeply inside her, that she had been carrying around with her for so long.

***

Not wanting to disturb Alex from his sleep, she freed herself from his arms, that were so lovingly wrapped around her, holding her tightly to him through the night, hoping that it would help to make her feel secure again. She got out of bed putting on her lemon, towelling dressing gown, before going through the house into the kitchen, to answer the ringing telephone there, that had awoken her from her deep, sleep at eight o'clock on Sunday morning, knowing the caller would be Stan in Australia.

"Hi Stan so you called me!" She said, answering the phone.

"Hello Olivia, and don't sound so surprised to hear my voice, I told you I'd phone you today, didn't I? Or did you think I'd forget?"

"So why didn't you ever get in touch with me all those years ago, when you left me? If only to just see if Antony and I were doin okay, eh?"

"But I did Olivia. I wrote to my friend Ian for over six months, asking him about you and Antony and telling him where I was, as I moved around Australia doing odd jobs. I also asked Ian to tell you, that I was missing you like crazy, and still loved you very much. And would you come and join me, over here in Australia? But I never heard a fucking word back from Ian, not a word, he never answered one of my letters!"

"Oh did you?" Olivia asked, not knowing whether to believe Stan or not. "Well Ian never once told me that he'd received a letter from you, or that you were wanting me to come to you over there. So I guess that is something I'll never really know the truth about."

"I want you to know that I loved you very much Olivia, and did so for many years after we parted. And that it took me a long long time to get over you, but I never ever forgot you and always wondered where you were and what you were doing. So if you ever feel like having a break sometime from Canada, and want to see Australia, I'd very much like to see you again. And I would like you to meet my wife Sandy, and my two sons John and David."

"Maybe," Olivia replied with a big yawn. "Maybe if I could ever find some compassion inside of myself, to ever forgive you for what you did to me. But I find it hard to forgive, and I certainly never ever forget things, or what people do to me. Anyway I'm still very tired, so I'm now going to go back to bed, and curl up to my loving husband Alex. So goodbye Stan."

"Goodbye Olivia, and always remember I'm very sorry about everything, and I did really love you for a very long time."

******

Chapter 50

Over the next few weeks Olivia and Stan, mailed letters and tape recordings to each other, saying how their lives had been over the last twenty years. She listened to Stan's tapes most days, over and over again, telling her how very, difficult it had been for him, to begin his new life in Australia without her, and how he couldn't get over losing her, for such a long time. And how homesick he was for Bradwell and her, for many many years. Until he finally met Sandy, in Sydney at a place where he was working, and they started to go out with each other, and eventually got married. Sounding as though there was nothing wrong at all, with expecting Sandy, to put up with, his drinking every night, his gambling on horses, his constant changing of jobs, often being out of work for months on end, and his quick nasty temper, which had never left him. But he was never physically violent to her, and hit her, like he had done to Olivia. *Yeah well she should be so fucking lucky, not to get hit by him*, Olivia thought. And she really didn't care about the fact, that they lost their first baby boy, who died two days after he was born. And later on had John who was now fifteen and David who was twelve, with their birthdays being on the same day. He also reluctantly felt that he should tell her, that due to what he had been through, with leaving his home in Bradwell. He began to suffer badly with his nerves, having to take a medication for them!

They also sent photographs of themselves and their families to each other, and when Olivia looked at the photographs of Stan, it was like seeing an older version of her Son Antony, who was the image of his Father. With his Sons John and David looking nothing like Stan at all, but more like their Mother Sandy, whose photo's of her, showed a small, petite girl with a very, plain face, and mousy blonde hair, hung limply, and straight on her shoulders. Olivia of course had sent Stan, some lovely, photos of herself taken over the years, up to how she now looked at the age of thirty-six, with her hair looking very, shiny, soft and fluffy, as it fell in large, dark, curls around her shoulders.

Stan enjoyed often looking at the photographs Olivia, had sent to him. Telling her that he thought, she had a lovely family, and she looked very, much like he thought she would, at the age she was now, still beautiful looking, with those large, cat looking, green eyes of hers, that he remembered so well.

***

"I think that maybe I should go to Australia to see Stan again," Olivia told Alex, Ivan, Antony and Shawna, one evening.

"Don't go Mum please?" Antony replied. "You don't owe my fucking aboriginal Father, a fucking thing, not even a visit."

"No Olivia please don't go to see Stan?" Added Ivan. "'Cause from what you've told us about him, I don't get very good vibes about you seeing him again. I just feel it could be very dangerous for you Olivia, what do you think Alex?"

"Well, I certainly don't want her to go there either," Alex replied. "But you all know Olivia, she will always do what she wants to do, and no one will stop her. Eh Olivia?"

"Let's just call it some unfinished business, maybe that's why I have to go there to see him," Olivia said. "Because I still don't know if he knew that I was pregnant again, when he left me. He says he didn't, but I don't know whether to believe him or not. I just need and want to see the look on Stan's face, when I ask him again. Because then I'll know if he knew or not."

"I think it's something that Olivia feels she's got to get out of her system, eh?" Shawna stated. "And as a female I can understand her, she just wants to know the truth. I'll go to Australia with you, if and when you decide to go, so I know that you'll be okay then. 'Cause you won't be by yourself."

"Well thanks Shawna, but hey I'll be okay you guys, and I'm sure I won't need any bodyguards, I'm going to see Antony's Father, not some mass murderer. And I think you're all over reacting 'cause there is no reason at all now, why he would ever want to hurt me again.

And I think he's still feeling guilty about what he did, and treating me so badly all those years ago. Anyway wouldn't it be good if Stan and I could become good friends in time? Because I have a feeling that's what he'd like to do, be friends with me," Olivia replied with a smile.

"Look it Olivia," Alex said, putting his arm around her. "Too much water has passed under the bridge now, for you to even think of getting any revenge on Stan, even if he did know that he'd left you pregnant. And if he did know, what difference will it make now after all these years? So just let it be, try and let it all go now, please Olivia?"

"The poor guy's not had an easy life down under," Olivia replied, now beginning to feel some compassion for Stan. "And in one of the letters that he wrote to me, and on a tape, he tells me that he's had a bit of a problem, with his nerves, and had a complete breakdown just a few years ago."

"Yeah probably because he's a fucking losing psycho schitzo," Ivan replied, feeling uneasy about Olivia wanting to go to see Stan. "And look Olivia, I've got a good friend called Scooter, who went to live in Sydney Australia, just a few years ago when he got a job there. So I'll go over there with you if you like, then we can all go to visit Stan. And I'm sure we could both stay at Scooter's home, so we won't have to be paying out to stay in expensive hotels. And I'd like to see if Scooter's still got his good, gun collection, that I hope he managed to take over there with him. So just let me know when you're thinking of going and I'll go along with you. 'Cause yes I'd also like to see what life is like down under, to see if they've all got it as good as us North-Americans."

"Yeah, that's a good idea. So why don't we all go down under for our next vacation? It'll make a change from 'Disney World' and 'Niagara Falls' next year," Alex agreed, with a laugh.

***

As the summer of 1987 was now slowly, turning into the fall, Olivia became very restless and withdrawn in herself. Her mind would often wonder back to when she was seeing Stan, in the year of 1967 and how she had once loved him so much, thinking that this puppy love of hers, at one time could have turned into a promise of marriage to him, forever. She also very, fondly remembered, the fun she'd had with her Sister, Suzanne and close, school friends, Angel, Jill, Brenda, Cheryl, Jane and Sandra. And how they had all supported her, with their loving help and moral, support, to get over Stan, when he had run away and left her. All feeling that it was the best, thing that he could have done for their friend Olivia, knowing how he had started to knock her around, after he had been drinking, which was most nights of the week.

She thought of David, the guy who was very, protective towards her, and so much wanted to marry her, to help to save her reputation around the village of Bradwell. She remembered the first time she ever went to a discotheque, it was with him to 'The Marquis Of Granby' near Bamford. And the fight that had taken place outside in the car-park, between David and some guy, who had rudely insulted her. Remembering with a smile how David had knocked the poor, guy over a lovely, white sports car, cutting him deeply, above his eye, and the blood from it going all over the white car.

The fun that she'd had working at the 'Flamingo Night Club', when her Uncle Brian was the 'Chef' there. The good friends she had made with the other people who worked there, who never sat in judgment on her, with being an unmarried Mother to her Son, Antony. And willingly learning about another way of life in a very, much kinder, grown up adult world. Before returning home after a few months, to Bradwell.

Meeting these Hippies, called Kenny Dee, Bozo, Bucket, Lassie, Snifter, Skippy, Egg, and Willie. Who while she was away had turned up from Dronfield, in the small village of Bradwell, beginning to date her Sister and friends. And how she had so much eagerly, enjoyed becoming one of them, a Hippy herself. And the loving, gentle, romance that she had with the very, tall good looking, blonde haired guy, called Bozo. The meetings and fun happenings that they all had shared together, in their wonderful 'Rock-Canyon', that was up the Dale by the rocks in Bradwell, that became their secret Hippy meeting place, 'Their-Private-Playground'. The big, bright, red, Standard-Car that they had painted colourful flowers all over, making it their symbol the 'Flower-Power-Car'. The lovely, big colourful, flower that Bucket had painted, high up on one of the rocks on the 'Rock-

Canyon' walls, so that it would be in memory of them all, in many, years to come, the loving Hippies that they were. With the different thoughts and ideas they had all shared about life. Never thinking or ever, believing that they would one day, all grow up becoming much older, and allowing the system to eventually get them all, to fall in line with how things are and really went in the real, world. Because back in those days nothing ever seemed to matter or bother any of them then, as their Hippy years were filled with such good, innocent, laughter, fun and love for each other, with them all wanting to believe that this wonderful, way of life, could and would go on and on forever.

How she met Clive Lemons at her parents' pub 'The White Hart', with him becoming the first man that she married, and the very, bad car smash, that she was involved in with him. Nearly losing her young, precious life! How after her months of recovery, Clive always seeming to be away on business for long periods of time, now leaving her all alone by herself.

With Kenny Dee, becoming a mobile DJ by then, and feeling sorry for her, being left at home alone. So she accepted his offer of becoming a Go-Go dancer for him, when he was out on the road with his mobile disco called 'Highway 68.' Oh how much she loved being his go-go dancer for a few years, before deciding that it was time for her to have a baby, and wanting so much to have one, sweet little, baby girl.

Remembering meeting Alex at the 'Spinning Wheel Discotheque' one night, and going back to his hotel room with him, and having a wonderful, night of passionate, lovemaking. Realizing a month later that she was at last, finally, pregnant!

Her best friend, Angel, being killed in a car smash while she was pregnant with twins, and the shock of hearing this news about her very, good friend, it sending her into labour. James and Cassandra, getting her to the hospital, where she gave birth to twin-girls herself, just four hours later, after Angel and her twins had died.

Spending a lot of time with Diana, whose daughter Lulu was the twin's best friend. Alex coming back into her life, and the divorce from Clive Lemons.

Moving house and marrying Alex, and being so happy and in love with her new husband, until Alex hurt her one night, by making out with some girl, that he had met in a disco. And how after that night, it had taken her many many years to forgive and trust him again!

During her estrangement from Alex, meeting and becoming good, friends with Cindy, whom she'd met at the bottom of her road at the bus stop. And that same day meeting Winston, who worked at the 'Crazy Daisy', being introduced to him by her new friend Cindy. And the loving intense affair that they had together for many years.

The wonderful platonic, friendship she had, knowing that a friendship like the one they had, could never be replaced, was her milkman Danny. And the 'Aikido' he'd taught her when she was afraid of meeting the 'Yorkshire Ripper'.

And all of the games that she enjoyed playing, with different, men, to get even with Stan, Alex and Winston, whom she felt had seriously, hurt her, very much. Until Alex came to ask her one day, to come and live with him in Canada, and knowing that she was making the right choice to go with him. Saying good-bye to all of her family and friends. And before leaving England, spending her last night with her family, at Danny and Gayle's home, before flying out to her new life in Canada.

Yes I think everything was all planned out for me in my life, and it was meant to be, whatever happened to me back then, through all of those years. And I think that I've now come a full circle of twenty years in my life, from the year 1967 to 1987 all the way back to Stan! But why? Why this? And why now? Olivia thought. After looking back at all the things that have happened in her life, all the good and the bad times, that she'd experienced over the last twenty years, since Stan had left her.

***

Her dreams at night now always seemed to be about Stan and her, going back to the time of when she was a young, teenage girl, around the age of 16 years old. She was running away from him, and he would be reaching out his arms to her, and calling her back to his side, whilst crying out in dreadful pain. "Olivia help me? Please I need you, I love you, don't ever leave me, or I will die!"

She would awake from these horrid, nightly dreams, in a wet, cold, sweat, sitting up in her bed feeling very, confused in her mind, whilst looking at Alex who was asleep at the side of her.

She would lay back down wrapping her arms tightly, around him, feeling secure as she tried to go back to a dream free sleep, while thinking most nights, *Please wake up and help me with all of this Alex?*

But Alex couldn't help Olivia at all, because he didn't know anything about these bad, dreams that she was having, because she never told him about them.

And during the daytime, when she eventually allowed herself to think about her weird night-time dreams, hoping to see if she could analyze or make any sense of them, by trying to understand them and work them out. But no matter how hard she tried, she couldn't make any sense of them, and Stan's crying out for her. Because in reality it was Stan, who had left her, not she who had left him!

******

Chapter 51

A few weeks later after Alex had gone to work one morning, and the twins had just got the school bus outside their front door, to take them to their high school. Olivia was sat at the kitchen table, drinking her morning coffee and reading the newspaper, when the telephone began to ring.

"Hello is that Olivia?" Said an Australian voice, on the other end of the line, when Olivia answered her phone. "I was hoping that it would be. This is Sandy, Stan's wife phoning you. And I'm sorry to bother you Olivia, but do I need your help so badly. You see love, it's like this, since you contacted Stan the other month, and told him those things that had happened to you after he left you, well it's now put him in a very bad state love, and I think he's about to have another serious breakdown."

"Well I'm very sorry about that, I didn't expect him to have a breakdown over it," Olivia replied. "I just thought that he'd be pleased to hear from me again, that's all. But what do you think I can do to help him?"

"Well he can't stop thinking or talking about you Olivia, and he feels so bad about leaving England when you were pregnant again. He keeps saying he has to see you, to tell you how sorry he is. And I was wondering love, if there was any chance of you coming over here to see him, before he gets any worse, and has to go back into a mental institution again. 'Cause I'm afraid he won't come out for a long time, if he goes back in again. You see love, Stan's just started working for himself, less than twelve months ago. He's opened a stall in the outdoor market, selling hardware and cleaning products, it hasn't been easy for him to get a business going, and it only just seems to be making any money for us now. I'm sorry if I seem to be rambling on a bit love," Sandy continued, in a teary, worried, nervous tone of voice. "But I feel if he saw you again Olivia love, and you two could have a talk about things, Stan would start to be okay again."

"Yeah I understand what you're saying to me Sandy. And I'm sorry, I didn't know Stan had been in a mental hospital, I didn't mean to make him ill, even if I did give him a fucking blasting out, when I've talked to him. So yes if you really do think that it would help him? I'll come over there to see him for a few days. I'll go and pack a case and then get down to the airport, sometime today and get myself a flight over there. Okay I'll see you later Sandy."

"Oh thanks so much love, it's so good of you. And please don't tell Stan that I've phoned you, will you? 'Cause he'd be ever so annoyed at me if he knew. Bye Olivia, and I'll see you later."

Wow! What a poor desperate sounding lady, thought Olivia, hanging up her telephone. *I'd better get myself showered, pack a suitcase, and then off to the airport to get myself a flight.*

***

Just before she was ready to leave the house, she placed a call to Alex at his work, but she had to leave a message for him, with his secretary Jill, because he was in a long, business meeting. "Okay then Jill, will you please tell Alex from me, that I've had to go to visit someone over in Australia? And that I'll probably be staying at a 'Holiday Inn Hotel' in Sydney over there. And that I'll call him as soon as I get there. And please do make sure that Alex gets my message, as soon as he gets out of his meeting? Thanks Jill, Bye."

***

When she arrived at the airport she was just in time to take a flight to Vancouver that was leaving at 10:30 a.m. From Vancouver she got another flight that was going to Honolulu, and from Honolulu a flight across to Australia, with her plane touching down at Sydney airport at 6:10 a.m. Australian time, the next morning.

She was now feeling very tired and didn't get much sleep on the thirty-hour flight, beginning the day before in Montreal. She quickly got herself a taxi from the airport, to take her to the nearest 'Holiday Inn Hotel' in Sydney. Where she got herself a room, and ordered a drink before taking a nice, long, hot, shower, then collapsing into the bed and falling fast sleep.

***

"Oh no! I really hope not!" Alex said, with a deep, moan in his voice, when he came out of his meeting later that day, reading the message from Olivia, that his secretary, Jill, had left for him on his desk, before she left the office for the evening.

He then found Ivan before leaving work, telling him that Olivia had gone to Australia, and she was by herself.

"I just don't like the feeling of this, that Olivia's gone to Australia and she's gone there by herself. It's pretty obvious that she's gone to see that guy Stan, but why didn't she tell you that she was going?" Ivan said.

"I've been in a meeting that's lasted all day when she called, so she left me a message with Jill. But something must have happened for her to just up and go, to take off just like that, without talking to me first about it and her plans. Because I know that she had nothing planned to go over there just like this, so I'm like you Ivan, I don't like any of this one little bit, and I have a bad feeling about it all. So I'm going over there myself after her, I just hope that I'm not too late."

"Yeah you know I feel very much like you about all of this Alex, not very comfortable, so I'm coming with you. Come on let's get to the airport and get the next flight."

***

Olivia had a lovely, long, dreamless sleep in her hotel room, the best sleep she'd had in weeks. She awoke sometime around midnight and looking at her watch thought, *'God I must have been tired. I never meant to sleep as long as this. And it's too late to go and see Stan at this time of night, so I'll wait until morning'.* After a visit to the bathroom, she went straight back to bed falling quickly asleep again.

***

The next morning she took a shower, put on a pair of tight jeans and a T-shirt, and went to the hotel Dining-room for breakfast, now feeling very, refreshed from her sleep, after her long journey over here from Canada.

After breakfast, she asked someone at the hotel desk, if they knew where the outdoor market was, and she was told, that there was a big one, called 'Sydney's Barrow Market', on Green Lane, which was about a couple of miles away from the hotel. She thought that the Australian people, whom she talked to, seemed very, nice, helpful and friendly, but they all spoke with a strange, weird accent, that she was glad wasn't hers.

She went back to her room and phoned her home in Canada, but there was no answer. As she thought that, *Alex must be at work, and the twins would be at school.* So she then went outside of the hotel, flagging down a passing taxi, to take her to the 'Barrow Market'.

On arriving there she paid the taxi fare, and began to walk through the market, looking at the stalls with their wares, and the people's faces.

She finally saw Stan, whose stall was near the centre of the big market. He was leaning back against some large, wooden crates, with his arms folded, looking very, deep in thought with his head down seeming to look at something on the ground. He had no idea at all that Olivia was close by him, stood looking at him, from just a few feet away. She began to slowly, walk up to his stall, not wanting it to be too much of a surprise and shock to him, when, and if, he did recognise her face. "Hi Stan, remember me?" She said, with a smile on her face, standing in front of him. "You've been looking very deep in thought about something."

Stan lifted his head up slowly, looking at Olivia in disbelief. He took hold of her hands, and looked into her green eyes, smiling at her. "Hello Olivia, so you've come to see me at last, I hoped you come to see me one day. Oh it's so good to see you again, after all this time. You just don't know how much this means to me, seeing you again." Stan said, putting his shaking arms around her, and holding her as close to him as he could.

"You look so good Olivia," he said, now looking closely at her. "You're still so lovely and slim, with a terrific figure, you're just beautiful. And your hair suits you that way, it really does."

"Yeah it's so good to see you again Stan, after all this time. Anyway how's business doin? Have you sold very much this morning? I could help you if you like. I've never worked behind a market stall before, and I guess it's fun."

"No, no, you're not going to start working for me," Stan replied, laughing nervously. "It's quiet on the market today. Anyway I'm going to pack up now and take you sightseeing around Sydney, would you like that? And when did you arrive here?"

"Okay I'll help you to pack this stuff away. Then I'd like to see the opera house, Sydney harbour, some Kangaroos, Koala Bears and some Aborigine people. I arrived here yesterday, but due to all that jet lag, I seem to have been doin a lot of sleeping since I've got here."

Olivia helped Stan to pack his market stall goods, into the large, boxes and crates, and load them into the back of his large, blue van. Then setting off to look around Sydney and the outskirts of it, on into the bush country, where she saw some Aborigines, who were living in Government, built houses. She was so happy when at last, she saw some lovely Koala Bears, holding onto the branches of some trees, and some kangaroos hopping about. "Oh it's all so really lovely and very interesting to see all of this," she said. Before Stan told her, that he was now going to take her back to his home, to meet Sandy and his two Sons. "It reminds me of when I first saw Canada and the States, because until I saw them, I was never really aware of how big those countries are. They seemed to go on forever, like Australia does. You could fit England into a small corner of any of them, and not really notice you'd lost any space, where you'd placed it."

"Yes I thought that when I arrived here. Did you miss England Olivia? Were you homesick? Have you made many new friends in Canada?"

"Yes I guess I did miss England for a while, and I really missed my friends, 'cause I have some great friends back home there, that I could never replace, and I still keep in touch with most of them. But no, I was never really homesick, like you said you were. But I left England under very different circumstances to you Stan, didn't I? I went to North America with Alex and my kids, not by myself, like you came to Australia. And yes I guess it must have been very hard for you Stan, being so young and all alone in a big, strange country, like this one."

"Yes you were lucky, you didn't go to Canada by yourself at all did you? You had Alex with you," Stan replied, his whole body beginning to shake nervously now.

"Yes Alex has always been there with me. Hey are you okay? Or have I touched a raw nerve about something? 'Cause I can see that you're starting to shake badly," Olivia asked, beginning to feel some concern for him, as she gently, touched his arm.

"Oh don't worry I'll be okay soon, it's just that I haven't been feeling too good lately. I'll take a tablet when we get home. We'll be there soon, and Sandy will be very pleased to meet you."

"Look it I really don't want to impose on your family Stan. You could take me back to the hotel and I could get something to eat there, 'cause I'm hungry after breathing in all this fresh Australian air."

"No, no, I wouldn't dream of it. And Sandy will cook us all a meal, she'll be home from work by now."

***

An hour later Olivia followed Stan through a wooden, white painted door, down a small, carpeted Hallway into a small, Kitchen. It appeared to be a very, clean small, modest home that Stan and his family lived in. Certainly not like anything as big as Olivia, and her family lived in Canada. With her thinking that, *They probably couldn't really afford to live like her and Alex, with the very, good job and wage that he made with it, in Canada.*

"And this is my wife Sandy, Sandy this is Olivia," Stan said, introducing Olivia and Sandy to each other in the Kitchen.

"Hello Olivia," Sandy said with a smile, shaking Olivia's hand warmly. "I'm very pleased to meet you at last, after I've heard so much about you."

"Hi Sandy, and it's good to meet you too," Olivia replied, smiling back at the lady, who looked just the same as in her photographs. "You've heard a lot about me have you? And was it all so bad?"

"Oh no, no! It was all good things that Stan's told me about you love. Anyway I've got a piece of lamb cooking in the oven Olivia, so I hope you'll stay to eat with us," Sandy asked, while turning the heat down on the stove, under pans of potatoes and vegetables that were cooking.

"Okay thanks, yes I'd like to," Olivia replied, looking across at Stan, who was stood at the sink drinking water from a glass, and putting three capsules into his mouth to swallow.

Sandy noticed Olivia watching Stan taking his tablets and said, "They're for his nerves love, he has to take them a few times a day now."

"Olivia and I are going to sit in the other room Sandy," Stan said, in a stern voice, after taking his medication. "And I'd like a cup of tea brought in, and one for Olivia."

"No thanks, not tea, I'll make myself a coffee if you don't mind," Olivia said to Sandy, smiling at her.

"No, Sandy will make it for you," Stan replied.

"Hey, just a minute you," Olivia said, looking at Stan. "I don't expect Sandy to wait on me, she's been out working today and she's cooking us all a meal. Don't you think that's enough for her to do? And why can't you make your own tea Stan? What happened to women's lib in Australia Sandy? Did no one ever think of it over here? Or are you still all slaves to your men?"

"It's all right Olivia love, I don't mind really," replied Sandy, pushing her hair back from her warm, face, now beginning to look very flustered and afraid of Stan. "I expect Stan's had a hard day working at the market, haven't you love? So you go through into the other room to talk with him, and I'll bring tea and coffee through for you both when it's ready, it won't be long."

Olivia now began to feel sorry for Sandy, as she looked into her sad, pleading eyes, thinking, *Yes I wonder if that's how Stan would have wanted me to be, if I'd have married him? A slave to his every wish? No way!*

Olivia sat down next to Stan on a dark red, well-worn couch, with a long wooden coffee-table in front of it. With Sandy soon bringing their tea and coffee in the room to them. "Do you take milk in your coffee love?" She asked.

"No thanks, just sugar," Olivia replied with a smile. "I like it black and sweet."

"Oh do you?" Stan asked, staring hard at Olivia questioningly, while drinking his tea.

"Yes I do," replied Olivia, staring back at him, thinking that, *Yes, he could be a somewhat prejudiced guy.* And wondering what he would say, *If he knew about the affair that she'd had many years ago, with Winston, the black guy from Jamaica?* "Anyway there's something that I've come over here that I must ask you Stan," Olivia said, putting down her coffee cup, before lighting a cigarette and inhaling the smoke from it deeply, while looking into Stan's eyes. "When you left England, did you know or have any idea, that I was pregnant with our second baby?"

"No I didn't," Stan replied quickly, taking hold of her hand and looking down at it, making sure that his eyes now, avoided looking back into hers. "I really don't think so, but to be honest with you, it was all such a long time ago, I can't really remember. Anyway I couldn't have left you, if I'd have thought that you were pregnant again. And I'm so very sorry about it, and everything that you went through, I really am."

"Oh yes so you have kept telling me, but I'm still wondering if you did know that I was."

"Hey listen, that's John and David coming into the house, come here boys, I'd like you to meet an old friend of mine from England," Stan happily announced, very eager now to change the subject, getting it away from Olivia's dead baby.

Two boys with short 'crew cut' hair came running into the room and stood in front of the coffee table, looking at Olivia. Stan stood up and put his hands on the boys' shoulders, as he proudly introduced John and David to Olivia. They both shook hands politely, with her, saying, "Hello," in their strong, Australian accents. "How do you know my Dad?" David asked, "And have you come over from England to live in Australia?"

"Oh no, not at all," Olivia replied, with a laugh. "I live in Canada, the Great White North, where we get lots of snow in the winter. Have you ever seen any snow?"

"Only on television," John replied. "But how do you know my Dad?"

"Olivia used to be my girlfriend, many years ago when I was younger, and we both lived in Bradwell in England," Stan explained. "We were very much in love, and were going to get married. We had a baby Son called Antony, that I've told you both about, and he's your Step-Brother."

"Well what happened?" David asked, looking at his Father with questioning eyes. "Why didn't you two get married then?"

"Because we fell out and I came to live in Australia," Stan replied, answering his boys with a nervous laugh at the end of his sentence.

"Dinner's ready, come and get it," Sandy shouted from the kitchen. "Boys, go and wash your hands please."

"This is a lovely meal you've cooked, Sandy," Olivia said, eating the roast lamb, baked potatoes, mashed potatoes, peas, carrots and gravy. "You're a good cook."

"Are you a good cook like my Mum, Olivia?" David asked.

"I guess so, and I'd like to think so" Olivia replied laughing. "Well Alex and the twins say I am, and I know I make a mean lasagne."

"What's lasagne?" Asked John.

"Oh it's a pasta dish with sauce and cheese," Olivia replied.

"I'm afraid we're not into pasta," said Stan. "I don't like it, so we never eat it."

"Are you guys into pizza? We eat a lot of pizza in North America," Olivia asked.

"No Stan doesn't like pizza, so we don't eat that either," Sandy quickly replied. "Do you like living in Canada, Olivia? And have you been back to England for a visit, since you left?"

"Oh yes I like Canada very much, and I just love Montreal," Olivia replied. "And I've been back for a short visit to see my family and friends, the other year. I'm seriously thinking of going back over there for a visit again soon."

After everyone had finished eating the delicious, meal that Sandy had cooked. Olivia offered to help her to do the dishes, that she began to clear from the table. But Stan told Olivia, that there was no need to, that Sandy could manage them by herself. So there was no need for any of her help.

"Yes I'm sure Sandy has to manage by herself often," Olivia snapped at Stan. "But I can see you haven't got a dishwasher, so I will help her to wash and dry these dishes. Then I want to get back to the hotel, and take a shower, 'cause it's been a long, hot day, and I'd like to freshen up before I go to bed. And it's getting kinda late now."

"You're very welcome to stay here Olivia, instead of at the hotel if you'd like to," Sandy said. "You could sleep on the couch in the other room."

"No thanks Sandy, I prefer to go back to the hotel, if you don't mind? And I've got to call Alex and the twins in Canada, to tell them that I'm okay, and I'll be back home in a few days time. And I think that the twins will probably ask me to bring them a Koala Bear back home with me. Anyway could you call me a taxi soon please Sandy?"

"Oh no, you're not going back to the hotel in a taxi Olivia. I'll drive you back there myself," Stan said.

"Oh okay but only if you insist, because you know that I can get myself back to the hotel in a taxi. And do you mind Stan giving me a lift back there Sandy?"

"Oh no not at all, it's the least we can do for you."

After helping to clear up the kitchen, Olivia said good-bye to Sandy and the boys at the doorway, and told them she'd probably see them again tomorrow.

As she was leaving their home, Sandy took hold of Olivia's hand, squeezing it very, gratefully, and thanking her so much for coming over to Australia to see Stan, as she knew it was helping him, because he seemed to be looking and feeling better, already.

***

Alex and Ivan had managed to get a plane from Montreal into La Guardia airport, in New York City. Then changing planes at Los Angeles, to fly over to the Honolulu airport in Hawaii, from there they boarded another plane to fly them to Australia.

They both kept glancing at their watches, as the plane was now starting to descend lower, from the night sky.

***

Stan drove Olivia back to the Holiday Inn Hotel, asking her if it would be okay if he came up to her room with her, because he felt they had lots more to talk about, things that he hadn't wanted to discuss at the house. So she told him that she understood, and it would be okay with her, as long as he didn't stay too long, because she was feeling tired. She also then went on to tell him not to think for one minute, that anything could have been any different between them, in their life's. That they could not have changed anything that had happened between them, because it was all destined to be, that one day they would both have to go on, in their own separate ways.

From her hotel room she phoned down to the bar, and ordered a bottle of 'Canadian whiskey', Coca-Cola, ice cubes, and a couple of bottles of 'Fosters Lager' to be sent up to her room, while Stan laid himself down on her bed, very deep in his thoughts.

The drinks soon arrived, and she poured herself a Rye and Coke, while Stan opened his bottle of Lager. "Salut, and it's been great seeing you again Stan, it really has," Olivia said, lifting her glass to him before taking a drink. "I think you've got a lovely family, and it's really good to see that you're so settled over here, in this beautiful country. I think we can both also put all our fears to rest about each other, now that we both know we came out of our puppy-love okay. Yes it was hard for us both Stan, but we got through in the end, didn't we?"

"Yes I suppose we did. But do you still love me Olivia? And wish that it was you living as my wife, over here with me in Australia?" Stan asked, looking at her very, intensely.

"No thanks Australia's a lovely country, but I do so much prefer North America," Olivia replied with a laugh, thinking that Stan was just teasing her. "Yes I'll always have a place in my heart for you, Stan, 'cause if my memory serves me well, I did once love you very much. But all of that was a long long time ago now, when you were my one and only first love, my puppy-love. And yes I'll always be very fond of you. But it's Alex that I love very much now, and he will always be my true love forever."

"But I thought that by now you would have realized that, I still love you very much Olivia, and I've never ever stopped loving you. I've just waited for you to find me, to come to me, and I think I've waited very patiently for a long time now, for this moment, this time of ours together. So why don't you come and lay down on the bed, here at the side of me?"

"No thanks I don't want to," Olivia replied, in a very, definite voice. "And please don't try anything Stan, 'cause I'm not bloody interested. Now just drink your Lager up and go home, back to your lovely wife Sandy, and you know that she will be waiting for you. And maybe it's time for you to take another one of your pills, for your nerves. How many times a day do you have to take them?"

***

At last their plane came into land at the airport in Sydney, with Alex and Ivan running out of the airport, as fast as they could, once they had cleared customs, getting a taxi to take them straight to the 'Holiday Inn Hotel'. "Are we anywhere near Houghton Road?" Ivan asked the taxi driver.

"Yes we will be passing it soon," the driver replied. "It's quite near the 'Holiday Inn'."

"Oh good," Ivan said, with a sigh of relief. "I just want you to stop at 316 Houghton Road first, before we go on to the hotel."

"But what are you going there for?" Alex asked anxiously. "We've got to find Olivia."

"It's okay, just trust me," Ivan replied, smiling at Alex. "It's something I want to pick up from my friend Scooter, just in case, and it'll only take me a few minutes, honestly."

"I just hope we get to Olivia in time, 'cause this horrid feeling that I've got, about her being in danger, is still with me, and I don't even know this guy Stan."

"I understand Alex, and I sense it too. Especially after what Olivia's told us, in all innocence about Stan, this guy she once loved. I've picked up on a few things that I didn't like, about these strange moods and this temper, that he seems to have."

***

"Olivia, I've been working things out in my mind for a while now, and it's all fallen into place today, now that I've seen you again," Stan said, after now opening his second bottle of Lager, and drinking it out of the bottle. "You were the piece that was for a long time now, missing from my puzzle. But now you're here, now you've come back to me, it all fits into place. So come on Olivia, come and lay down on the bed with me?"

"No I won't, and you're talking a load of fucking bullshit!" Olivia shouted, starting to feel afraid of Stan now, and the funny look that was beginning to appear on his face, and in his eyes. "And why do you have to go and spoil the good day that we've had on our reunion? And what the hell do you mean, now I've come back to you, it was you who left me, remember? I didn't go anywhere."

"No, no Olivia," Stan said, getting up off the bed and going to stand next to her in the room. "You wanted to run away from me, when you said it was over between us, and I tried to stop you. Don't you remember? You wanted to leave me, finish with me, but I didn't want you to. So it was meant to be that we would get back together again sometime, can't you see that? And think about it Olivia, we can't part again now, or it will spoil and break my puzzle and plans for us again. And that baby boy of ours who died, he had to die because we weren't together. That's why Sandy lost our first baby boy also, because it wasn't from you and me, our baby together. And you had those twin girls, they should have been ours, and I have two boys whose birthdays are both on the same day. You know? I could never understand why they were born on the same day, three years apart from each other. But I do know now, it was a sign to me, to tell me about you. But I couldn't pick up on it until all these years later, until you found me again, and told me that you'd had twins. Can't you see it all for yourself now Olivia? Because now we're back together again, as we should be, we can now have our baby boy Oliver again, and this time he will live. I promise you that he will live, he's just been waiting for us to be together again, so he can come into this world and live happily with us as his Mom and dad, but without us being together he couldn't."

"My-God! You're just fucking crazy Stan!" Olivia said, moving as far away from him, in the room as she could get. "Sandy told me that you were a bit sick in the head. And I thought that it was just a bit of depression that you were having, something that everyone gets from time to time, not that you were very seriously mentally ill. Now I know why Sandy seemed to be so afraid of you, you fucking bastard, you have beaten her up, haven't you? But she still loves you Stan, she must do because she hasn't left you. And what about Sandy and Alex? What would happen to them if we got back together? What about their feelings for us two? Wouldn't they both be so hurt? If we left them to get back together?" Olivia said, trying to talk some reasonable sense into Stan. Hoping to get him to change his mind about loving and wanting her.

"Oh don't you go worrying about those two, 'cause they'd be happy for us, I'm sure they would," Stan replied, moving across the room, and getting closer to Olivia. "They both know we loved each other very much a long time ago, and they'll understand we want to be back together again, don't worry about Sandy or Alex, they'll be okay. What really matters now is us two, so come on Olivia? Let's make our other baby Son? That we've both been waiting for? And I only ever got to love you, when you were a young girl, so show me how you make love as a women."

"No!" She screamed, smacking Stan hard, across his face, and pushing him away from her, before running across the room towards the door, to get away from him. But just as she tried to open the door, she felt Stan's hands pulling her away from it, and shoving her towards the bed.

"No Stan! No! Please not like this! No never!" She screamed. "I don't want another affair with you, I thought we could just be friends."

"Of course we can be friends Olivia, and when we're married..."

"Married! We can't get married. I'm married to Alex, and I love him, not you. And you're married to Sandy, and you love her, not me. So I want you to now go back home to her. Go Stan, go home to Sandy and your Children. Just get the fuck out of my room Stan, because this stupid game of yours has gone far enough. And I'm now going home to Alex."

"Oh no you're not Olivia, you're not going anywhere ever again," Stan said, pushing her back up against the wall, and beginning to stroke her face and neck with his hand, as he was kissing her face all over. "You're not going to go anywhere ever again, you're going to stay here now, with me forever."

Olivia was terrified when she felt Stan's hands stroking her face and then around her neck, as his fingers beginning to squeeze there gently at first, and she began to have a feeling of déjà vu. "No Stan, please, please don't do this to me again," she begged, holding on to his hands, trying to pull them away from her neck. Completely forgetting the Aikido, and how to defend herself in a situations like this, that her friend Danny had taught her years ago.

"But you don't understand Olivia," Stan said, kissing her on the cheeks and lips, and beginning to squeeze her throat even harder. "I love you, and if I can't have you, no one else ever can. I'll never lose you to anyone else again."

Stan's squeeze, tightened around her throat, and she began to gasp for air, while still trying to push him away from her. Her head began to spin, and her world went black as she slowly, lost consciousness, and slid down the wall to the floor, with Stan's hands still squeezing her throat tightly.

At that moment the door to Olivia's room flew open, and Alex and Ivan looked into the room in horror and disbelief before running in, with Alex shouting out Olivia's name, as Ivan quickly pulled a small handgun out of his pocket, aiming it at Stan, pulling back the trigger and firing it.

Feeling the bullet enter him somewhere in the middle part of his back, Stan's hands, very slowly, let go of Olivia's throat, as he slumped to the floor with a deep moan.

Ivan then picked up the telephone, and asked the operator to get the ambulance and the police immediately.

Alex gently lifted Olivia up off the floor, and laid her on the bed, as she slowly opened her eyes looking thankfully into his face. "Thank God we got here in time before he killed you," Alex said, kissing her gently on the forehead and holding her hand. "I love you Olivia, and please don't ever go away like this again."

"Thanks for saving me Alex, my once again 'Knight in shining armour', that I will always love." Olivia replied, with tears running down her cheeks. "But could you please take me back home with you? Because I now know that I have at last closed the 'Full Circle'."

******

PERSONAL ACKNOWLEDGEMENTS.

I would like to extend my heartfelt thanks to the following people for their invaluable help, time, co-operation, advice, support, encouragement and belief in me, in the writing of this novel:

My very good DJ & TV presenter friend, Mark Krisky, at KTLA Television Station, Los Angeles, who listened and discussed with me in the beginning, the idea I had of writing this book. He said, "It sounds good to me, go for it Judi, I'm sure you can do it, and never give up on your dream of it being published."

Many thanks to my dear friend Isaac, who listened to my idea of the story line, and told me, that he hoped that I would write it, because there is a strong message in the story to help other girls, to learn by their mistakes in life out there -- because all the things that happened to Olivia, could happen to any other girl, anywhere in the world

My very special ex-Hippy and DJ friend Allan, whom I will always feel close to and love dearly. He told me that the best days of his life were when he was a 'Hippy'. Thanks for reminiscing those happy, precious Hippy-days with me Allan. And for helping me so much with my research.

A very special thank-you I want to give to a kind-old-school-friend of mine, my 'Sunflower-Earth-Angel'-Angela, for leading me in the direction towards the right publishing-house.

My wonderful friend Andrea, who always kept saying to me, "Judi I want you to write a book" Thanks so much for putting that crazy idea into my head, all those years ago!!!! And thank-you for always being there as my friend.

My hairdresser and friend Lyne at 'Coupe-que-Coupe'. Thank-you for trying so hard to understand and always supporting me, while listening to me and my ideas, in my much too fast talking English.

Pierre II, thank-you for sharing your knowledge of guns with me.

Neil Kushnir, Assistant Music Director at CHOM 97.7 FM, Montreal, who helped me by sending me lots of titles of songs with artists names, over the years I was covering.

Many, many thanks to my two favourite business men Benjamin and Kent, who gave up their precious time to help me with the business side of writing and whom to trust. I will never forget how much you guys helped me, and saved me from that disaster with that so called agent, in Toronto. Who told me, that I had no idea how to write a book and he thought that my work was rubbish

Thank-you Steve, for the box of pencils and the pencil sharpener you gave me in Venezuela, I will always keep them in memory of you. I will never forget you and I do hope you have found happiness and peace where-ever you are now!!

Thanks to Laura and Patrick at the Wal-Mart portrait studio in Cornwall, for the good photograph they took. We will use your good idea for the next shoot Patrick.

Also I send my thanks to my other very special and dear friends, some who live close by and others so very far away, who were and always will be there for me with their support, when I get my crazy ideas. I love you all and will never forget: Pat, Jean, Anouk, Kenny, Serge, Joanne, James, Nadia, Collette, Sylvia, Diane, Rodger, Margaret, Tony, Sue, Scott, King, Neville, Sid, Kathy, Cathy and Diane.

Printed in Great Britain
by Amazon